Praise for Elizabeth Chadwick

"An author who makes historical fiction come gloriously alive."

—*Times of London*

"I rank Elizabeth Chadwick with such historical novelist stars as Dorothy Dunnett and Anya Seton."

—Sharon Kay Penman, *New York Times* bestselling author of *Devil's Brood*

"The best writer of medieval fiction currently around."

—Richard Lee, founder and publisher, Historical Novel Society

"The reader is well aware on every page that this is life as it was lived eight hundred years ago, yet the characters are as fresh and natural as if they were living in present time."

—*Historical Novels Review*

"One of Elizabeth Chadwick's strengths is her stunning grasp of historical detail...her characters are beguiling, the story intriguing and very enjoyable."

—Barbara Erskine

"Elizabeth Chadwick is to medieval England what Philippa Gregory is to the Tudors and the Stuarts, and Bernard Cornwell is to the Dark Ages."

—*Books Monthly*, UK

"Brilliantly weaving a strong plotline, historical accuracy, depth of character, and dialogue filled with intelligence and wit...

Elizabeth Chadwick is one of the very best of historical fiction authors."

—Passages to the Past

"When Elizabeth Chadwick writes about history, you feel like you are there in the thick of it."

—Long and Short Reviews

"Everyone who has raved about Elizabeth Chadwick as an author of historical fiction is right."

—Devourer of Books

"Chadwick's great strength lies in her attention to detail—she brings to life all the daily humdrum of the medieval age but also seduces with the romance of her characters and the raw excitement of their times. And as always, she provides fascinating information on the background to her research and the historical period, putting the people and places into perfect focus. *To Defy a King* is Chadwick on top form."

—*Lancashire Evening Post*

"You don't just read a Chadwick book; you experience it."

—Shelf and Stuff

TO
DEFY A KING

TO
DEFY A KING

ELIZABETH
CHADWICK

sourcebooks
landmark

Published by Sourcebooks Landmark, an imprint of Sourcebooks, Inc.
P.O. Box 4410, Naperville, Illinois 60567-4410
(630) 961-3900
Fax: (630) 961-2168
www.sourcebooks.com

Originally published in the UK in 2010 by Sphere.

Library of Congress Cataloging-in-Publication Data

Chadwick, Elizabeth.
   To defy a king / by Elizabeth Chadwick.
      p. cm.
   1. John, King of England, 1167-1216--Fiction. 2. Young women--England--Fiction. 3. Great Britain--History--John, 1199-1216--Fiction. 4. Great Britain--Kings and rulers--Fiction. I. Title.
   PR6053.H245T6 2011
   823'.914--dc22
                              2010048511

Printed and bound in the United States of America.
               POD 10 9 8 7 6 5 4 3

Also by Elizabeth Chadwick

The Greatest Knight

The Scarlet Lion

For the King's Favor

Lady of the English

One

IT'S NOT FAIR!" TEN-YEAR-OLD MAHELT MARSHAL SCOWLED at her older brothers who were immersed in a boys' game involving a pretend raid on an enemy castle. "Why can't I be a knight?"

"Girls don't go raiding," Will answered with the superiority that came from being male, almost fourteen, and heir to the Earldom of Pembroke.

She made a grab for his horse's reins and he snatched them out of her reach.

"Girls stay at home and embroider and bear children. Only men go to war."

"Women have to defend the castle when their lords are away," she pointed out. "Mama does—and you have to obey her." Tossing her head, she looked at Richard, who was twelve and could sometimes be persuaded to take her part; but, although a broad grin sprawled across his freckled face, he didn't leap to her defence.

"She has to do our lord father's bidding when he returns," Will retorted. "Papa doesn't send her out with a lance in her hand while he stays at home, does he?"

"I can pretend; it's all pretend anyway." Mahelt was determined not to be bettered. "You're not a man."

Richard's grin widened as Will flushed. "Let her defend the castle," he said. "She might have to do it one day when she's married."

Will rolled his eyes, but gave in. "All right, but she's not a knight, and she's not riding Equus."

"Of course not."

"And she can be the French. We're the English."

"That's not fair!" Mahelt protested again.

"Don't play then," Will said indifferently.

She shot her brothers a fulminating look. She wanted to ride Will's new mount because it was a proper, big, glossy horse, not a pony. She wanted to jump him over hedges as Will did and see how fast she could make him gallop. She wanted to feel the wind in her hair. Will had called him Equus, which he said was the Latin name the scribes wrote meaning "warhorse." Richard's docile grey wasn't the same challenge, and she had almost outgrown her own dumpy little chestnut, which was stabled up with a leg strain. She knew she could ride as well as either of her brothers.

Heaving a sigh, she stumped off with bad grace to defend the "castle," which for the purposes of the game was the kennel-keeper's hut. Here were stored the collars and leashes for the hounds, old blankets, hunting horns, various tools, baskets, and bowls. A shelf at Mahelt's eye level held chubby earthenware pots of salve for treating canine injuries. Mahelt took one down, removed the lid of plaited straw, and immediately recoiled from the vile stench of rancid goose grease.

"Ready?" she heard Richard shout.

Her left arm crooked around the pot, Mahelt emerged from the shed and, with a resolute jaw, faced the youths, who were fretting their mounts. Both boys bore makeshift lances fashioned from ash staves, and gripped their practice shields at the ready. Uttering simultaneous yells, the brothers charged. Knowing

Settrington
Middleham
York

Newark
Nottingham

E N G L A N D

Thetford
Framlingham
Bury St Edmunds
Ipswich
Dovercourt

WALES

Chepstow
Bradenstoke
Caversham
LONDON
Pembroke
Rochester
Salisbury
Winchester

Miles
0 10 20 30 40 50

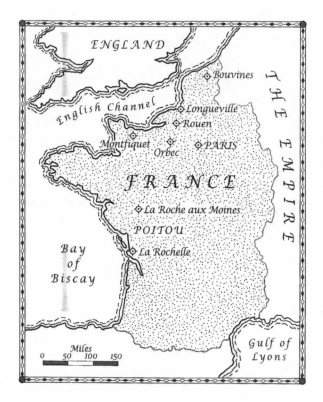

ENGLAND

Bouvines

English Channel

Longueville

Rouen

Montfiquet

Orbec

PARIS

THE EMPIRE

FRANCE

La Roche aux Moines

POITOU

Bay
of
Biscay

La Rochelle

Miles
0   50   100   150

Gulf of
Lyons

IRELAND

Carrickfergus ◇

◇ Dublin

Dunamase ◇

Kilkenny
◇

New Ross
(New Town) ◇   ◇ Wexford
◇ Waterford

Miles
0   10   200   30

SELECT BIGOD FAMILY TREE SHOWING TIE-IN TO SALISBURY AND THE ROYAL FAMILY

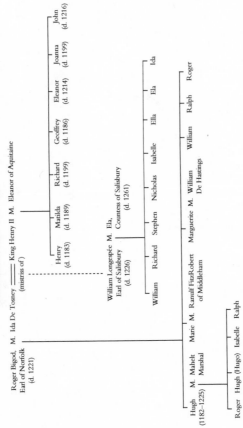

MARSHAL FAMILY TREE

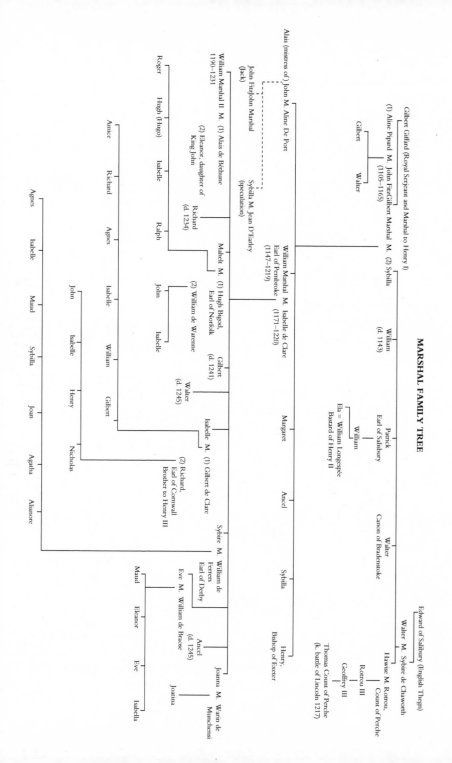

they expected her to lose her courage and dash back inside the shed, Mahelt stood her ground. She scooped up a handful of grease, feeling it cold and squidgy-soft between her fingers, and lobbed it at the oncoming horses. Will ducked behind his shield, which took the first impact, but Mahelt's next dollop struck him over the rawhide rim, splattering his cloak and the side of his neck. Another scoop burst on the shoulder of Richard's grey. His efforts to control his shying mount left him exposed and her fourth handful landed a direct hit to his face.

"Hah! You're both dead!" She leaped gleefully up and down. "I win, I win!" Triumph burned in her solar plexus. That was showing them.

Will was off his horse like lightning. Mahelt shrieked and tried to run inside the shed, but he was too fast and caught her arm. She spun round in his grip and struck his chest with her salve-covered hand, smearing his cloak with rancid grease.

"It's dishonourable to hit a lady!" she cried as he raised a threatening fist.

Will looked at his bunched knuckles and, lowering his arm, gave her a disgusted shove instead. "Look what you've done to my cloak! I pity whoever gets you to wife. You're a hoyden."

Mahelt raised her chin, determined not to show remorse or be browbeaten. "But I still won," she said. "Against both of you."

"Will, leave her," Richard said with exasperation, wiping his face. "Let's go. There are better places to practise. We'd get more hurled at us in a real battle than handfuls of old grease."

With a final glare, Will flung round and remounted Equus. "It looks as if you've lost after all," he said as he gathered his reins.

Through a blur of angry tears she watched her brothers ride away. Raising her hand to wipe her eyes, she found the stink of the salve on her fingers suddenly unbearable. She was cold, hungry, and empty. Her victory was a hollow one and she was going to be in trouble for wasting the hound-keeper's salve and dirtying her brothers' clothes. She returned the pot to its shelf and closed the shed door. When she turned round, she jumped, because Godfrey, her father's under-chamberlain, was standing behind her. "Your parents are seeking you, young mistress." He wrinkled his nose. "God's eyes, what have you been doing?"

"Nothing." She gave him an imperious look to cloak her guilt. "Defending the castle."

Godfrey said nothing, but his gaze was eloquent.

"What do they want?" Facing both parents at once was generally reserved for serious misdemeanours. Her mother had eyes in the back of her head, but surely she couldn't know about the grease-throwing yet and Mahelt couldn't think of anything else she had done recently to warrant such a command.

"I do not know, young mistress. Your lady mother just said to fetch you."

Decidedly on her guard, Mahelt followed him to the solar, pausing on the way to sluice her hands in the trough and wipe them on a net of hay tied to the stable wall.

Her mother and father were sitting before the hearth in their private chamber, and she saw a glance flicker between them as she entered. She could sense an atmosphere, but it wasn't angry. Gilbert and Walter, her two younger brothers, were playing a dice game on the floor and a nurse was attending to her little sisters, Belle aged four, and two-year-old Sybire.

Her mother patted the bench and Mahelt came to sit in the space her parents had made for her between them. The fire embraced her with warmth. The hangings were drawn across the window shutters and the mellow glow from numerous beeswax candles made the room feel cosy and welcoming. Her mother smelled wonderfully of roses and the arm she slipped around Mahelt to cuddle her was tender and maternal. Mahelt decided her brothers were welcome to their silly game. Parental attention was better, especially if she wasn't in trouble. She thought it odd that her father was holding her floppy cloth doll in his big hands and looking at it in a pensive manner. Seeing her watching him, he put it down and smiled, but his eyes were serious.

"You remember a few weeks ago, the Christmas court at Canterbury?" he asked.

She nodded. "Yes, Papa." It had been lovely—all the feasting and dancing and celebration. She had felt so grown up, being allowed to mingle with the adults. She had been wary of King John because she knew her mother disliked him, but she thought the jewels he wore around his neck were magnificent. Sapphires and rubies, so her cousin Ela had said, all the way from Sarandib.

"You remember Hugh Bigod?"

"Yes, Papa." The heat from the fire was suddenly hot on her face. She picked up her doll and began fussing with it herself. Hugh was grown up, but he had partnered her in a circle dance, clasping her hand and winding her through the chain. Later he had organised games of hoodman blind and hunt the slipper for the younger ones, joining in himself with great enthusiasm. He had a rich singing voice and a smile that made her stomach flutter, although she didn't know why. One day he would be Earl of Norfolk, just as one day Will would be Earl of Pembroke.

"Hugh's parents are seeking a suitable wife for him," her father said. "Your mother and I believe it would be good for Marshal and Bigod to unite in a marriage alliance."

Mahelt blinked. She felt the doll's soft dress under her fingers, the heat from the fire, her mother's arm around her. She looked at her father. If the law allowed it, if it were possible under God's heaven, she would marry him. She knew she was expected to make a great match to benefit her family. It was her duty and she was proud to do it, but she hadn't imagined the time to come like this—out of an ordinary day when a moment since she had been play-fighting with her brothers. Her stomach was suddenly hollow.

"It will only be a betrothal for the moment," her mother reassured her. "Nothing will change until you are older, but your father must make the offer now."

Mahelt's relief that she was not to be married off on the instant was immediately replaced by curiosity. "Why must you make the offer now, Papa?"

Giving her a grave look, he spoke as one adult to another. "Because, Matty, I want to secure an alliance with the Earl of Norfolk. He is powerful and honourable and his estates are prosperous. He knows the laws of the land better than anyone, and his son is a fine young man. You will be safe and cared for, and that matters to me. If we do not make the offer now, the earl may not wait. There are other families with whom he could match Hugh to great advantage. This is the best choice for you."

Mahelt tightened her grip on her doll—because she was thinking, not because she was upset. Will was betrothed to Alais de Béthune, who was five years old. Mahelt's cousin Ela, Countess of Salisbury, had married William Longespée when she was only ten. Mahelt was almost eleven now, nearly two years older. "I like Hugh Bigod," she said, swinging her legs. She liked Countess Ida too, who had given her a brooch at Christmas, enamelled with red and blue flowers. Hugh's father, Earl Roger of Norfolk, always wore magnificent hats.

"Then I am glad," her father said, "and very proud of you. I shall make the offer and we'll see what happens."

His approval made Mahelt feel warm and tingly. He hugged her and she abandoned her doll to squeeze him as hard as she could in return. He pretended to choke at the force of her grip, then made a different sound in his throat and drew away, grimacing. "Child, what have you been doing? What is that smell?"

Mahelt tried to look nonchalant. "It's just the salve Tom the kennel-keeper uses on the hounds when they're injured."

He raised his brows. "And why would it be on you?"

She squirmed. "Will said I had to defend the castle against attack because he wouldn't let me be a knight and ride Equus." Her eyes flashed. "He said I had to be French too, and then he got cross and rode off because he didn't win." She concealed a momentary quiver as she remembered him saying that she had actually lost. It wasn't true.

"And the salve?"

Mahelt set her jaw. "There was nothing else to throw. I wasn't going to yield, because they'd have taken me prisoner and held me for ransom."

Her father looked away and rubbed his hand across his face. When he turned back, his expression was severe. "You do know that Tom will have to make more salve now, and for that he will have to wait on the next pig-killing for the lard. He'll have to find the herbs too."

Mahelt fiddled with the end of her braid. "I'm sorry, Papa; I'll help him." It would be fun, she thought, all that mixing and stirring. Better than sewing in the bower.

He looked wry. "It is probably fortunate that there will be a gap between your betrothal and your marriage."

"I wouldn't throw things at my husband," she reassured him.

"I am relieved to hear it," he replied in a slightly strangled voice. "Go now and wash your hands properly and we'll toast some bread on the fire."

Mahelt jumped from the bench and hastened to do his bidding, relieved to have escaped so lightly. Besides, she was ravenous.

"She is still so young," William Marshal muttered to his

wife later as they glanced at their sleeping daughter on their way to bed. Illuminated in the small pool of candlelight, her rich brown hair shone with ruddy glints and she was fiercely clutching her doll to her heart.

Isabelle drew him away into their bedchamber before the light could disturb Mahelt's slumber. "You had to make a decision, and it was the right one."

He sat on the edge of their bed and rubbed his face. "Roger Bigod is a friend, but he will look to his own best interests first—as I would in his position."

"Of course he will," Isabelle agreed as she placed the candle in a niche, "but I suspect this offer will gladden his heart and be no second choice."

"I should think not!" William bridled. "Mahelt is a prize worthy of the highest in the land."

Isabelle set a soothing hand to the back of his neck. "Indeed she is, and you could not have done better for her than Hugh Bigod." She leaned round to kiss him, recognising his wistful sense of loss. Their other girls were still infants. Mahelt had been seven when her next sister had arrived, thus for a long time she had been William's only daughter. She was so like him. She had his prodigious energy and wholeheartedness and the same powerful sense of honour and duty, although, it had to be said, not his patience and tact. She knew her place in the world. As the Earl of Pembroke's beloved eldest daughter, it was an exalted one. Much as she loved her daughter, Isabelle knew that Hugh Bigod was going to have his hands full.

"Norfolk and Yorkshire are far away from danger too," William said, although his gaze was troubled.

Isabelle gnawed her lip. Their relationship with King John was uneasy. The latter neither liked nor trusted William. The feelings were mutual, but an oath of loyalty was binding, and John had given them the Earldom of Pembroke in exchange for that oath. William's strength had always been his absolute fidelity, but he served a man who put no trust in men's honour and had little of that virtue himself. Normandy was in turmoil and unrest seethed under a superficially calm surface. East Anglia, though, was a haven distant from trouble and its earl was a cautious man who kept a firm grip on his estates.

William shook his head. "Ten years ago, I carried her to her christening still with the marks of birth upon her body. It seems no more distant than yesterday, and now here I am arranging her marriage. Time is like riding a horse at full gallop that will not answer to your rein."

"The horse might not answer to your rein, but at least by planning ahead, you are less likely to lose your seat in the saddle."

William gave an amused grunt and, having removed his tunic, lay on their bed, his hands pillowed behind his head. "I am glad you said 'less likely,' my love." He watched her remove her veil and unpin her hair to let the heavy golden braids tumble down. "God knows there are sufficient obstacles in the road to unseat the canniest rider. I'll have the scribes write to the Bigods tomorrow, and then we shall see."

Two

SETTRINGTON, YORKSHIRE, FEBRUARY 1204

HUGH BIGOD DISMOUNTED TO EXAMINE THE WOLF HE HAD just killed, and wiped his spear in the tawny winter grass. Silver-grey fur ruffled in the wind. Her fangs were bared in a bloody snarl and even in death her amber eyes were baleful. She would have bred pups this year, but her swollen belly was not the result of fecundity, but of having gorged on the heavily pregnant ewe she and her mate had brought down the previous day. Wolves were a constant problem at lambing time, slinking round the sheepfolds, grey as twilight, waiting their moment. The shepherds and their dogs kept close watch, but they could not be everywhere at once and even when the flocks were brought in close to the homestead, there were still casualties.

Pellets of icy rain drove slantwise into his face and he turned his head away from the wind. Although his fingers were encased in mittens, his hands were numb. It was a frozen, hungry time of year, the dregs of winter hanging on even though the dawns arrived earlier and the light was slower to leave the sky at night.

"I can have a wolfskin rug for my bedside now," said his thirteen-year-old brother Ralph, a gleam in his dark grey eyes.

Hugh smiled. "With a sheepskin the other side for balance, and to remind you why we hunt wolves in the first place."

"I don't know why you want a wolf pelt anywhere near you;

they stink," said William. At almost fifteen, he was the closest of the brothers in age to Hugh.

"Not if they're properly tanned and aired," Ralph argued.

William shook his head. "The only good place for a wolf is a midden pit."

Accustomed to their verbal sparring, Hugh took little notice. It meant nothing. They squabbled cheerfully among themselves—sometimes even came to blows—but the rancour never lasted and they were always united against a common foe. Hugh remounted Arrow. The mare was so named because of her ability to fly into a fast gallop from a standing start. She could outrun any wolf and she was his pride and joy. Gathering the reins, he studied the sleet-laden clouds scudding in from the east coast while he waited for Ralph to swing the bloodied corpses across the pack pony's saddle. The wind was as vicious as the bite of a wild animal. It was a day when any sane man would remain by his hearth, and only venture outside to empty his bowels—or deal with wolves.

He had been lord of Settrington for five years, ever since his father had granted him ten knights' fees of his own following King John's coronation. He had been sixteen then, old enough for responsibility under supervision, and he had cut his teeth on these Yorkshire estates, preparing for the day when he would inherit vast tracts of fertile land and coastal villages in East Anglia including the castle at Framlingham with its thirteen great towers. His father was still hale and fit, but one day, Hugh would be Earl of Norfolk, and his knights' fees would amount to more than 160.

He paused by the shepherds' hut to give the herders the good news about the wolves, and then rode down to the manor. As the afternoon settled towards dusk, the horses churned their way through the icy mud of the track, bitter air clouding from their nostrils and steaming from their hides. Lantern-light gleamed through the cracks in the shutters of the manor house and grooms were waiting to greet the hunting party and take their mounts.

"Sire, your lord father is here," the head groom told Hugh as he dismounted.

Hugh had already noticed the extra horses in the stables and the increased number of servants. He had been expecting his father because King John and the court were at York, and Settrington was only twenty miles away. Hugh nodded to the groom, stripped off his mittens, and, blowing into his cupped hands, entered the manor house. His waiting chamberlain presented him with a cup of hot, spiced wine, which Hugh took with gratitude. His father was sitting before the hearth, legs crossed at the ankle, sipping from a cup of his own, but when he saw Hugh, he stood up.

"Sire." Hugh knelt on one knee and bowed his head.

"Son," Roger Bigod replied, pride in his voice. He raised Hugh to his feet and kissed him on either cheek. Hugh felt the solidity of his father's body beneath the fur-lined mantle as they embraced. He was as hard and sturdy as a pollarded tree.

William and Ralph arrived to be similarly greeted and for a while the conversation was all of the foul weather and the wolf hunt. More hot wine arrived, and platters of hot fried pastries. It was Lent so they were neither filled with cheese nor dusted with sugar and spices, but the tongue-scalding heat and the lard-fried crispness were still welcome to men who had been at hard exercise in freezing weather. Hugh's hands and feet began to throb back to life. Chilblains were another good reason not to leave the fire on a bitter February day. He pushed away the nose of a hungrily questing dog. "How is my lady mother?"

His father wiped his lips on a napkin. "Well enough, but longing for spring like all of us—and eager for news of you, of course."

"As soon as the weather improves I'll ride down to Framlingham and see her."

"It might be sooner than that."

"Oh?" Hugh arched a questioning eyebrow.

The earl glanced at his other sons. "After dinner will do. I want to talk to you alone and uninterrupted."

He would not be drawn and Hugh had no choice but to control his curiosity.

❖ ❖ ❖

After a modest Lenten supper of fish stew and bread, Ralph disappeared to skin his wolves. William, too fastidious to join him, went to play dice with the knights, having been ordered to make himself scarce.

As he waited for his father to speak, Hugh was tense with anticipation. Something momentous was afoot.

Standing with his back to the fire, the earl cleared his throat. "William Marshal has approached me and offered his eldest daughter Mahelt in marriage to you."

The news came as no surprise but Hugh's stomach still sank. His father had been studying prospective brides for some time. The Marshal's daughter was one of several names on the list.

"I told him we would consider the proposal and I would give my answer when I had spoken with you."

"She is not yet eleven years old." Hugh's initial thought emerged as words, although he had only half meant to speak.

"She will grow swiftly and you are still young for marriage. I was beyond thirty when I wed your mother, and the Marshal almost twice your age when he took Isabelle of Leinster to wife. What matters is the honour and prestige of a tie with the Marshals, and the affinity the girl will bring."

Hugh thought back to dancing with Mahelt Marshal at the Christmas feast in Canterbury. She was tall for her age and as lean as a gazehound. He remembered her hair in particular—shiny dark brown glinted with rich bronze. He had enjoyed her nimble, lively company, but she was a boisterous child, not a wife to wed and bed. Indeed, when he thought of the Marshal family, the earl and countess came to mind, not Mahelt. At court, he had been far more smitten by Countess Isabelle who, in her early thirties, was a strong and alluring woman.

"It bothers you, I can see."

Hugh cupped his chin. "There may not be many years separating girl from woman, but what if she should die in the meantime? Her dowry will no longer be secured to our estates and other offers will have passed us by."

"That is a risk we take," his father conceded, "but Mahelt Marshal is not sickly; all of her brothers and sisters are as robust as destriers." A gleam entered the older man's eyes. "Good breeding stock."

Hugh exhaled with sardonic amusement.

His father sobered. "There will not be a better offer than this."

Hugh knew his father's astute brain and reasoning abilities were what made the king value him as a judge and counsellor. He would have weighed the advantages and pitfalls of the match, and have answers for every point Hugh might raise. "I bow to your will, sire," he said. "I know my duty to the family and my concerns are not objections."

His father's lips curved in a half-smile. "Nevertheless, your doubts are commendable. I am pleased to have raised a son who can think for himself. The lord Marshal desires only a betrothal at this stage, and to leave the marriage until the girl is old enough for the full duties of a wife."

"Is she to live with us?" Hugh's tone was bland, but he was secretly unsettled at the notion of having a child-wife to his name, even if she would be mostly under his mother's wing.

"Not until the marriage, which will not take place until she is of an age for successful child-bearing. The Earl of Pembroke suggests the betrothal itself take place at Caversham after Lent."

"As you wish, sire," Hugh said with relief that he was not imminently to be saddled with a bride.

His father held out his cup for Hugh to refill. "Good then, it is settled, apart from negotiating the fine details of dowry and bride price. The king will have to give his permission, of course, but I foresee no trouble. We are in good favour with him and he values our support. I've taken the precaution of bringing a jewelled staff to present to him, and a copy of Aesop—given his enjoyment of gems and reading, they should put him in a good mood."

"Is there any news from Normandy?" When last Hugh had attended court, King Philip of France had been making deep inroads into the province and not only the Bigod lands near Bayeux were threatened, but also the considerably larger holdings belonging to William Marshal.

His father shook his head. "None that is good. As long as the castle at Gaillard holds out, Rouen is safe from the French, but there have been no gains on our part and when the campaigning season begins again..." He made a gesture that described without words how much of a predicament King John was in. Eastern Normandy had been overrun by the French and Anjou was lost. "Queen Eleanor is four score years old and in poor health. When she dies, there will be war in Poitou." He looked sombre. "I used to think she would be a part of the landscape for ever, but people are not as enduring as the stones."

Hugh said nothing, for it was the way he thought of his parents—as immutable as rock—when the truth was that they were as vulnerable as trees in the forest.

"The king will raise an army to try and push Philip back, but whether or not he succeeds..." Roger gazed into the fire, his air one of grave sobriety. "The minor Norman vassals will go over to Philip in order to keep their lands. Why should they be loyal to a lord who, as far as they are concerned, has fled across the sea and left them to cope as best they may? John will lose all the small men, and it is the small men who uphold the great."

Hugh gave his father a sharp look. "What of our own estates? What of the stud?"

"I was going to talk to you about that. Time I think to bring the horses to England. Even if I must lose Corbon and Montfiquet, I am not gifting the king of France with my horses. Come the better weather, I want you to go and fetch them back to East Anglia."

"And our people?"

"We will cross that bridge when we come to it." His father folded his arms inside his furred mantle. "Your great-grandfather came to England and fought on Hastings field because the Norman lands would not sustain him. They are a useful addition, but hardly a patrimony." He pursed his lips. "It will go hard for the Marshal if we lose Normandy because he does have castles and estates of great value to think on. He stands to lose his second son's inheritance. The lad's rising thirteen years old and the Marshal needs to hold on until he can despatch him to Normandy in his own right and create separation that way." He heaved a deep sigh. "We all walk knife edges of one sort or another, but better to walk them in strong company. That way there is less chance of being eaten by wolves." He raised his cup in toast. "To your betrothal."

"My betrothal," Hugh responded wryly.

Three

*J*OHN, KING OF ENGLAND, RUBBED AN APPRECIATIVE THUMB over the carved ivory panels protecting the cover of the book in his hand. "My magnates complain of their poverty, but they still have the wherewithal to gift me with items like this." Opening a page, he pointed to an illuminated capital. "Crushed lapis and gold," he said. "How much did that cost the Earl of Norfolk?"

"I do not know what is in his coffers, sire." William Longespée, Earl of Salisbury, shook the dice in his fist and cast them on the gaming board.

"Do you not?" John's eyes held a sardonic gleam. "You spend enough time in Bigod company. I thought you might have a notion."

"The earl keeps his coffers to himself, and it is not the kind of thing a guest asks."

"But you are more than a guest; you are family too," John said silkily.

Longespée silently cursed as the dice fetched up on the trestle as a two and a one. John's luck might be uncertain in other areas, but he had been winning at dice all night. The words, just spoken so pleasantly, were intended to sting. His royal half-brother was well aware of the tangled emotions Longespée harboured for his Bigod relatives, and exploited them without remorse. "I am your family too, but I do not know the amount of silver stored in your strongbox."

John laughed unkindly. "You know that there is soon to be at least another mark of silver," he said, indicating their game with his free hand. "The pity is I always have to lend you more in order to win it back. Does the Earl of Norfolk bail you out when you visit your mother?"

Longespée flushed. "We do not game."

"No, I suppose not. Roger Bigod wouldn't take the risk." John delicately turned the pages of the exquisite little book.

Longespée reached for his wine. It was a privilege to keep close company with John; to sit in the king's private apartments in the castle at York, drink the ruby Gascon wine, and lose his silver in games of chance. But for the stain of bastardy, he would have been a prince himself. His mother had been a girl of fifteen when John's father, King Henry, had taken her for his mistress and got her with child. She had married Roger Bigod, Earl of Norfolk, when Longespée was an infant, and Longespée had been raised to manhood in the royal household. She had since told him how much she had grieved at being forced to part from him—that his father the king had given her no choice in the matter. She had gone on to bear her sanctioned husband a litter of legitimate but less exalted offspring, and raised them far from royal circles in Yorkshire and East Anglia. Longespée was contemptuous of his womb-mates and at the same time he envied them what they possessed and he didn't. He paid sporadic visits to their great fortress at Framlingham. The experience was always a mingling of joy and pain and he was usually relieved to make his farewells—but reluctant too.

"So." John carefully closed and latched the book—he had more respect for literature and the written word than he did for people. "What do you think about this marriage contract between the Marshal's eldest girl and your half-brother?"

"It seems sound policy to me," Longespée replied cautiously.

John ran his tongue around the inside of his mouth. A sneer entered his voice. "Bigod ever has his eye to profit and advancement, but all done to the letter of the law, naturally." He cocked a speculative eye. "Your Ela was nine years old when you married, wasn't she?"

Longespée gave a cautious nod. "Thereabouts."

"Luscious sixteen now. How long did you wait?"

Longespée's complexion darkened. "Long enough."

"No belly on her yet, though." John flashed a wolfish smile. "Still, the trying keeps you busy, eh? You'll have plenty of advice to give your brother when his time comes."

Longespée said nothing save by his rigid posture and expression. He hated it when John spoke of his private life in that tone of voice. That was the problem; John didn't see it as a personal matter, but Longespée did. He adored Ela and he was protective of her. Knowing what a predator John was, he seldom brought her to court. He was careful not to speak of her either, because he had observed how jealous John was of anything that came between him and those whom he considered his individual territory. Longespée knew he was one of John's possessions and was not unduly bothered by it, because it gave him prestige and a place at the heart of the court. There was a price to pay, but then there always was. He strove to be honourable in his own life, and looked the other way when things happened that he could not control.

Smiling, John picked up the dice, shook them in his fist, and cast a six and a five. "Come now," he said. "Do not make that face at me; I did but jest. Good fortune to your Marshal and Bigod kin. They are most deserving of each other." He managed to make it sound like an insult, which probably it was.

❖❖❖

In the morning, the court prepared to go hunting, and Longespée made his way through the mêlée of dogs and horses in the stable yard to find and congratulate his half-brother on his forthcoming nuptials. He would rather have avoided Hugh, but one had to preserve the courtesies.

Longespée saw the glistening silver mare first, her harness arrayed in the red and gold Bigod colours, and his heart swelled with envy. His stepfather kept the best stable of horseflesh in England and Hugh, as the heir, naturally received first pick. The latter was deep in conversation with a groom and Longespée gave a contemptuous shake of his head. There were intermediaries to deal with servants. Drawing himself up, he adjusted his cloak and went forward. "Brother," he said, forcing the word out before it stuck in his throat. "Well met. I hear congratulations are due."

Hugh turned and smiled, although his sea-blue gaze was tepid. His hair gleamed like dull gold in the pallid winter sunlight. "Thank you." He looked dubious. "I am still growing accustomed to the notion. How is Ela?"

"She is well." Longespée replied stiltedly, remembering what John had said about advice and feeling awkward. "Will your bride come to Framlingham?"

Hugh shook his head. "Not immediately. I still have some bachelor years left to enjoy."

"Make the most of them then—but you will take pleasure in a wife too, I think. Ela is a constant delight to me." Formalities complete, Longespée moved around Hugh to examine the mare. "Fast?" He checked her legs with knowing hands.

Hugh nodded and relaxed a little. "Very. She'd beat any courser in this stable over a mile."

"You reckon she could beat de Braose's black?" Longespée nodded in the direction of the entourage belonging to the lord of Bramber. A groom was tending a powerful Spanish stallion with arched neck and broad rump. The horse was fresh and sidling, eager to run.

"Easily," Hugh said with a hint of bravado.

"Easily enough to wager on it?" Longespée felt the familiar burst of excitement that always accompanied a gamble. He imagined himself astride the silver mare; her speed, her strength. Knowing Hugh, he'd not have tested the half of her mettle yet.

Hugh hesitated.

"Or was it just an idle boast with no proof behind it?"

Hugh's blue eyes flashed. "It was no boast."

"Then you'd race her?"

"I..."

Longespée turned at a slap on his shoulder and faced another of his half-brothers: Ralph. "Hah, the whole family's here!" He greeted the newcomer with a heartier embrace than he had given Hugh. He could bear Ralph; indeed he enjoyed his company. The lad was younger, his admiration was obvious, and he wasn't the heir to an earldom three times the size of Longespée's.

Ralph laughed. His voice had a deep adolescent crack. "No, there's just me and William and Hugh with our father. The others are still in Norfolk. We've been helping Hugh hunt wolves at Settrington."

"Catch any?"

"A male and female. They'd have started a new pack if we hadn't taken them. I've got the pelts."

Longespée's nostrils flared. "They stink."

"That's what William says."

Longespée rubbed his jaw. "So," he said, getting down to business, "do you reckon your brother's mare would beat de Braose's black?"

"What, Arrow?" The youth put his hands on his hips. "Of course she would. There's no faster horse in England!"

"Well then, you have nothing to lose." Longespée turned to Hugh. "What do you say? Will you lend her to me?"

"Go on, Hugh, do it!" Ralph's grey gaze shone with enthusiasm.

"What about the hunt?" Hugh prevaricated.

"You've got other mounts, haven't you?" Longespée waved an impatient hand.

With great reluctance, Hugh handed over the reins. "Be careful with her."

Longespée flashed a condescending smile. "Don't worry, I know horses. I could ride before I could walk." He patted the mare's neck, set his foot to the stirrup, and swung astride. Exhilaration warmed him as his perspective changed and he was able to look down on Hugh from a superior height—which was appropriate and as it should be, since he was the son of a king. He sent his herald to make the challenge and wagered five marks on the outcome.

De Braose was amused by the bet and eager to compete, although given his bulk and maturing years, he put one of his squires in the saddle. "You're never afraid of the odds against you, Longespée, I'll say that for you," he chuckled, his breath clouding the air. He smacked his hand against the black's solid neck, making the stallion flinch and sidle.

The king arrived, cloaked and booted, ready for the chase, and eyed the proceedings with a mingling of interest and scorn before strolling over to Longespée. "I hazard de Braose's stallion will win." He handed up his whip of plaited black leather. "You'll be needing this to stand any chance."

Hugh's heart began to thud. "Sire, I never whip my horses, and neither does my father—"

"Then perhaps you should." John looked contemptuous. "Horses, dogs, women, and bishops. All benefit from the lash to quicken their paces from time to time." He waved his hand at

Longespée. "Make her fly, brother, because my lord de Braose will give you no quarter."

Longespée reined the mare towards the castle gate in a tight turn that pulled on her mouth. Ralph sprang to his saddle and followed his half-brother at a rapid trot. Hugh swallowed a repeat warning, knowing they would think him an old woman, and instead snapped at a groom to saddle up his remount. He had to leap aside as de Braose's big black came shouldering through, sweat creaming against the line of the reins on its neck. Hugh's stomach was hollow. He wished he had left Arrow at Settrington, or stayed there himself. There was less danger in chasing wolves.

A crowd had gathered in a field beyond Micklegate Bar and other men were wagering their swiftest horses against the main contenders. The Earl of Derby had put his squire up on a lean chestnut, and another of the king's half-brothers, Geoffrey, archbishop of York, had sent his bay courser with a young groom astride.

Hugh chewed the inside of his mouth as the distance was measured to four furlongs and a wooden post thrust into the ground as the turning point. He thought about making Longespée dismount and riding Arrow himself, but matters had gone beyond that point; all he could do was watch and pray. He was concerned at the way Arrow was sidling, swishing her tail and dancing on her hooves under Longespée's hands. The competitive light in his half-brother's eyes, the tension in his body, worried him too.

He was briefly distracted as his father arrived in the company of several Bigod retainers.

"What's happening?" Roger cocked his head towards the milling men and horses.

Hugh told him. His father's expression remained unchanged, but Hugh sensed his displeasure. "I should have refused," he said.

The earl nodded. "You should, but you will know better next time. Learn from this—both of yourself and of other men. William Longespée covets that which is best. He has a soldier's courage and a gambler's heart—and that is why Ralph loves him as he does."

Riders and horses clustered at the start of the impromptu course, eight in all by now, their mounts prancing and eager, the riders fretting the reins and casting intimidating glances at each other. De Braose's black snapped and lashed out at all who came near. Someone quipped that the horse was not unlike de Braose's acerbic wife, if somewhat less ridden. There was ribbing too for Hugh's mare amid remarks about untrammelled virginity. Longespée laughed aloud. Hugh forced a smile, although he had never felt less like smiling in his life. He felt queasy as he watched Longespée pull on Arrow's ears and slap her sweating neck with all the intimacy of an owner.

A starting line had been marked across the grass with floor sand from the king's chamber and the horses jostled and milled behind it. A herald arrived bearing a horn, set it to his lips, and blew the away with gusto. As if flung from a catapult, mounts and men hurtled over the line. Clods churned and flew, showering the onlookers. Hugh followed Arrow's surging white rump and the banner of her silver tail. Briefly she was hemmed in by a sea of bay, chestnut, and black, but soon edged in front and sped away from them like a wind-blown cloud.

"He's riding her too hard." Hugh craned on tiptoe as the horses disappeared from sight. "He should be pacing her; she'll be caught!" Hearing the strain in his own voice, he collected himself, aware that people were watching him. As heir to the Earldom of Norfolk, he had a duty to appear strong before his peers, especially when speculation was rife concerning the Marshal alliance. A man who showed weakness over a horse was a man who might be weak in other areas.

The rapid drumming of hoofbeats vibrated through his boot soles. Ralph was yelling in a voice like a raw knife blade: "They're winning! They're winning! Come on, girl, fly like the wind!"

Arrow was indeed still leading as the horses hurtled back towards the starting line, but with each stride, de Braose's black was gaining ground, and so was the archbishop's bay. The mare was galloping hard, but that first spark had been spent on the outward journey and now she was straining and under pressure.

"Go on!" Ralph roared, punching the air. "Go on!"

Arrow's ears were pressed against her skull as she lunged for the next stride and the next, while the black closed her down on the right and the bay on the left. A length, half a length, a head. Longespée raised his arm and the whip came down once and again and the mare almost flattened herself to the ground in a final burst of speed that brought her over the sand line a head and shoulders in front of the other two. Still galloping, still carried forward by her momentum, she stumbled, pitched, and went down, mane over tail, legs thrashing. Longespée rolled clear, staying down and curled up as the rest of the horses thundered past. Uttering a howl of denial, Hugh ran out to the mare and fell to his knees at her side. Scarlet rivulets streamed from her nostrils and although she was still breathing, and struggling to rise, he knew he was looking at a dead horse.

Longespée lurched to his feet and staggered across the churned grass to the dying mare. "Christ," he gasped, ashen-faced, and wiped his hand across his mouth. "Dear Christ."

Hugh didn't hear him. He was watching the light go from Arrow's eyes and the shuddering of her limbs as the effort to rise became death throes. Her blood flowed hot against his folded knees. Leaning over her, he cupped her cheek and rubbed the coronet of hair starring her forehead.

Her last breath fluttered out and her limbs ceased to twitch. Hugh felt his own blood congeal. People crowded round, looking, exclaiming, drawn to the tragedy and the spectacle. William de Braose arrived, stared for a moment with curling lip, and then shoved a heavy pouch into Longespée's hand.

"Count yourself fortunate that the line wasn't ten yards further," he growled. "No good having a fast horse if it's going to drop dead under you." With a single, scornful glance over his shoulder, he stalked off in the direction of his sweating stallion.

Rage flickered through Hugh's numbness. He lurched to his feet, the hem of his blue tunic blotched with Arrow's blood. "You used the whip," he accused Longespée in a fury-clogged voice.

"Only the once." Longespée drew shallow breaths, one hand pressed to his ribs. "God's life, she died because she wasn't sound, not because I struck her. It could have happened at any time. Better now than in the midst of a hunt or a battle campaign."

The excuses shattered Hugh's control and he seized Longespée by the throat. "You rode her to death!" he sobbed, his voice breaking. "Her blood is on your hands!" But the blood was on his own, rimmed around his fingernails, staining the creases in his knuckles.

His father dragged him off Longespée and put his bulk between them. "Enough! Whatever has to be said and done, let us not make it more of a spectacle than it already is."

White-faced, clearly in pain, Longespée responded with a stiff nod. Hugh clenched his body, squeezing down upon his own raw anger.

"I shall recompense you for your loss," Longespée offered. "I'll buy you another courser—one that is sound of wind and limb this time."

Hugh bared his teeth. "I want none of you. I would not take silver from your hand even if I were starving and destitute.

That horse was worth more to me than money—but you wouldn't understand that!"

Longespée said nothing, although his expression implied that he thought Hugh a fool to harbour sentiments over an animal. There was reproach too that his offer was being rejected with such bad grace.

The king arrived. Someone had retrieved his whip from where it had fallen as Longespée rolled clear from the stricken horse, and now John gripped it in his hand. "A bad business." He shook his head. "My condolences, Bigod. Your mare had a turn of speed, but speed is not everything." He gave Roger and Hugh a pointed look. "You need to look to your bloodlines, and have a care to how you breed your next generation."

"Sire, thank you for your concern and your advice," Roger replied in a neutral tone. "Be assured I will take it to heart. No bloodline is immune to failure."

John looked sourly amused. "Indeed not, my lord." As he started to turn away, he directed a look over his shoulder at Longespée. "You have leave to use my chamber while I am gone should you need succour for your injuries."

Longespée shook his head. "Thank you, sire, but I will join the hunt."

"As you wish. Your devotion is commendable—if fool-hardy." John tapped Longespée's arm lightly with the whip and took his leave.

With the king gone, Longespée handed the pouch containing the five marks to Roger, who did not refuse it. "I regret what happened," he said, breathing in shallow bursts, "but the horse would have foundered sooner or later."

"So you have said already, and so I accept," Roger replied impassively. Hugh couldn't bring himself to speak because, unlike his father, he didn't accept it at all.

Longespée managed a bow before walking gingerly towards

his own courser. Ralph, who had been watching wide-eyed on the edge of the fracas, hastily fetched the horse to the mounting block. By the time Longespée gained the saddle and gathered the reins he was white and sweating, but resolute.

As the hunt rode out, grooms from the Bigod household fetched ropes to drag the mare away. Hugh eyed the bag in his father's hand with revulsion. "It's blood money," he said, his throat working. "He gives us silver from the wager that cost the life of my mare and he thinks his debt is paid, but I tell you this, sire, I will never lend or give him anything of mine again, and that is a vow unto the grave."

Four

*M*AHELT DARTED HER FUTURE HUSBAND A LOOK THROUGH her lashes as he slipped a ring of plaited gold on to her heart finger. Three months ago, he had held her hand and danced with her at the Christmas feast in Canterbury. Now the gesture was part of a ceremony as binding as marriage itself. Hugh's manner was serious, lacking the light exuberance he had possessed before. This time she was strongly aware of being in the company of a grown man with whom she had nothing in common beyond their mutual status and the obligation of performing a family duty.

Mahelt pressed her lips together and tried to ignore the fear uncoiling in her stomach. It wasn't as if she had to go and live with him right now. This was just a promise for later. All she had to do was make her responses, just like the progression of steps in a dance. She made herself look at him properly. His eyes were a summer sea-blue and a brief smile lit in them as they met hers, giving her a glimpse of the humour she remembered from the Christmas court. Reassured, Mahelt smiled a reply before looking down again in modest decorum.

From Caversham's chapel, the company repaired to the hall and a feast to honour the betrothal. Hugh's mother enveloped Mahelt in a sweet-scented embrace and welcomed her to the family. Hugh's father was expansive with satisfaction and reminded her of a cockerel with fluffed-up feathers. As usual he wore a magnificent hat, red today and adorned with curling plumes. Hugh was also more relaxed in the aftermath of the formalities, but his behaviour towards her remained courtly and polite, and he showed no inclination to play as he had done at Christmas. Mahelt kept her eyes downcast as befitted a future bride, although under the table she was swinging her legs. Had it been feasible, she would have kilted up her gown and run and run, just to be rid of her surplus tension and energy.

Hugh placed the choicest morsels before her, but she wasn't hungry. Lent might be over and dainties once more allowed in the diet, but she was too tense to enjoy the succulent young duck and fragrant barley grains perfumed with cardamom.

"When we are married, I will take you riding and show you around our estates," he said. "Would you like that?"

Mahelt nodded. "I have a new palfrey," she volunteered. "She's called Amber."

His eyelids tightened and she thought she had said or done something wrong, but then his expression smoothed out and he smiled. "Indeed, and very fine too. I watched you arrive on her and thought what a good rider you were."

She felt a glow of pride at his praise. "Do you still have that white mare I saw you riding at Christmas?"

The dark look returned to his face. "No," he said, "I don't, but I'm going to Normandy soon to bring our stud herd to England, and I'll choose a new horse then."

Mahelt swung her legs harder and toyed with a piece of bread. She decided not to ask what had happened to the mare because she could tell from Hugh's expression that he didn't want to speak about it.

Towards the end of the meal an armourer arrived with some

sword blades that Mahelt's father had been expecting and the men went to try them out, leaving the women to their talk.

Mahelt's second cousin Ela took the opportunity to admire the betrothal ring. "It's beautiful," she said, a smile in her hazel-grey eyes. Ela had been married to Hugh's half-brother William Longespée since she was nine years old. She was sixteen now, and a modest but confident young woman. Her husband was serving the king at court, but Ela had been glad to attend the betrothal.

Studying the ring, Mahelt tried to imagine being a wife, but it was like putting on a new dress that was too big for her, and people saying she would grow into it.

"Do you know when the marriage will be?" Ela asked.

Mahelt shook her head. "Not for a few years."

"Countess Ida is lovely," Ela reassured her. She cast a fond look in the direction of her mother-in-law. "She has taught me so much."

"I like her," Mahelt agreed, knowing that no one would ever match up to her own mother.

"What about Hugh, do you like him?" An impish sparkle lit in Ela's eyes. "He's handsome, isn't he?"

Mahelt felt her cheeks grow warm as she nodded.

"And kind too," Ela added. "You cannot set too high a price upon kindness in a match—and respect. My husband is good to me and I love him dearly. I only wish that he and Hugh were fonder of each other. I am sorry for it because they are both fine men in their individual ways, and they come from the same womb."

"Why aren't they fond?" Mahelt asked, her curiosity thoroughly aroused.

Ela's brow furrowed. "My Will refuses to talk about it; he becomes irritated with me if I broach the subject, and pretends it is of no consequence, but I believe it has to do with matters of family and belonging."

Mahelt's brow furrowed as she tried to puzzle out what Ela was saying. She supposed Longespée might feel awkward among the Bigods owing to his bastardy, although from what she had seen of Hugh's nature, she didn't think he would be cruel or unwelcoming to his half-brother because of it, and surely as the son and brother of a king, Longespée was well compensated.

"My husband has a foot in two worlds," Ela said. "He finds it difficult because the king expects him to tell him things about his Bigod family, and his Bigod family look to him to ease their path with the king. Balancing the two is not always easy for his honour and his duty."

Mahelt nodded. She understood that part because her father often had to tread a fine line between his duty to his family and his duty to the king. It still didn't explain the animosity between Hugh and Longespée though.

"It is the place of a wife to be a peace-weaver," Ela said. "I do my best, but Will is proud and stubborn, and Hugh hides behind a smile he doesn't always mean."

While Mahelt was trying to digest this food for thought, a messenger arrived at the gallop, dismounted, and hurried straight to her father. Whatever he said as he knelt made everyone cease their swordplay and gather around him, hands on hips, expressions concerned. Mahelt's stomach wallowed. Messengers were always coming and going at Caversham. Indeed, her father was seldom not in their company, but for one to approach him in the midst of a social gathering meant that the news would not wait.

As the group dispersed, Mahelt ran up to Will and grabbed his arm. "What's happened?" she demanded.

Her brother pushed his dark hair off his forehead in an agitated gesture. "The castle at Gaillard has fallen," he said. "It means Rouen is exposed to the French because Gaillard guarded the river approach. The king's lost Normandy for certain now."

Mahelt thought of the high castle walls at Longueville and the vista of undulating fields ripe with dark-gold wheat seen from its battlements. "Does that mean Papa will lose his lands too?" she asked.

Will shrugged. "Not if he can help it," he said, "but it's bad."

Five

MONTFIQUET, NORMANDY, MAY 1204

LYING ON HIS BED, HUGH LISTENED TO THE BIRDSONG OUTSIDE his chamber window. The rich warble of a thrush in the cool dawn air swelled his breast with emotion which threatened to overflow like the bird's canticle. Beyond the shutters, the manor was stirring to life. He could hear voices, the whinny of a horse, the squeak of the winch winding up the well bucket. In a moment he would have to stir too and join the bustle, knowing that by the time the sun was warming the spring grass, this place would be a memory he could never again refresh—unless a miracle happened.

He turned his head on the pillow to look at Nicolette. Her hair was a dark, deep red that reminded him of cherries and her mouth was soft and sweet. He could never get enough of kissing her. They had left the shutters open last night on a sky thick with stars, and had made love knowing that when morning came, their lives would not mesh again. He knew he was only one of several select clients, including a bishop and a wealthy wine merchant, but even so affection between them extended beyond the exchange of payment for exquisite services rendered.

As if sensing his scrutiny, she opened her eyes and yawned at him.

"It's light," he said. "We have to go." He leaned over to

embrace her one final time and she wrapped her arms around his neck and held him hard.

Outside the noises had increased in variety and volume. The grooms were out saddling up the horses. A woman was calling to the chickens. Reluctantly, Hugh drew away and, with the damp imprint of their kiss still on his lips, began to dress. She sat up and watched him, the sheet folded across her breasts and her ruby hair spilling down her spine. "I am going to miss your visits." She yawned again, like a cat. "Perhaps when all is settled between the king of England and the king of France, you will visit me in Bayeux."

"Yes, perhaps." He knew he wouldn't.

When they were both dressed, he presented her with a little embroidered belt purse with silk cords. The weight of silver within was generous and gave the pouch a pleasant heft. It was her fee, but bestowed as a gift rather than payment.

She thanked him with a last, lingering kiss. "Think of me sometimes," she said.

"I will think of you more than sometimes," he vowed. "The difficulty will be not thinking."

She stroked the side of his face and drew away. "For a while, my Hugh, but time will soften the edges. What is tender to the touch now will become nostalgia."

He knew she was right. These last moments were achingly sweet, but once the tie was severed, they would both move on to the next point in their lives.

Together they went down to the courtyard. Hugh cupped his hands to boost Nicolette on to her mount and for a moment stood by her saddle, his hand encircling her ankle. Then he opened his grip and let her go, accompanied by two of his men for escort.

She looked back once, and he memorised the pale oval of her face and the smile parting her full lips. When she faced the road again, he too turned away and, with determination, applied himself to the task of assembling his father's horses for the journey to the coast. He had chosen a new courser from among the herd—a four-year-old stallion with a coat the colour of polished jet. Hebon, named for his colour, showed the strain of Spanish blood in his convex nose and the proud curve of his neck, covered by a waterfall of black mane. Hugh had ridden him over the estate yesterday, bidding farewell to familiar boyhood haunts, knowing that soon the French would come and seize the land, breed their own horses here, mulch the apples, and make the cider. On the flat fields between the orchards he had taken his courage in his hands and put Hebon to the gallop: hard, flat out, the wind in his face, his cloak flying. He had experienced a feeling of release and, at that moment, had finally begun to put the incident with Arrow behind him and bid her farewell. It was in the past; live and learn.

So early in the season, the verges were green and the roads firm but not yet dusty as Hugh and his retinue of serjeants and drovers herded the horses towards the coast three miles away. Hugh's adolescent brothers rode with him, their father having deemed it useful experience for them to accompany him; and indeed they had pulled their weight and been of great help. With unusual tact, they had left him alone last night, although their nudges and smiles this morning were less than discreet.

Ralph cantered ahead, his hat set at a rakish angle on his dark curls. He had plaited a red ribbon in his mount's tail. Hugh shook his head but had to grin. To Ralph, life was one gigantic adventure. William joined Hugh, his own expression sombre with reflection. "Why do you think our father decided not to leave one of us in Normandy?" he asked. "Ralph or I could have sworn an oath to the king of France and kept the estates for our family."

"Neither you nor Ralph is of age and leading men would be

difficult—no matter what Ralph thinks." Hugh cast an exasperated gesture at their high-spirited younger brother. "The lands we own might give us good horses and cider, but they are a spit in the ocean compared to our English estates. Our father will not put one of us out on a limb here. Rather he will consolidate what we have that we can hold for a certainty and that won't cost us more to defend than it provides in revenue."

"The Marshal's not pulling back, is he? Not from the news I heard this morning."

Hugh looked at him sharply. "What news?"

"A jongleur arrived while we were breaking our fast and you were still...otherwise occupied. He was seeking employment, but since we were leaving, he moved on to the next ville."

"And?" Hugh's tone continued brusque.

"You know the Marshal has gone to see the French king to try and negotiate a peace settlement?"

Hugh nodded. "That's common knowledge."

"The jongleur told me that the Marshal has offered King Philip five hundred marks to let him keep his Norman lands for another year, and Philip has accepted with the proviso that after that time, the Marshal must either give them up or swear allegiance to France—unless John has recovered the territory, of course."

Hugh mulled the information and watched Ralph cantering up and down the line of horses. The Marshal lands in Normandy were much greater than their own. It wasn't just a matter of a few manors and orchards and horses. It was Orbec and Longueville and Bienfait and all the rest. King John was not going to take kindly to such news. Private arrangements between his barons and the king of France were the stuff of royal nightmares.

"I hope it doesn't cause difficulties for us, with you being betrothed to the Marshal's daughter," William said darkly. "What if we get caught up in any disputes that arise from this?"

Hugh made a gesture of negation. "Our father is too shrewd to let that happen, and the Marshal is no fool when it comes to keeping his hide intact. Why do you think he chose to settle his eldest daughter with us in the first place?"

William shrugged. "Because he and our father are friends and allies. He wants unions with all the great families in the land in order to strengthen his position, and he has the sons and daughters to accomplish that."

"Yes," Hugh agreed, "but he also knows our father treads a steady path. We are powerful enough to protect his daughter, and East Anglia is the size of a kingdom in itself, away from the hub of the court. We can live as we choose and none will interfere."

"You hope."

Hugh conceded the truth of William's remark with a tilt of his head. He suspected that, whether soldier or judge, the road ahead was going to be full of potholes and that each man would have to find his path as best he could.

Six

CAVERSHAM, SPRING 1205

ILL FOLDED HIS ARMS AND WATCHED HIS SISTER, A LOOK OF exasperated amusement on his face. "Surely you're not keeping that thing?"

Sleeves rolled up, linen apron tied at her waist, Mahelt was busy bathing a scruffy, scabby brown and white terrier with the same tender thoroughness with which she had bathed her wooden dolls as a smaller child. The dog in the tub shivered and whined, but tolerated the treatment. Now and then it tried to lick Mahelt's face. "Mama said I could," she replied without looking up. "He's just dirty and needs a bath."

Will snorted. "There's a lot more wrong with him than being dirty! For a start he's missing a foreleg, or had you not noticed?"

Mahelt scowled at him. "Father Walter says he probably got it caught in a trap when he was a pup and that someone managed to cut it off and save him—like old Adam." The latter was a one-legged cart driver, once a serjeant in her father's troop, who had been wounded in the calf by an arrow and had survived the ensuing amputation.

The chaplain had found the dog scavenging in one of the barns after a group of players had passed through, and it probably belonged to them. He was mangy and flea-ridden; his ribs stared through his coat like rake tines; but the vigorous wag of his tail and bright, beseeching eyes had stayed the priest's first inclination to fetch a guard and have the creature knocked on the head with a spear butt. Mahelt, grieving for a pet bird that had recently died, had seized on the stray and immediately given him her heart.

"He won't be able to run with the hunt or dig out foxes," Will said.

"Not all dogs hunt." She lifted him out of the tub, liberally wetting the front of her gown in so doing. "He'll live in the bower and bark at strangers."

The dog shook itself vigorously, spraying water droplets far and wide. Somehow it stayed on its feet. Mahelt giggled, while Will leaped backwards, cursing. "That's one part of your dowry the Bigods might think twice about accepting," he said with disdain.

"Hugh likes dogs." She gave him a superior look. "Anyway, I'm not going to be married just yet." Slightly over a year had passed since her betrothal and life had settled back into its usual rhythm. Mostly she forgot that she was betrothed at all. She was making items to go into her marriage chest, embroidered pillows, sheets and coverlets, fine table napery and the like, but while they were frequent reminders of her future, they were also part of an everyday background. She kept her ring in her coffer and only wore it on special days. Talk of her marriage was like a fairy tale about someone else. She kept Hugh Bigod in her prayers, but it was a routine thing to do. She did not know him well enough to have him colour her thoughts and had not seen him since the betrothal because he had either been about his father's business or following the court.

Will shook his head at her and the dog, but crouched and held out his hand to be sniffed and then licked. He produced a crust from his pouch that he had been saving for his horse. The tail wagged with enthusiasm, and the bread, although taken with the utmost politeness and delicacy, vanished in a gulp.

"Father Walter says we should call him Tripes." Mahelt dropped a towel over the dog's back and rubbed him energetically. "He says it's Latin for three legs."

"And it's English for guts." Will grinned. "Tell you what, I'll make him a collar and leash out of Equus's tail hair. Would you like that?"

Mahelt cocked her head at him. "So you think we should keep him too?"

He gave a nonchalant shrug. "Of course not, but you'll do it anyway; I know how stubborn you are."

Mahelt left off drying the dog to give him a fierce hug. There were times when she thought him unbearably arrogant, opinionated, and so sure of his masculine prerogative that she wanted to throttle him. But there were times like this too, when he exposed his kinder side and made her laugh. Besides, he was her big brother and she loved him.

"I can't wait for Papa to come home so I can show him," she said. "Do you think you'll have time to make his collar by then?"

"Perhaps," Will said. "It depends what happens in Portsmouth."

Mahelt shaded her eyes against the sun the better to see his expression. "What do you mean?"

"The king wants to cross the Narrow Sea and invade Normandy. The barons don't want him to become involved in a campaign until he has an heir. A lot of them are saying too that it's no concern of theirs what happens outside of England. Our father thinks the army will not sail at all."

Mahelt felt envious that her brother was a party to the political discussions that she, as a girl, was denied access to. Her brain was just as good as his—probably more so, because she couldn't fight her way physically out of situations but had to rely on her wits. Her mother was always involved in discussions pertaining to their lands, but her mother was a countess in her own right and her father respected that and gave her due credit. A daughter, unfortunately, did not have the same privilege. "Does Papa want to go?" she asked.

"He can't because of his oath to Philip of France. If he does, he'll be foresworn and lose Longueville and Orbec for certain."

"Won't he be in trouble with King John if he doesn't go?"

Will picked up a stone and aimed it at a fern growing out of a crack in the mortar of the castle wall. "Probably, but that's nothing new for anyone. There's hardly a baron manages to keep the king's favour these days. He takes money from us and pays his mercenaries to do his bidding in our stead. The Bigods are in favour, but that's because of William Longespée's influence, and because Roger of Norfolk doesn't put those hats of his on top of his battlements." He slung another stone hard after the first. "Just think, in the way of kinship ties, John will almost be your brother by marriage."

Mahelt sniffed. "Yours too," she retorted, "because you are mine by blood."

Will curled his lip at her, and then nodded at Tripes. "Is he supposed to be doing that?"

Mahelt whipped round and shouted in dismay, for the dog had found a heap of fresh horse dung and was rolling in it with luxurious abandon.

"Looks like you're going to need some more water." Will laughed. "Are you still certain you want to keep him?"

❖❖❖

At Portsmouth, Hugh sat under the awning of his father's striped pavilion and sheltered from the heat of the June sun. The tent had been set up to face the blue glitter of the sea. Around him the Bigod troops had begun striking camp. The cooking fire was being left to go out and men were folding up canvas and harnessing packhorses.

His father returned from the beach and flopped on to a stool. Hugh poured a cup of watered wine from the jug on the trestle and handed it to him. "The king is still at it," Roger said. "If he hopes to embarrass us all into embarking with him, he will be disappointed."

Hugh rubbed the sun-reddened back of his neck. "I have told the men to strike camp." For the last two days, the king had been trying to shame his barons into crossing the Narrow Sea by embarking himself and sailing up and down within view of those on the shore. Thus far the only men to join him had been his mercenaries and Longespée. Treading a delicate path, his father had declined to put his own men on ships, but had offered up the shield tax on his knights' fees so the king could buy mercenaries if he wished.

"Good." From beneath the broad, shady brim of his straw hat, his father gazed at the shimmering vista of tents. "I doubt we'll be here for much longer."

"What will happen to the Marshal?" Yesterday the latter and King John had quarrelled in public over the Marshal's refusal to embark because he had sworn allegiance to Philip of France for his Norman lands.

His father swatted away a persistent wasp. "If he is fortunate, then nothing. He has too many friends for the king to isolate him and pick him off, but he might find it wise to lie low for a while. He has dared more than I would, but then he has more to lose." He nodded towards the royal galley out on the water. "Look, they're coming in."

The king disembarked from the ship, followed by his household knights, mercenaries, and some of the crew, and stalked off in the direction of the royal pavilion. William Longespée crunched across the shingle and arrived at the array of tents lining the field beyond the shore. His own camp was still intact; indeed, his cook was applying the bellows to the fire and a spit of freshly caught grey mullet had been set to roast.

Seeing Roger and Hugh, Longespée diverted to speak to them. His complexion was the colour of tanned leather and weather-creases fanned at his eye corners. "The king is rightly furious," he told them, an air of checked anger in his own bearing. He set his hands to his hips and thrust out one foot, clad in dyed calf hide. "He cannot cross to Normandy without the backing of us all."

"There will be a more opportune time," Roger said evenly. "Better to husband our resources for now."

Longespée fixed him with a hard stare. "That is the opinion of some."

"Of the many," Hugh said. "As you can see with your own eyes."

Longespée shot him an irritated look. "That does not make it right."

Roger gestured to Longespée's pavilion. "I notice you are not packing up camp?"

"No." Longespée drew himself up. "I am to head an army to relieve La Rochelle. They have held out thus far, but they need men and supplies and at least the king can provide those for them, whatever else he is prevented from doing. It would be shameful beyond reckoning if the king of France were to devour Poitou as well as Normandy, don't you think?"

Roger inclined his head. His tone remained level and tactful. "I wish you success and may God speed your voyage and keep you safe."

Hugh repeated his father's sentiments, paying lip service to politeness, although his true feelings were somewhat more tepid. It was typical of his half-brother to see the thick of a military adventure as a superior duty and the right thing to do. Let others worry about the harvests and see to the welfare of everything that underpinned the world. *What else are servants for?* Longespée had asked on more than one occasion.

Longespée bowed in return. "I pray you greet my lady mother on my behalf and tell her I will bring Ela to visit on my return."

"I will do so."

Longespée continued on to his tent and began issuing commands. Hugh let out his breath on a hard sigh, unclenched his fists, and flexed his hands to ease the tendons.

"At least sending troops to La Rochelle with a commander he can trust is sound strategy on John's part," Roger said. "It will keep him a thorn in King Philip's rear and it is something that's feasible to accomplish. It's good employment for Longespée too. He might be as irritating as a hair shirt, but there is no denying his skill as a soldier."

Hugh wrestled with his antipathy. In fairness, despite his insufferable air of superiority, his half-brother's military and maritime abilities had to be acknowledged. Realising that his father was watching him with knowing eyes, he stilled the motion of his hands.

"Longespée is valuable to the king, and valuable to our family because of it," Roger said. "Your mother cherishes him; he is my stepson and your half-brother. For all these reasons I make him welcome..."

"Sire," Hugh replied stiffly.

"...but he is not a Bigod."

The subtle humour in his father's remark changed Hugh's expression. He began to grin, and then could not help a chuckle. "God forbid."

His father slapped him on the shoulder. "Come," he said. "The horses are saddled and we can leave. Let the baggage follow at leisure."

Seven

HAMSTEAD MARSHAL, BERKSHIRE, JULY 1205

*M*AHELT SAT ON RICHARD'S BED IN THE CHAMBER HER brothers shared, her world in tatters. Will's bed was a stripped frame. The mattress had been rolled up, secured with straps, and put on the packhorse together with the sheets and bolsters. His clothing chest was empty, his gaming board and box of bone counters gone. No garments draped the hanging poles and no mantle or hood occupied the wall peg. Two nights ago they had played dice together in here, bantering with argumentative pleasure, the atmosphere full and vibrant. Now nothing of his presence remained to say he had even existed. Mahelt stared down at the small, colourful piece of green and yellow silk folded in her hands. She could not believe King John had demanded Will as a hostage for her family's loyalty and she was still reeling from the knowledge that her father had agreed to give him up. There had been trouble at court because her father had pledged himself to the king of France for their Norman lands in order to safeguard them until Richard came of age. Now, in retaliation, John had demanded Will. She had been told that her brother was going to be a squire and it was a positive thing for him: it would broaden his horizons and be a valuable part of his training; but Mahelt knew the words were a colourful gauze covering a turd. Her parents had quarrelled over John's demand. Her mother had wanted to refuse, but her father said they had no choice—and his word was law. Never before had Mahelt's security been threatened by division in the household and she was deeply upset and angry.

The door opened and Will entered. He was cloaked and booted for his journey, a dark cap with a rolled brim covering his hair. His set expression gave nothing away, but Mahelt knew he didn't want to go—not to John.

"What are you doing here?" he asked curtly. "Everyone's waiting in the yard."

Mahelt lifted her chin. "I could ask the same of you."

"Making sure I haven't left anything behind." He crouched and extended his hand to Tripes, who had been snuffling round the corners of the room but came to lick him, then rolled over for a tummy rub.

Her throat constricted. "That's what I was doing...but you haven't; I've checked." Tears filled her eyes as she held out the piece of folded silk. "I was going to give you this when I'd finished it properly, but you'll have to have it now."

Will rose from fondling the dog, took it from her, and opened it out to reveal a small silk pennant designed to fly from a lance. It bore the Marshal blazon of a red lion snarling on a background half green and half gold.

He swallowed manfully. "I'll keep it with me always," he promised.

Mahelt couldn't bear it. It was all ending. Nothing would ever be the same again. What was it going to be like without him? With a small cry, she flung her arms around his neck and hugged him fiercely. "I won't ever let you go!"

He hugged her in return and swung her round. "I'll never leave in spirit. You'll always be with me, I swear."

She felt his skin and his hair and tried to reach inside him because she knew the embrace might be their last one. Whether it was or not, this moment closed the door on her childhood.

He had to use firm pressure to unlock her arms and push her away. "It'll be all right, Matty." He smiled, trying to make light of it. "I think you are just jealous because you want to be a squire in my stead and ride a fine big warhorse."

The use of her nickname made her want to howl aloud with grief, but she held it in until her stomach ached. "I would take your place if I could."

"I believe you would, but I don't think I would have much skill at embroidery and the Bigods would certainly receive a shock."

Mahelt forced herself to play along, and gave him a watery smile and a nudge of reproof.

"Besides, it's my duty." He cast a final, lingering look around the room. Mahelt put her hands behind her back, gripping them together in an effort not to throw herself at him again.

He ushered her ahead of him down the twisting stairs and out to the courtyard. The summer sun blazed upon the saddled horses and sumpters; it glittered on harness and trappings. Will had a new grey stallion for his journey, with Equus as his second string. Her father, who was escorting him, was already astride his horse and wore his customary air of calm. Mahelt wondered how he could be so strong and implacable. She tried to emulate him, but it was impossible. Her mother's complexion was pale and her eyes were full of grief, but she held her head high.

"We'll not be broken," Mahelt heard her say softly as they watched Will mount up. "We'll never be broken." Her voice became no more than a breath. "But oh my son, oh my child."

Mahelt's own grief welled up, as did her fury at King John for tearing into her family like this and opening such painful wounds. As the final horse trotted out of the gate, she whirled round and fled to the chamber she shared with her little sisters, threw herself down on her bed, pummelled her pillow, and wept.

After a while, her mother came and sat on the bed. Taking Mahelt in her arms, she stroked her hair. "Courage, daughter," she said, her own eyes puffy and red-rimmed. "Weep now, but tomorrow be strong. Remember who we are and that whatever else is taken from us, they will never strip our honour and our pride."

❖❖❖

Watching Ralph wander around the bedchamber with the distracted air of a lovesick swain, Hugh wrestled the urge to grab him by the scruff and shake some sense into him. It was on the tip of his tongue to snap that William Longespée was a mortal man, not a god, but telling him would only result in rolled eyes and hostility. Ralph had to discover such a thing for himself.

Ralph had been in this condition for a week now, ever since Longespée had come to visit, full of ebullience following his successful campaign at La Rochelle, and offered to take him into his household as a squire. Ralph had been ecstatic and desperate to seize the opportunity. Longespée had basked in the adulation and although nothing was said, it was plain he thought he was being gracious and bountiful towards his Bigod kin.

"It's all packed." Ralph glanced at the two baggage rolls at the side of his bed. He fixed wistful eyes on the pair of wolf pelts spread on the floor.

"Longespée won't thank you for bringing those," Hugh said. "Indeed, I suspect he won't allow you. He doesn't have that kind of tolerance."

Ralph sighed. "I suppose you are right."

"I know I am. I tell you what. I'll keep them to remind me of you, and they'll be here when you return—unless Mother throws them out."

"She won't," Ralph said. "She'll keep them, like she's kept all of our baby teeth and our first tunics and shoes."

Hugh grinned wry agreement, thinking of the chest in his mother's chamber filled with a motley assortment of mementos from their childhood. (His first hobby horse was in there, patched and refurbished, if a little bald around the ears.) Not that he could imagine her adding two wolf pelts to the collection. Even now, a year later, there was a heavy, unpleasant aroma when they were shaken out.

"I'm going to miss you." Hugh pulled Ralph into a rough, bear-cub embrace. "The Earl of Salisbury had better look after you well or I shall be down upon him with all the force of a stone from a trebuchet." He rubbed his knuckles over the top of Ralph's head. Ralph struggled free and aimed a swipe, but Hugh ducked out of the way.

"Don't worry," Ralph said. "I can take care of myself. I promise not to return swirling my cloak and posing as if I expect everyone to look at me." He struck an attitude.

"If you do, I'll be down on you also," Hugh warned, but he was laughing.

Ralph flashed an exuberant grin. "You'd have to catch me first." He dodged Hugh's cuff and, going to the bed, slung a satchel over his shoulder and hefted one of the baggage rolls. "I'm going to miss you too," he said. "And home." He looked around the chamber. "But not enough to stay."

Hugh lifted the second baggage roll and together the brothers left their bedchamber for the hall.

Longespée was seated talking to their mother. His garments were immaculate and draped with a casual artifice that left Hugh wondering how much practice it had taken to achieve such nonchalance. Their mother was listening attentively to him, her face alight with maternal pride. He was regaling her with a story about a school of dolphins that had played across their bows on the homeward journey from La Rochelle. He was good at telling tales, knowing how to make the gestures and flourishes so that one could almost see the steel-silver leap of the creatures from sea to sky and back to sea. Ralph's arrival was the signal for the conversation to break up and everyone to go out to the courtyard where Longespée's entourage awaited the order to leave. More fervent embraces ensued; shoulder slaps; exhortations to take care. Ralph knelt to his parents and received their blessing and an extra hug from his mother. A groom strapped his baggage to the packhorse and Ralph mounted his bay palfrey. His grey eyes were bright and he was quivering with the thrill of imminent adventure. Nevertheless, as he gathered his reins, he pushed out his chin and affected a straight-backed dignity.

Ida sniffed and dabbed at a tear, and Hugh curved a comforting arm around her shoulders. Hands gripped around his belt and legs squarely planted, his father stood a little aloof to watch his son ride out. "Count your blessings, madam," he said with an exasperated look at his wife. "At least he is going of his own free will and not as a hostage to Longespée's royal brother as the Marshal lad has done. May we always avoid such a situation."

Hugh felt his mother shiver under his hand. "Amen to that," she said. "I pray for the Marshals and their boy."

They returned to the hall; it was quiet now the visitors had gone. Hugh didn't miss Longespée's presence one bit, but there was a gap at his side where Ralph had been, and suddenly he was glad he had persuaded his merry younger brother to leave his pungent wolfskins behind.

Eight

ITTING AT HER NEEDLEWORK, MAHELT LISTENED TO THE patter of heavy rain outside the shutters. She was working on a bolster case to put in her wedding chest. Knowing how skilled her future mother-in-law was at embroidery, she was trying to make a neat job of the delicate whitework. Each time she set the needle into the fabric, she was reminded of how swiftly time was passing. Three months ago she had begun her fluxes. The flowers they were called, because, like a flower, her body had begun to produce seed and thus she was capable of conceiving a child, if not yet possessing the pelvic width to successfully birth one. Mahelt had been both proud and apprehensive at the appearance of the monthly blood because it marked her transition into womanhood, and brought her marriage a step closer. No one had raised the subject beyond a few teasing smiles and general talk while they worked on her trousseau, but she knew that what had been a distant speck on the horizon had moved significantly closer.

She raised her head towards the open window as she heard the sound of a horn blowing to announce her father's arrival and, with a quickening of relief, put her sewing aside.

Her mother left her own needlework and issued brisk orders

to build up the fire. "They'll be soaked to the skin," she said, glancing at the teeming rain.

Mahelt leaped to her feet, already reaching for her cloak. "I'll go down!" She flurried from the room, eager to be the first to greet her father and have him to herself for however brief a moment. Her soft goatskin shoes were no barrier to the bailey puddles, but she paid no heed nor to the water soaking upwards from the hem of her gown. As her father rode through the gateway, her excitement soared. For an instant she was a little girl in Normandy again, overjoyed at his return, demanding to be taken up on his saddle. That memory drove her forward now. Wearing a smile as wide as the sun, she reached his stirrup, half hoping he would remember old times too and reach down to her.

He had been hunched over his pommel, but he made an effort to sit up. "Matty." His voice emerged as a hoarse croak. "Matty, where's your mother?"

Mahelt's dazzle of excitement became a plummet of fear. His eyes were glittering and opaque at the same time, like polished but scratched stones. His cheeks wore a scarlet flush. "In the keep, instructing the women—"

"Fetch her then, sweetheart..." He dismounted but clung to the horse as his knees almost buckled. Mahelt felt the heat emanating from him like a brazier. "Go, child...do not come too close, there's a good girl. I'm tired from the journey; I wouldn't want to fall on you."

Mahelt heard him trying to make light of his difficulty and not succeeding. An attendant came to support him as the horse was led away. Mahelt raced back to the keep, splashing through the puddles. Her mother was in the hall, becloaked and on her way to greet her returning husband. Mahelt grabbed her arm. "Come quickly! Papa's sick. He's got a fever and he can't stand up!"

Her mother gave her a horrified look and took to her heels.

By the time she and Mahelt arrived in the lower ward, he was being supported towards the keep, his knight Jean D'Earley on one side and a sturdy groom on the other. After a single exclamation, Isabelle tightened her lips and hurried to help.

Mahelt would have joined her, but Isabelle ordered her to go and see that the bed was prepared and extra blankets and bolsters fetched. Mahelt sped to the task, snapping at the women to make haste. She plumped and shook the pillows herself, expending some of her frightened energy on them. When her father arrived, staggering badly, she ran to him, but he fended her off. "Let the men tend me, Matty. They are just as wet as I am. I'll be all right by and by."

Her mother sent her to deal with matters in the hall and liaise with the chamberlain and steward to see to the needs of the returning knights. Mahelt didn't want to go, but someone had to, and it obviously couldn't be her mother. The rest of the family was sent from the room too, to give her father peace, her mother said, although Mahelt suspected it was also to protect them from any evil vapours he might be exuding.

"What's wrong with him?" she asked Jean D'Earley once she had finished speaking with the chamberlain. He was her father's foremost knight, and a trusted family friend. Where her father was, Jean was invariably at his side.

Jean's attempted smile of reassurance did not reach his eyes, which told a different story. "He is tired and chilled after a hard journey, and has a touch of fever," he said. "I'm sure it is only a cold and he'll be better by the morning."

Mahelt fixed him with a challenging stare. "He's never ill."

"That is not true, but usually he shakes things off so quickly or with so little effort that no one sees. He's in the best place to be looked after—at home with his family; he'll be all right, you'll see." Jean chucked her under the chin.

Mahelt wanted to believe him but was not sure she did.

Jean might be one of the most dependable members of their household, but that didn't mean he would give her the straight truth if he was trying to protect her.

The steward arrived to ask her a question about which wine to use and she had to divert her attention, by which time Jean was busy among the men, settling them down, organising and making everything seem routine and normal, but Mahelt knew it couldn't be while her father was sick and her oldest brother might never come home at all.

❖ ❖ ❖

Breathing hard, Hugh cleaned his sword on the tunic of a dead French soldier. Four knights had been taken for ransom and the serjeants and footsoldiers had either fled or died. They had abandoned their baggage, including two cartloads of armour and eight pack ponies laden with sacks of flour and other supplies. The French army that had been besieging the town of Niort was melting away before the English advance, but those who had left it too late, or chosen the wrong roads to make their escape, were coming to grief at the hands of King John's troops.

Hugh's arm ached fiercely from the clash of the fight but he was unharmed; none of his men had been wounded and the outcome was successful. The armour they had seized would be very useful and the cooks would be glad of the flour.

Hugh organised his men, saw the prisoners tied on horses, and rode to rejoin the main Bigod force from which he had originally detached in order to reconnoitre. The troop, led by his father, had also caught some stragglers, but had let them go with their lives, although minus their mounts, weapons, and money.

"They're well on the run," his father said with satisfaction. "The scouts report that the road into Niort is open. The French have drawn back."

Hugh gave his father the tally of profit from his skirmish. "No wounded," he said. "Four good destriers and eight sumpters as well as the armour carts and ten bushels of flour."

"Good grist to the mill." His father chuckled at his own weak pun. "I did not think King Philip would linger to face us. He can't afford to chew too hard on Poitou while he still has Normandy to digest." His smile faded because although he had acknowledged some time ago that the Bayeux lands were lost to their family, it had still caused a pang to let them go.

"Perhaps we can make other gains—Montauban, for a certainty."

His father nodded. "Once Niort is secure, that will be our next target."

As they approached Niort, other foraging parties converged with theirs. Banners and pennants rippled and the heat of the late-morning sun intensified the pungent aromas of an army on the move: sweat, faeces, dust, grease, and blood. Hugh sweltered inside his mail shirt. He feared he would have to be poured out of his armour when the time came to remove it. His father was scarlet in the face with exertion and sunburn. He was approaching his sixtieth year, and although hale and well, he was carrying too much weight.

A shout from behind made both men turn to watch a bay palfrey cantering up the line towards them. Hugh suddenly grinned. "Ralph," he said.

His father rolled his eyes. "I ought to have known."

Hugh reined Hebon out of the column and cantered to meet his brother. The two horses met in a puff of dust and a near shoulder-clash, Ralph having to haul hard on the reins. Several enamelled pendants decorated his belt buckle, all displaying the blazons of French knights.

"You're still alive then," Hugh said nonchalantly. He had last seen Ralph as the troops left La Rochelle. The lad had been reeling in the saddle, baggy-eyed with exhaustion, having spent most of the previous night polishing armour so that Longespée could ride in full splendour. However, he was certainly bright and exuberant now.

"Course I am. I can take care of myself."

"And these?" Hugh indicated the pendants.

"They're from knights we've captured for ransom. My lord said I could wear them on my belt."

"That's a good tally."

Ralph nodded. "I helped to capture this one and this one," he said, proudly pointing. "So did Will Marshal." Turning in the saddle, he beckoned to another youth astride a grey gelding, who had been following in his wake. "We pulled them down off their horses and my lord Longespée took their oaths of surrender."

The youth bowed to Hugh, and then to Hugh's father. Will Marshal, heir to Pembroke, had recently turned sixteen years old. He was a handsome lad, more finely built than his illustrious sire, but no weakling. His body spoke of whipcord strength; his dark gaze was wary and watchful. He was supposed to be attached to King John's household, but during the Poitou campaign had been spending a lot of time delegated to Longespée's camp. The youth's father had sent troops to Poitou, but he was not here in person and the king had not permitted the young Marshal to fraternise with his father's men.

"So how is life in Longespée's retinue?" Hugh asked Ralph as they rode on towards Niort. "Is he working you to the bone?"

Ralph cocked his head while he considered. "He likes his harness and equipment polished until you can see your face in it," he said. "He gets upset if there's a speck of dirt. He expects his bed to be properly made even if we're camping in a field in the rain, but he's fair, and I like training with him. There's always something to do."

Hugh exchanged a knowing look with his father. When he had had care of Ralph at Settrington there had always been things to do there, but matters of demesne rather than adventurous warfare. "How are you finding a squire's life, Messire Marshal?" Hugh enquired of Will, who had been listening to Ralph without remark, but smiling slightly at the mention of Longespée's fastidiousness.

"I'm learning a great deal," he said neutrally.

Ralph made a spluttering sound which he turned into a cough and blamed on the dust rising from the trail of horses and carts.

Earl Roger looked pointedly at his younger son. "That is the entire point, is it not?" he said sternly. "To learn?"

❖❖❖

Later that night, safe inside the walls of Niort, fêted as its liberators, the English army set up billets and camps. In the hall of the donjon, Hugh sat at the fire with his father, Ralph, Will Marshal, and Longespée. The latter was in an expansive mood following the day's successes and the consumption of two cups of good red wine relieved from a French supply wagon. A third measure rippled at the halfway mark in his goblet as he balanced it on his thigh and his cheeks were flushed with bonhomie. A scurrilous drinking song about Frenchmen and virgins was being sung in the round and he had relaxed enough to join in the chorus.

"Once Poitou is back in our hands, we can look to Anjou," he announced, wafting his goblet. "My brother will hold court in Angers before this campaign is finished, mark me. We have the French on the run."

Men toasted the sentiment and cheered because it was good fighting talk and, after today, anything seemed possible. Tonight no one wanted to think that it was spitting in the sea.

A cold sensation at Hugh's nape made him look up, and suddenly he was on his feet and then down on his knees. Everyone else made shrift to follow as the king himself walked into the firelight, jewels winking around his neck and rings glittering on his fingers. John gestured to the company to resume their seats and praised them all fulsomely for the day's accomplishments. His gaze settled on Longespée. "I have a desire to throw the dice tonight," he said. "What say you, brother?"

Longespée inclined his head. "If that is your wish, sire, nothing would please me more."

John smiled around the gathering. "You see, my lords, how easy it is to accommodate me."

Roger of Norfolk raised a laconic eyebrow. "Indeed, sire, but I also wonder how much my lord of Salisbury is going to lose."

John chose to be amused by the remark and thus everyone else felt safe to laugh. "Nothing of his own, for certain," he retorted, "because everything he is or he owns has been vouchsafed by his royal family. His life, his lands, his wife, his privileges: all in our gift. He knows well not to bite the hand that feeds—unlike some." His glance darted with brief eloquence over Will Marshal before settling on Longespée with the benevolence of an owner eyeing up a favourite hound. Longespée flushed and lowered his eyes. John took a pace as if to move on, but paused and turned, one hand fiddling with the jewels round his neck, the other gripping his black leather belt. "While I think upon it, Marshal," he said. "I was sorry to hear of your father's grave illness. I shall pray for him."

Will stared at John in shock. "My father's illness, sire?"

"You did not know?" John looked concerned and apologetic. "Ah well, I suppose my messengers are faster than those from your family. They can't have forgotten you, surely? A congestion of the lungs, so I understand, and quotidian fever. Such things are dangerous for a man of his years. As I have said, I shall pray for him, as should we all." John went on his way, gesturing to Longespée with a flick of his fingers.

Looking uncomfortable, Longespée hesitated. He reached out to grip Will's shoulder. "If this is true, I am deeply sorry. I shall pray to the Virgin for your father's safe recovery, and I'll try to find out more." He rose and left in John's wake.

Will stared round, breathing hard. "I should not be here; I should be at home. Why haven't I been told?"

"Because as the king says, his messengers are swifter," Roger said. "Perhaps it is nothing. Your father or his representatives would not write unless there was real need. Calm yourself, lad. We'll find out the truth of the matter on the morrow."

Hugh well understood the eloquent look his father sent to him. By the word "messengers" John had meant spies. Probably the Marshal was sick, and he did not want the world at large to know, unless it was strictly necessary. But then John was renowned for his casual cruelty and was not above fabricating stories in order to cause people grief. If it were true, they would have to watch the situation carefully and take stock. Even if it was a lie, John's remark to the youth revealed how much the Marshal's oath of fealty to Philip of France still rankled.

❖❖❖

Mahelt knelt before the altar in the family chapel at Striguil and crossed herself repeatedly. "Holy Mary, Mother of God, Holy Mary, Mother of God, mercy, mercy for my father's life." To her own ears, her voice sounded small and ineffectual. She had never felt so helpless, and because of it she was angry—furious that this was happening to her beloved father and not to King John. He was the one who should be suffering.

The priest had come to sit with her father this morning. At first Mahelt had been terrified that his condition had worsened and that he was about to receive final unction. Reassurance that the visit was only for spiritual comfort had brought no relief because she didn't believe it. She knew she was not always told everything. People thought they were protecting her, but not knowing made her feel powerless and frustrated. She preferred to meet trouble head on, rather than turning aside and pretending it didn't exist. That was the coward's way.

Her father had been ill for so many days that she did not know how much longer he could endure. Much of the time he had been delirious with high fever and congested lungs. He refused to have any of his children in the sickroom lest they contract the same illness, and he was even reluctant to have Isabelle sit with him, although she had overridden his protests with fierce insistence. That made Mahelt angry too—that her mother could disobey the rules, or at least take them into her own hands, whereas she had no power to do the same. She swore that once she had her own household as a grown woman, she would rule it as she chose, not as others saw fit to tell her.

Her knees were red and sore from spending long hours on the tiled chapel floor, begging the Virgin to hear her plea. Imagining her father dead under a cold tomb slab terrified her. *Not him, please don't take him, please!* If he died her world would collapse because that encompassing, unconditional love would be gone. Will would become more than just John's hostage. Being underage, he would become his ward too. They all would, and John would sell them off to the highest bidders. Her own betrothal would stand, but her three little sisters would be at the king's mercy, as would her four brothers, not to mention her mother, who was a wealthy countess still of child-bearing years. They would all be subject to John's will, and it would be an ill will, she knew.

She rose to her feet and dragged herself to the piscina to wash her face using water from the priest's jug. The cold splash revived her, but it made her shiver too.

"Mahelt?" her mother said.

Mahelt spun to face her and for a terrifying instant thought she was the bearer of the worst tidings. Backing away, she shook her head. "No, Mama, no!"

"It's all right." Isabelle made a swift gesture. "Matty, it's all right. The fever has broken and he is asking for you." Isabelle smiled, and then laughed a little and wiped her wet cheeks with the heel of her hand. Then she opened her arms and Mahelt ran into them and clung to her.

"Is he...is he going to get better?"

"Of course he is!" Her mother's voice was quivery but determined. "But he is as weak as a kitten. We mustn't tire or vex him. He needs gentle tending."

"I can do that. I'll look after him." Mahelt's voice shook with eagerness. She wiped her own face. "I'll play to him on my lute and I'll sing him songs and tell him stories."

"But not all at once," Isabelle cautioned. "He must have peace and quiet."

"I can be quiet too!" She would do anything to have her father better and back as he should be.

"And first you must eat and drink something and tidy yourself. Your father will want you to gladden his eyes. God knows he must have had enough of me being a wan scarecrow these last few days." She tugged at her crumpled dress.

Mahelt shook her head. "Mama, you are beautiful."

Isabelle snorted. "I doubt it just now."

Mahelt hugged her again and then ran from the chapel, but remembered at the entrance to curtsey and cross herself in gratitude to the Virgin. She vowed to give her best brooch as an offering as soon as she could fetch it from her coffer.

Her father was sitting up in bed when she entered the room, propped up on numerous pillows and bolsters. A cloak of red soft wool lined with miniver was wrapped around his shoulders and fastened with a gold pin. His face was drawn and gaunt, but he managed a smile. Mindful of her mother's warning, Mahelt approached the bed decorously and gave him a peck on his stubbly cheek rather than her usual full-blooded embrace. His skin was cool to the touch and his eyes, although dark-circled with exhaustion, were clear.

"Sweetheart," he croaked.

"I've been praying and praying. You are going to get better, aren't you?"

He gave a weary smile and closed his eyes. "I certainly hope God will be so merciful. Play me some music, there's a good girl."

Mahelt fetched her lute and sat down at the bedside. "What shall I play?"

"You choose. Something soft."

Mahelt bit her lip. She had taken her mother's news in the chapel as an indication of a fuller recovery and had not expected him to be so weak. Tentatively she set her fingers to the instrument and began to pluck the strings. His eyes remained closed, but he nodded his appreciation of her delicate notes.

"I have much to think about, Matty," he said after a while. "It is long past time I put my affairs in order."

"Papa?" She stopped and looked at him, but he shook his head and gestured her to continue.

"Let me hear the one I taught you. The one your mother likes about the Virgin and the Christ child."

❖❖❖

Day by day, Mahelt watched her father recover from the sickness that had threatened his life and been a chill warning to all about mortality and how swiftly the scythe could cut the corn. He was in no great haste to force the pace, for which everyone was glad because there had never been such a sustained period when he had dwelt at home with his family. Always, before, the world had taken him away from them, but now, briefly, time stood still.

In the early days of his recuperation, Mahelt spent her time in the sickroom perched on his bed, talking to him, singing, or playing her lute and citole. As his concentration improved, she played games—chess and merels and tables. Sometimes she would catch him looking at her with a pained and concentrated stare, but when she asked him what was wrong, he would smile and make light of the moment—say it was nothing, or that he was proud of her and the lovely young woman she was becoming.

As his health and strength returned, he began to ride out and regain the use and tone of his muscles. He was no longer content to sit in his chamber or in a sheltered warm spot of the keep and be passive. Once more he gathered the affairs of the earldom into his hands and began to spin policy and intent.

"He's going to ask the king's permission to go to Ireland," Richard told Mahelt as they watched a ship unloading its cargo of wine at the castle's water gate on the river Wye. Tripes snuffled along the base of the wall, pausing now and again to mark his territory.

"How do you know?" Mahelt eyed her brother. His hair glinted like bright copper wire in the autumn sunshine and his greenish eyes were shrewd. She felt a twinge of jealousy that Richard was party to something she wasn't. Just because he was older; just because he was a boy. It wasn't fair.

"I heard him talking to Jean D'Earley in the stables. He said he needed to go to Leinster and sort matters out—that he had let it slide for far too long, and that he was going to write to the king and ask his permission to go."

Mahelt listened to the hornsman blowing the signal and then the squeak of the winch hauling the net of wine barrels aloft. She had visited Ireland when she was a little girl. Her grandmother Aoife had been a daughter of the high king of Leinster and still alive then, and Mahelt could remember the bare, cold fortress of Kilkenny, with its leaky roof and musty chambers. She had vague memories of the bustle of repairs and of the new building work her father had undertaken there, including founding a port on the river Barrow to bring prosperity and commerce to Leinster. The rain too. Always the rain, but her father had sheltered her under his fur-lined cloak and kept her warm and dry. "He has people there who can look after it for him," she said.

"Yes, but they are not doing the best job they can, and some of them are King John's creatures. Leinster is Mama's dowry."

Mahelt shrugged. "What of it?"

Richard looked sombre. "Well, it's what Mama would have to live on if she was widowed."

Mahelt hit him. "Don't say that!"

"It must be faced. That's what Papa's doing. He's saved our Norman lands so I can inherit them. Now he has to safeguard the rest for Mama and Will and all of us."

Mahelt shivered and resumed walking. She hugged herself to keep warm. "Will is the king's hostage," she said. "Some people never return from the king's custody. Everyone knows Prince Arthur disappeared whilst he was John's prisoner. I've heard the rumours saying John murdered him—and Arthur was his own nephew." Arthur had challenged John for the English throne and control of Normandy and Anjou, saying he had the greater right. Arthur had been captured during the battle campaign that followed, had entered the Tower of Rouen as a prisoner and not emerged.

Richard looked apprehensive for a moment, but then shook himself. "It's all hearsay. Papa wouldn't have given Will to John if he thought John was going to kill him."

"But if Papa goes to Ireland, he won't be nearby if anything does happen…"

"Don't you trust his judgement then?"

"Of course I do!" Mahelt quickened her pace as if by striding out she could escape her fears, not least the changes that would happen in her own life if her father decided to cross the Irish Sea.

Nine

A THIN LAYER OF SNOW DUSTED THE GROUND LIKE SPILLED flour around a kneading trough as Hugh mounted Hebon. Dogs and horses milled in the yard as men hastened to mount up in readiness for a winter deer hunt in Framlingham's great park.

The earl was nursing a strained back and had declined to follow the chase, preferring to keep warm by the fire, drinking spiced wine and dealing with affairs of estate. Let others bring fresh venison to the table if they desired. However, swathed in his fur-lined cloak he came out to the yard to salute them on their way.

Longespée was visiting and keen to hunt. His bay courser stamped and pawed, tail swishing, and Longespée was in a similar state of impatience. Having returned from the Poitou expedition covered in glory, his opinion of himself was particularly high just now. Roger exchanged a knowing smile with Hugh. They had done their own duty in Poitou and acquitted themselves without dishonour, but they were not fame-seekers, whereas Longespée was determined to live his life trailing banners of glory.

Roger eyed Ralph who was fretting his own horse. The youth's cold-reddened lips were parted in a dazzling smile. A long dagger hung at his hip as well as a shorter knife. He looked every inch a soldier-squire and courtier, tuition under Longespée having sharpened both elements.

"Good hunting." Roger slapped the rump of Ralph's courser.

"I hope so. We'll bring home enough venison for a banquet!"

Roger grunted. "I hope you've warned your mother and the cooks." His focus left Ralph and fixed on the messenger just riding in. The man's horse bore the Marshal blazon on its breast-band pendants and saddle cloth. Suddenly Roger was even more keen to sit by the fire and attend to business. Although the Marshal had recovered from his serious bout of illness, he had yet to return to court. Various rumours were circulating, but it seemed certain from what Roger had heard that William Marshal was bound for Ireland as soon as he could obtain King John's permission. Such a move had wider implications to men who were Marshal allies. As the hunt streamed out of the postern gate and galloped towards the deer park, Roger retired indoors and told his chamberlain to bring the messenger to him immediately.

❖❖❖

Although it had snowed, the ground underfoot was still soft and the going treacherous. Hugh was careful with Hebon. It was one thing to risk a horse in a battle, or when one's life depended upon it, quite another when the concern was sport, and after Arrow, he was wary. He would rather have stayed behind with his father, but he was expected to accompany Longespée and play the good host. Longespée didn't see it that way, of course, but then he would ride a horse to death in order to win a bet. He had already taken the lead at full pelt, his cloak flying behind him, his features ablaze with fierce exhilaration. Hugh didn't attempt to keep up, knowing if he did the stakes would only rise.

The beaters were out, shouting, blowing their horns, smacking the undergrowth with besoms and sticks to make noise and startle the game from cover. The hounds strained at their horsehair leashes and gave tongue. Suddenly a louder halloo sounded as a fallow buck sprang from a thicket of young hazels and bounded away, his coat a flash of dappled red-brown through the winter trees. The hound-keepers loosed the dogs and the riders spurred in pursuit. Hugh reined Hebon in a tight circle as the buck ran in the direction of the steep-sided ditch separating the edge of the deer park from the fields beyond. Following off the pace, he rode along the edge of the ditch, noting where a section had crumbled and needed repair.

The buck doubled back on the hunt and burst out of the trees on Hugh's left. Shooting past Hugh, it bounded along the crumbling rim of the ditch, and then, with a wide sideways leap, shot back into the forest. Startled, Hebon flinched and lost his footing, pitching Hugh off his back and over the side of the bank. As Hugh tumbled down the muddy, precipitous slope, he scrabbled for a handhold, but found none, finally landing at the foot of the ditch, bruised, winded, and plastered in thick, clinging mud. He could hear Hebon snorting at the top of the leap, and the thud of the stallion's hooves on the churned forest floor. His right wrist stung from a long, bloody graze and his ribs and his left hip were booming with pain. Hugh wiped his hand on his cloak, but since he was caked all over in mud, it made little difference.

The hunt came hurtling back in pursuit of the buck, first the dogs in full cry, then the men, shouting and hallooing. Hugh had lost his hunting horn in the fall, but he cupped his hands and hallooed back, unsure if he would be heard in the commotion. Surely they would see his riderless horse? With great relief he heard someone blow a summoning note. Moments later, Ralph's face appeared over the edge of the drop. "Hugh?"

"Down here!"

"Oh Christ. Are you hurt?"

"No. Just get me out. Have you got Hebon?"

"Yes. What happened?"

"The buck startled the horse and I was thrown." The shouted exchange was one Hugh would rather not be having. He felt like an idiot. He hadn't fallen off a horse since he was six years old.

"What is it?" Longespée's voice demanded impatiently. "The deer's going to escape!"

"Hugh fell, but he's all right," Ralph said.

Longespée muttered something derogatory that Hugh didn't quite hear, then he peered over and shouted down, "Can you climb out?"

"No, the sides are too slippery. I need a rope or a ladder."

"And you're not hurt?"

"No!" Hugh snapped, ignoring the pain in his arm and flank.

"Good. We'll send someone back for you as soon as we can."

Ralph's voice rose in astonishment. "We can't just leave him!"

"We're not. We'll come back for him." Longespée's reply was terse with impatience. "We can't do anything without a ladder anyway. I'll send one of the beaters to get him out when we've caught up with the hunt."

"But…"

"That's an order."

Hugh listened to the jingle of harness and the sound of horses being reined about and ridden away, the pace gathering from trot to gallop. He couldn't believe they had left him. He made several attempts to climb back up the slope, but the mud was greasy and wet and the angle too steep. There were no hand- or footholds except dead grass and clumps of moss that came away in his grip. Eventually, having added several more scrapes and bruises to his tally, he gave up. Crouching down, he wrapped his cloak around himself, pulled his hat down over his ears, and prepared to endure.

The sky was bruising towards dusk when Hugh finally heard

people approaching. He felt as stiff as a corpse several hours dead and the winter cold had seeped deep into his bones. "Hola!" Ralph shouted. Looking up, Hugh saw his brother's dark shape at the top of the bank. His father was there too and a couple of huntsmen. A rope ladder came snaking down the bank, banging the sides, collecting mud and debris on its way. Hugh's fingers were numb with cold and his legs like boards. His bruises had set and it was an effort to grasp the rungs and agony to haul himself out of the ditch into the red winter dusk. Strong arms grabbed him as he breasted the rim, and dragged him out.

"I'm sorry, we got caught up in the chase and Longespée thought you'd probably be able to get out on your own," Ralph said in a voice breathless with effort and chagrin.

"Then let us put him down here and see how quickly he succeeds!" Hugh snarled. "He deliberately left me here!"

"No," Ralph said on an anxious note. "I'm sure he just forgot in the heat of the chase. He wouldn't do that."

"Wouldn't he?" Hugh said with utter contempt.

His father handed him Hebon's reins. "Are you fit to ride?" He gestured to Hugh's scraped and muddy hands. Although he said nothing, the earl was shocked at what Longespée had done. You didn't just leave a fallen man for hours on end; you got him out. It was your duty and your responsibility.

"I'll manage," Hugh said with a terse nod. Although he was in pain, he gained the saddle and turned for home.

When he walked into the hall at Framlingham, draggled and frozen to the marrow, Longespée was taking his ease on a padded bench before the fire, talking to their mother. He was richly dressed in a robe of wool so thick that the nap shone like silk. A gold brooch gleamed at his throat. He looked warm, relaxed, and well fed. Their mother was smiling at him with a doting look on her face. Hugh fought the urge to do murder.

"Why didn't you send someone back before now?" he spat. "How in the name of God's bleeding eyes did you expect me to get out of there on my own?"

Longespée coloured. He made an apologetic gesture and smiled as if he thought Hugh was making a fuss over nothing. "I am sorry; I knew you were unharmed."

"And hunting deer is more important than rescuing a fallen member of the party and your own kin to boot?"

"I have said I am sorry. Come, sit by the fire; have some hot wine." He pointed to the jug warming on the hearth. Hugh caught the pleading look on his mother's face—an expression that managed to intimate they were children squabbling over a prank one had played on the other, and that he should accept the olive branch.

"I think not," he replied. "I need to be rid of these befouled garments and I'm not good company just now. I pray your leave." With a stiff bow to his mother and ignoring Longespée, he left the hall and climbed to the private chambers on the floor above. A hot tub had been prepared in anticipation of his return and an earthenware pot of meat broth simmered on the hearth. Bread and wine stood on a small trestle near the tub together with some spicy pastries.

As Hugh was disrobing, the door opened and shut quietly as his father entered the room. Obviously he too was disinclined to remain in the hall and drink wine with their guest.

"He thinks because I do not run headlong into danger and because the song of the sword is only one of many to me that I am soft." Hugh winced at a long red graze on his forearm that matched a tear in the shirt.

"It is because for all that his father is a king and I am but an earl, he is a bastard and you are born in wedlock to twice his wealth," his father said pragmatically. "He'll always begrudge you that circumstance of birth. For your mother's sake I make him welcome; besides which he is useful to have at court where our interests are concerned—even if today's behaviour goes beyond the pale."

Hugh immersed himself in the waiting tub and began to feel better as the hot scented water lapped around him, easing taut muscles, soothing his aches and bruises. The wine was hot and spiced; the pastries contained ginger and it was not long before he was aglow. "I know what Longespée is," he said. "I realise we need him at court and I know how my mother dotes on him. I understand why he is welcomed here, but after today…" His mouth turned down at the corners and his voice hardened. "For my mother's sake and for the earldom, I will tolerate his presence, but do not expect me to keep his company."

"I do not," his father said. "I am glad of this private opportunity to talk though, because there's another matter we need to discuss."

"What?"

"Your marriage to Mahelt Marshal."

Hugh left the tub and, after a vigorous towelling, donned soft, fire-warmed clothes and comfortable kidskin shoes. "Why, are you having second thoughts?" he asked as he latched his belt.

His father gave a distorted smile. "It is a little late for that. A betrothal is a binding promise to wed and annulment would be fraught and difficult—not that I desire such a thing." He stroked the fur collar of his cloak. "The Marshal has written to say he plans to go to Ireland once he's obtained the king's permission. His wife's dower lands in Leinster must be brought to heel. The countess will need their income to support herself should anything happen to him, and I would guess he is considering his mortality after his recent illness."

Hugh refilled his cup. "How does that affect us?"

Roger smoothed the soft squirrel pelts. "The Marshal is not

taking his eldest daughter. He wants her to stay in England and he's requested that her marriage to you be solemnised—preferably before Lent."

Hugh stared at his father in dismay. "That's only two months away!"

"The girl will be almost fourteen years old. Her family say that she has begun her woman's courses, but she is still too young for child-bearing. They have requested we guard her chastity until her fifteenth year day."

"And a marriage without consummation is one that can still be dissolved," Hugh said.

"It is something to be aware of, I agree, but they are taking as much of a risk as we are," Roger replied shrewdly. "William Marshal wants his daughter kept safe and is asking us to be her guardians. A year is not long to wait and you will have time to come to know each other before you share a bed, which is all to the good while she learns our ways."

Hugh thought of the brunette-haired child to whom he had made his betrothal vows two years ago. He could imagine cajoling the lass and teasing her in the same manner he did his younger sisters, but the notion of courting her, let alone sharing a bed for procreation, was like a foreign language. "The king might well refuse his permission to let the Marshal go to Ireland."

"Indeed yes. It will not be to John's taste to have him meddling there and upsetting his interests. The countess is Irish royalty. Knowing John's suspicious nature, he might think the Marshal intends to carve himself a kingdom there."

"Do you think he intends that?"

His father looked thoughtful. "I believe the Marshal wants to be away from John and pursuing his own projects because they have been too long neglected, but there has to be balance between one's own desires and what the king will tolerate.

We have been fortunate thus far, but that is because we have kept within the bounds of John's acceptance and not roused his suspicions."

Hugh pondered his father's words. The Marshal must think there was a strong possibility of gaining royal permission or he would not have written to them about the marriage. "And if we decline Earl William's request?"

"I do not believe it is in our best interests to do so. William Marshal is no fool. He needs us, but he also knows the value of this marriage to us. No other great men have daughters of comparable stature. We'll need to keep our eyes open and our wits about us, that's all."

Going to the hearth, Hugh crouched to spoon himself a bowlful of hot broth.

"I thought after his illness the Marshal might do something like this," his father mused. "A prudent man should look to the future and the security of the next generation." He eyed Hugh knowingly. "You've been well educated on the domestic side by your mother and sisters and doubtless you have learned plenty more about women in your own private dealings. I expect you to be able to handle Mahelt Marshal should the marriage be brought forward."

Hugh used sipping his broth as a good excuse not to comment.

"She'll have her own chamber at Framlingham, of course. The solar in the old hall can be refurbished as her quarters while she receives guidance from your mother and learns our ways." Devouring a ginger pastry, Roger headed to the door. "Longespée will be gone soon enough," he said. "I trust to your good sense to keep the peace."

The face Hugh pulled made his father chuckle before he went out. Hugh sat down on the hearth bench to finish his broth. The notion of an imminent marriage left him nonplussed. He was going to be landed with the responsibility for a young bride. A child who was neither his sister nor his daughter, and who must be kept chaste in the eyes of all. He groaned. Longespée had been through a similar situation with Ela, and would likely have some sage advice, but Hugh had no intention of asking him. He knew if he did, Longespée would behave like a tutor trying to educate a witless dolt, rather than a brother and a friend.

He looked up as the door opened again and his mother came softly into the room. Her delicate features were anxious. "Are you all right, my love?" she asked. "I was worried when I heard you had taken a fall." Setting her hand on his shoulder, she kissed his cheek.

Hugh forced himself to smile. "Yes, Mother; there's no lasting harm."

"I do hope you and William can patch up your differences before he leaves. I hate to see the pair of you fighting." Her soft brown eyes were troubled. "You are brothers when all is said and done."

It was too much to swallow without a retort. "Then perhaps he should remember it. If Ralph or William or Roger fell down a slope and couldn't climb back up, I wouldn't abandon them to go off and hunt deer. I'd go myself and bring a rope."

"He has apologised," she said on a pleading note. "I don't think he realised that you couldn't get out."

"Oh, he realised, Mother." Hugh bit his tongue. She was utterly blind where Longespée was concerned, and since that blindness was caused by her guilt and remorse at being forced to give him up as a baby, she would never recover her sight. He sighed. "Very well, I will speak to him—for the sake of peace and diplomacy—but do not ask me to do it out of brotherly love."

She kissed him again. "Thank you, I'm proud of you. Has your father spoken to you about Mahelt Marshal?"

"Yes, he has."

Dimples appeared at her mouth corners. "It will be so good to have a young girl around the house again. I miss that kind of company now that your sisters are married. She will be without her own family, so we'll have to become her family instead." The smile faded slightly. "There's going to be a great deal to organise if there's to be a wedding so soon after Christmas." Hugh could tell from the far-away look in her eyes that she was making mental tallies of tablecloths and napkins, goblets, salvers, and the like. Then she shook herself and refocused. "Are you coming to join us in the hall? We need your voice for the singing."

Hugh hesitated. He had not intended to do so, but if he lurked here, he would only seem churlish and unable to take blows like a man. "Very well," he said with a resigned sigh, and the way his mother's face lit up filled him with a mixture of pity and exasperation.

In the hall, a space was waiting for him on the bench by the fire and he was greeted with cheers and toasts and bonhomie. Longespée did his utmost to welcome him, even pouring him a cup of spiced wine rather than getting a servant to do it— something unknown. Hugh suspected his half-brother realised he had gone too far and was now attempting to make amends.

At first, Hugh had to force himself to smile and respond, but as the evening wore on and the singing grew fervent, he mellowed. His voice, rich and full-toned, was far superior to Longespée's and rang out for all to hear, while Longespée had to make do with joining in the chorus. It was a small thing, but it made Hugh feel better.

Ten

FRAMLINGHAM, JANUARY 1207

HUGH KNELT BESIDE MAHELT IN FRAMLINGHAM CASTLE'S chapel to receive the sacrament. He had set a wedding ring on his new wife's heart finger, spoken his vows, and endowed her with the nine manors of her marriage portion. She was very young, but not quite the child he had been envisaging. She had grown considerably since their last encounter and was taller than his mother. Her wedding gown of subtle silver-green silk enhanced her recently developed curves and showed off a figure that was lissom yet strong.

Hugh was perturbed, wondering how he was going to deal with her. It was a huge responsibility and a new stage in his life for which he was unprepared, and although the instructions concerning his conduct towards his bride were strict, the situation left much opportunity for confusion and conflict. She was his wife but was not expected to fulfil a wife's duties; she was a woman but she was still a child. She was to be treated like a guest, yet she was also a full member of their household. Aware of Mahelt's father looking on, Hugh was over-conscious of every word he said and every action he performed, lest it meet with disapproval. It was almost like being an adolescent again, when he had been his own man for several years.

The wedding party emerged from the chapel and processed

across the ward to the new hall which had been decked in evergreen and ribbons to mark the occasion. Trestles dressed in snowy linen lined the perimeter of the room and brightly clad musicians and players waited to entertain the guests during and between the various courses of the marriage feast. Mahelt's parents were leaving at dawn on the morrow to return to Striguil and prepare their departure for Ireland; thus the celebrations, although colourful and magnificent, were not to be a protracted affair.

Diversions and dancing were held between each course of the feast and Hugh and Mahelt were the focus of attention as they stepped and turned in a marriage carole, their feet crushing underfoot the herbs with which the dried rushes had been strewn and releasing brief moments of lavender and rosemary. Mahelt flashed swift looks and smiles at Hugh. Her eyes intrigued him for although they were dark, their hue was mutable and it was like looking into a dye-pot with all the deep colours swirling and changing. Her hair, long and loose to proclaim her virginity, shone the colour of polished oak and was as lustrous as damask silk. She was a little shy, but she was not uncertain. This girl knew her worth.

They both danced with other wedding guests, and Hugh found himself partnering his mother-in-law, the magnificent Isabelle de Clare.

"I am glad we are leaving her in safe hands," she said to him as they met, parted, and turned. "It is one less burden for us to carry across the Irish Sea."

Hugh bowed to her. "She will be precious to everyone at Framlingham, my lady mother." Calling Isabelle "mother" made his face burn, not least because he was still rather smitten by her.

Isabelle looked amused. "I wanted you for her, you know," she said. "I am glad my husband was of the same mind."

Hugh cleared his throat, feeling like a tongue-tied squire. "I shall do my best to care for her, my lady."

Her smile was warm. "I know you will."

The dancing continued. Hugh partnered his mother who was tense behind her bright exterior, anxious that matters should progress without mishap. He reassured her that all was well and made her laugh by twirling her around on his arm. His sisters, Marie and Marguerite, both married, offered him a glut of matronly advice. Do this, don't do that, be attentive but do not crowd her. Give her presents, but don't spoil her. Eventually Hugh managed to escape to the company of his sister-in-law Ela, Countess of Salisbury, who was resplendent in a gown of blue silk embroidered with little golden lioncels. "You are kin to me on both sides now," she teased. "Half-brother to my husband, and now cousin by marriage through your wife."

"I'm glad of the bond," Hugh replied, and meant it, because whatever he thought of Longespée, he was genuinely fond of Ela. "Do you have no words of wisdom for me today?"

She gave him her very sweet smile. "Surely you have already endured a surfeit of those!"

Hugh chuckled. "I certainly know all the things I am not supposed to do, although I'm in no danger of being near enough to my wife to be put to the test. I've hardly had a chance to speak to her and I'd not know what to say if the opportunity did arise."

"Trust me, you would." She patted his arm. "My own wisdom, for what it is worth, is to let everything unfold in its own time."

Hugh snorted. "The timing thus far has been well ahead of me, but I'll try to keep abreast of where I'm supposed to be."

Longespée arrived to claim his wife with a possessive hand. Hugh made a few stilted comments to his half-brother and excused himself to go in search of his bride.

There was no sign of her in the hall, or outside. A guest who had over-indulged was vomiting into the winter-sparse rose trellises against the wall. Shaking his head, Hugh crossed the courtyard to the old hall where Mahelt had been given her lodgings, climbed the outer stairs to the solar chamber, and opened the door.

Mahelt was sitting on the bed, cuddling the strange little three-legged dog she had brought with her from Striguil.

Looking up, she drew a swift, short breath. "I...I came to check on Tripes." Her cheeks were as bright as rosehips. "He's been shut in here a long time."

"Indeed you must make sure of the dog's welfare," Hugh said gravely. "I know everything is strange just now, but I hope you will grow accustomed."

"Yes," she said, with doubt in her eyes.

He gestured round. "You can arrange this room just as you desire. Everyone will do their best to welcome you."

She gave him a serious nod. "Thank you."

Footsteps sounded on the stairs and Richard Marshal put his head round the door. "They're looking for you, Matty." His glance darted between her and Hugh.

"Can I not even visit my dog without everyone hunting for me?" She glared at her brother. "Am I to have an audience even in the privy?"

"Quite likely," Hugh said with a straight face. "Tongues and opinions are busier today than flails at threshing time."

She rose to her feet and lifted her chin. Bidding Tripes stay, she walked to the door like a queen, her silver-green gown shimmering like water. Then Hugh saw her surreptitiously pinch away tears with her forefinger and thumb and felt a pang of compassion. Poor lass. She didn't even have a haven where she could go for a good weep to release her tension. In silence, he stood aside and courteously ushered her before him.

"Perhaps it would be better if you escorted your sister to the hall," he said to Richard.

The youth's cheeks brightened with embarrassment. "I didn't think you were doing anything dishonourable in here."

Mahelt gave her brother a glare filled with furious reproach.

"Of course not," Hugh said, smoothing the path, knowing full well that Richard had indeed come to check on them for that purpose. "But she is your sister and an agreement has been made that you desire to see honoured in every way." He gestured to the door.

Chagrined, Richard extended his arm to Mahelt and she took it. Hugh inclined his head in courtesy and stepped back to follow at a short distance.

"I'm sorry," Richard muttered from the side of his mouth. "I just wanted to make sure you were all right."

"You're a fool," she hissed. "Of course I am. Besides, it's a bit late to be worrying about the state of the Bigods' honour now, isn't it?"

"I'm going to miss you," Richard said glumly. "I never thought I'd say such a thing when we squabbled as children, but it's true. Who else is going to tell me what a dolt I am?"

Mahelt's precarious control threatened to desert her. "Don't say anything else, Richard, in God's name do not! You will make me weep and I will not have my new family or our parents see me in tears. This is a joyful occasion!"

"Of course it is." The enthusiasm in his voice rang like a knell.

"Then do not be such an idiot!" She gave him a swift, fierce hug and he returned the embrace full measure. "I'm going to miss you too." He was like a young bear and her ribs almost cracked under the pressure. I will not cry, she told herself. I will *never* cry.

A new dance had begun and Richard led her into the first set of steps, and then passed her to their father, and Mahelt fixed the smile to her lips, even though her heart was aching and all she wanted to do was latch on to the security of her childhood and not let go.

"Sweetheart," her father said, and touched her face. "I am proud of you."

She made herself smile up at him, as if this was the happiest moment of her life, and hoped that he had not felt the dampness of her tears under his thumb. And he smiled back. She saw the warmth in his eyes and also the sadness. He wore his own face but with the courtier's mask over the top. She would be like him, and no one would know of her anxiety and grief.

Her father passed her gently on to Hugh. "Take care of her," he said, his voice coming from deep in his chest.

"With my life," Hugh answered and Mahelt felt her new husband mesh his fingers through hers and put his hand to her waist for the lift and leap. She went with him, light and lithe, and when he set her down, it was in a different place to where she had been before, not between her brother and her father, but between Hugh and his father, so that in changing places in the dance, she had also changed families.

Eleven

FRAMLINGHAM, FEBRUARY 1207

MAHELT LOOKED OUT OF HER CHAMBER WINDOW AS SHE pinned a brooch at the throat of her dress. The February morning was mild and bright—a teasing forerunner of the spring that was still a month away. The first skinny white lambs were staggering beside their mothers and the evenings had started to lengthen.

She was slowly settling into her new life, but found many aspects awkward and strange. The Bigod household was very different to the Marshal one, and although everyone was kind to her, she missed being the centre of attention and the apple of her father's eye. She couldn't be the apple of Hugh's while they were not truly man and wife, nor could she get to know him properly as a partner when they were always chaperoned. He had ridden out two days ago to deal with affairs in Yorkshire, so for the moment she didn't have his company at all. She was wary of Hugh's father, who was not bound in affection to her; his attitude towards her was informed by duty and responsibility. He was protective, but he was strict about the niches people occupied in his household. His opinion was that if everyone knew their place, all would run smoothly, but if they deviated from their allotted roles, chaos would ensue.

Straightening her dress, Mahelt left her chamber and crossed the courtyard to the new hall and Countess Ida's solar, which overlooked the gardens and the mere. Ida sat at a frame weaving a length of braid. Her women were busy with other textile crafts and the shutters were open so that the morning light streamed in to illuminate the fabrics and enrich their colours. The sight reminded Mahelt of similar industry at home. This might almost have been her mother's chamber at Pembroke or Striguil. Such dedicated work was not particularly to Mahelt's taste, although she was competent. She preferred more energetic pursuits that yielded a swifter reward, although at least whilst engaged in weaving and embroidery she could learn the castle gossip and find out whom to cultivate and whom to avoid.

Going to Ida, Mahelt curtseyed. "My lady mother," she said. The address still sounded strange in her ears.

Ida kissed her cheek and pinched the edge of Mahelt's silk wimple between finger and thumb. "This is lovely," she said.

"It belonged to my grandmother, the Princess Aoife," Mahelt replied. "She wore it when she married my grandsire, Richard Strongbow."

Ida nodded in approval. "It is good to pass things on through the family." She gestured to her work, which bore a repeating design of the red and yellow Bigod shield, embellished with gold thread. "I am making a new belt for the earl."

"It is very beautiful." Mahelt admired Ida's expertise, while hoping she would not be expected to create work to a similar standard.

Ida beamed with pleasure. "I think so." A waft of breeze blew through the window aperture and ruffled the wall hangings. Mahelt gave a yearning glance at the arch of light and sniffed the fresh air like a hound.

Ida followed the direction of her gaze. "Come," she said with sudden decision. "I want you to see what lies beyond our walls.

At this time of year, fine weather is a gift we should not waste. Besides, I wouldn't want you to think you were a prisoner here."

Mahelt felt a moment of resonance deep inside as Ida used the word "prisoner." The thought of Will as the king's hostage, her parents far away in Ireland, and Hugh absent in Yorkshire gave her a queasy feeling of isolation. Walls were made for protection, but they could confine too. "I would like that very much, Mother," she replied.

"Bless you, child." Ida hugged her. Instructing her women to continue with their work, she sent a messenger to the stables to order the horses saddled. A boy was despatched to tell the earl she was taking Mahelt to show her the demesne and very soon the women were trotting under the portcullis and taking the path by the mere. They were both well wrapped in warm cloaks and they rode astride as if for hunting rather than using the platform side saddles that would have been correct in formal circumstances.

"It is a long time since I have done this," Ida said wistfully. "Indeed, too long."

Mahelt gazed around, taking pleasure in being out on the demesne instead of just looking at it over the castle wall. "I used to ride most days when I was at home...I mean before I was married."

If Ida noticed the remark about "home" and its correction, she gave no sign. "With your mother?"

"Sometimes, but just as often with my brothers or my father. We'd inspect the demesne together. It was good to breathe the air and it stopped the horses from getting stale."

A mischievous glint lit in Ida's eyes. "We own the finest horses in England," she said. "I wouldn't want them to go stale for want of regular exercise."

Ida and Mahelt eased their mounts from trot to canter as they entered the park. Thickets, coppices, and woodland provided cover for the deer, and were dappled with wide grass rides to aid the coursing of hares and create a diversity of habitats. Filled with delight, the women urged the horses to gallop. Mahelt revelled in the feeling of speed, in the wind streaming against her face, and the surge of her mare along the ride, clods showering from beneath her hooves. Ida's cheeks were flushed and suddenly she laughed aloud, the sound high and clear, belonging to the ghost of a much younger woman.

At a brook, where the water ran as clear as brown glass, they dismounted to drink from their cupped hands. The hems of their gowns darkened from contact with the stream's edge and their knuckle joints reddened and ached from the pure coldness of the water. The escorting grooms hung back, exchanging glances with each other, causing Ida and Mahelt to giggle.

"Ah," said Ida. "We must return here in the summer with fishing lines and a picnic basket."

Mahelt agreed fervently. Her fondest memories were of such days spent at her father's manors of Hamstead and Caversham when he was able to cull time from his duties.

Beyond the pale of the deer park, Ida showed her dark fields of rich arable land soon to be sown with spring wheat. The skies were wide and bare and seemed to stretch for ever, and Mahelt was awed in spite of herself. She was accustomed to the majesty of mountains and fierce coronal sunsets behind the Welsh hills, but this cool eastern light had its own regal splendour. The wide stretches of land and sky made her realise the power of the family into which she had married. They didn't have as many castles or knights' fees as her father, they didn't have a province in Ireland or estates in Normandy, but they did own vast tracts of fertile, productive farmland. They had coastal territories rich in fisheries, salt pans, and commercial ports. Ida told her about the profits they made from the wheat they grew and how important it was to the demesne economy. She showed her the stud herd of mares, the fine destrier stallions, the cows, the pigs, and the poultry. "Not all your life will be spinning and weaving in the bower," Ida said. "There are matters of estate to see to as well."

Her voice held a hard note that made Mahelt wonder if Ida was unhappy with her lot. She knew her mother-in-law had once been the old king's mistress and had dwelt at court. The life she led now was so different that it must have taken some adjustment.

When they returned to Framlingham, Mahelt discovered that a messenger had arrived from her father with letters for the earl and one for herself. It was accompanied by an embroidered purse containing a coil of red silk hair ribbon, and a mark of silver. The gifts, however, were the sweetener to news that made Mahelt sit down abruptly on the hearth bench and put her hand across her mouth.

"What's wrong?" Ida was swiftly at her side.

Mahelt shook her head in distress. "My brother Richard's been taken by the king as a hostage too—before they sailed for Ireland." She lifted brimming, furious eyes to her mother-in-law. "King John thinks my father is a traitor, but he's not, he's not!"

"Of course he's not!" Ida put her arms around Mahelt. "Oh my dear, there has to be a mistake."

Mahelt shivered with revulsion. "Why does he do this? He has no right to take away my brothers. I hate him!"

"Hush now, hush now. It will be all right." Ida looked round at her women and warned them by her expression to say nothing of this outside the bower. She was appalled. It was disturbing but understandable that John had taken the eldest Marshal boy. Roger said the king was quite within his rights and that William Marshal had been sailing very close to the wind over the issue of his Norman lands. But to take the second lad too—that was beyond the pale. Obviously John did not want the Marshals to go to Ireland, but Mahelt's father had ignored him and gone anyway. Where was it all going to end? Dear God, there might even be repercussions for her own family; what if John demanded her sons too?

"No it won't," Mahelt said through clenched teeth. "It will never be all right!"

"Come," Ida said. "There is nothing you can do on your own, but if you ask God's help, surely He will listen."

Mahelt allowed Ida to coax her to the chapel where only a few weeks ago she had been married. She gazed at the painted pillars, the candles burning on the altar, the statue of the Virgin and Christ child smiling down with inane serenity. If God really was listening, she thought, He would strike John dead with a thunderbolt. But she also thought that God often needed the hand of man to bring His schemes to fruition, and perhaps it was true that God helped those who helped themselves.

❖❖❖

"I heard about your brother; I am sorry," Hugh said.

Mahelt shook her head and watched Tripes snuffle along the path in front of her. "I don't know why the king acts like this towards my family. It's not just and it's not fair." She rubbed her arms. The weather had turned cold again, but the sky was clear and wide. They were walking side by side in the pleasure garden under the castle's west wall. Hugh had returned from his duties that morning, three days after she had received the news about Richard being taken hostage.

"Your father is a powerful man," Hugh said. "The king wants him at court where he can keep an eye on him and take advantage of his advice and counsel. John is losing one of his most important men, perhaps for a long time. Your father was away from court much of last year too."

"That's because he was sick," Mahelt protested.

"Indeed, but John didn't know how truly ill he was. He probably construed it as avoidance. While your father is in Ireland, he will be serving his own interests above John's. The king is probably thinking of all the gifts and rewards he has given to him and deciding that he has not received good value in return, especially after the business of the French allegiance."

Mahelt's eyes flashed. "My father doesn't make hostages of the sons of his vassals when they go home to their estates. Neither does yours, so why should the king be different?"

"You are talking about two different things." Hugh gave her a look that said he knew she was being deliberately obtuse because she did not like what was being pointed out to her. "The stakes are not so high, for a start. One manor is not a province or a kingdom, and our fathers do not have the king's suspicious nature. Your father's departure to Ireland seems like a betrayal to John—a sign that he has no time for him. Your father is so powerful and popular that he could threaten the throne if he chose." Hugh raised his hand as Mahelt prepared to do battle. "I know he would not, but John sees it differently. He thinks your father has gone to Ireland to feather his own nest at royal expense."

"He will have no nest left if the king has his way," Mahelt snapped. "He's constantly encroaching on our lands and taking bites out of our rights and privileges. Why shouldn't my father go to Ireland? Leinster belongs to my mother. He's not stealing it from anyone. John is the one who takes what does not belong to him!"

"Your father is a strong man, well able to take care of himself, even against the king," Hugh replied evenly. "And you are well protected here because we have a similar strength. We'll not let anything happen to you."

Mahelt bristled at the humouring patience in his voice. She

was not a child and she resented his cozening. "What of my brothers? Who will protect them?"

He shook his head. "I do not believe they are in any danger. Your father is not without allies; there are men who will keep an eye on them at court. Baldwin de Béthune for one, my brother William Longespée for another. He is your kin by marriage and mine by blood."

As Mahelt considered this, her agitation diminished to a dull ache but the pain did not go away. "They should be with their family, not hostages to a king's whim. Would you say the same if it was your brothers who were held captive?"

Hugh rubbed his chin. "I would take such things into consideration, but perhaps you are right; I would think on it more."

She shivered. "A monster does not go away even if you have walls to guard yourself against it."

"Indeed, but knowing what kind of monster you are dealing with helps when it comes to defending yourself against it. I know you thought I was belittling your cares, but truly, I want you to feel safe at Framlingham."

"I do feel safe." She thawed enough to give him a look through her lashes.

"Good." He smiled at her and Mahelt felt a glow in her solar plexus. She wondered what it would be like to be a wife in all senses of the word rather than a wife in waiting. The glow spread upwards from the feeling and became a blush. Suddenly she needed to be in motion. Disengaging from him, she picked up a stick from one of the soil beds and threw it as hard as she could for Tripes. As the dog scampered off to retrieve it, she ran after him, encouraging him in a bright voice.

Watching her play with her pet, Hugh smiled at her mercurial change of mood. He appreciated her coordination and lithe grace with a physical surge in his gut and the pleasure of an artistic eye. He felt compassion too. She was having to mature quickly and the growing pains must be difficult. He made a silent promise to protect her as best he could and smooth the transition. And with that decision came a warm feeling of possession too. Not only was the responsibility his, but so too would be the reward.

Twelve

*I*T WAS A SEWING DAY. MAHELT SAT OVER HER EMBROIDERY, pecking away at the stitches with determination but little enthusiasm. It was time-consuming and there was so little to show for it, but in loyalty to Ida and in the interests of being a good daughter-in-law, she was applying herself. One of the few advantages to the task was that it gave her time to dwell on thoughts of Hugh and daydream about his smile and his vivid sea-blue eyes.

She had been enjoying his company these last three months and felt deprived when he had to be elsewhere. She went out riding with him most days, and although servants or companions were inevitably present in the background, there were still moments when they managed to be alone; indeed it had become a kind of game. Sometimes he would hold her hand when they went for walks with the dogs, playfully swinging her arm and his in unison, and he had not minded when Tripes had chewed his best kidskin shoes.

He talked to her of music and poetry. Often he would read to her from the family's collection of books: fables of Aesop, tales of King Arthur, the romances of Marie de France. She loved to listen to him read for the dual pleasures of hearing the story and the richness of his voice embracing the words and giving them life.

Today he had been closeted with his father and brothers for most of the morning, discussing a matter pertaining to the earldom. The atmosphere had been tense, although nothing had been said in front of the women. When Mahelt tried to speculate to Ida about what was worrying the men, her mother-in-law shook her head in warning. "Let be," she said. "They will deal with it; they know what's for the best." Mahelt wasn't so sure about that. Her mother was always saying that men thought they knew what was for the best, which wasn't the same thing.

She had stilled her needle and was gazing out of Ida's chamber window as the meeting broke up. Hugh's brothers Roger and William emerged into the ward and headed purposefully towards the stables. So did a messenger, already slinging his satchel at his shoulder and breaking into a run. Moments later, Hugh himself entered the room with brisk intent. The startled serving women curtseyed. Ida set down her sewing. "What's wrong?"

Mahelt tensed. When the lord closeted his retainers and sons together for a meeting, and when a man entered the women's sewing chamber in a hurry, it always meant trouble.

Hugh gripped his belt either side of the buckle. "Nothing..." he said, looking round the room as if seeing it for the first time.

The "nothing" was typical too. Next would come the "but."

"...but we've to move some things out of Framlingham for a while." He strode to the fabric cupboard and opened the doors. "Your silks, Mama, and the best bolts of wool and linen. Just keep what you immediately need." He looked round again, his manner that of a predator on a scent. "Also we'll take down the good bed hangings and that hunting scene." He gestured to a costly embroidery on the wall that had come from Flanders. "William and Roger have gone to muster the carters and the sumpter men."

"But why?" Ida stared at her son in alarm and crossed to the cupboard, her arms outstretched as if to protect a precious child.

Hugh heaved a deep sigh. "The king has ordered a tax on a thirteenth of all moveable goods and revenues. No one is exempt and his officers are authorised to make inspections and check tallies. We've heard that Richmond Castle has been seized because its constable Ruald FitzAllan would not declare what he owned."

Ida looked blank. "I do not understand."

Hugh gestured at the bolts of cloth, the silks shimmering like deeply coloured water, the linens muted and subtle. "We need to move our valuables for safekeeping before the sheriff's inspectors arrive. How much do you think a thirteenth of that cloth of gold is worth? Or the wall hanging? Or those cups with the rubies and rock crystals? We always pay our dues, but this is beyond fair asking. If we don't move them now, we're going to land ourselves with a demand for thousands of marks."

"Now?" Ida looked dismayed. "You mean at this moment?"

He nodded. "Yes. We don't know how much time we have before they come looking and Framlingham will be a prime target."

"Where are you going to take them?" Mahelt was more interested than shocked. The king was always demanding taxes. Other than the usual scutage that everyone paid to provide soldiers, John had demanded a fine of a seventh on all moveable goods four years ago.

"It'll be best to spread it far and wide," Hugh said. "If we store it all at one location and we are caught, we may as well not have bothered and we'll receive a fine on top of a fine." He ticked off on his fingers the names of various religious houses of which his family were patrons. "We'll take some to Thetford, some to my grandmother's foundation at Colne. Then there's Hickling, Sibton, and Walton. They'll all do their part."

"But if Framlingham is stripped bare, surely the king's officers will become suspicious," Mahelt said. "Perhaps you should 'slightly' hide a few good things—but nothing too precious—just so they are easily found, and that will put them off the scent."

Hugh's eyes gleamed with amused approval. "Precisely. We shall place decoys, but we have to move things now."

Mahelt wondered about her own family paying out a thirteenth part of their moveable income. Her father was bound to have contingency plans. Tintern and Cartmel could be used and he had probably taken much of his wealth to Ireland with him anyway.

"I'll help," she said eagerly. Anything that thwarted John was to be embraced with fervour.

Hugh grinned. "You're a true Bigod wife."

Mahelt blushed.

She spent the rest of the morning helping to pack the baggage carts with fabrics and napery, with wall hangings, cups, silver plate, and all manner of sundry items that would be considered taxable goods by the king's officers. She revelled in the work, much to the indulgent amusement of her husband. Even his father chuckled as she ordered the servants to arrange a casket just so in the cart to protect the inlay. The earl was of the opinion that women should keep to the bower and mind the domestic business, but her enthusiasm and her undoubted organisational skills, not to mention her youthful spirits, made him tolerant.

Ida looked on, bemused by it all, but showed her own spark of determination when her husband wanted to take away a particular bolt of red silk, which she insisted she needed for her next project. She stood in front of the cloth, her chin up and the battle-light in her eyes, daring him to take it. The earl grumbled about the contrariness of women and what it was going to cost him, but Ida got her way. Mahelt suspected the earl had capitulated because he intended Ida's precious bolt of red silk to be one of the decoys if the royal agents came calling.

When the carts were finally loaded, Hugh left his groom saddling Hebon and told Mahelt to prepare for the journey too. "What could be more natural than moving my household to Thetford and paying my respects at the tomb of my ancestors?" he asked. "If there are women present, it will add veracity to anyone we pass on the road. Father Michael, your maid, and my brothers will travel with us and bear witness that pledges of chastity are being upheld."

Mahelt didn't need a second bidding and flew to pack a baggage chest. Smiling plaintively, Ida helped her. "It is going to seem very quiet without you." She looked rueful. "Especially with the fabric cupboard so empty!"

"It will only be for a few days." Impulsively, Mahelt hugged her mother-in-law and received the embrace back twofold.

"Godspeed you," Ida said as she watched Mahelt almost skip from the room. She was like a leggy colt, young, vibrant, and full of life. The sight made Ida sigh. How swiftly the river carried everyone downstream and far out to sea. She went down to the courtyard to wave the carts on their way and thought how handsome Hugh looked as he boosted his smiling, excited girl-wife into the saddle. God grant them happiness, she thought, and had to wipe her eyes on her sleeve. She leaned a little closer to her husband, who was watching the entourage with his hands on his hips and his lips pursed. "Let's hope the weather stays fine for them," he said.

Ida glanced up at him, thinking it was rather romantic of him to say so.

He clucked his tongue against the roof of his mouth. "I'd hate the cart to bog down in the mud and questions to be asked."

Sighing, Ida turned back to her devastated fabric cupboard.

❖❖❖

At Thetford the designated goods were taken to the prior's house. A few sacrificial pieces were concealed in such a way that a moderately determined search would discover them. Most of the treasure went into safe hiding where, without tearing the priory to rubble, it would not be found. While Hugh and his brothers dined with the prior and delicately negotiated a fee for the safekeeping of the goods, Mahelt entertained the wives of some of Thetford's worthies at the Bigod house across the river. She had seen and helped her mother in similar circumstances so often that it came easily to her and she enjoyed the opportunity to have sole charge, rather than deferring to Ida.

When Hugh and his brothers returned, Mahelt's final guest had just bidden farewell and the servants were clearing away the scraps to dole out in alms.

"They don't like this thirteenth tax either," Mahelt told Hugh as he removed his cloak and sat by the fire. "Half of them have been hiding things or omitting to declare all that they own."

Hugh lifted his brows in surprise. "They told you?"

She laughed. "In a backwards manner of speaking. There was a lot of talk about how much they *did* have—meaning that which they were prepared to put on show and declare."

He gave an amused grunt.

"By the same light, they know we're not just at Thetford to visit your grandsire's bones. They know there's more going on than that. But they need our patronage, and they feel we are all allies against injustice, so we are safe."

Hugh folded his arms. "You enjoy this, don't you?"

She cast him a look filled with pride and masked her uncertainty by jutting her chin. "I was raised to listen and watch and to sift what words and actions really mean."

Hugh glanced over his shoulder. His brothers had drawn off to talk between themselves and share a cup of wine. The servants were all busy. Turning back to her, he stroked the side of her face with the back of his hand, and then kissed where he had stroked and lingered just a moment with the delicate rose-water taste of her skin under his lips before pulling away.

"I will not ask you what you construe from that," he said. "Other than approval."

Mahelt gave him a melting, mischievous look. "Then I am pleased to please my lord," she answered. The look in Hugh's eyes and the feel of his lips against her cheek made her tingle all over. She half hoped he would do it again, but he drew back from the intimacy and brought her instead to join his brothers by the fire.

❖❖❖

Following their return from Thetford, Hugh had to set off immediately for Yorkshire with more of the family assets to squirrel away. He had also to ensure that the thirteenth did not make too large a hole in his own revenues.

Mahelt was sad to see him leave. The time they had spent travelling to Thetford, staying there for three days, and riding home again had changed their relationship. She had discovered the delightful pastime of flirting with Hugh and having him reciprocate. It gave her a frisson to mesh her fingers through his as they sat by the fire, telling stories and singing songs. His hands weren't big and powerful like her father's, but there was strength in them, and grace. When they had shared a trencher at their last meal at Thetford before their return, their shoulders had touched and if she had shifted her leg just a fraction, it would have pressed against his. She hadn't, but she had wanted to. He had fed her morsels from their meal and Mahelt had been aware of how close his fingers were to her teeth, and that she could have bitten him if she had wanted. When she had reciprocated and wiped a trace of sauce off the side of his mouth and then sucked her thumb, he had flushed and she had seen his breathing quicken. On their ride home he had kept more distance between them, but even so there had been scope for jesting and laughter and more songs. Oh yes, she enjoyed the heady pleasure of flirting. Framlingham was going to be a very dull place without him, when all she had were daydreams instead.

The king's officers visited the castle and Hugh's father issued pledges concerning his goods and chattels and gave the men an open hand to search where they willed. "We have nothing to hide," he said, spreading his arms.

Mahelt was a model of demure diligence when the officers came to inspect her mother-in-law's chamber. The fabric cupboard, when unlocked by Ida, revealed several bolts of everyday linen, a decent green wool, and Ida's red silk, although it was only a quarter of its previous size. Tripes growled at the men and bared his teeth. His collar of red braid was a match in hue for the glorious silk gown his young mistress was wearing. "He's only got three legs," Mahelt said pertly to the searchers. "He's already paid his taxes."

When they had gone, Mahelt caught Ida's eye and the women burst out laughing. Partly it was a release of tension and even anger that the king could send men to search their personal chambers and raid in the name of his greed. Mahelt thought it an enormous pity that Tripes hadn't bitten their ankles.

"I wonder how long it will be before I can have my other cloth back," Ida said with a wistful sigh.

Mahelt frowned, considering the problem. "You'll just have to buy some more in Norwich to tide you over," she said and that started Ida laughing again. Eventually she sobered and wagged a mock scolding finger.

"You had better change out of that gown, my girl, if you are going to help me with the cheese-making this afternoon," she said.

A week later they heard that their house at Thetford and the priory had been searched and a set of four silver cups and a flagon discovered and confiscated. Earl Roger was smug because he had expected the king's officers to discover the Flemish wall hanging too, but obviously they had not probed hard enough. Not that anyone relaxed their vigilance. One always had to be on guard.

❖❖❖

Mahelt was sitting in her chamber putting her hair to rights. While riding the demesne, she had followed the dogs through a thick coppice. A branch had snagged in her wimple, which had been half pulled from her head. She had lost a couple of gold pins in the incident, and returned to Framlingham in a state of dishabille most displeasing to her father-in-law. He was of the opinion that she rode out too much with no purpose but pleasure and that she ought to spend more time involved in domestic duties. She had hastily curtseyed to his scowl, and retired to tidy herself, having dismissed her maid, Edeva, who as usual had been making a fuss. Sometimes Mahelt thought it was like being surrounded by hens, all clucking and fluffing, even if they were trying to be maternal and tuck her under their wings.

She was drawing her comb through the strong, silky strands when the door opened and Hugh walked into the room. He stopped and stared, drinking in her exposed hair with quickening breath. Mahelt leaped to her feet with a joyful cry and ran to him. "Hugh! Oh, it's so good to have you back!"

He set his arms around her waist and swung her round. He couldn't resist stroking her hair. Its length fascinated him; its sheen, its strength and vibrant colour. No woman wore her hair unbound except in the private chamber, and it was an exclusive privilege of a husband to see it thus. "Where's Edeva?" Glancing round, he released her.

Mahelt tossed her head. "Oh, she was twittering as usual, so I sent her to help your mother." She sat back down on her bed and resumed her toilet. "It got into a tangle when I was out riding. I went into that mature coppice the other side of the mere after the hounds got the scent of a fox, and a low branch snagged my wimple."

Hugh stooped to pat Tripes who rolled over, inviting a tummy rub. "You've been keeping busy in my absence then," he said drily.

She made a face. "Despite the bare cloth cupboard you left us, there's still been plenty to do. I only escaped for a while this morning because my horse was stale and needed to gallop."

"And you didn't?"

"A little," she conceded with a smile. "The king's officers came, you know."

"Yes, my father wrote to me."

"Did they visit your manors?"

He nodded. "They found nothing. They were thorough, but no match for me. I'm used to seeing off wolves." He left the dog and, sitting on the bed, took the comb from her hands and began to groom her hair. "It's like a dark waterfall," he said softly.

Mahelt closed her eyes and leaned back into the gentle tug of the comb and the smoothing follow-through of his hands. Then she turned towards him, lifting her face to his in mute invitation. His kiss was the merest touch on her brow and the points of her cheekbones. She held her breath, willing him to do more, wanting the moment to last for ever.

He stroked her hair back from her brow with the edge of his thumb and sought her lips. Mahelt closed her eyes and gave herself up to the delight of being kissed and learning how to kiss in return. It was like holding a butterfly, she thought, and feeling the delicate sweep of its wings in the palm of your hand.

They lay full length on the bed and he continued to caress her hair between kisses that went no further than a gentle initiation. There was no play of tongues, no moist, swift urgency.

And yet in stroking the long sweep of her hair he touched the parts of her body that it covered: her waist, her arm, the curve of her breast. His thumb grazed her nipple, once and again. Mahelt almost dissolved at his touch. Her head felt light and her body warm and heavy, drugged with a slow languor that centred in her loins and made her turn towards him. While she was innocent, she was not naive and she wanted more.

Outside the window one of the grooms shouted to a companion, and Elswyth the laundress joined in with a raucous cackle and a quip about a good, stiff wash pole.

Hugh threw back his head and gasped. What had begun as a brief tender moment of welcome to his return was rapidly developing into something else. He had vowed not to consummate the marriage until next spring, but set against that vow was the fact that this girl was his wife; she had the curves of a woman and the way she had been responding to him of late had not been in the manner of a child. Yet he didn't want their first time to be in haste, listening for footsteps with the bawdy talk of the servants floating through the window. It had to be in honour. It was one thing to court her and lead her gradually down the path to joy in the marriage bed—he had that right— another to break a vow.

Summoning his will power, he kissed her again, shortly and playfully this time, and, pushing away from the embrace, stood up. "Come," he said. "Cover your hair before you unravel me completely. I've got something for you—a present from the North."

Mahelt licked her lips, her expression hazy and disorientated.

"I brought it for you because of your father and his father before him," he enticed, holding out his hand. "Don't you want to see?"

Reluctantly, she rose from the bed and came to where he stood near the door. She looped her arms around his neck and hung against him. "Can't you bring it here?" She laid her head against his chest. Hugh closed his eyes and swallowed. Standing up was no safer than lying down, as once again he found himself pressed hip to hip and his imagination running riot. "I could," he said in a congested voice, "but it would be difficult." Determinedly, he set her to one side and picked her cap and wimple off the bed. "Make haste, or it will be dinner time."

"You'll have to help me—unless you want me to call for Edeva."

Hugh gave a breathless chuckle. "That wouldn't be wise."

She braided and coiled her hair and together they tucked and pinned it in place, then arranged her wimple to cover all, by which time, although still flushed with desire, they were laughing too, and the mood had lightened. Once she was decent and could leave her chamber, Hugh grasped her right hand firmly in his and, with a feeling of release and escape, tugged her out of the room and across the ward. A rich meaty smell wafted from the kitchens as they passed and the sound of a ladle banging against the side of a cauldron suggested that dinner was indeed imminent.

In the stables, a small, fat piebald pony occupied one of the stalls. Its forelock covered half of its face and the tip of its full black tail touched the deep straw of its bedding.

Mahelt looked at Hugh askance. "For me?" she said.

Hugh bit the inside of his mouth at the sight of her baffled expression. "I was reading a charter the other day from your grandsire's time. It said that it was the Marshal's privilege to have all the pied horses captured during a battle campaign. I know I've not been to war, lest it be in our efforts to avoid paying undue taxes, but I thought since you are of Marshal stock he was an appropriate gift."

Mahelt clapped her hands and burst out laughing. "Oh Hugh, you rogue! He's beautiful!" She took a handful of oats from a grain bin and held them out on the palm of her hand. The pony greedily whiffled them up and before she could fetch more, took a sudden fancy to her newly restored wimple and gripped it firmly between its teeth. Squealing with laughter, Mahelt struggled to free herself. Hugh began to chuckle, and then to laugh harder as he watched the stubborn tug of war. By the time Mahelt finally managed to wrench the fabric out of the pony's grip and stagger free, her torn wimple edge was covered in slobber and half-masticated oats and Hugh was doubled over, helpless with laughter. Clutching her own stomach, Mahelt fell against him, tears pouring down her face. He couldn't resist kissing her again until she was rosy and flushed, and when finally he surfaced to draw breath, it was to see the stable lad easing out of the door, his gaze studiously lowered. Hugh realised belatedly that the dinner horn must have sounded without them hearing. Hastily he drew back and straightened his tunic, then he helped Mahelt rearrange her wimple, although there was nothing to be done about the mess the pony had made.

Their late and flustered entrance to the hall was witnessed by a room full of spellbound diners. Putting his head up, Hugh walked to the dais as if there was nothing untoward about the moment, and Mahelt walked beside him with the dignity of a queen, although he could sense her quivering and dared not look her way lest he begin laughing again.

On the high table, the knights and retainers exchanged glances and there were some knowing, low-voiced chuckles. The earl, although somewhat red around the jowls, compressed his lips and said nothing as the couple took their places. Ida gave Mahelt a reproachful look. "There is straw on the back of your gown," she whispered fiercely. "What have you been doing?"

Mahelt flushed as she washed her hands in the fingerbowl. "Hugh brought me a pony from Yorkshire. We were in the stables."

"Did you not hear the dinner horn?"

Mahelt shook her head and explained about the pony eating her wimple, showing the stained, torn edge of the garment as proof. Ida looked relieved, but, nevertheless, put a warning hand on Mahelt's wrist. "We only have your welfare at heart, my dear, and the honour of both our families. A promise made should be held sacred."

"Yes, Mother," Mahelt said meekly, although she felt resentful. Why did people have to think the worst? Why couldn't they leave her and Hugh alone?

The main dish was lamb, dressed with sharp mint sauce—a rare treat, for lambs were not usually killed for meat. However, on this occasion, their skins had been required to make parchment and a dozen surplus males had been slaughtered. Hugh and Mahelt exchanged smiling, conspiratorial glances as everyone settled to their meal. He sliced the meat on their shared trencher, brown on the outside, pink and succulent in the middle. Mahelt daintily took a sliver between forefinger and thumb, dipped it in the mint sauce, bit half off and fed Hugh the other half. He responded in kind. They shared a cup, each drinking from the same place. Mahelt knew full well that her father-in-law was watching her and disapproving. Desire and rebellion tingling in her blood, she deliberately fed Hugh another morsel.

❖❖❖

Dinner was over. The scent of roast lamb still lingered on the air and everyone was greasily, comfortably full. Ida took Mahelt off for some sewing, and supervision. The earl eyed their departure with a jaundiced eye and turned his irritation on Hugh, who had remained with him in the hall.

"I know you are newly returned from Yorkshire and that absence makes the heart grow fonder, but you should be more careful in your behaviour," he grumbled.

"Sire?"

"Do not give me that innocent look. You are becoming too intimate with the girl. We made a promise to her parents that we are honour bound to keep. No one will say that the Bigods break their word. If you have needs, satisfy them elsewhere. You know what I mean."

Hugh reddened. "We have done nothing untoward," he said stiffly.

His father raised his brows. "Coming from the stables covered in straw?"

"That wasn't..."

"What's more, I came to look for you before dinner and I saw the marks of two bodies on her bed, not one. What does that say of behaviour and intent?"

"She is my wife. I have not touched her beyond kisses." Hugh's voice strengthened with anger. "Surely we are allowed a little courtship?"

The earl unbuckled his belt to give himself stomach room. "You can do all the courting you want in the hall, or out riding in company, or chaperoned by your mother and her women, but not in the stables and not alone in her chamber—especially not on a bed. I do not want to have this conversation with you again, understood?"

"Perfectly, sire," Hugh said with a set jaw, feeling like a child being reprimanded for stealing cakes from the kitchen.

❖ ❖ ❖

Mahelt was sewing in Ida's chamber, darning her torn wimple. Nothing had been said, but Mahelt had registered a general air of reproach and although she still felt wild and restless, she was doing her best to mend broken bridges. When Hugh entered the room, she kept to her sewing and barely looked up, although her cheeks grew hot. He greeted his mother formally and sat for a moment, talking to her in a quiet voice. Whatever he was saying dissipated Ida's tension and she kissed him and patted his cheek. Peace made, he came to the window-seat where Mahelt was bending over her task.

"My father says we should be more careful about our conduct," he said and then sighed. "I suppose in truth he is right."

Mahelt's irritation boiled up. Why did her father-in-law have to interfere? She wondered if the old earl had ever known the sweet intensity of courtship and desire. She couldn't imagine it. Certainly he never shared the countess's bed these days, preferring to keep to his own chamber and pore over his charters and tallies. "Do you always do as he says?" she challenged.

"I do my duty and obey him," Hugh replied evenly. "Do you not do the same for yours?"

Mahelt compressed her lips and felt mutinous. She hated the way everyone watched them, judging to a pin-point what was suitable and proper behaviour. Ida said she did not want Mahelt to feel she was a prisoner at Framlingham, but it often seemed that way.

"Then I suppose we must do as he says…" she said with a deep sigh, before flashing him a wicked look from under her lashes, "…in public." Leaving him, she went to ask Ida a question about the embroidery pattern, making sure her leg brushed his in passing.

Feeling more than a little masculine bemusement at the ways and wiles of women, Hugh escaped the bower for the straightforward company of his brothers and the business of the demesne, which at least was uncomplicated.

Thirteen

A LINEN APRON TIED AT HER WAIST, HER HAIR BOUND IN A kerchief, Mahelt dipped a ladle in the cauldron of rich pork and bean pottage and emptied it into the bowl that a cowherd's wife was holding out. The woman bobbed a curtsey, gave Mahelt a shy smile, and moved on to a trestle piled with small loaves of good white bread. Mahelt dipped the ladle again and served the next woman waiting her turn. It was a Michaelmas tradition for the demesne tenants to attend a feast provided and served by the lord and his family. Whilst the earl and his sons doled out food to the men, the countess and her ladies served the women and children.

Mahelt was enjoying herself immensely. This was much better than needlework. While acknowledging and rewarding folk for their diligence and hard work, she was in return receiving their appreciation and goodwill. The duty came naturally to her and she was performing it so well that she was in her father-in-law's good offices and he had a ready smile for her today. The blacksmith had brought his bagpipes, someone else had a drum, and several children and adolescents had linked hands to dance. Mahelt watched and smiled. Under the trestle from which she was serving food, Tripes contentedly gnawed on a hock bone.

Taking a momentary respite from his own serving and carving, Hugh sauntered over, a dapifer's towel slung over his shoulder and his blue eyes alight with pleasure. Mahelt returned his look and felt joy spark through her body. Since his father's warning about their behaviour, they had become more circumspect, but their courtship play had continued. Yesterday they had gone hunting and he had helped her settle her hawk on her wrist. His closeness, his fingers on her skin, the swiftness of his breathing before he moved away had been achingly delicious. And all under the watchful eyes of his father and within the bounds of propriety.

"You are doing well, lady wife," Hugh said with a grin.

"I'm enjoying myself." She dipped the ladle and raised it to offer him a taste.

"So am I." He drank with his eyes on hers, and, although it was an ordinary exchange, it was meaningful and suggestive too and Mahelt's cheeks blazed. Belatedly she noticed her father-in-law observing them and had to restrain herself from poking out her tongue. A messenger stood at his side, drinking thirstily from an earthenware cup. Taking the ladle from Hugh, Mahelt resumed her duty. Hugh, in good part, plucked the empty bowl from the hands of the little girl next in line, presented it to Mahelt to fill, and then returned it with a courtly flourish. The child giggled and fluttered him a coy look over her shoulder as she walked away. Hugh continued to assist and the queuing women nudged each other and cackled.

The earl joined them and the laughter stopped. Mahelt felt a frisson of anxiety. She was almost as tall as he was; he couldn't look down on her from a physical advantage, but even with a serving towel over his shoulder, he still possessed enormous power and presence.

"A word with you," he said to Hugh, casting Mahelt a shrewd glance that she didn't understand. She suspected she was about to be reprimanded yet again, and her irritation surged because she was on her best behaviour. She knew how it would go. He would deliver the reprimand to Hugh and expect Hugh, as her husband, to administer it.

Hugh bowed to his last customer and secretly squeezed Mahelt's hand before following his father away from the trestles.

Mahelt returned to doling out the pork stew, but she had to force her smiles now as she waited for the blow to fall. It wasn't fair. Once everyone had been round at least once, she left the ladle in the stew and untied her apron.

Ida joined her, still wearing hers. "You have done so well." She beamed, kissing her. "I am proud of you. You have a true talent." Her look became teasing. "I can tell you prefer this to sewing."

"I cannot deny it," Mahelt said, trying to engage with her but feeling distracted.

Ida glanced round the gathering. "It is good to have days like this to remember."

"Yes," Mahelt agreed, but she didn't want to live for memories. She wanted to live for now and in the moment. She saw Hugh returning and his troubled expression confirmed her fears, especially as Ida suddenly found a reason to be busy elsewhere.

Facing him, Mahelt stood erect and prepared to fight her corner. "What has your father said to you this time?" she demanded, prepared to make attack her defence.

"Come." Hugh took her arm and drew her to a bench, shooing away the two children who were sitting on it, swinging their legs and sucking on pork rib bones. "It's not what you think."

"Then what is it?"

"He's just had word from the court—from my brother Longespée." His eyes were sombre as he took her hands in his. "Your father's in England. He's been summoned back from Ireland by the king."

She had been prepared to defend herself against the petty foibles of her father-in-law and Hugh's words stunned her. She did not know whether to be overjoyed or terrified. "Why? Is my mother back too, and my brothers and sisters?"

He shook his head, looking serious. "No, they are still in Ireland. But your father's been summoned before the king to answer in a dispute between himself and Meilyr FitzHenry."

Mahelt tossed her head. "I know about the dispute. It's one of the reasons my father had to go to Ireland in the first place. Meilyr FitzHenry has been stealing our land and he has to be stopped before we have nothing left." Her eyes darkened with anger. "It's criminal that he's the justiciar in Ireland but he commits acts of thievery against decent men."

"FitzHenry has been summoned to court too, and some of your father's Irish vassals...but I am afraid there are difficulties."

She began to feel cold. "What kind of difficulties?"

Hugh sighed. "FitzHenry has plundered your father's port at Newtown and attacked his men and positions."

"The whoreson!" Mahelt sat upright, her eyes flashing. "The craven turd! How dare he!" Rage and fear shimmered through her. "My father will not let this go unpunished; he won't stand for it!"

"He has left his best men to protect your mother and your brothers and sisters," Hugh said with brisk reassurance. "Jean D'Earley has been given the charge and he is strong and loyal to the core." He didn't add that her father was trapped at court and powerless. The Marshal couldn't return to Ireland without John's permission and in the meantime FitzHenry's henchmen could wreak mayhem as they pleased. The king not only had Mahelt's two oldest brothers hostage now, he had her father too. His own father was deeply worried about the implications, and Hugh was concerned for Mahelt. Who knew where this situation would lead? It might take more than this to bring the

Marshal down, but what was happening showed how dangerous it was to be on the wrong side of a distrustful, vindictive king.

"Your father will weather this," he said, allowing none of his doubts to show on his face. "He is a great man. We'll protect you at Framlingham. Nothing will harm you here."

Mahelt gave an irritated shrug because she didn't care about that. She wanted to fight. Glancing around at the feasting, singing, and dancing, it suddenly seemed silly and all her work with the ladling a waste of time because it wasn't helping her father. Her hatred for John was so strong it curdled her stomach.

"Longespée wrote that your father was trying to obtain the king's permission to return to Ireland, but that John will take more than a little persuading. For the moment all we can do is watch and wait."

Mahelt's expression contorted. Watching and waiting was a trial worse even than needlework. Her restless energy and impatience was desperate to engage and do something. The knowledge that action was impossible drove her mad. She jerked to her feet, needing to be in motion, and set off at a rapid walk, striding out like a man, wishing in truth that she was a man and could take up a sword and hew her enemies into little pieces.

Finally, at the side of the mere, she stopped, her feet almost in the sedges bordering the water. A half-grown family of mallards flustered away, quacking in alarm. Mahelt compressed her lips. Her head ached with pressure and her eyes were smarting. Hugh had followed her, and now, without a word, he set his arm around her shoulders.

"The king won't win," she said between clenched teeth. "I swear he won't." And then she turned into the comfort of his chest and hid her face against the soft blue wool of his tunic.

Fourteen

A MONTH LATER, EARL ROGER BROUGHT HIS HOUSEHOLD TO Thetford for several days and Hugh took the opportunity to go hunting in the forest with his brothers and the household knights to secure fresh meat for the table.

In the time since learning the news of her father's return to England, Mahelt had heard little concerning his dispute with Irish baron Meilyr FitzHenry. Debate was continuing and her father was being forced to drag his heels at court where John was keeping him close to hand.

Having spent an hour exercising her mare, Mahelt was dismounting when a pedlar arrived riding a larger version of Pie, the black and white pony Hugh had given her. Several cat skins dangled from his pack basket and although his hose were an expensive shade of scarlet, they were wrinkled and torn. He stank of old smoke and the ingrained dirt of weeks of travel. Mahelt made to avoid him and go inside the hall, but he crossed her path, removed his greasy hat, and bowed. Then he swiftly handed her a sealed, folded parchment that had been tucked under the brim. "Lady Bigod, I was bidden to give you this by a certain young lord I encountered on the road. He said to tell you that a lion is always a lion, the more so when it belongs to a Marshal."

Mahelt hastily concealed the parchment into her belt beneath her mantle, glancing round to see if anyone had seen the exchange, but the pedlar had picked his moment well and the groom was busy with her horse. "Thank you," she said breathlessly. "Ask at the kitchen for bread and ale and tell them Lady Mahelt Bigod said you were to be fed."

"My lady." He flourished another bow, vouchsafing her a sight of the lice crawling through his hair, before shambling off towards the kitchens. Mahelt sped to her chamber, dismissed Edeva with an impatient flick of her fingers, and sat down in the window-seat to read what was written on the parchment. Tripes leaped on to the seat beside her and settled down to a spot of grooming. Mahelt gazed at the splotchy writing that had obviously been penned in haste, and laughed while she wiped away her tears. However, as she read the words, her heart began to race. Will, in the custody of his gaoler's son, John FitzRobert, and a knight of the court called Robert Sandford, was on his way north, but would be staying at Edmundsbury on the morrow night. He desired her to come there and meet him. Frowning, she bit her lip because it was easier said than done.

She made herself tidy, ensuring that her head covering was straight, her gown smooth without a dog hair in sight, and that everything about her appearance was modest and decorous. Affecting a demure air, she took a deep breath, and went in search of her father-in-law.

He was busy with his scribes in his alcove, but he beckoned her within the small chamber and broke off his discussion. "Daughter?" He raised his brows. "Is all well?"

"Yes, my father." Her heart in her mouth, Mahelt showed him Will's letter and asked his permission to ride out and visit her brother.

Her father-in-law steepled his hands under his chin and

considered her out of shrewd grey eyes. "I think not," he said eventually, his voice calm but imperative. "It is not a woman's place to go gadding about, especially when she is as young and unknowing as you are. I can spare neither the men nor the horses for such an escapade. And receiving private letters from passing vagabonds is unseemly and not the kind of behaviour I expect of my son's wife."

Mahelt stared at him in dismay. "But Will's my brother! I haven't seen him since he was taken hostage!"

The earl was implacable. "I am sorry for that, but I must look to your safety and the interests of my family first, and that means keeping tight rein on all that happens here. I will not have this household called into question. By all means you may socialise with your brother, but openly and appropriately. This smacks to me of clandestine doings. For all I know you could be riding into a trap."

"Please!" Mahelt implored. "You can't deny me, you can't!"

"Daughter, I can and I do," he replied icily. "I suggest you repair to your room, calm yourself, and think on the subject of obedience."

Mahelt had always been able to wind her own father around her little finger and Hugh could be cozened to an extent. But her father-in-law had no such chink in his armour. He was steely. She gave him a perfunctory curtsey and swept from the room. He watched her exit with narrowed eyes and then turned back to his business, but he did not dismiss her from his mind.

❖ ❖ ❖

The autumn dusk had fallen. In the west the sky was pimpernel-red, struck with primrose and bruised with violet. Feeling queasy, Mahelt lifted her cloak off its peg and fastened it around her shoulders. A hood and cape followed. She had been sick twice, lending veracity to her declaration that she was unwell, and had begged leave to retire and sleep off whatever was ailing her. Her father-in-law thought she was sulking over his refusal yesterday to let her visit her brother, but had given her the benefit of the doubt and bade her good rest and hoped she would feel better in the morning.

Earlier in the day he had granted her permission to write to Will, wishing him well and telling him that it was unwise for them to meet. That letter had gone with a merchant heading for Edmundsbury. But there was another letter too, sent via the pedlar who had left at dawn wearing a fine new set of hose, his pack laden with bread, cheese and sausage, and three silver pennies in his pouch. With the letter, he carried a gift to her brother of a silk scarf bearing the motif of the red Marshal lion. She hoped Will would understand its meaning.

"Mistress, please, you shouldn't do this!" Edeva wept, wringing her hands. "It is too dangerous. Do not defy the earl, I beg you!"

"It is only dangerous to me if you open your mouth!" Mahelt snapped at the maid. "You will serve me best by telling anyone who comes to my chamber that I am sleeping. I shall be back long before dawn. Now, let the ladder down."

"Mistress...I dare not!"

"Jesu God, then I'll do it myself!" Mahelt opened a coffer and took out the rope ladder she had sneaked into the chamber earlier in the day, concealed under a pile of spinning wool. The earl's gatekeeper might be vigilant but there was still the wall. Going to the window, she threw the shutters wide. The air held a scent of frost and the sunset was a narrow ribbon of blood-red on the western horizon. Although terrified, Mahelt also felt a flush of wild exhilaration. "In Christ's name, don't be such a milksop!" she hissed at the maid's continued weeping. "If it was your brother you'd do the same!"

Finally she coerced the trembling girl into helping her with the ladder. Edeva begged Mahelt not to go, but Mahelt had the bit between her teeth and made her way over the wall with rebellious determination. Nothing would stop her now. If Hugh could go hunting in the forest with his cronies for a night, then she could certainly visit her brother.

In the trees beyond the house, Will's groom Tarant was waiting for her with a spare horse, true to her instructions sent with the pedlar this morning. Within moments, Mahelt was in the saddle and riding hard for Edmundsbury.

❖ ❖ ❖

Roger glared at Edeva who stood weeping in front of him, her hands wrung almost to the bone. "Over the wall," he said, barely able to enunciate the words because his jaw was so stiff.

"Yes, sire," Edeva sobbed. "I told her she should not, but she refused to listen. I had to help her for fear she should fall or do herself an injury."

"You didn't think to raise the alarm there and then?"

"I…I didn't know what to do…Oh sire, I beg your forgiveness!" Tears streamed down her face.

Roger wasn't in a forgiving mood and this silly wench was exacerbating his ire by the moment. Nevertheless, his years as a judge on the bench held him in check. At least she had come and told him. If she hadn't this entire, disgraceful exploit might have passed unnoticed and have left room for escalation. "Enough," he said. "Go to your chamber for now and talk to no one. You were right to come to me, and in so doing you have saved yourself."

"What will…what will happen to my mistress?"

"Let me concern myself about that. Away with you."

When the woman had gone, Roger paced across the room to expend the energy of his temper. He glanced at Ida who was sitting near the hearth, her sewing frozen in her hand. "We have given the girl too much leeway," he growled. "Why hasn't she been more closely watched?"

Ida shook her head. She too looked as if she might burst into tears at any moment. "Mahelt has always been well chaperoned. If not by me, then by one of her women, or a chaplain."

"But no one was by to prevent her from doing this, were they?"

Ida looked hurt. "I was in the hall with you and about my duties. As far as anyone knew she had a sick stomach. What else could we have done?"

Roger reached the end of the chamber and turned round to stalk back the other way. "She should have been curtailed long before this ever happened," he snapped. "You go out riding with her and you act like a pair of wild women. I thought you would teach her how to be a good wife, but instead, she is teaching both of you how to become hoydens!"

Ida gasped and put her hand to her mouth, feeling as if he had struck her. She was appalled at what Mahelt had done and filled with remorse and self-blame, wondering what she herself had done wrong. She couldn't think of any way she could have made things better for the girl and had believed they had a good relationship. Her husband was indeed right; it had been fun to laugh and ride and enjoy the company of a bright young woman—something she had sorely missed since her daughters had married into other households. Mahelt had lifted the clouds, but at what cost? "It is just a foolish thing, a childish prank," she said.

A muscle ticked in Roger's jaw. "But she is not a child any longer, and this is not a prank. Indeed, it could be dangerous to all. And Hugh is no better. He lets her lead him on like a lovesick mooncalf, and then he abdicates his responsibility to go hunting and socialising. The girl needs more to occupy her time, because obviously she has too much of it on her hands."

"What are you going to do?" Ida asked, feeling sick and frightened. "Will you go after her?"

He shook his head. "No. I need to know if there is more to

this before I decide, but she will be brought to heel. I will not have this insubordination in my household."

❖❖❖

As Mahelt dismounted outside a merchant's house on the outskirts of Edmundsbury, Will was waiting to greet her in the moonlight. She gasped his name and flung herself into his arms, crying with joy and the release of pent-up tension. He hugged her to him and kissed her so hard on either cheek that she felt her flesh bruise against her teeth.

"It's so good to see you!" His voice cracked with emotion. "I'm so glad you came!"

"Do you think I would let anyone or anything stop me!" she answered fiercely. She looked him up and down. He was much taller than she was now.

His laugh was wry. "I don't think anyone would dare, sister, but even so, I know the risk I have asked you to take."

She jutted her chin. "I don't care. I'd have ridden through hell to get here."

They entered the house, which was warm and well appointed, and Will guided her to a seat by the hearth and poured her a cup of hot wine from a jug resting near the embers. "I told Sandford and FitzRobert that I had a liaison with a young lady." He sent her a quick look from under his brows. "Which is true, but they don't realise it's my sister. They've gone off to drink wine elsewhere for a while to give me some peace."

"They are your gaolers though?"

Will shrugged and looked rueful. "It's more that I'm in their custody for the moment. John's sending me north away from our father—for a while anyway. He doesn't want us colluding with each other at court. FitzRobert's father is constable of Newcastle, where I'm to be held. In truth, I am glad to be away from the royal train." Deep lines furrowed his brow. "You do not know. It is like trying to survive in a pen full of hungry rats. Some of John's mercenaries…" He broke off and swallowed. "I will not speak of it."

Mahelt sipped the wine but the heat didn't touch the frozen lump of fear at her core. "What of Papa, and Richard?"

"Richard's all right. He has that way about him that gets him by. He's constantly teased because of his red hair and his size, but he shrugs it off. Our father…" Will's mouth twisted. "He shrugs all off too, but at what cost? He just answers whatever humiliation John heaps on him with a smile or a calm look, but the insults and treachery must be ripping him to shreds inside where it doesn't show. I cannot bear to see it. And as to what's happening in Ireland, God help us." He tossed back his own drink and poured another cup.

Mahelt clenched her fists at the thought of her beloved father being hounded like this. She dared not think about Ireland beyond the superficial because she would become a screaming harpy.

"Our mother's with child again as well," Will added. "Due in the early spring, Papa says. They wanted one of us at least to be Irish born."

Mahelt gave him a shocked look and wondered how much more could be piled upon them before everything broke down. The news of a pregnancy was usually a cause for celebration, but the thought of her mother coping alone in Ireland as her condition advanced, and this her ninth time, only compounded her agitation.

Will hesitated, and then said, "I have something for you." Reaching down between shirt and tunic, he produced a piece of parchment folded small.

"What's this?"

He looked furtively round and handed it to her. "Letters from the king about sending soldiers to Ireland. It concerns numbers of men and which castellans he's sending where—instructions to his agents."

Mahelt's stomach plummeted. "Where did you get this?" she whispered.

"One of FitzRobert's messengers happened to leave his letter satchel unattended when he went for a piss. I daren't keep this with me lest they search my baggage, but if you can find a means to pass it on to our mother and Jean D'Earley, it will be of great value to them. Don't let anyone else see it because it will be our downfall. I didn't know whom else to trust and I can't keep it with me."

Mahelt shivered at his words, but stiffened her resolve and tucked the parchment into the pouch at her belt. "Don't worry," she said, her confident aplomb concealing terror. "I'll deal with it. I'll write to Mama and pass this on as soon as I can."

Will offered her food, but although she nibbled at a crust of bread and a wedge of cheese, she was too apprehensive to be hungry. The letter and the knowledge she should not be here were preying on her mind. "I have to go," she said, finishing her wine. "The earl refused me permission to see you and if he finds out I've gone…" She let the sentence hang.

Will nodded. "I understand. Roger Bigod is set in his ways." He gave her a quick look. "What about your husband?"

Mahelt flushed guiltily. "Hugh's away hunting in Thetford forest. He doesn't know." She toyed with a loose thread on her cloak. "He makes me laugh, and he sees the layers in things. He's not rigid like his father."

"Can you rely on him?"

Her flush deepened as she stood up. "I wouldn't tell him about this," she said, "but I do trust him…" She put her arms around Will again and squeezed him close, absorbing the touch and feel of kinship, not wanting to let him go, but knowing she must. "Take care of yourself, and I pray to see you again soon. Don't worry about the parchment. It's safe with me."

"I don't remember what it was like at home any more," he said, his voice muffled against the hood of her cloak. "I daren't because it would unman me. Besides, I can never go back and neither can you...Ah, I say too much. Go, Matty, and do what you can." He kissed her temple and her cheek.

A boy brought a fresh horse and Will boosted Mahelt on to its back for the thirteen-mile ride back to Thetford. "Godspeed," he said. "Tarant will see you safe." He nodded at the groom.

Mahelt blew her brother a kiss from the saddle and nudged the horse with her heels. Looking over her shoulder as she rode away, she fixed in her memory Will's image outlined in the torchlit doorway, his arm raised in farewell.

❖ ❖ ❖

Mahelt woke late in the morning and lay in bed, reorientating herself. The happenings of yesterday were like a dream, but when she reached to the small tear in the mattress and felt the curled edge of the parchment Will had given her last night, she knew it was true. Her thighs were stiff from hard riding and her arm twinged where she had banged it on the wall whilst clambering back up the rope ladder and through the chamber window an hour before dawn. Edeva had been waiting for her, and trembling so hard she had barely been able to draw the shutters closed. Mahelt had not been much better herself, but she had been awash with excitement too and it had taken her a long time to fall asleep. What had woken her now was Edeva tiptoeing about the chamber. The maid had brought her a cup of buttermilk and some bread and cheese. Mahelt was still too keyed up to be hungry, but she made herself drink the buttermilk at least. If the tray returned from her chamber with the food untouched, it would give credence to the fact that she was unwell.

Edeva kept her eyes downcast as she helped Mahelt to dress,

and her chin kept dimpling as if she were about to burst into tears. Mahelt felt like snapping at her not to be such a goose, but she held her tongue. Pretending nothing had happened was probably the best way to deal with matters. She was about to send the maid for parchment and ink so she could write to her mother when a squire came to the door saying that the earl wanted to see her in his chamber immediately. Mahelt swallowed panic. He couldn't know. He couldn't! Unless... She looked at Edeva but the maid was busy smoothing the bedclothes. The servant was waiting, making it clear she was to go with him, and Mahelt knew that claiming sickness would not stand in her father-in-law's way.

Filled with dread, she followed the man to the earl's chamber. He stood in the middle of the room waiting for her, and Mahelt gasped in horror as she saw her brother's groom Tarant draped between two household knights. He was beaten and bloody, his hands bound with cord. She felt as if a vast hole had opened up beneath her feet and that she was falling and falling even while she stood her ground.

The earl's grey-blue eyes were as cold as a winter sea. "Do you know anything of this business, daughter?" he demanded. "Do you know this man?"

Mahelt shook her head. "I have never seen him before in my life," she lied, her mouth dry with terror.

"Well then, I can only assume since he has no business being on my lands, and he won't say what he was doing, that he is a traitor or a spy and must be dealt with accordingly." He gave her a hard stare. "What do you think we should do with him, my girl? String him up?"

Fear made her voice hoarse. "Perhaps he is just passing through on his way elsewhere, sire."

"Elsewhere is not here, and what business does he have in the dead before dawn?"

In the long, uncomfortable silence, Mahelt dug her nails into her palms and wondered whether to confess that she had been to see her brother. She was almost certain the earl knew and that this was her punishment. Should she own up, or brazen it out?

"He wears your father's colours. Are you sure you know him not?" The earl opened his clenched fist, palm upwards, to show her a small enamel horse pendant bearing the Marshal lion on the familiar green and gold background.

Her knees almost buckled. "He may be part of my father's household but I don't know all of the servants," she said faintly.

The earl's top lip curled. "We'll find out one way or another. I can always write to the king and let him know we caught this man prowling."

Mahelt's eyes widened. "No!"

"Ah, so you do know him."

Mahelt looked down, avoiding the earl's gimlet stare, and gave an infinitesimal nod.

"So what was your business with him? I will have it out." His voice thickened. "By God, I will have the knowledge of what goes on in my domain!"

"I only wanted to meet with my brother," Mahelt whispered. "I haven't seen him for so long." She wiped her sleeve across her eyes. "It was my only chance. I had to know he was all right."

"And in so doing, you disobeyed my will," Roger said harshly. "You put a ladder over the wall. You endangered both your moral and physical welfare. But what is inexcusable is that you compromised the safety of this household. I will not have it."

Mahelt had never before received a tongue-lashing of this power. Before her marriage she had been the darling, the favoured daughter. Her heart thudded against her ribs. She was scared, cornered, and angry. "He is my brother," she repeated.

"Indeed, and you will have fitting opportunities to see him that do not involve irresponsible escapades in the dead of night. I want you to go now and fetch me the business that this was about."

Mahelt's breath locked in her throat. "I don't know what you mean."

"Then perhaps a look inside your mattress will remind you. Bring me that parchment now. I will not be played for a fool. Hamo, go with her." He gestured to one of his knights.

Mahelt tottered from the room on wobbly legs. There wasn't a hope of getting rid of the parchment or defacing it with a hard-faced knight at her side, and since her father-in-law knew about its existence, he was already one step ahead of her in the game. When she entered her chamber, Edeva was still there and Mahelt knew who was to blame.

"I had to tell him, my lady," Edeva wept, wringing her hands all over again. "I was so afraid for you..."

Mahelt said nothing because she was so full of rage and so hollow with terror that dealing with Edeva, even speaking to her, was impossible. As she removed the folded parchment from the slit in the mattress under Hamo's frigid, watchful stare she wanted to die. Her brother had trusted her and she had not been up to the task. Had the ladder still been there, she would have thrown it over the wall again and run away. As it was, she retreated within herself and it was as if a stranger walked down the stairs, re-entered the chamber, and handed over the parchment to the waiting man, while she watched in angry shame from a distance.

The earl read the page with a closed expression on his face. "This does not reflect well on your brother, or your brother's loyalty, does it?" he said icily. "Or yours for that matter." He compressed his lips. "You need to be taught whose side you are on, my girl, and whose interests you serve. Not your brother's, not your birth family's. You serve the blood into which you have married. While you are under this roof, your loyalty is to the Bigod name and honour above all other considerations. Is that understood?"

Mahelt gritted her teeth. "Yes, sire," she said, knowing she would never forgive him for this humiliation. Raising her head like a queen, she went to stand beside her brother's groom in a gesture of solidarity.

"Were you born to me, I would have had you tied at the whipping post for this," Roger growled. "A pity your father did not lay on with the lash when it was needed. I have been too lenient. If you have time for this sort of caper, you are being under-employed. I will have no more of this...this wasps' nest." He thrust the parchment into the brazier and watched it curl and blaze up, before being licked to ashes. Then he gave a brusque wave of his hand. "You can take your accomplice out now and tend to him. After that he may go, and I will hear no more of this business—ever. Cut his bonds." He gestured to Hamo.

Mahelt made herself curtsey to the earl and helped Tarant away to the tack alcove in the stables. She had a youth fetch her a bowl of water and a cloth so she could bathe the groom's purple, swollen eye, and she brought him bread and ale herself. He drank, but did not eat because the inside of his mouth was ribboned with cuts and he had several loose teeth.

"He knew, mistress, he knew," Tarant slurred as she dabbed at him. "But I didn't tell him, I swear I did not."

"I know that." Her throat was tight. "I only wanted to help my family." She felt as if her burden was too much to bear. She was sorry for Tarant and guilty too, but it was as if she too had been beaten. "Do you think the earl really will tell King John?" she whispered.

Tarant swallowed a mouthful of ale and gasped with pain.

"No, mistress, because then the king might suspect he is implicated too. I believe he was trying to frighten you."

Mahelt bowed her head. "I only wanted to do what was best, but it is all such a mess," she said.

Tarant gestured her to stop dabbing at his bruises. "Have courage, young mistress. Let all settle down for now."

She felt ashamed that out of his pain he was yet trying to comfort her, and she was sick with anger too. She knew the earl thought he was teaching her a lesson about actions and consequences, but she had only been trying to help her family and she fiercely resented the way he had humiliated her.

"I don't want you to return to my brother," she said. "I want you to go to Ireland, to my mother and Jean D'Earley." As she helped him to his horse, she told him all that she could remember from reading the details on the parchment. It wasn't perfect, but it was better than nothing. It was a little bit of defiance and it felt good.

❖❖❖

When Tarant had ridden out, hunched over his saddle, nursing his bruised ribs and tender stomach, Mahelt went to Ida's chamber, knowing it was expected of her and that, no matter how unpleasant, she had to face this out.

Ida had been weeping and her face was blotched and puffy. She sat near the window with her sewing, taking neat, fast stitches, as if by doing so she could mend the world and make everything right again. Mahelt paused on the threshold, washed by guilt at the sight of the older woman's bowed head and sorrowful air. She crossed the room and put her arms around her. "I am sorry if I brought trouble upon you, my lady mother," she said, and meant it. She would not hurt Ida for the world.

Ida was rigid at first, but eventually softened to accept the embrace, although she did not reciprocate. "Do you know how much danger you were in?" Her voice trembled with distress.

"We are bound in sacred trust to look after you. What would we tell your parents if you had taken a fall and been killed or abducted? You may believe you are immortal, but you are not. You should think on all the grief you have caused those who care for your welfare." Tears bloomed in her soft brown eyes. "The earl blames me. He says I have not been giving you enough to do, and he blames Hugh also for not being a strict enough husband."

Mahelt gasped. "That's not fair!"

"No." Ida raised her hand. "The earl is within his rights—and whatever you may think of him, he is never less than fair."

Mahelt disagreed with that, but said nothing.

Ida drew a deep, steadying breath. "I know you do not care for sewing, but you are good at supervision and you have boundless energy. It is only right you should take over more duties now you have been here awhile. The earl thinks it will steady you to the yoke. I should have seen to it that you had more tasks before now, but I did not want to burden you too soon into the marriage. I see now I was wrong."

Mahelt was stung. "I know how to be responsible."

Ida arched her brow. "Going over the wall in the night hardly shows maturity, even if you thought you were doing the right thing. It is time you learned more about your responsibility to this household." Her mother-in-law emphasised the last two words. "I know it is upsetting to have your family far away and your brothers sent hither and yon at the king's whim, but your life is with us now, and you must learn to live by our rules."

"Yes, Mother," Mahelt said with a mutinous pout.

"Come." Ida left her sewing and rose to her feet. "We're returning to Framlingham on the morrow and we need to pack. Let me see how responsible you truly are."

With a feeling of resignation, Mahelt followed Ida to the baggage chests in the corner of the room.

"Once we are back, the earl wants you to oversee the mulching of the apples for making cider and storing over winter," Ida said as she opened the lid of the nearest chest. "It is something I usually do, but it will be your task now, from start to finish."

"Yes, Mother," Mahelt said dutifully. She supposed that, on balance, apple-mulching was better than being given a mound of sewing to do, but it was still a mundane, domestic trifle when set against her family's struggle to survive.

Fifteen

THETFORD FOREST, OCTOBER 1207

RAWING ON HIS CLOAK, HAIR RUMPLED FROM SLUMBER, HUGH parted the tent flaps and stepped into the autumn forest morning. Smoke twirled from the camp fire and his companions were stirring lethargically to life in the aftermath of last night's conviviality. Hugh had a sore head and a tannic taste in his mouth, but counted them a small price to pay for the enjoyment he had had.

His brother William and his brother-in-law Ranulf were nursing their heads as they sat by the fire, eating bread and cold sausage and drinking weak English ale. Joining them, Hugh playfully tipped William's hat over his eyes.

"It was a good night, eh?" He glanced across to where the huntsmen were securing butchered deer carcasses on to the packhorses. There would be good prime venison for the table and the smoke house. The dogs had also coursed several hares to add to the tally.

"I think so, from what I remember." Ranulf gave a theatrical grimace. His light green eyes were narrowed against the sharpness of the morning light. "Marie says you are a bad influence. You always manage to lead me astray."

Hugh laughed. "My sister would say that. In truth, you're quite capable of going astray all by yourself."

Ranulf snorted and made a rude gesture, then he looked up as a messenger rode into the camp. "Trouble," he said.

Frowning, wondering what was so important it couldn't wait, Hugh went to the man and took the folded parchment he produced from his satchel. It bore his father's seal and the image in the wax was very solid, as if impressed with a decisive, perhaps angry hand. With a hollow feeling in his belly, he broke the seal, opened out the letter, and began to read. The words on the page inflated within him until finally he could take no more and let out his tension on a huge sigh.

"What is it?" William asked, looking anxious.

Hugh made a face. "What do you think? Mahelt."

"Ah." His brother rolled his eyes and grinned. "She's been disturbing the order of the household again, I take it?"

"You might say that." Hugh handed the parchment to William, who shared it with Ranulf while they finished their ale.

William looked up at Hugh, no longer laughing but serious. "What are you going to do?"

Hugh puffed out his cheeks. "I don't know. If I bat her down too strongly, then I lose her trust and the very part of her that makes her individual, and I would not do that for the world."

"But you must do something," William said. "This was more than just folly. It could have had serious repercussions for all of us."

"I know." Hugh bit his thumb knuckle. "She doesn't think before she acts."

Ranulf cleared his throat. "The men accompanying your wife's brother..." He paused and shook his head. "De Sandford is a loyal king's man, but John FitzRobert is known as a hothead in my neck of the woods."

"His father is loyal to the king though, and constable of Newcastle."

"Yes, but the son keeps company with John de Lacy, who

is a rash one too, and de Lacy's father is close kin with the Irish branch of the family. De Braose, de Lacy, and Marshal." Ranulf counted the names on his fingers. "John would curb all three if he could because he fears their power." He wagged a warning forefinger. "Even if he is a hostage, your wife's brother is keeping suspect company—and the king will be watching, because his spies are everywhere."

"But Roger de Lacy is as solid as a rock," Hugh said, thinking of Pontefract's dour, trap-mouthed constable.

"You are talking of the father, not the son," Ranulf replied. "It doesn't always follow. Old King Henry had four grown sons and they all defied him." He reached for the ale jug. "I am just saying you should look to your security the way a good shepherd tends his flock against wolves."

❖❖❖

When Hugh arrived at Framlingham, Mahelt came flying out to greet him. Watching her in vibrant motion, Hugh's heart constricted. How in God's name was he going to tame her without breaking her spirit?

As he dismounted, she hesitated and then hastened forward again and bestowed him a proper curtsey. Her cheeks were deep pink, which might be the result of her dash, although knowing what he knew, he suspected the cause was emotional—and that her speed was probably caused by her desire to reach him before anyone else did.

He raised her to her feet, kissed her cheek rather than her lips, and then pulled back, still holding her hands, and gave her a grave look. "My father wrote to me," he said. "Mahelt, what have you done?"

She raised her chin. "Nothing I am ashamed of. Your father doesn't underst—"

Hugh held up a warning hand as he saw his father approaching them at a brisk stride. "Sire," he said, and bowed.

Mahelt curtseyed stiffly and compressed her lips.

The earl's grey stare flicked between them. "A word, my son." He dismissed Mahelt with a brief nod that said she might run faster and be first to the greeting, but he had the ultimate power and she should learn that lesson.

Mahelt had no option but to curtsey again and retire to the women's chamber. Her shoulder blades burned as she felt the speculative stares of the hunting party on her as she walked. She put her head in the air and pretended not to see them.

❖❖❖

"Good hunting?" Roger asked curtly as the servant closed the door to his chamber, leaving him and Hugh alone.

"Yes, sire. I spoke to the foresters about making that new coney warren."

"Perhaps it would be better to set your house in order at home before you go ordering dwellings for coneys."

Hugh's chest expanded with indignation. "You said it was a good idea for me to go. You raised no objections!"

The earl gave him a narrow look. "That was before your wife absconded in the middle of the night to indulge in treasonable activities with her brother. *Your* wife, Hugh, not mine! She is your responsibility and quite obviously you are not teaching the girl hers!"

"Sire, that is not tr—"

"What do you mean by allowing her to run wild?" His father drew himself up. "What do you mean by giving her such freedom? She is a hoyden and a disgrace to the name of Bigod!"

Hugh's gut tightened. His father seldom boiled over, but when he did, his rages were concentrated and powerful. Hearing his tirade against Mahelt filled Hugh with consternation. He loved his young wife for her energy, her forthright ways, the funny things she said, but he could understand his father's fury.

"She is still very young, sire," he said. "She probably didn't realise the harm it would cause."

"She is swiftly becoming a woman to judge from the way you have recently been treating her," his father snapped. "You say one thing about her and you do the other. That girl needs keeping in her rightful niche and it is not the one she is carving for herself with your blind yeasay! She must be moulded to fit and, as her husband, it is your task to do so." He stabbed a forefinger in emphasis. "She must not be allowed outlets for this sort of behaviour in our household."

"I agree," Hugh said, but his father was in full flow, determined to have his say.

"Remember that this is indeed *our* household, *not* the Marshal one. I will not be a sub-house for that family and I will not have them dictating what we do. That girl is but a pawn in their game."

"I don't—"

"And if they think so little of her as to put her in so much danger, then beware, because they will think little of her husband too—and of us, mark my words." He finished speaking and stood before Hugh, his chest heaving, sweat on his brow, and the room scarcely big enough to contain his ire. Hugh hadn't seen his father this riled since the time when he, as a youth, had dropped a large stone in the cogs of a mill's machinery to see what would happen and completely ruined the workings.

Hugh poured wine for both of them and then went to sit before the hearth, giving himself an opportunity to reflect and his father a chance to calm down. He didn't think his sire was right about the Marshals' attitude towards their daughter, and besides, it was her brother who had involved her in the first place, but he did agree on the main issues. However, he had Mahelt to consider too, and he didn't know how he was going to put her in a niche. She was like a cloud: changeable of mood, impossible to grasp, often stunningly beautiful but quite capable of wreaking havoc.

If he used physical discipline on her, he sensed it would only turn her against him and make her more wilful yet. He had been raised in a household where correction was generally meted without fist or whip. In boyhood he could only remember receiving a serious thrashing once—for endangering his little brother by using him as a tourney target. His father had whipped him before the entire household. But he couldn't do that to Mahelt and a strict lecture would just be water off a duck's back. It boiled down to harnessing all that vibrant energy she possessed and guiding it in positive directions.

He suspected the way to lead Mahelt was by appealing to her loyalty and her love. Those qualities had been fostered in her since birth, but for her blood family alone. To win her, he would have to find a way to change her focus. He did not want to lose her. She was the humour and spark in his life and he felt protective of her too.

His father had remained standing. Although his shoulders had ceased to heave and his colour was more natural, his expression still said he intended to have this out to its conclusion.

"Sire, I am sorry," Hugh said. "I realise I have been remiss and perhaps too indulgent with her, but I am in a difficult situation—with respect, one you never had to face."

His father raised his brows.

"When you married my mother she was already a woman grown and the mother of a child. But how do you deal with a girl to whom you have a right, yet no right at all? How do you care for her when she is not your daughter but not yet your wife? When you do not know from one moment to the next if she is a child, or a woman?"

His father inhaled with a closed mouth and his nostrils flared.

"I do not know, but you must make haste and find a way because I will have no more of this in my household. Curb her."

"Sire, I will, but give me a little time to ponder the matter." Finishing his wine, Hugh stood up.

His father grunted and raised a forefinger in warning. "Do so swiftly," he growled. "Because if you do not, I will."

❖❖❖

Seated at the high table in the hall that night, Mahelt had never felt more miserable and upset. She knew whatever Hugh's father had said to him about her must have been damning. Since emerging from his father's chamber looking grim, Hugh had barely spoken a word to her and paid her even less attention, something she found intolerable—and frightening. She needed him to notice her; she needed him to take her part; but it was clear he believed his father's version of events.

The meal was a formal affair and Hugh sat beside his mother and served her trencher while Mahelt was forced to share with the earl. The tender beef in sauce stuck in her throat. Hugh's father behaved towards her with impeccable, glacial courtesy and Mahelt responded in the same wise that she ate—forcing herself and with meagre result. Her own family would never treat her like this. Even the earl's other sons were distant with her and barely spoke, their eyes filled with wariness and disapproval.

Following the meal there was dancing and singing. Normally Mahelt loved such entertainment, especially when Hugh was home. It was an excuse to touch, to laugh, to be in motion. But tonight Hugh was formal and remote. He only danced with her once and he was distant, although she was aware of him eyeing her in a thoughtful, speculative way.

Eventually, unable to bear the atmosphere, Mahelt begged leave to retire to her chamber, where at least she could have a cry and be miserable behind the privacy of her bed curtains. The earl granted her the mercy with a gesture of his hand.

"Sire, I shall escort my wife to her chamber." Hugh rose and bowed to his father, who gave him an eloquent look and inclined his head.

Hope surged through Mahelt as she left the hall with Hugh. Now that they were out of his father's presence, it would be different, she thought. She could tell him what had really happened, and win his support. However, as they walked across the courtyard and started up the steps to her chamber, he spoke first.

"You must be careful not to go too far afield from your quarters tonight." He gestured towards the soldier pacing the ward with a mastiff held on a short leash. "As you can see, the guard has been tightened and everyone is being very vigilant."

His voice held neither warmth nor humour and Mahelt's wretchedness increased. There was wine on his breath and his enunciation, although not slurred, was careful. She stamped her foot and turned on the stair, tears stinging her eyes. "I will not be treated in this way!"

He advanced two more steps so that he was immediately beneath her but almost on level because of his greater height. "Unfortunately you will until you learn what proper behaviour is in this household. Don't you realise the upset you have caused by your foolishness?"

Mahelt was stunned. "You do not know what proper behaviour is in this household!" she lashed out from the depth of her misery. "It would take a Marshal to teach you right from wrong."

There was a moment's silence, then Hugh said with quiet scorn, "Pity then that you are a Bigod, my lady wife."

Mahelt gasped and raised her hand to slap him, but he grabbed her wrist and held it high and to one side. She struggled, but his grip was a soldier's, strong and sure. He pushed her against the wall and she felt his body against the length of hers. Dear God in heaven, dear God! He put the index finger of his other hand to the tip of her nose. "Be very careful whom you provoke, my lady, for who knows what the consequences may be," he said on a hoarse whisper. Taking away his finger, he kissed her on the mouth, parting her lips, running his tongue around them, while their bodies fitted together as a perfect match at breast and thigh and groin. All the blood of her anger raced to her pelvis. She was quivering, melting; her knees were buckling. When he pulled away, she had to grip the wall for support.

"We'll talk more about this in the morning when I am sober and we have both had time to think," he said. "And then we will decide where we go from here. For now, I bid you goodnight, and tell you to bolt your door for your own good."

Mahelt gave a sobbing intake of breath and pelted up the rest of the stairs. Once inside her chamber, she did indeed bolt the door, and then leaned against it, panting like a hunted deer that has reached a hidden cave just ahead of the hounds.

Gradually, she became aware of Edeva standing near the turned-down bed. The maid's eyes were lowered and she was trembling almost as much as her mistress. Mahelt's anger came surging back. She thought of Hugh saying that she was going to be watched. Mayhap so, but not by this woman. "Get out!" she spat. "I don't want you here!"

Edeva bit her lip. "My lady, I was only doing my duty."

"Not to me you weren't. Go, I don't want to set eyes on you again!"

The maid gave her a reproachful look but sidled towards the door. Mahelt unbarred it and stood aside to give her room to make her exit, suppressing the urge to give her a shove, and then shot the bolt once more with an almighty slam. She leaned her head against the cold stone wall and allowed herself to cry, her sobs wrenching up from deep inside her. She wanted her old life back where she was the cherished daughter and everyone loved her. Here she was viewed as a junior member of the household and a nuisance, although they were keen to have the wealth and prestige she brought to their family. Oh yes, they wanted that. Her body still tingled from Hugh's kiss. A dull ache suffused her pelvis and she felt restless and frustrated. If she could she would have run out to the stables, saddled a horse, and galloped for miles and miles. But she couldn't. It wasn't allowed. Indeed, she wondered if she would ever be able to gallop again.

❖ ❖ ❖

In the early morning, Mahelt walked among the trees in the orchard, her gown trailing in the wet grass and the hem growing dark. Edeva had not returned and she had had to dress herself and drink the dregs of the stale wine from the jug left in her chamber. No fresh water for washing had been brought and no food. She was still being punished, but she refused to come to heel like a cowed dog. Rather than go to the hall to break her fast and make an appearance in public, she walked among the trees instead, and breathed the crisp, clear air.

Passing under a low branch, she reached to cup an apple in her hand and give it a slight tug to see if it detached easily. It did, but when she tasted the flesh it was tart and sour, although with an underlying sweetness. Good for cider or verjuice then.

At the sound of a soft footfall, she turned to see Hugh advancing on her bearing a wooden board laden with bread, cheese, and two mugs of ale. "Here," he said. "Unless you want to break your fast on green apples and pay for it later. I saw you walk past the hall."

"I suppose you were watching me and being vigilant?" she asked, curling her lip. "Perhaps you thought I was about to abscond over the wall?"

"I honestly do not know what you might do," he retorted with a shake of his head. "Neither does anyone else. Come, eat." He placed the board on a bench curled around one of the trees and sat down. Mahelt joined him, but waited a moment to show it was of her own accord and not obedience to an order. After last night she was on her guard with him, but wondered if this gesture was by way of an apology that was not going to be voiced.

The orchard workers were beginning the day's tasks and bustled about with their ladders and baskets. A few last, lazy wasps crawled among the windfalls and droned around the trees, causing sudden flurries of alarm amidst the apple-pickers.

Hugh broke the bread and cut up the cheese with his knife. Mahelt watched his hands at work. His hair fell over his brow and the summer sun had dipped it in gold at the ends. Task completed, he set down his knife and looked at her. In the fine morning light, his eyes held every shade of blue from woad and speedwell to charcoal and slate.

He bit into a piece of crust and chewed with enjoyment and vigour. Even if he had been drunk last night, he was evidently not suffering a malaise because of it. Mahelt's stomach was churning. She picked at the cheese and nibbled on the bread and waited for him to speak.

"So," he said eventually as he lifted his cup. "What are we going to do about this mess? You have caused more flurry in this household than a fox in a chicken coop."

Mahelt continued to play with her food and said nothing.

He drank, appraising her over the rim of the cup before lowering his arm and sighing. "Don't you realise the harm you could have caused? If the wrong people found out it could destroy us all. How can my father help yours and be a force for stability if the king turns upon him for treason? He has to be above reproach!"

Her eyes widened. It had not occurred to her to think of Hugh's father helping her situation. She viewed him as a stuffy and self-satisfied little cockerel with a pedantic need to have everything in its place. She had seen the way he arranged his dish at the table, placing everything just so. Heaven forbid that a knife or a cup should be slantwise on the cloth, or that the cloth should have a drip on it. "I did not know your father was helping mine."

"There's a lot you don't know." He took her hand and ran his thumb back and forth over her wedding ring. "Your brother may hand you what he believes are clandestine messages, but we are not uninformed dolts. We know what goes on at court; we have to for our own safety."

Mahelt shivered at his touch. "I fear for my father and my brothers—as you would if your kin were held hostage."

"Indeed I would. I know you felt desperate and did what you thought you must, but it can't happen again. Come to me if you are troubled and we will see what can be done."

Mahelt wondered if he was offering in oblique language to help her pass messages, and that made her anxious as much as it melted her, because while she might be a Bigod by marriage, it certainly did not make Hugh a Marshal. She wanted to trust him, but knew he was honour bound to obey his father. "I have some apples to mulch," she said, avoiding a straight reply. "Your father seems to think it a fitting occupation for women."

Hugh's lips twitched. "What he desires is a commitment from you that shows him you are prepared to be part of this household. Mulching a few apples seems to me a small price to pay to keep the peace and to prove you can be a good chatelaine. Do this well, and the pressure on you will ease."

Mahelt rose to her feet and fixed him with a challenging stare. "And will it always be this way? Shall I always be a prisoner of his opinions and dictates?"

Hugh rose too, and slipped his arm around her waist. "My love, you are not a prisoner, except of your own choosing, but you must learn to compromise."

"Why?" she pouted. "He doesn't."

Hugh's grip on her tightened. "There are ways around. You don't have to butt down walls with your head when there's an open door beside you—unless you enjoy hurting yourself. My father is a judge and a lawyer. He understands justice and he's fair. If you are prepared to be reasonable, then he will be reasonable too."

"He wouldn't allow me to see Will; I don't call that reasonable!"

"And do you call going over the wall at night and accepting secret letters reasonable too? Which is the more reasonless? That is something you should think on, my love." He kissed her, once on the mouth, tenderly this time, without last night's smoulder, and then again, lightly, on the cheek. "Don't put your fingers in the fire unless you are prepared to be burned," he said. "As I told you, deeds have consequences."

Watching him walk away to his own duties, Mahelt set her fingertips to her lips. Her body was tingling. She felt light and heavy at the same time. Full and empty, needing, but not knowing what would satisfy her. He was right. She did have a lot of thinking to do. Drawing a deep breath, she turned to her task. If mulching an orchard full of apples was what it took to restore her to grace, then it had best be done, but what lay beyond that was open to question.

Sixteen

FRAMLINGHAM, JANUARY 1208

*O*N A SLEETY, FREEZING JANUARY DAY, MAHELT WAS PLAYING
a boisterous game with the younger members of the
Bigod household. One person was rendered blind by a woollen
hood worn back to front. The other players used their own
hoods as soft weapons to dart in and bat the victim. The latter
had to try and catch one of the other players, so that they
became the hoodman instead.

Mahelt swiped her brother-in-law Ralph, who was the
hoodman, and leaped away. She was aware of her father-
in-law observing her, but for once he was smiling, even if
his gaze was watchful. Meeting her glance for a moment, he
toasted her with a cup of cider pressed from the apples she
had mulched in the autumn. Mahelt swept him a dutiful if
less than heartfelt curtsey. She had been doing her best to
fit into the mould required since the events of the previous
October. She still found it difficult to sit and sew, but she
had taken over supervision of the dairy and helped out with
arranging the welcome of guests and visitors to Framlingham.
She enjoyed the latter and was good at it, but knew she
was closely watched lest she used it as a means of passing
on information. She only wished she could. Her father was
still kicking his heels at the court and her brothers remained

hostages. She did not want to think about any of them being trapped and powerless.

She lunged at Ranulf but he was faster and he caught her with a yell of triumph. Mahelt both laughed and screwed up her face as she changed places with him. Somehow it seemed appropriate that she should be in darkness. The play began again, hoods flicking against her body while she snatched at thin air and heard the teasing laughter. A soft knot tapped against her side, once and then again, taunting. Flick, flick. She pretended to ignore it, but then turned with a sudden leap, her hand seizing the tassel attached to the end of a hood. Hugh, she realised, because his was the only one with such decoration. "Got you!" she cried in triumph, pulling her own head covering off.

He flashed a grin. "You mean I saved you," he retorted.

Mahelt put her nose in the air and her hands on her hips. "Not so!"

He tweaked her nose and kissed her cheek.

Physically she and Hugh remained balanced on a knife edge. Since November, he had often been away, attending to various duties concerned with the earldom and his own estates. During his absences, she was kept under the earl's unwelcome and strict supervision. When Hugh was home, he was careful and restrained. Nevertheless, it had still been possible to snatch a few vivid moments alone. His father could not watch them all the time, and even he allowed that a certain degree of formal courtship was permitted, providing it stayed within limits.

The earl's chamberlain walked up to his lord and pressed a sealed package into his hands with a murmured word. Mahelt's stomach clenched as it always did when she saw a messenger because of the news he might be bearing from Ireland, or from the court. The earl broke the seal and read the contents. His face remained expressionless, which might mean everything or nothing. She threw herself into the game with reckless abandon and was caught again. Hugh shook his head. "What am I to do with you?" he said sorrowfully. "I can't save you from yourself!"

She tossed her head. "I don't need saving," she sniffed, her manner haughty because she was on edge. Fiercely she donned the hood, darkening her sight. The next time she caught someone, it was her sister-in-law Marie, and as Mahelt blinked in the light and looked round, she realised that Hugh and his father were not in the hall. Making an excuse that she needed to visit the privy, Mahelt left too.

❖ ❖ ❖

Hugh closed the door of his father's personal chamber. Sleet tapped against the closed shutters like fingernails and the flames in the sconces leaned away from the windows, pushed by an icy draught.

"Sire?"

Roger handed a roll of parchment to Hugh. "It's from Ralph. I don't know what to believe any more. The rumour at court is that the Marshal's men have been brought down in Ireland."

Alarmed, Hugh swiftly read the news his brother had sent. The parchment bore the imprint of the sheep's spine like a ghost. Meilyr FitzHenry had returned to Ireland and the king had ordered all the Marshal's best knights to come to court and answer for their conduct. They had refused and the king claimed to have received news of heavy fighting in Leinster resulting in the death of Jean D'Earley and the seizure of the pregnant Countess Isabelle and the other Marshal children.

Hugh gazed at his father, appalled. "How can this be true? The country would be in uproar if that had happened, and Longespée himself would have written to us, not left it to Ralph!"

"I no longer know anything with this king at the helm," Roger said brusquely. "Nothing he says or does can be trusted as the truth. If the Marshal does fall..." He did not end the sentence, but shook his head and said, as if to convince himself, "It won't come to that. Rumour is only rumour and we know how John likes to make men squirm and hang them with words."

"It must be true about sending FitzHenry back to Ireland though."

"Yes, but Ralph says FitzHenry has only been gone a fortnight. It isn't long enough for those claims to have happened and the news to be brought back. I suspect the king is causing mischief because it is in his nature." His father drew his furred cloak more firmly around his shoulders as another hard gust of wind flurried sleet against the shutters. "We'll discover the lie of the land ourselves when we go to court."

"Should we tell Mahelt?"

His father considered, and then shook his head. "There is no point until we have sifted rumour from truth ourselves. Whatever has happened, nothing we do can alter it now. The only advantage is that forewarned is forearmed."

Emerging from the chamber, Hugh almost bumped into Mahelt and saw from her white face and blazing eyes that she had heard at least some of the discussion. Hugh cursed, looked over his shoulder, sent up a prayer of gratitude that his father hadn't noticed her, and dragged her forcefully into the corridor beyond. "Listening at keyholes again?" he whispered. "I thought you'd learned your lesson!"

Mahelt jerked out of his grip. "Why should I not when it concerns me! I heard you talking with your father—about mine!"

Hugh scrambled to remember what had been said. He seized her again and pulled her further away from his father's chamber while he assessed the damage. The door was thick and she had been playing hoodman blind when he left. She couldn't have heard it all.

"What do you mean if he falls?" she hissed. "What have you heard?"

Hugh glanced round again and said in a low voice, "The

king has sent Meilyr FitzHenry back to Ireland and demanded your father's senior knights come to court. Ralph thought we should know."

Mahelt blinked fiercely. "They won't come," she said. "Jean would never desert my father's instructions or leave my mother on her own."

"I am sure he would not."

"Why is he doing this to my family? Why can't he leave us alone! I hate him!" She began to weep.

"Ah, Mahelt, don't." He folded her in his arms and kissed her. He wanted to protect her from the hurts of the world, and King John was one of those hurts. In a different way he suspected that her father and brothers were hurts too because whatever was done to them, she felt as a blow to herself. She might be a Bigod in law and supposedly this family was her first allegiance, but he suspected that whatever lip service she paid to that fact, she would always be a Marshal first. Nothing was ever going to alter that.

❖❖❖

Roger hadn't been to court for several months, but thought it prudent to put in an appearance, show himself to the king, and give the right sort of impression. It was one thing to have representation in the form of deputies and kin, but they were only a presence to mark his place, rather than to carry matters forward.

Standing in the busy hall at Marlborough, Roger rested his glance briefly on Hugh who was talking in a group that included Longespée, Ralph, and the Earl of Oxford. Mahelt's hostage brothers were present too, the older one having been brought south again. He wasn't being kept in one place for long. The Marshal brothers stood amid the group, yet slightly apart from it, as if there were an unseen barrier between them and other men. At least the rumours Ralph had mentioned in his letter were only half true. Meilyr FitzHenry had indeed returned to Ireland with a remit to summon the Marshal's men, but the tale about the fighting and capture of the countess was merely the overflow of John's malice and wishful thinking. Foul weather in the Irish Sea meant no ships had made the crossing in the last month.

To Roger's pleasure and satisfaction, Hugh was proving popular at court. He used his good humour and fine looks with subtlety; he wasn't brash like some of the other young bloods. Nor was he affected in his mannerisms or the way he wore his clothes—Longespée's failing. Roger judged that his son needed to learn to present a less open face to certain men, but that would come with time and experience.

Glancing further round, he noticed that William Marshal, who had been talking to the bishop of Norwich, was now alone save for two of his knights who stood either side of him like wary guard dogs. Men were avoiding him, because being out of favour with King John was contagious. A man had to watch with whom he spoke and measure every word. It was one of the reasons Roger was keeping a close eye on Hugh's progress.

Roger took a deep breath because he was not relishing the next few moments, but things had to be said, and when he remembered what had happened behind his back at Thetford, it still made him hot with anger. Putting his head down, he walked bullishly across the room and joined William Marshal with a formal bow.

The Marshal had kept his looks into late middle age. The flesh was taut upon his handsome long bones, but close up Roger could see how gaunt he had become since Hugh and Mahelt's wedding. There were hollows under his cheekbones and haggard shadows beneath his eyes.

William gave Roger the smile of a professional courtier. "I hear the court is moving to Freemantle on the morrow," he said.

Roger inclined his head. "At least the roads are dry," he replied, feeling irritated. He did not want to involve himself in stilted chit-chat and, for his own good, he could not afford to be seen talking for too long to the Earl of Pembroke.

"How is your daughter faring?" William asked after a moment, still smiling.

Roger was well aware that William was referring to Mahelt, not Marie or Marguerite. He said curtly, "I was under the impression she was your daughter, my lord."

There was a taut silence as each man absorbed the meanings underlying the words. A muscle flickered in William's cheek. "Alas, not any more now that she is a Bigod, but I hope she is doing sterling service and I...I think of her often..."

Roger was taken aback to hear a sudden crack of emotion in the other man's voice and see a glitter in his eyes. William Marshal was usually a consummate courtier, hiding all behind an attitude of genial, relaxed calm. In that moment, Roger realised how much the man truly cared for Mahelt, but that in itself was dangerous. Life should have balance and that balance should not be on a knife edge. "Be assured of our care for her welfare," he replied. "We will do everything in our power to nurture and protect her." He gave William a strong look. "I keep a vigilant eye on all that happens within our jurisdiction."

William bowed. "As indeed you should, my lord."

Roger returned the compliment. "I am glad we understand each other," he said and moved to join another group. He rubbed his sweating palms together in a gesture that encompassed both washing his hands and dusting them off. It was over and done with. Closed. Glancing back, he saw that William's erect stance had slumped a little. A part of him felt triumphant and vindicated, but it was the smaller, meaner part. In his greater self he was alarmed and even sympathetic because, in truth, any man in this room could find himself in William's difficult position at a moment's notice. Two years ago, the Marshal had said he was a mirror for all of them, and he had not lied.

❖❖❖

Hugh found himself alone with his brother by marriage as they made their way to the latrines. His father had approached William Marshal. Now it was his duty to talk to Will. Making sure no one else was within hearing, Hugh said, "You should not have involved your sister in your activities. You put her in grave danger."

The young man shot him a look from eyes the same changeable dye-pot hue as Mahelt's. "You do not know my sister," he said with an air of contempt.

"I am swiftly coming to do so," Hugh replied, unsmiling. "She would put herself in peril of her life for you and your father and her birth family. She does nothing by halves and her loyalty is fierce and true. You should not involve her in your schemes. As her husband I am duty bound to care for her welfare and her honour and I will have neither compromised."

Will continued to look scornful. "Then do not put her on too tight a rein because she will not thrive."

Hugh narrowed his eyes. "Neither will she thrive if she is endangered by your rash behaviour."

Will's lip curled. "We are all endangered, 'brother,' and all of the time."

Hugh resisted the urge to seize Will by the throat. "Maybe so, but for the moment, at Framlingham, she has stability. You endangered her by your reckless scheme and you incurred the wrath of my father when he found out. Now he does not trust her and her life has become a cage because of it. There is little I can do to mend her situation because my father's word is the law and because he is right. Not only have you caused damage to our household and your sister, you have strained the bonds between my father and yours. There have been consequences and you should realise that—'brother.'"

A red flush starred Will's cheekbones. "I know the meaning of honour," he said curtly, "and so does my sister. We do not need you to teach it to us."

"Then learn prudence to go with it," Hugh snapped. "Think on what I have said—and think on your sister's welfare."

Seventeen

FRAMLINGHAM, MARCH 1208

RIDING INTO THE VILLAGE OF KETTLEBURGH, MAHELT STARTED and looked round in consternation as a woman's hysterical screams and the shrieks of children pierced the bright spring air. "What's that?" she demanded.

Ida took a firmer grip on her mare's reins, looking worried. "I do not know."

Their escort closed ranks around the women and the laden pack ponies. Ida and Mahelt were returning to Framlingham from a week's visit to the Bigod house and quay in Ipswich. The roads were mostly safe for those who travelled with the protection of armed men, but times were becoming increasingly troubled.

As Mahelt and Ida reached the turning that branched off to the small church, they were astonished to see a wailing woman, wrists tied, being dragged along at the tail of a soldier's horse. Tears streamed down her face. Her headdress had been torn off and unkempt grey braids snaked around her shoulders. Behind another horse, two children were being similarly tugged along—a weeping girl of about ten and a younger spindle-legged boy with grubby knees.

The soldiers were hard-faced men wearing mail shirts with swords at their hips and cudgels in their hands, but they reined back at the sight of the Bigod entourage and gave them right of way. Mahelt's brother-in-law William was marshalling their journey homewards and he drew out of line to speak with the men, while the woman and her children continued to weep and howl.

"It's the interdict," William reported, rejoining Mahelt and his mother. "The king says that if priests will not serve the country, then he will no longer tolerate their lax ways." He nodded at the soldiers and their captives. "They're sheriff's men and they've been sent to arrest any woman known to be a priest's concubine. She says she's been his wife for twelve years, but since priests aren't allowed to marry, they say she's his whore and those are her bastards."

"What's going to happen to them?" Mahelt cast a sympathetic look at the mother and children, but knew there was nothing they could do. The interdict had recently been pronounced on the king and the country by papal decree because there was a dispute over who should be the next archbishop of Canterbury. John had refused to accept the pope's candidate, Stephen Langton, and in retaliation Rome had applied sanctions to all of England. The dispute had been simmering for two years, giving plenty of scope for dissatisfied men to use its momentum to make trouble. Mahelt hated John, but in keeping with most folk she thought the pope's behaviour heavy-handed and that it was not his business to reach out from Rome and say who should be the next archbishop of Canterbury. An interdict meant that the clergy had to refuse to perform their offices. No church bells were to be rung, no masses celebrated, no marriages blessed, no confessions heard, no bodies buried in hallowed ground. The only services undertaken were baptism of the newborn and extreme unction for the dying. In reply to the sanctions, John had ordered Church lands to be seized and put into administration, but this policy of arresting the families of priests was a new twist—an ingenious and spiteful one.

William shrugged. "They'll be taken to Norwich and thrown in gaol. If the priest wants to see them again, he'll have to pay a ransom to get them back."

Mahelt exchanged pertinent glances with Ida as they rode on towards Framlingham. Michael had a "wife" who worked as a seamstress in Ida's chamber. They had a little girl of two years old and a baby in the cradle. "Will the sheriff's men come for Wengeva?"

"I don't know." Ida looked anxious. "I hope not. The sheriff is a king's man but he has no cause to harry us at Framlingham."

Mahelt shifted uncomfortably in the saddle. Ida was not accusing her or even making oblique reference to the incident with her brother, but Mahelt's own guilt was a hard taskmaster. She did not regret going over the wall, but she had come to realise how dangerous it had been for more than just herself and Will.

Framlingham was bustling with activity when they arrived. Mahelt stared round at the sight of the horses and carts. "Hebon!" she cried, seeing Hugh's black courser tethered to a ring in the wall where a groom was rubbing him down. The earl's big chestnut was there too, and the mounts belonging to various knights and squires. Without waiting for her groom's assistance, Mahelt flung down from her mare and sped towards the hall in an unfettered way that made Ida shake her head ruefully, but smile despite herself.

Hugh was just emerging and Mahelt almost bounced off him. He caught her and steadied her before picking her up and swinging her round. Mahelt flung her arms around his neck and kissed him. Hugh laughed, hugged her close, then held her at arm's length to look her up and down.

"We've been at Ipswich," Mahelt said. "We didn't think you'd be back for another week at least."

Hugh's smile quenched a little. "We felt it was time to come home," he replied and went to kiss his mother and clasp his brother's shoulder. The earl emerged from the hall on Hugh's heels, and Mahelt curtseyed to him with the decorum she had not shown when greeting Hugh.

"Daughter," he said gruffly. "I have letters in my baggage from your father. He sends you his greeting and gifts—and bids you remember you are a Bigod wife now."

His words dissolved Mahelt's propriety. "You have seen my father?" she said eagerly. "Is he well, my lord?"

The earl's sea-grey gaze warmed slightly. "Your father is well indeed. To set your mind at rest, let me tell you that the Irish matter has been resolved. Your mother and your brothers and sisters are safe. Your father has agreed a new charter for Leinster with the king, and has returned there to deal with his affairs. Meilyr FitzHenry is to be replaced as justiciar of Ireland by the bishop of Norwich." He nodded to terminate the conversation and cast a meaningful look at the hectic courtyard. "I shall not keep you from your duties."

For the next several hours Mahelt and Ida were kept busy directing the servants and organising food, arranging sleeping spaces, unpacking essential baggage, and dealing with all the sundry tasks that accompanied the return of two households. Finally, order secured out of chaos, Mahelt took a moment to sit in the garden below the west wall and read the letter from her father. The words, penned by his scribe, were reassuring. He was well and there was no cause for her to worry. There was neither censure nor reference to the incident with her brother, although he did bid her cleave to her husband and obey her father-in-law. Mahelt's brow puckered at that and she wondered what had been said at court. He had sent her a small casket of jewels: a silver Irish brooch, gold finger rings and wimple pins, and silver pendants for her mare's breast-band. He loved her; he wished her well. Mahelt squeezed her eyes shut but still, hot tears trickled down her face.

Hearing a sound, she turned swiftly and saw Hugh walking towards her with Tripes snuffling at his heels. She hastily wiped her eyes on the hem of her sleeve.

"Tears?" Hugh looked concerned.

"I am just glad my father is all right," she said, sniffing. "He sent me these." She showed him the contents of the casket. "He says he is well."

"He is." Hugh sat down beside her.

"I wish I could have seen him for myself."

"Doubtless you will once his business in Ireland is in hand. He had to return immediately to set all to rights."

She nodded. "I know he is needed there." She tried not to sound disappointed. "Perhaps John will leave him alone now."

Hugh hesitated and then said, "The danger is not over yet. The king is replacing Meilyr FitzHenry with John de Grey and he is more than able, and a loyal king's man. Your father and de Grey are on good terms, but there will be no quarter given in the matter of John's rights." Hugh crossed his leg over his thigh and toyed with the leather lacing on his boot. Tripes flopped down, nose between paws, and heaved a sigh. "I also suspect de Grey is going to Ireland to avoid pronouncing the interdict on the king."

Mention of the interdict reminded Mahelt of the scene on the road at Kettleburgh and she told Hugh about it now. "It mustn't happen to Michael," she said vehemently. "I don't want them to throw Wengeva and her children into prison and we can hardly hide them like rolls of cloth or silver candlesticks."

Hugh touched her arm. "I've already spoken to Michael. He will continue to perform our services in the chapel and all are welcome to attend, which means there will be no conflict and no need for the king's agents to come visiting."

"But will he not be disobeying his bishop and the pope?"

Hugh shrugged. "Since the bishop of Norwich is going to be very busy in Ireland, neither he nor his officials will be checking on every priest and chaplain in the diocese. And the pope is in Rome. Michael is sensible enough not to bite the hand that protects his woman and children. There will be no change here." He leaned to kiss her in reassurance. Mahelt kissed him back, melting into him. She had missed him so much.

Delicately, he removed her head covering and stroked her burnished dark braids, murmuring how beautiful they were. Then abruptly he stopped and drew back. Following his gaze, Mahelt saw that his father was watching them from the wall walk. She couldn't see his expression, but knew it would be censorious. Feeling uncomfortable at having been observed, she hastily bundled her hair back inside her undercap and covered it with her veil. Hugh gently rearranged the latter so it was straight and set the pins in neatly. "Soon," he said. "Soon we will have our own room and our own bed."

Mahelt made a face and stood up. "It won't stop ears at the door and eyes at the keyhole," she said, "and people measuring the time we spend alone and watching to see how swiftly my belly swells."

Hugh rose too. "We'll find moments and places."

"Like now, in the garden?"

"I promise you."

She shook her head. "I must go. I have duties." She said the final word with a twist to her mouth.

Hugh caught her back as she reached the door in the wall. "I swear it," he said, kissing her again, cheek and brow, throat and lips. Mahelt gasped, but slipped under and away from him.

"We shall see," she said, but there was a smile on her lips left by the kiss as she went out into the courtyard and rejoined the castle activity.

Hugh touched his mouth and tried not to think of all the things he had not told her about Ireland.

Eighteen

HUGH SAT IN HIS FATHER'S CHAMBER AND FOR THE THIRD time attempted to read the letter demanding his attention. It was a draft charter granting lands to Colne Priory and he was supposed to be checking the wording, but he couldn't keep his mind on the matter in hand and the characters were as meaningless to him as they had once been when he was six years old, struggling to learn his letters and his Latin. Uttering an oath of frustration, he cast down his quill and went to the window. His whole body felt as if the sap was uncoiling through it, burgeoning with the warmth of spring and the flourishing abundance that was all around. Horses grazed in the lush fields with foals afoot. On the mere, the water fowl trailed strings of fluffy youngsters. There were fledglings in the nests, new pups in the kennels, kittens in the stables. All had their young at foot. Even his father-in-law had had a new son waiting to greet his return to Ireland. They had received the news of little Ancel's birth three weeks ago. Glancing over his shoulder, he sighed at the tallies and parchments waiting his attention. Mahelt had recently celebrated her fifteenth year day, but Hugh had been away in Ipswich. His father said there must be a formal bedding ceremony, to conclude the agreement they had made with the Marshals, but it was going to be another two months before the household was gathered in Framlingham at the same time. His father was serving at court and it would be past midsummer before he came home, and in the meantime, Hugh needed to go to Yorkshire to deal with his own estates.

Continuing to gaze out of the window, he pondered his dilemma. Mahelt was of age and the agreement had been kept in good faith. The waiting time was over but the occasion needed to be a proper rite of passage; yet he recoiled from the notion of a grand bedding ceremony with the bloody sheet displayed in the hall as proof to everyone of a deed accomplished. He knew Mahelt would be mortified. That prying aspect set them both on edge each time they kissed or touched, knowing they were under scrutiny like a mare and stallion in the mating season.

Muttering under his breath, Hugh returned to the board and tried to work. Framlingham's constable William Lenveise arrived to ask him about employing some crossbowmen for the garrison and wanted to discuss their wages. After he had repeated the same question twice, he began to look a trifle irritated.

"Sire?" he said pointedly.

Hugh waved his hand in apology for his distraction. "Take on four," he said, "and we'll employ others as required. We don't need more at the moment."

Lenveise bowed from the room. Hugh rubbed his eyes, gazed at the parchments, and with another oath, abandoned them and went downstairs.

Ida put down her sewing and looked at her son in surprise. "You want my blessing to take Mahelt to Settrington?"

"Yes, Mother." Sitting down beside her, he picked up a length of ribbon from her sewing basket and wove it through his fingers.

"Does this mean what I think it does?"

Hugh looked at the silk gleaming on his hand. Over and

under and through. "Yes," he said. "By all means let us have a ceremony at Framlingham when my father returns and for formal purposes, but I need to be alone with Mahelt—properly alone."

His mother's expression filled with concern. "And what of your father's wishes?"

"He can still have his ceremony," Hugh said with quiet determination, "with a phial of chicken blood to deflower the bedsheet if he must have all in order. I have obeyed him thus far, but I am not him and he has to give me room to breathe. I know my wife as he does not—and I would know her better yet. How can I concentrate on what I'm supposed to be doing when she is here all the time—at my side but out of bounds?"

Ida gave him a pensive stare. "And will you able to think any better when she is within bounds? Will you get anything done at all then?"

Hugh met his mother's soft brown gaze. Usually her looks for him were tender. Often her eyes held a lively sparkle but just now they were tired and sad. She hadn't said the words with her usual twinkle and she was considering him sombrely. "Yes, I will," he replied firmly. "I will be whole and complete—and so will she. While we are here we are as children under your eye. We need time on our own to become man and wife."

His mother was silent for a long time. Then she sighed again. "When I married your father, he brought me to Framlingham. It was in the days before the towers and the new house were built and there was just the old hall. He wasn't an earl then, but a young man trying to make his place in the world. I had lived at the court for many years, but I was glad to come here. We had time together, alone, and I valued those moments above gold and above the coronet of an earldom." Her eyes glittered with moisture. "Indeed, those weeks we spent then have been a blessing and a curse down the years."

Hugh raised his eyebrows.

"It was the sweetest time of my life. We were just an ordinary newly wedded couple with only ourselves to please and to do as we chose. Your father toasted bread over an open fire in the bedchamber and we fed each other on love..." She swallowed hard. "We have not had so many moments since then. What the world has not taken away the changes of time have wrought." She gave him a sad, poignant smile. "Yes, go; have your time and with my blessing. I will not deny either of you that sweetness."

Hugh knelt to his mother and felt her light touch on his head.

"Once you stood no higher than my knees," she said with a catch in her voice. "Now you have to bend to yours."

"In honour," Hugh replied and she took his hands between hers and kissed him on either cheek.

When he had gone, Ida wiped her eyes and looked round the room at her various needlework projects. Each stitch was a tiny mark in time, building up from that single starting point into a garment or a wall hanging, or a length of braid, speaking of months and years of work—time that she had not spent with Roger except for the odd occasion. All of these pieces were tangible keepsakes of industry and loneliness. The reminders she had of the shared times with her husband were their children, but one by one they had cut the threads and woven lives of their own beyond her sphere—just as her husband had gradually distanced himself from her and spent his time with the business matters of the earldom. Grandchildren would fill the gap, she supposed, and of course there was always more sewing. She gave herself a brisk mental shake. Thinking that way was foolish and unproductive. She ordered her women to bring the coverlet of pale silk on which she had been embroidering white and pink roses in preparation for the bedding ceremony. It was almost finished and if they all applied themselves to it today, it would be ready for Hugh to take in his baggage to Yorkshire as a tangible gesture of her love and blessing.

❖❖❖

Mahelt dismounted in the stable yard of Hugh's manor at Settrington and gazed around, drinking in her surroundings. The house reminded her in many ways of her family's home at Hamstead. It was of a comparable size and even had a similar river flowing nearby. There was the same pleasant, cared-for air, and because it reminded her of a piece of home, she was immediately endeared to it. The arched windows made her think of surprised eyes and a smile of light streamed through the doorway.

Riders had gone ahead so that the servants had had time to prepare for the arrival of the main party and enticing smells wafted from the kitchen buildings. The hall was clean and bright; the interior walls wore a coat of fresh white limewash given splashes of colour by shields and banners. The furniture was sparse, but of good oak that gave off a honeyed smell of beeswax.

They had come to Settrington via the coast, sailing up from Yarmouth to Bridlington, and had then ridden westwards to Settrington. Mahelt had loved every moment. Unlike her father she wasn't prone to seasickness and had enjoyed the wind in her face and the spray sparkling over the gunwales and salting her lips. Hugh had sea water in his blood and she had watched him with pride and desire as he helped reef the sail and took his turn at the steerboard. It had felt so right to sit beside him under the awning of the deck shelter, a shared cloak protecting them from the wind, as the galley surged northwards and the seabirds rode the updraughts from the smudged coastline on the port side.

Hugh made her comfortable before the fire in the hall and had servants bring water to wash her hands and refreshments of good wine and dainty little pastries. He murmured that he had something to do and would return on the moment. Mahelt smiled and nodded, and used the time to settle her thoughts and absorb the atmosphere. The bench she was sitting on was old but well cared for and gleamed with a soft patina.

She suspected Ida's stitchwork in the beautifully embroidered cushions. She leaned her head back, savouring the wine and the feeling of tranquillity and freedom.

Returning, Hugh sat down on the bench at her side. His face was flushed and he seemed very pleased with himself. "Do you like it?" He gestured around.

"Very much." She smiled at him. "It's just like being married, isn't it?"

Hugh threw back his head and laughed aloud. "I would not know, but I am ready to find out." He ate a pastry and washed it down with the wine. "This place has been mine since I was seventeen years old."

She gave him a flirtatious look through her lashes. "We should have come here sooner."

"I thought about it, but then I certainly wouldn't have been able to keep my promise to your parents and mine."

Mahelt's stomach gave a small, pleasant lurch.

"I have something to show you." He put his cup down and held out his hand. "Come with me?"

Mahelt laughed. She felt warm and weak. "It's not another pony, is it?"

Hugh's eyes were luminous. "Not this time."

Mahelt took his hand and followed him outside and up the stairs to the door leading to the chamber over the hall. He removed his hood and covered her eyes with it as if about to start a game of hoodman blind.

"I don't want you peeking through your fingers," he whispered against her ear. His voice was muffled by layers of cloth, but the laughter and the tension in it were still unmistakable and a small, luxurious shiver ran down her spine.

He took her hand again, opened the door, and led her step by step across a room. She felt the firm but yielding springiness of rush matting under her feet and sensed a soft draught from a window against her cheek. He guided her sideways to avoid an item of furniture. Deprived of her sight, she found her other senses were alert and tingling. His hand was warm in hers, leading. She felt the heaviness of a wool curtain and knew he was raising his arm to clack it aside on its rings. He pulled her gently over a threshold and closed the curtain again behind them.

"You can look now," he said and removed the hood.

Mahelt blinked, then stared and stared. They were in a bedchamber as she had thoroughly expected, but what a chamber! A low fire flickered in the hearth, taking the chill off the room. The walls shone with white plaster and were painted with a frieze of delicate green scrollwork interspersed with pink dog roses. Open shutters of warm madder red allowed the afternoon light to stream across the floor and flood the bed in radiance. Sheets and bolsters of crisp white linen contrasted with a coverlet that was a field of embroidered roses. There were rose petals too, scattered upon the pillow. The bed was without hangings, so that all was open to the bright day. A delicate scent of mingled flowers and spices filled the air.

Mahelt was dumbstruck with wonder and a little tearful. Her chest felt as if her heart had expanded and there was no room to breathe. Hugh cupped the side of her face on his hand and with great tenderness unpinned her headdress and removed her netting cap to let her braids tumble down.

"I have dreamed and dreamed of this," he said hoarsely, running his hand down one of her lustrous plaits. "I know we are to have an official ceremony with witnesses, but this is for us. On land that is mine and without interference from anyone. Just me and you, if only for a few days. I swear I shall not hurt you. You will come to no harm in my hands."

Mahelt's breathing quickened. "I am not afraid of this, or of you," she whispered.

Hugh lifted her up and carried her to the bed and the full spring light dazzling on the coverlet. All would be luminous clarity for this first time, sanctified in light. He wanted to see her body; to know everything there was to know about her so she could truly become a part of him, and he a part of her.

He uncoiled her hair from its braids and let its dark silkiness twist around his hands. The sun shot the filaments with tones of gold, ruby, and royal purple. Her eyes were midnight and charcoal, rayed with amber around the pupils. As her lips parted under his, he tasted honey and wine. Now that the moment was here, Hugh no longer dwelt on a knife edge. He wanted to make it last for ever. He wanted them to have all the time in the world.

He undressed her slowly, clothing her in kisses to replace the garments he stripped from her. He explored her skin, admiring with the eye of a lover and artist the lithe lines of her body. Her legs were long; her breasts were small and round; he could easily cup them in his hands like sun-warmed apples. Her nipples were a marvellous shade of rose-brown. He kissed the elegant sweep of her collar bone, her slender, pale throat, and gloried in the sight of the spring sun gleaming on her skin. He tugged his tunic over his head and taking her hands, set them to the fastening at the top of his shirt. She needed no more hint than that and untied the strings. He pulled the garment off and her eyes met his for a moment before lowering to contemplate his body.

Mahelt had seen him half-clad before, but never as intimately as this. Always they had touched with their clothes on and it was the first time she had explored his bare skin when they were alone. He was supple and muscular, all in proportion. His hair was surrounded by a nimbus of sunshine and it was as if they were both beings of light.

The rose petals were damp under her hips and buttocks

and the sheets were cool and pristine. She shivered, gooseflesh rising on her arms.

"Are you cold?"

"No..." Ripples ran through her from head to foot. She saw her own luminosity reflected in his gaze and returned to her a hundredfold. "Hugh," she whispered and touched his hair, before burying her face against the strong pulse beating in his throat. She could feel the rapid thudding of his heart against her ribs and her own pounding in unison. As they stroked and touched and kissed, she began to feel as if they were one person. One flesh, as the Church said that a man and wife became when they took the marriage vows. Adam's rib restored. Feeling the undulation of his hips, she responded in similar wise. He gasped and pulled her over on top of him and threaded his fingers through her thick hair, bright and dark at the same time. Mahelt trembled with excitement and fear. She disliked being caught in a situation where she was at a disadvantage and thus she dared herself to push on a stage further and with that daring came wildness, as if she were in the midst of a battle and it was the only way to survive.

And Hugh harnessed that wildness and used his own experience to bring her to his will even while he was desperate with his own need. He entered her and the sun played over their bodies as they moved within the light. He kissed her eyelids, her nose, her throat, then her mouth, timing each motion of his lips and tongue with the surge and retreat of his hips. The smell of perfumed sheets, the sharpness of their mingled sweat, the spicy scent of her hair filled each breath he took and became part of him. He felt Mahelt tense beneath him and thrash her head on the bolster, and knew it could not last for much longer but he wanted it to go on for ever because it was perfect and perhaps it would never be this perfect again. He gathered her in his arms and she wrapped her legs around him and in turn gathered him in, giving and receiving and giving back, all melding into one.

In the aftermath following the blinding sunburst of release, Hugh flopped over on to his side to avoid squashing her with his weight. Her hand moved against his heaving rib cage. "Your heart will tear through your breast," she murmured.

"Then it will be in your keeping." He stroked her hair. "And that is as it should be because you are its owner." As a peaceful lassitude washed through his bones, he felt that the world could go and do as it wanted; he didn't care. Only let him and Mahelt stay here in this moment for ever. "I have my wife," he said, and then added with a smile: "My woman."

Mahelt glowed when he said "my woman." Because she truly did feel like a woman now. She knew what other women knew. She had the experience and she was grateful to him for making it so good. Leaning up on her elbow, she traced her other hand over his body. The sunlight had shifted and mellowed from white to pale gold. His hands and wrists, face and throat were darker than the rest of him, making him look as if he was wearing an undergarment of flesh—one she had recently reached beneath to touch his true self. She felt such a welling of love for him that it brought tears to her eyes. "My husband," she reciprocated. "My man."

❖❖❖

Over the ensuing days, Hugh took Mahelt riding around the demesne and showed her the fields, the woods, the sheep pasture. He gave her little surprises: a dainty ring depicting two clasped hands; a crown of roses for her head; silk garters for her hose and gold ribbons to dress her hair. They played like children and this time there was no one to stop them or cast censorious glances, and they made love with the windows open and the light upon the bed until they were sore and sated.

One day a traveller visited the manor, headed for York.

He carried jewels in his knapsack: glossy black jet, garnet, and amber from the Baltic. Hugh was particularly taken by an irregular lump of amber that had a strange insect trapped inside it, looking as if it had been drowned in honey. The detail was so clear that he could see the delicate veins on its outspread wings and the fine hairs on its legs. He bought the piece from the packman, together with a deep red garnet for his father's hat and a large blue jewel to set in a pendant for his mother. And pearls for Mahelt, to wind like stars through her hair.

The packman's name was Matthew; he was a garrulous young man who, although aware of his place in the world, was not obsequious and plainly took great pride in his profession. He was hoping to sell most of his stones to the goldsmiths of York.

"You should have a care," Hugh warned him. "Men will rob you for what you have in your pack."

Matthew shrugged. "If they do, they do, but all they see on the outside is a poor pedlar not worth their time. I don't wear rich clothes; I don't have a fine horse, just my donkey, and a common pack saddle."

Hugh nodded, seeing the sense in this, and it made him thoughtful. Perhaps Matthew would be useful to foster should he need to send messages to his father or others less obviously than by a messenger wearing Bigod livery.

❖ ❖ ❖

Mahelt opened her eyes and, as she returned from the oblivion of sleep, gazed through the open shutters. She was fascinated by the way the light changed through the window from white, to gold, to ochre as the day progressed. Hugh was still asleep beside her, his hair a sun-streaked tangle, his mouth relaxed in a natural curve, encircled by a sparkle of stubble. A fierce pang of love arrowed from her heart to her loins. He had said last night that it was time they returned to Framlingham. She knew he was right but she was keen to enjoy these remaining few days and wring from them every last droplet of gold that she could, because once they returned to Suffolk, their lives would immediately become constrained by their duty to others. She was just contemplating kissing him awake when she heard the sound of hoofbeats in the yard, the jingle of harness and voices bantering back and forth.

Mahelt threw on her chemise and, binding her hair in a plait, hurried to the window. To her utter astonishment her brothers Will and Richard were dismounting, together with another young man she had not seen before. Looking upwards, Richard saw her peering out and gave her a grin and a wave. Mahelt hastily backed out of sight and ran to shake Hugh. "Wake up!" she cried, her voice vibrant with excitement. "Wake up, my brothers are here!"

Hugh grunted, forced his eyes half open, and groped for his shirt. "They took their time," he mumbled.

Mahelt paused in donning her dress to stare at him. "What do you mean 'took their time'? You knew?"

"I heard they were at Newcastle, so I wrote to Robert FitzRoger, their custodian. I thought he'd be sympathetic enough to allow them to ride down to Settrington for a couple of days."

"You didn't see fit to tell me?" She laced the sides of her gown with swift fingers.

"I didn't know for sure that he'd let them off the hook, so I preferred to keep it secret and hope for a surprise."

Mahelt leaned over the bed and kissed Hugh hard on the lips. "I love your surprises!"

"They do reap their rewards," he replied with a chuckle.

Mahelt nipped his lower lip between her teeth and he swatted her buttocks. She gave him a mock glare as she bundled her hair into a net and secured a veil over the top with gold pins. "You'll pay for that."

"I'll look forward to it," Hugh retorted, not in the least set down, and laughed to himself as she flung from the room like a whirlwind. Gradually, however, his smile faded and his expression grew thoughtful. He pushed aside the knowledge that his father would not approve of what he had done. He considered it better to let Mahelt flout the rules when he was with her, rather than letting her go off on her own wild tack. This way he could keep his eye on what was said and done, and perhaps learn something too.

❖ ❖ ❖

Mahelt hurried across the hall to greet her brothers, flinging her arms around them and exclaiming with joy. With less exuberance, she curtseyed to John FitzRobert, eldest son of her brothers' gaoler. The young man had the pitted marks of smallpox upon his face and a fierce expression in his eyes, but he was well spoken and his manner was courtly enough.

Hugh arrived in the hall still fastening his belt. "I am sorry, we are slugabeds this morning," he said with a smile as he greeted their guests. He brought them to the dais table where servants were setting out jugs of wine, fresh loaves, cheese, and honey.

At first as they sat over their food, the talk was all light banter and family matters. Will and Richard told Hugh the tale of their sister throwing rancid salve at them while defending her "castle" and Mahelt put her nose in the air. "I won," she said. "Didn't I?"

"Yes, you did," Will said with a quirk of his lips. "My cloak was never the same again."

Mahelt sniffed and looked superior. The talk turned to Ireland and discussion about their new baby brother, Ancel. "Let us hope we get to meet him before he's a grown man," Will said.

"If we don't, we'll all be greybeards," Richard remarked.

Mahelt nudged him. "Don't say that; we'll all be together soon."

Will shook his head. "Do not be so certain. Meilyr FitzHenry may have been defeated, but the king won't let things rest as they are."

Mahelt eyed him. "What do you mean?"

"John hates to lose and he's vindictive. He won't let our father alone in Ireland, especially now William de Braose has fled there."

Mahelt's eyes widened. "De Braose has fled?" She gazed at Hugh in bewilderment, but he was avoiding her eyes. "Why?"

Will looked surprised. "I thought you would know. He's run to Ireland with his wife and family. The king says de Braose owes him thousands of marks, and he's ordered him to pay up and give hostages for his good faith." Will spoke the word "hostages" with grim revulsion. "But it's much more than a matter of owing money."

Hugh shot Will a warning look. "This is not a conversation for company."

"Then when else shall we have it?" Will demanded. "Shall we sweep it into the midden like everything else and pretend the stench beneath our noses doesn't exist?"

"Will knowing make a difference?" Hugh shook his head. "No one goes poking in a midden unless they must."

Mahelt glared at Hugh. "Tell me. I will not be left in ignorance."

Hugh compressed his lips.

Will turned to her and said, "De Braose was the last person to see Prince Arthur alive and he knows what happened to him." He glanced round the gathering. "John murdered his own nephew in cold blood."

"That is mere rumour," Hugh snapped.

"Enough of a 'mere' rumour for de Braose's wife to refuse to give her sons as hostage to John," Will retorted. "Enough to raise de Braose on high for his silence, and then bring him down like a rat scrabbling at the end of a sealed tunnel. Enough to destroy him and his kin. How much rumour is needed before it becomes a truth? How much more do we have to suffer of this tyrant's rule?"

"That is enough." Hugh's voice was hard with anger. "Be welcome to visit with your sister and hunt on my lands, but know that I will not harbour such talk at my hearth."

Will matched his stare. "Not talking about it will not make it go away. It will grow and grow while you ignore it—*because* you ignore it—and one day it will swallow you whole and you will wish you had listened."

"Not if we take pains to protect ourselves. There are more ways than one and within the letter of the law. In East Anglia we have been little troubled."

Will's expression said without words he thought Hugh was deluded.

"Perhaps because you are comfortable in East Anglia turning a blind eye," FitzRobert said.

It was on the tip of Hugh's tongue to say better a blind eye than blinded in truth, but he held back. FitzRobert's sire was not only constable of Newcastle, but the sheriff of Norfolk too and it was prudent to tread carefully. "I have clear enough vision to see how close we all are to the edge," he replied with finality. "Enough of this talk. Would your fathers approve if they were sitting here? How do you think they would respond to your words?"

An uncomfortable silence ensued. Then Will muttered an apology into his chest and Richard asked a deliberate question about one of the gazehounds dozing near the fire, and the conversation lurched into safer waters.

❖❖❖

Mahelt finished combing her hair and watched Hugh pace their chamber with restless energy. Her brothers and FitzRobert had retired for the night to a chamber off the hall and would leave with the morning light to hunt and then travel back north.

Hugh let out a deep breath. "Will is treading a dangerous path."

"What path would you tread if you were him?" Mahelt demanded. "If you had been taken from your family and subject to whim and cruelty?"

Hugh rubbed his brow. "If you stick your head over a parapet you are asking for an archer to put an arrow through your eye. Better to stay down."

"And what of truth and justice? What if all your friends and allies were being killed? Wouldn't you go to their aid?"

Hugh gestured impatiently. "Of course I would, but putting my head over the parapet would just mean joining them in death. That I have invited your brothers to visit is already close enough to peering out through the crenel gaps!"

Mahelt lifted her chin and said with scorn, "My father once stood in the way of Richard Coeur de Lion to stop him capturing old King Henry when they were at war. He was willing to sacrifice himself. He never counted the cost."

"I've heard that story dozens of times," Hugh snapped as he unlaced the ties on his shirt. "King Richard was unarmed and your sire knew he had the advantage. Your father has done many great things, but he has never taken an uncalculated risk and he has never defied the king—only sought to protect himself from attack. My father is a great man too, but not in the same way as yours. King Richard used yours to fight his wars in Normandy and to hold fast against adversity. He used mine to administer justice, apply the law, and keep peace in the shires. Now we have a different king and times have changed.

We must all make adjustments, but staying true to one's path is the best way."

"But what if you are turned from your path?" she persisted. "My brother should never have been made a hostage and my father should never have been persecuted. That is gross *injustice*. Surely, if there is an obstacle in the way, you remove it."

"Or you go round it, or change it."

"To do that you must have knowledge."

"Knowledge is one thing, I agree, and often hard won, but plotting and treason are another matter entirely. There is a line that must not be crossed. Your father and mine know this, but I am not sure your brother and his friends do."

"My brother is loyal!" she flared.

"To his family, yes, but if he crosses that line and he is found out, there will be repercussions for everyone. It is not just himself he will bring down."

Mahelt busied herself arranging her combs and pots of salve on her coffer. Hugh was right but she wasn't going to admit as much because she felt protective of Will and she hated conceding an argument. "What about de Braose?" she asked, taking a side-step. "Do you think the king did murder Arthur? Do you think de Braose is being persecuted because he knows too much?"

Hugh heaved a deep sigh. "I believe it very possible that John killed Arthur, but there is no proof. I think de Braose has become too arrogant and powerful, and John has set out to bring him down—as he tried to bring your father down. He fears men who have the potential to be stronger than he is."

"You didn't tell me about de Braose."

"No," he said. "What good would it have done?"

"That is not the point. You should have told me, not kept me in ignorance." She folded her arms around herself. "Do you value me as more than just a breeder of your heirs?"

"Of course I do!" Hugh's eyes flashed. "You are in my thoughts all the time. I wear you like my skin! I didn't want to concern you when there was no need. I have gone out on a limb for you by inviting your brothers here, because I knew they could not come to Framlingham. I see you, Mahelt. I see through to your heart. I want you to bear me sons and daughters. I want to give them to you, but if you think that is the only reason I need you at my side, we might as well inhabit separate chambers as of now."

Her lip curled. "As your parents do?" It was like the sparring matches on the tourney ground where opponents tested each other's mettle and boundaries—often drawing blood.

"We are not them." Softening, he leaned forward and cupped her face in a conciliatory gesture.

She closed her eyes at his touch. "I want to trust you."

"I want to trust you too...but can I? It is a sword that cuts both ways, my love."

"You can trust me to the last drop of my blood," she answered fiercely, "but you must swear to me the same..." She bound him to the moment with the intensity of her stare. Her breathing quickened and her pelvis grew heavy as she saw the expression and purpose in his.

"On my soul," he said hoarsely and, pulling her against him, kissed her hard.

Mahelt kissed him in reply with an equal strength, and in mutual agreement they took each other to bed to seal the pact and tend each other's wounds.

Nineteen

*M*AHELT PLACED HER HAND ON HER WOMB AS SHE FELT THE baby kick and turn. Her waistline was still slender at the sides but her belly revealed a proud curve as she entered her sixth month. The announcement of her pregnancy at the feast of Candlemas after she had missed her second flux had been greeted with joy and celebration by her marriage family. Her father-in-law was being mellow and indulgent towards her and very tender of her welfare because she was fulfilling her role as the bearer of the next generation. In her turn Mahelt had called a truce. Her nature had gentled as her pregnancy developed. She found herself wanting to sit and sew with Ida rather than be in constant motion. She couldn't pass a cradle without looking into it, and had suddenly discovered an interest in infants and small babies. When Ida's daughter Marie visited with Ranulf and their offspring, Mahelt watched the infants with new eyes. It gave her a pleasant shiver to think about having a child of her own—Hugh's child—becoming a mother, making Hugh a father, and giving her own parents grandchildren.

She and Hugh finally had a private chamber in the old hall and a bed of their own. They could be alone together with every right and sanction. For Mahelt it was bliss. The earl had insisted on an official bedding ceremony when they returned from Yorkshire, and the rosebud coverlet had been formally spread on their new bed and blessed by Michael the chaplain, who continued to serve the household even though the interdict had taken a tighter grip on the country. In the chapel at Framlingham, the castle inhabitants still went to mass and confession, were married with blessings, or buried with hallowed respect.

News arrived occasionally from Mahelt's brothers and from Ireland, but all of it was innocuous. Will had heeded Hugh's warning, and Mahelt's pregnancy meant she was less keen to be involved in matters beyond the household.

"Are you well?" Ida touched Mahelt's sleeve, a note of concern in her voice.

Mahelt turned from her reflections and smiled at Ida. "Yes, Mother. The babe is lively this morning, that is all. He's a little whirlwind." Her tone was wry. In the month since quickening, the movement in her womb was constant. She was sure the child never slept; he or she already possessed the wherewithal to be a champion jouster.

Ida laughed with pleasure and sympathy. "Come. Lie down. Let me rub your feet."

"You are very kind to me." Mahelt went to the bed and slipped off her soft shoes. It was so good to be pampered. Ida, who had a talent for such work, began to massage her feet with firm strokes. Mahelt half closed her eyes and relaxed. Had she been a cat, she would have purred. Even the child calmed its kicks and somersaults, as if attuned to Ida's soft voice and soothing hands.

Ida sang softly under her breath as she worked, but after a few verses of a lullaby, paused to speak. "I am so glad you have settled down with us, my daughter."

"Now that I am doing a woman's duty, you mean?"

Ida looked apologetic. "When you first arrived, I loved you

immediately, as I would a daughter, but I did not know you. I tried to draw you into the family and make you welcome, but after…after what happened I feared for you."

"I know, and I am sorry," Mahelt said contritely, because she did indeed regret causing Ida upset. Yet she knew she would still act in defiance again if she had to. "I have grown up since then."

"Indeed, a great deal." Ida hummed the tune through another verse and continued her rubbing. "It is better for everyone now that you can live as a true wife and have responsibilities that are your full due. You make my son happy, for which I bless you, and the earl is well pleased."

Mahelt almost made a face at the mention of her father-in-law.

Ida sighed. "I know you and the earl have had your differences, but he has always had your welfare and the welfare of this earldom at heart."

"Yes, Mother," Mahelt replied with muted diplomacy. She knew Ida wanted everything to be splendid and right, but it wasn't always possible. Earl Roger desired all to be in its place and performing its proper function, but things needed room to stretch and grow to survive, and he didn't seem to understand that. Her mother-in-law had become resigned, but Mahelt was determined that no matter how many children she bore down the years of her marriage, no matter how much domestic responsibility was laid at her door, she would never allow herself to become squashed into a box.

Hugh came into the chamber and joined them, bowing to and kissing his mother in formal greeting, and then embracing Mahelt similarly. He had been busy with his father going over the business of the earldom and the preoccupied look on his face made her anxious. He hadn't come to his mother's chamber for the pleasure of passing the time of day.

"The summons has come as we thought," he said. "We've to muster in York at the end of July with our levy and then move north to deal with William of Scotland." He flicked a sombre glance at Mahelt. "There are rumours of a conspiracy against the king by the northern barons. He's intending to secure the Scottish border and deal with any wayward ambitions King William and others might be harbouring."

Mahelt felt a qualm on Will's behalf. "There are always rumours of conspiracy," she said. "John could see conspiracy in a cup of water."

Hugh shrugged. "That may be so, but it does not alter the fact that we must obey the summons."

Ida heaved a sigh. "I had better go and begin sorting out your father's baggage," she said tactfully and, giving each of them a kiss, left the room.

Hugh sat down in his mother's place and took Mahelt's feet into his own lap. He loved their strong, graceful shape, the high arches, fine long bones, and alabaster skin, but his move was as much pragmatic as it was indulgent. While he was holding her feet, she couldn't leap up and pace about the room.

"So what are these rumours of conspiracy?" she demanded, as he had known she would. "And how have you come to hear them? You said to me before that rumours are only rumours and nothing until proven."

"Yorkshire is not so far from the Scottish borders and my mother has kin at the Scottish court; so we hear things. King William has been exchanging letters with Philip of France discussing an invasion of England. There's also trouble simmering in Ireland. Roger de Lacey at Chester is under suspicion because his son has been writing letters to France and stirring the brew and the family are powerful across the Irish Sea also."

Mahelt bit her lip. "Is…is Will involved in any of this?"

Hugh gently rubbed her feet. "I do not know—and I do not want to know. Christ, I hope not, for his sake. From what we can tell, Ireland, Scotland, and France are preparing to unite and John cannot allow that to happen. Scotland is the easiest kingdom to deal with first. He doesn't have to cross the sea and plundering over the Scots border is a pastime that everyone will take to with delight whether they love John or not."

"And what of my father?"

He saw her eyes darken with anger and fear. "I esteem your father and he is a strong, shrewd man," he said carefully. "He will deal with matters as they fall."

"You think he is involved too, don't you?"

He hesitated and then said, "I think he knows what is happening and I think he will keep his distance. He has reached agreement with the king over Ireland and even if de Braose is his ally, King John is his liege. For the moment John's eye is fixed upon Scotland; there is no cause for immediate worry."

Mahelt withdrew her feet from his lap and, leaving the bed, went to look out of the window. "Will you see my brother?"

"Probably."

"Tell him...tell him to be very careful."

"I shall do so," Hugh said, thinking it would be wasted breath because Mahelt's brother, like Mahelt herself, did not take kindly to advice. Rising to his feet he came to stand behind her, close but not touching. Beyond the window the fields and meadows sparkled in tranquil summer sunshine.

"And you be careful too," she said in a tight, hurting voice that made his heart go out to her.

"I am not about to become embroiled in anything, my love." He set one hand to her shoulder and curled the other across the gentle swell of her womb. "I have too much to lose."

She turned in his arms and traced his jaw with the tip of her index finger. "Oh Hugh..."

Looking down into her eyes, filled with trouble and love, he realised he still did not know what colour they were, only that they held the world in them.

Twenty

RAISED UP ON HER ELBOWS IN HER CONFINEMENT BED, MAHELT watched the nursemaid bathe a squawking baby boy in a bronze bowl at the fireside. He was pink and perfect with a damp quiff of dark hair, long limbs, and a lusty cry. A son and future successor to the Earldom of Norfolk and her father's firstborn grandchild. She was proud of herself, satisfied, and elated, if a little sore. He was to be named Roger for his grandsire because it was a traditional Bigod name.

Mahelt had retired to confinement a fortnight ago as Hugh rode out to the royal muster in the North. She had expected to be brought to bed at the beginning of September, but the child had arrived early and caught everyone out—including his mother. One moment she had been sitting by her chamber window watching the sky and wishing she could ride out beneath the vast expanse of blue, the next she had been overtaken by a sudden gush of water from between her thighs and cramping, powerful contractions. It had been short for a first labour, so the midwife had said. Less than four hours all told and everything had gone well; Mahelt had been indignant because the midwife had patted her hips, commenting that she was a big strong girl, just as if she were a mare or a cow. Today, with her breasts suddenly burgeoning into massive udders, Mahelt acknowledged that the woman probably knew something she didn't.

Since the baby had not been expected for at least another three weeks, Ida was away in Ipswich dealing with the earl's business and Mahelt's only companion had been Ela of Salisbury who had come to keep her company during the confinement.

Ela watched the nurse and baby with yearning, troubled eyes. "He is beautiful," she said.

"All the more so now I no longer have to carry him around!" Mahelt laughed. "He has Hugh's nose, I think, but my eyes. Hugh will say he has my temper, but I think that is all to the good."

Ela forced a tepid smile and placed one hand to her belly. She was wearing a fashionable tightly laced dress and her figure was as flat as a board. Mahelt said quickly, "It will be all right. The queen has only just borne King John a son and they've been married for seven years."

Ela looked pensive. "I have been praying and doing the things that the midwives tell me, but William has been away a lot and we have not shared a bed in a while." She looked down at her hands. "My husband is such a proud man."

Mahelt heard what went unsaid. Hugh having a male heir would gall Longespée who always felt he had to be the best because of his royal blood. "Then you must get him into your bed," she said. "Prayer and midwives are useless if you do not have the other ingredient. It's no use having a prepared flowerbed and no one to plant the seed."

Ela flushed. "I know that." She watched the nurse pat the baby dry, bind him in swaddling, and lay him in the cradle. "But I do not want my husband to think I am being forward or immodest."

"I do not think you will have to worry about that," Mahelt said, suspecting that little Roger's birth was going to make

Longespée very attentive in that department, opportunity permitting, and she could not imagine Ela being immodest if she tried.

The baby settled to sleep and Mahelt lay down for a nap too, but she did not miss the way that Ela tiptoed from the room and went into the adjoining chapel to kneel and pray.

❖❖❖

The next morning, Ela was reading to Mahelt from a *lai* of Marie de France, when they heard the light dash of footfalls on the stairs. The door flung open and Ida hurtled into the room, breathless and flushed, the bottom of her dress all muddy from travel. "Where is he?" she cried, her eyes alight. "Where is he?" She beamed at Mahelt and Ela and at the same time hurried over to the cradle and peered into it. The nurse was fetching clean swaddling and the baby was naked on his fleece cover. As Ida leaned over him his small fingers accidentally caught the blue jewel hanging around her neck and tightened in a fist.

"Oh!" Ida was immediately and utterly besotted. "Look, he's already reaching for things and he's scarcely born! He'll be a bold warrior, this one!" With tender care, she picked him up and cradled him to her bosom while gently untangling his fingers from the chain around her neck. "The firstborn of my son and his wife and a future earl." Tearfully she kissed and dandled him, and came to Mahelt's bedside. "You have done so well!"

Mahelt smiled. "He is beautiful, isn't he?" she said a little smugly.

With great reluctance, Ida handed him to the wet nurse to be swaddled and then sat down at the bedside, oblivious to the mud-splattered hem of her gown. "Was it painful? I am sorry I was not here, but you took everyone by surprise!"

Mahelt screwed up her face. "It was worse than the stomach ache I had from eating green apples when I was little, and it was hard work, but at least the result is more rewarding." She glanced at the nurse who was busy with the yards of swaddling bands. "Ela has kept me kind and good company."

Ela reddened and smiled, although the curve of her lips was a little strained.

"You're a good girl," Ida said with warm approval before addressing Mahelt again. "Have the messengers been sent out with the news?"

"Yes. To Hugh and the earl and to my parents in Ireland."

Ida's gaze shone. "Their first grandchild. They will be so proud of you, and I know Hugh will be ready to burst."

There was such warmth in Ida's voice that Mahelt felt choked. "Come," Ida said. "Let me comb your hair and sing to my grandson as I work."

Ela rose. "I shall have food and drink fetched, Mama, and water for you to wash away the dust."

"Oh don't worry about that!" Ida laughed, but then looked down at herself and chewed her lip. "Although I suppose I do resemble a harridan!"

"Never!" both daughters-in-law protested in unison.

"You are sweet girls," Ida said. "Now I think on it, wine and food would not come amiss, and perhaps a clean gown."

Ela hurried from the room on her errand. Ida fetched combs and a pot of nutmeg-scented powder and set about grooming Mahelt's burnished dark tresses. "I had hair like yours when I was a girl," she said. "You would not think it now, but once it was as lustrous and thick as the richest damask. Now it is best hidden under a wimple of that cloth instead." Her tone was wistful as she dipped the comb in a bowl of rose water and smoothed it through Mahelt's hair, leaving behind a warm summery perfume.

"Ela worries about being barren," Mahelt said.

Ida's smile faded. "What will be, will be, although I pray she and my son will be blessed in time. I hope God does not punish them because of me."

"Because of you?" Mahelt stared at her mother-in-law with surprise.

"I fornicated with King Henry when I was a young girl at court and my son was the result. I have done penance for my sin ever since and tried to live as a virtuous wife and mother, but I cannot help wondering if it is my fault."

"Of course it isn't!" Mahelt was shocked that Ida was still suffering for something that had happened so long ago. Her mother-in-law had occasions when she was quiet and brooding, but Mahelt had never really thought about the cause, or else had blamed the earl. "It's just that they haven't been together very often. The king is always sending him away from home. It will be all right; I know it will."

"I hope so." Ida removed the blue jewel from around her neck and tied it to the top of the cradle where it winked and sparkled as she set her foot to the rocker. "I want all of my children to fulfil themselves and be happy, and their children after them. If I could have one thing in all the world it would be this, but I know it is more easily wished for than accomplished."

❖❖❖

Hugh and his father sat in their tent at Norham near the Scots border, drinking wine that was sour from several weeks in the barrel, having been sloshed around on shipboard and then jogged on pack pony and cart all the way here. The tents of the English army spread as far as Hugh's eyes could see, like fairy rings of autumnal mushroom. Opposing them, William the Lion of Scotland had fewer troops to command and even fewer resources. He didn't possess as many knights and their equipment was not up to the standard of the English. It was said that what they lacked in numbers they made up for in ferocity, but then again, what they had in fierceness they lacked in discipline.

All that day, John and the Scots king had been in conference, hammering out a harsh understanding—namely that John would not send his English army across the border to ravage Scotland to bloody bones, providing that King William disbanded his own army, paid the sum of fifteen thousand marks, and handed over his two legitimate daughters as hostages with the agreement that in future they would be married to English barons of John's choosing. The terms had been put forward in diplomatic language, but the discussions had been robust.

Longespée paused at the Bigod tent on his way to his own pavilion to change his tunic for the forthcoming banquet. As he tasted the proffered wine, a muscle ticked under his eye.

"Reminds me of the old days at court," Roger said to him ruefully. "Your father's barrels were notorious for the vinegar in them."

"I was too young then to be a victim. But I've heard about it." Longespée sucked in his cheeks and swirled the contents of his goblet. "Wine never travels well on campaign." He shot a look at Roger and Hugh. "What do you think about the king removing the shrievalties of Lancashire and Yorkshire from Roger de Lacey?"

Roger shrugged. "John needs a solid backbone in the North. At least with this treaty the Scots won't bother us again for a while and if the northern border has loyal men in place, we won't have to constantly watch our backs. I'm not saying de Lacey is disloyal—I like the man—but his son is fickle and the family has relatives across the Irish Sea who are not trustworthy."

Hugh eyed his half-brother. "What is John going to do with that fine of fifteen thousand marks from the Scots?"

Longespée's expression immediately closed. "He has several irons in the fire."

"When doesn't he?" Hugh looked up as a messenger arrived at the tent entrance. He had obviously ridden hard and the stink of horse and sweat was so pungent it was almost visible, but there was a huge grin on his face as he took a packet of sealed parchments from his satchel and knelt to the men. "My lords, I am bidden to greet you and tell you that the lady Mahelt Bigod was delivered of a fine healthy son four days since on Assumption eve."

Hugh seized the message, broke the seal, and read the words before grabbing the man, hauling him to his feet, and embracing him as if he were his best friend. He yelled to a lurking squire to bring more wine. "Find the best we have, or go and buy it. I want to toast this in sweetness. A son! The first time and I have a son!" From hugging the messenger, Hugh grabbed Longespée and gave him a smacking kiss on the cheek.

Longespée held himself rigid under such common onslaught. "Great news," he said with a half-hearted smile as Hugh went to throw his arms around his father, who was wearing a satisfied grin.

Hugh turned back to the messenger. "My wife is well, you say?"

"Yes, my lord, and sends you her greetings. The babe has been baptised Roger as you wished."

The squire returned with a barrel of wine he had managed to cajole from the Earl of Oxford's steward, Oxford being blood kin to the babe about to be toasted. The barrel was swiftly broached and measures handed around.

"To my son and to my grandson, future Earls of Norfolk!" Roger declared, lifting his cup above his head. Everyone drank and the wine this time was actually half decent.

"To my wife!" Hugh responded. "And to my father the reigning earl, long may he prosper!" Again men drank and cups were refilled.

Longespée stayed for the first two toasts but declined to refill again and observed with disdain that the messenger and other servants were being allowed to stay and drink. It was all highly inappropriate but it was typical Bigod behaviour. A terrible weight of envy swelled within his chest. That Hugh had begotten a son before him was unbearable. It sickened him to see Hugh puffed up with pride and the old earl looking like a bullfrog. Excusing himself, he flourished in a mannerly fashion from the tent but once outside, he clenched his fists and stalked back to his own pavilion in a foul mood.

Hugh pressed an extra day's wages into the messenger's hand. "Go and find a billet for yourself among my men. I will write a letter to my lady, but tell her I'll be home as soon as I may. Two weeks at the most."

"My lord." The man tugged his forelock and left the tent.

"I remember when you were born," his father said in a nostalgic tone. "I thought I was the king of the world. When I saw you lying in your cradle, I knew there could be no better moment in my life...and now my son has a son."

They embraced again and emotion prickled Hugh's eyes. His father cleared his throat in a gruff businesslike manner. "Your wife. I may have seemed harsh on her, but she had to know the boundaries. I am well pleased at the way she has settled down and done her duty."

Hugh felt a glimmer of irritation at the remark, but he understood why his father had said it and for him, when everything was in its place, all was right with the world. "I had better go and tell her brothers they have a new nephew."

His father nodded, but raised a finger in warning. "Do not stay with them for too long and mind what you say because I have no doubt we are being watched."

"I have their measure." Hugh managed to keep the impatience out of his voice. His father's lecturing was wearisome, even if it was born out of concern.

He found Will and Richard in the company of the two Johns: FitzRobert and de Lacey. Although such a gathering was predictable and almost expected, Hugh's nape still prickled because this was not safe company. Richard gave Hugh a cheerful grin and made room for him to join them over a pile of harness which they were ostensibly cleaning.

"Do you want to assist?" he enquired. "There's a nice bridle here that needs a polish. Plenty of embellishment and fiddly bits."

Will had propped his feet on a low camp table and was leaning back on his chair. "Don't be an idiot, Richard," he said archly. "Our good brother-in-law isn't staying. His father won't let him."

Hugh's eyes narrowed at being talked to in so insolent a manner by a lad of nineteen years old, but he held his peace because this was a moment for joy not rancour. "I've come to tell you that I have a son and you a nephew. Mahelt has been safely delivered of a boy child."

Richard immediately gave a loud whoop, leaped to his feet, and clapped Hugh across the shoulders. "Great news!"

A slow smile spread across Will's face and the caution and belligerence faded from his expression, revealing the winsome dark-eyed youth lurking beneath the hard exterior of world-weary man. He took his feet off the table and came to embrace Hugh. "I am delighted for you and Mahelt. Give her my love, and blessings to the child." He laughed. "The girl has made me an uncle. Suddenly I feel all ancient and responsible."

"It doesn't show yet!" quipped de Lacey and received a rude finger gesture from Will.

Hugh decided to take up Richard's offer and join them for a while, because, despite the danger, there was something uplifting and refreshing about their company. He drank a mug of the local ale, which was much better than the far-travelled wine, and even picked up the bridle Richard had indicated and began to work on it with a cloth swiped round a pot of beeswax.

After a while Will said, "I suppose you've heard that the king is going to take away the shrievalties from John's father?" He indicated de Lacey.

"Longespée told me, yes." Hugh looked up from rubbing the leather. "I also heard that my lord de Lacey will be engaged in fulfilling other duties for the Crown. He is just being deployed elsewhere—which the king has the right to do."

De Lacey shot Hugh a scornful look. "It seems he has the right to do many things," he said with a curled lip. "There was no cause to remove my father."

Will leaned towards Hugh. "What do you think he is going to do with all this money he has obtained from the king of Scotland?"

Hugh shrugged. "There are many things for which he could use it—building ships to protect the coast from the French for one thing."

"Or funding a campaign in Ireland," Will said.

"That may be so. I think it a good thing the Scots are not going to be raiding over our borders, because my Yorkshire fees stand in the way. I have enough trouble with wolves of the four-legged nature without dealing with raids by Galwegian wild men." He drank up his ale, aware of Will's brooding scrutiny. "I have to go." Standing up, he put the refurbished piece of harness on the trestle. "I've more people to bring the news. I hope you will soon be able to visit and see Mahelt and your new nephew."

"Will I be welcome?" Will asked, the cynical expression back on his face.

"That is up to you."

Hugh ducked out of the tent into the evening and puffed out his cheeks. The younger William Marshal was hard work. A chilly wind had sprung up with the arrival of sunset and he paused to pin his cloak higher up on his shoulder. Richard stepped out of the tent and caught up with him. "It was good news you brought us," he said. "Will meant it too but his mood is sour. Pay no heed."

Hugh stopped and faced his earnest, freckled brother-in-law. "I don't," he said. "And the offer to visit remains. I want my son to know his Marshal uncles."

Richard's grin shone out. "Is that a responsible remark for a new father to make?"

Hugh laughed and, feeling lighter in the heart, slapped the young man's shoulder. "Likely not, given the circumstances. I hope not to regret it."

"You won't."

Hugh gave a non-committal shrug. "We'll see," he said and went on his way. And soon he forgot about Mahelt's brothers because there were other camps and other celebrations, and it was as if a light was shining over his world because there was a new little being in it.

❖ ❖ ❖

On his way home, Hugh bought gifts for Mahelt: a ruby cross on a gold chain; a belt with a delicate gold buckle; a silk head-dress and hair ribbons; a teething ring and a rattle for the baby. The generosity of his love tumbled over into the generosity of his purse and he had to rein himself back because while the former was bottomless, the latter wasn't. His father had stayed with the king who was travelling south to Marlborough where all his vassals-in-chief had been summoned to swear allegiance to him and his own infant son Henry. Superficially there was peace, but it was tense and flawed, threatening to break like badly spun yarn.

His mother bustled out to greet him as he rode into Framlingham. Her face was alight and he had not seen her so animated for a long time. She embraced him with fervour, her brown eyes aglow. "Your son is beautiful...and so is your wife," she said as the grooms led the horses away. She gave him a kiss and a gentle push towards the stairs. "Go to them; they're waiting for you."

The first thing Hugh saw when he entered the chamber was the cradle set near the bedside. Going to it, he looked down at his son and was filled with wonder. Seeing Mahelt's swollen belly and knowing she was with child was not the same as seeing that child in the cradle. The baby was not bound in swaddling but was wearing a long linen smock. His little arms and legs were waving and he was making noises to himself, not fretful, but more as if he were accustoming himself to the sound of his own voice and exercising his limbs. His hair was soft and dark and his eyes were his mother's dye-pot blue-brown.

"Well now, my young man," Hugh said softly and chucked the child under the chin with a gentle forefinger. The baby gurgled and turned his head. Father and son looked at each other and Hugh was certain that the infant was focusing on him. His whole being flooded with warmth and joy. He turned to Mahelt, who was standing by the bed, watching his reaction and smiling radiantly.

"Isn't he beautiful?" she said with pride. "And so strong and clever already. He tried to grab your mother's blue jewel the first time she saw him. See, she's hung it on the cradle."

Hugh tenderly took her in his arms and kissed her. Her waist was slender, but her stomach was still rounded from the birth. "You are well?"

She screwed up her face. "They tell me it was an easy labour, but it didn't feel like it at the time. I have great sympathy for my mother and yours—and any woman who endures this year upon year. As a penance for Eve's sin, it is well exacted!" She stopped over the cradle and lifted the baby out. "But worth it." Her touch was confident, for she had been old enough to handle her sisters when they were born, and was used to infants.

Smiling, she placed him in Hugh's arms, and he too was well at ease, since he was the eldest of many. He tickled the baby under his chin and laughed to see him wriggle. "I promise not to tax you year upon year, but I cannot complain at the result." He kissed her again. And for the moment nothing else mattered in the world but being in the heart of his home with his wife and his son.

Twenty-one

FRAMLINGHAM, DECEMBER 1209

THE GROUND WAS HARD WITH FROST AND THE AIR BITINGLY
cold. Winter sunlight reddened the yard where the men
were sparring and practising with their weapons, their bodies
haloed in expended breath. Mahelt sat by the open shutters
in the hall, watching the sport with Ela and Ida and the other
women of the household.

Ida said to Ela with a wistful note in her voice, "You are
welcome to stay for the Christmas feast, you know that."

Ela turned her neat, small head. "Thank you, Mother, and
I would accept, but the king expects my husband at court."
There was genuine regret in her reply. Her expression was
carefully neutral as she spoke of the king.

"Yes, of course." A forced smile concealed Ida's disappoint-
ment. "At least you can enjoy yourselves while you are here."

"Are you saying they won't when they are with the king?"
Mahelt asked with a gleam of devilry in her eye. Christmas
would soon be upon them and Longespée and Ela were visiting
for a few days before attending the royal gathering at Windsor.
There had been the usual tensions and undercurrents, but
everyone was managing to be civil and thus far their stay had
passed without incident. Ela was very taken with little Roger.
She loved to cuddle him and make him giggle. Mahelt had

noticed how Longespée watched his wife and the baby with a look that was half yearning and half sick. She suspected he would not want to dally beyond the days he had allotted to spend here, and that Christmas at court would be easier for him to bear than Christmas here.

Ida flushed. "Of course not, but at court they will have more duties and responsibilities. Here they are both family and welcome guests."

Suitably reproved, Mahelt focused her attention on the sparring men. The sound of quarterstaffs clacking together drifted up to the window; the shouts of advice and Ralph's expletive as he was hit on the thumb. Mahelt smiled to herself. That was a new one. She would have to remember it.

❖❖❖

Down in the courtyard, Hugh paused to catch his breath. The frozen air burned in his chest and although he was warm in his quilted tunic and sweating with exertion, he was still aware of the bitter cold. He would rather have spent his afternoon by the fire roasting sweet chestnuts, telling tales, and singing songs, but Longespée had wanted to come out to the tiltyard and exorcise his demons, and since he was the guest, and Hugh's other brothers were keen, he had obliged rather than be a killjoy.

As his breathing eased, he watched his half-brother twirl the long sword for which he was famous and demonstrate several slick, polished manoeuvres. The others tried to emulate him but none possessed Longespée's skill. Ralph, who had also paused for respite and was now recovered, challenged Hugh to a sparring match. Hugh obliged, lifted his shield and went through the manoeuvres, turning Ralph's blows with ease and economy.

Longespée stopped to watch them, his hands on his hips, his expression critical. After a moment, he gave a small shake of his head. Hugh noticed the unspoken remark from the corner of his eye and, as he and Ralph broke apart, he lowered his sword and turned. "Do you have anything to say?" he demanded, shoulders heaving. "We might as well hear it."

Longespée folded his arms. "To Ralph that he is good, but he should keep on practising and go more for the legs since he does not have the advantage of height."

Ralph reddened at the praise and criticism, and nodded with the eagerness of a young dog in training.

"And to me?" Hugh enquired.

"That you fight defensively, and perhaps you do not have enough killer instinct to be a battle commander."

Hugh narrowed his eyes. "I was unaware that this was a battle. Perhaps next time, to please you, I should cut off Ralph's head." He sheathed his sword and folded his arms. "You have great skill in the military arts and I commend your abilities, but it is not everything, nor does it mean that those with less… dazzle are not competent. A tunic does not serve a man better just because it is edged with thread of gold—indeed sometimes a plain one gives better service."

Longespée's nostrils flared. "Your meaning?"

"I would have thought it obvious to a man of your wit."

Longespée looked pained. "I do not know why you take such a hostile tone when I am only telling the truth."

Hugh refrained from saying that Longespée's vision of the truth was not the same as his. If they continued in this vein, there would be a bitter argument and for his mother's sake he would keep the peace. "Then let us agree to see the truth differently. You will excuse me." Hugh left the gathering to approach the man he had just seen leading his laden donkey into the courtyard. It was Matthew the gem-seller, and this time he had a woman with him and a little boy of perhaps five years old. Hugh greeted Matthew with pleasure and, gesturing him to rise, patted him on the shoulder.

"I am glad to see you, and by the looks of your load you are hoping to lighten it here."

"Indeed, sire, that is part of my errand," Matthew said. "This is my wife Godif, and my son Edmund." The woman curtseyed. The tow-haired little boy flourished a most proper bow that caused Hugh's lips to twitch.

"Go and take your donkey to the stables and tell the grooms I said you were to bring him there. Then seek out Simon the chamberlain and have him bring you to my mother's solar. The women will want to see the contents of your pack for certain—although perhaps I shouldn't be so swift to send you to them in consideration of the grief to my purse!"

Matthew smiled, and then straightened his mouth and added, "Sire, I bring news as well as jewels. The king has been excommunicated by the pope. There's been a decree issued but not enforced." He glanced beyond Hugh to Longespée who had come forward to listen, drawn by curiosity about what Hugh would actually find to say to such lowly people.

"How do you know this?" Longespée demanded.

"I heard it from one of my clients, sire." A red flush crawled up Matthew's throat.

"Hah!" Longespée snorted. "As if someone like you would be told such information."

"Matthew carries jewels to great men of the Church as part of his employment," Hugh answered curtly. "As I said, a man doesn't need a fancy tunic to show off his importance to everyone." He turned to the gem pedlar and his family. "Go to. I'll join you in a while and make sure you haven't made too good a job of emptying my coffers."

"One of your spies, I suppose," Longespée said with a curled lip as Matthew and his family departed towards the stables with the weary donkey.

"Not in the least; merely a man who bears news wherever he

goes and whom I like and can trust." Hugh gestured to the squires to start tidying away the equipment. A bruised dusk was creeping up on the horizon and even had it not been time to pack up, he no longer had even the semblance of interest in weapon play.

"What happens if the king is excommunicated?" Ralph wanted to know.

"It means his seat on the throne becomes less secure, for one thing," Hugh said. "He must have known this was going to happen. That's why he had everyone swear allegiance to him at Marlborough and why he was so keen to pin down William of Scotland."

"We cannot let Rome dictate to us," Longespée said indignantly. "The king has been thoroughly reasonable over the matter of archbishop of Canterbury."

"He was right to defend his choice of candidate," Hugh agreed, "but he has chosen not to be conciliatory. He is often his own worst enemy."

"He will not stand for this; I know he will not." Turning on his heel, Longespée strode back to the hall.

Hugh sighed and glanced towards the solar window as the women closed the shutters. At least Longespée would definitely be leaving now, which was a personal positive thing to come out of this, but having an excommunicate king on top of the interdict was like ripping a wheel off an already damaged cart. It was unlikely to stay on the road for much longer—and Longespée must know it.

❖❖❖

Sitting on the bed with Hugh in their private chamber, the baby slumbering in his cradle beside them, Mahelt said thoughtfully, "What would happen if the king were brought down?" She held one of Matthew's clear garnet stones up to the light and shivered as the notion struck her that it was like looking through a clot of blood. "Who would take the crown?"

"Well, John's infant son would be the figurehead, but someone would have to make all the decisions," Hugh replied. "Or the king of France would invade. Some men might welcome him to the throne, especially in the North."

"Would you?"

"Would your father?" He took the garnet out of her hand and as she had done, held it up to filter the light through it.

"That isn't what I asked."

"No, but I gave you an answer. Would you welcome a French king who will set up his own favourites? Would you want to see the earls and barons squabble over who rules in John's stead? To remove John would not make matters simpler, mark me." He handed the garnet back to her. "Do you want blood on our hands?"

"No, but when I think how much there is on John's, and all the wrongs he has done to people...to my family...Things might not be simpler, but they have to be better."

Hugh moved closer. He slowly unbraided her hair and then ran his fingers through its thick brunette strands. "John is still an anointed king. Your father recognises that and you are surely no less than your father's daughter."

Mahelt tossed her head, making her hair ripple over his fingers. "I am a Bigod now, so I am told." In a mercurial change of mood she pushed Hugh down flat and sat across his body, her eyes gleaming. "A dutiful, submissive Bigod wife. What would you have me do?"

Hugh slid his hands under her dress and ran them over her calves and up her long thighs. Suddenly he was tight to bursting. "Your duty," he muttered in a congested voice.

Mahelt gave a breathless laugh and with a few quick movements had him free of his braies and inside her. It was completely shocking for a woman to be on top of a man during lovemaking; indeed it was a sin because it upset the world order, but Hugh found such daring behaviour arousing and it certainly kept that surprise element in their relationship. There was always that edge. He never quite knew what to expect. It was something his father would not do; he knew with absolute certainty that it would shock Longespée and such knowledge only served to increase his desire.

Mahelt closed her eyes and clenched upon him in climax, crying out, and as she finished, Hugh with a tremendous effort wrenched her off him and spilled himself outside her body. It might be another terrible sin to waste one's seed, but he had seen what happened to women who bore children in rapid succession and he wasn't going to let that happen to Mahelt, whatever the strictures of the Church. He didn't want to see her body slacken into a series of shapeless sacks, and her beautiful hair grow thin and sparse. Even if the pleasure of coupling was lessened because he could not let go within her, he had chosen to forbear, at least until their son was walking.

Mahelt fetched a cloth dampened in rose water to clean them both off and they curled up together in the contented afterglow. "Was that duty enough for you?" she purred.

Hugh grunted sleepily. "I suppose it will do for now."

Mahelt leaned over and nipped his ear, making him yelp and swat at her with a fatigue-heavy hand. "That was not so dutiful," he grumbled, and thought that her deed was a perfect reflection of her personality—a mingling of sweetness and thorns. The honey and the sting. The notion made him smile. She was mettlesome and he loved her for it, and for the moment he was too pleasantly tired and sated to think further on the news that Matthew had brought. For now it was enough to watch from a distance and observe how matters unfolded.

❖❖❖

Mahelt sat at her weaving frame making a long strip of braid to edge one of her gowns. She was in a reflective, contented mood and rather enjoying the work. The pattern was turning out well; the colours were strong but subtle at the same time, being varying shades of blue like the sky, the mere, and Hugh's eyes. Their son's eyes had changed from their first kitten colour to hazel-brown, and his dark natal hair had been replaced by a softer mid-brown tinged with gold. He was a vigorous, energetic baby, always reaching and grasping for things when released from his swaddling. Just now, for once, he was taking a respite from hurling himself at life and was asleep in his cradle, although there was an intensity about his slumber that reflected the vigour of his character when awake. Marshal and Bigod. It was a devastating combination. Every now and again, Mahelt glanced at him, her heart bursting with pride.

Firm hands suddenly gripped her shoulders and she half turned with a little jump and a cry to meet Hugh's smiling gaze. He pushed her veil aside and stooped to kiss her behind the ear. "What are you doing?"

She leaned back a little, enjoying the touch of his lips against her skin. "Milking a cow," she said pertly. "Does my lord not have eyes to see?"

"Well I do," he chuckled, "but I am not sure I believe them when I see you weaving of your own free will." He had spoken quietly in order not to wake the slumbering baby. Now he stepped lithely over the bench and sat down beside her so that their shoulders were touching. For a while he watched her weave, and then said, "You move your hands like reeds in water. It's beautiful to watch."

She laughed and blushed and became a little self-conscious.

"Those blues blend perfectly...Let me have a try."

Mahelt eyed him askance to see if he was being serious and saw that, although he was smiling, he meant it. She showed him what to do, how to turn the tablets and knock down the weft to secure the pattern into shape. He grasped the technique swiftly, his fingers deft and dextrous. He understood the language of the textile and he had a good memory for the pattern. "There," he said as he completed another turn and beat it into place. "Now this length will have a part of you in it and a part of me, for always—like our son."

A jolt of love shot through her like lightning. She lifted her face to his and they kissed, sealing the moment, although by far the most intimate part lay on her loom, winding in a river of sunlit blue. The sound of a throat clearing behind them caused them to leap apart on the bench and turn guiltily to see the earl standing in the doorway. He was red-faced with embarrassment and also, Mahelt thought, shock. To see his son sitting at a weaving frame must sorely upset his sense of order. Colour had flooded Hugh's face, but he gave his father a direct stare.

Mahelt rose from the bench and curtseyed. "Sire, would you care for wine?"

Her father-in-law shook his head. "Thank you, daughter, no. Hugh, I need to speak with you." He was already turning towards the door and Hugh had perforce to follow him, the implication being that it was men's business to be discussed in private. Mahelt clenched her fists. Her own father never excluded her mother from discussions. Hugh gave her an eloquent look over his shoulder as he left.

Mahelt heaved a deep sigh and looked at the piece of braid she and Hugh had just woven together and a sour smile curled her lips. Her father-in-law didn't have a say in *everything,* even if he thought he did.

❖❖❖

Sitting down in his own chamber, the earl rubbed his leg and winced. Of late the pain in his knees was worse than toothache. He was also recovering from a head cold and his skull appeared to be stuffed with wet fleece. Seeing Hugh at the weaving frame with Mahelt had shaken him. It was completely outside of the manly order of things, unless one was a professional weaver. Next thing Hugh would be taking up an embroidery needle, or worse still a distaff. But there had been something so tender and nurturing in the sight of his son and young wife sitting together, the baby cradled at their side, that Roger was filled with a feeling that would have been grief had he allowed it to settle. Once he and Ida must have been that close, but the detritus of the years had built a wall between them. There were times when they had knocked it down, but never to the foundations, and now the accumulations were too thick and the wherewithal lost. To see his son and wife shoulder to shoulder, kissing so affectionately, made him feel almost bereft.

Hugh had remained standing, and his gaze was wary. That saddened Roger too. Everywhere he looked these days there were barricades. "The king has called a muster of his tenants-in-chief in Pembroke at the beginning of June," he said. "He is taking an army to Ireland to deal with de Braose, his de Lacey kin and, if necessary, the Marshals. We are summoned to answer our military obligations, and our sailors are to man the ships."

Hugh eyed his father in dismay, although he had suspected for some time that this news would come.

"It was always likely," Roger said dourly. "The king is determined to secure his grip and he has William of Scotland's money to fund the expedition. We've to muster in Bristol by the fourteenth day of May."

"But what about Mahelt's father?"

"What about him?"

"He has sheltered and succoured de Braose. What if he chooses to defy the king?"

Roger's mouth twisted. "William Marshal can take care of

himself, and I mean that both as a reassurance and a warning. He will do what he must to survive. I do not believe he will openly declare against John. He is a man who stands by his word, even if the interpretation of that word is sometimes open to question. That part is out of our hands. Your part is to take the men to this muster."

Hugh stared. "You want me to lead the men?"

His father's tone was caustic. "It's a bit late to declare yourself incapable, but if you would rather sit at home and weave pretty patterns, say so and I'll send one of my other sons."

Hugh stiffened at his father's tone. "I am quite capable of leading the men and I have never shirked my duty, sire, but I thought you would want to oversee things yourself."

Roger shook his head. "It is time you had the responsibility of absolute command on a campaign. I have aches and pains like any man of my years. I may not be in my dotage, but I do not relish riding all the way across England, crossing the Irish Sea, and spending the summer fighting and sleeping in a tent when there are younger men fully capable of performing the task. I've got the scribes working on summons to our vassals and orders for supplies. You'll be on the road within the fortnight."

Hugh was still reeling as he returned to Mahelt. His head was full of apprehension and expectancy. He had never been to Ireland before, nor been in sole command of the Bigod troops. A large part of his trepidation was knowing he might have to face his wife's father across a battlefield. Such a position was untenable.

Mahelt no longer sat at her loom, but was standing by the window looking out. He studied her outline, slender and taut in her red dress. "Do you want to come out riding?" he asked.

She regarded him with knowing eyes. "Your father must have told you something serious."

"Please, if you will. I'd like to." He opened his hand in a gesture of courteous request, knowing she would not refuse him because she loved riding over the demesne.

While she was donning her riding dress and boots he had their horses saddled: Hebon for him and a black mare with a white star for Mahelt. Side by side, escorted by a pair of grooms and accompanied by a motley assortment of enthusiastic dogs, they rode out of the postern entrance and past the garden and the mere that his father had had landscaped to show off Framlingham at its best. Not just a defensive fortress, but a home of grandeur and elegance built from the wealth of the East Anglian grain exported from the bustling ports of Ipswich, Yarmouth, and Hunstanton. Hugh looked over his shoulder at the crowning turrets. They could live a richly fulfilling life if only circumstances would let them.

They rode out into the deer park, their mounts trotting almost knee-deep through clearings of lush grass, and threading through broad woodland, the tree canopy still wearing the delicate pale green of spring. The dogs snuffled at their heels and chased along the trails. In the distance several does and fawns bounded into a thicket and Hugh whistled his gazehounds to heel. Then they rode in silence for a while. Since carrying and bearing a child, Mahelt had learned to better control her impatience and bide her time. Nevertheless, she was concerned, because whatever he had to tell her must be dire if he needed to bring her out riding in order to broach the subject.

At length Hugh pointed down to the left and said casually, "I was thinking that when I return from Ireland we could put in some lime trees for shade and divert that stream over there."

Mahelt swivelled to stare at him. "Ireland?" she said. "What do you mean when you return from Ireland?"

He made a face. "The king is going there to deal with his

Irish vassals. We've to muster in Bristol by the fourteenth of May." He hesitated. "My father wants me to lead the men because his health is failing."

Mahelt looked sick. "When you say the king is going to 'deal' with his Irish vassals, does that include my father?"

"That will depend upon your father's actions."

"Am I to see you and him in opposite camps?"

Hugh shifted in the saddle and avoided her furious, frightened gaze. "It won't come to that."

"Then why else has a muster been called?"

"There was a muster called to Scotland too, but there wasn't a fight. John wants to set down a new constitution for Ireland, so that everyone is clear on the boundaries."

Mahelt lashed her reins down on the mare's neck and dug in her small silver spurs. Snorting with indignant surprise, the mare bolted across the clearing at a hard gallop. Muttering an oath, Hugh spurred Hebon after her, pushing the stallion to his fastest pace. He thundered alongside Mahelt's black mare and reached to grab her bridle, hauling her in close as he would have done with an opponent at a tourney. The mare chopped to a standstill just before the tree line.

"Your father is too shrewd to be caught," Hugh panted. "The king isn't after him anyway. He's after de Braose and the de Laceys."

"Yet but for the grace of God it could be my father too!" she spat. "We all know why he's after de Braose—and it's not because de Braose owes him money, is it?"

"No, it's because his wife couldn't keep her mouth shut!"

"If you see that as the sin, then I have nothing more to say to you." She wrenched the mare around and began to trot back towards the castle.

Hugh cursed and rode after her. "I didn't say it was the sin. I said it was the reason. You are putting words into my mouth."

"But it is all a matter of degree. You will help to destroy de Braose and then you will be condoning the murder of Prince Arthur. Do you not think John should be brought to account over that before he makes others accountable?"

Hugh said harshly, "Out here there is only me to hear you say this. Your father knows well when to bridle his tongue. I would hope that for all our sakes you have the same skill."

Mahelt kicked her mare to a gallop again and this time Hugh let her go.

❖❖❖

Hugh jiggled his son in his arms. "Be a good boy for your mother while I am gone." He kissed little Roger's cheek. The baby laughed and reached to pull his father's hat off. Hugh grinned and plopped it over the soft round head.

Watching them together, Mahelt's stomach clenched. Ever since Hugh had told her he was going to Ireland, there had been a wall between them. She didn't want him to go, but there was nothing she could do to prevent him. She was angry with him, with the king, and with her father-in-law for forcing him to this duty. The earl wasn't so elderly or ill that he could not attend in person. She was furious with herself too because she did not know how to mend the situation. Certainly not by apologising, because she knew she was right. Supposing there was a war? Supposing she lost both her husband and her father? The notion terrified her. She had never been clingy or weepy. She had always stood fast with her head high and she hated the feelings filling her heart. This was a side of loving and loyalty that was unbearable.

Hugh retrieved his hat and handed his son to his nurse. The baby's face puckered as he prepared to bawl and the woman shushed him and bore him away to the window to look at the activity in the yard.

Hugh went to Mahelt. "It's time." Tentatively he traced

the side of her face with his thumb and then stooped to kiss her mouth.

Mahelt closed her eyes, desperate to absorb this last imprint before he went to war. "Dear God," she whispered, "I do not want you to go."

"I do not want to go either, but I must; it is my duty."

"Yes," Mahelt said bitterly. "Your duty." She knew she was not being fair, but for the moment could not go beyond her own distress. She rose, went to the window, and took the baby from the nurse. Holding him against her, she kissed his soft cheek, and then stared at the courtyard until her eyes were so dry they stung. Behind her, she heard the door latch lift and drop as Hugh left the room.

Lips compressed, Mahelt forced herself to move before it became impossible. Still carrying her son, she went down to the courtyard to bid farewell. The earl was already waiting, and Ida too. Stepping out into the overcast morning, Mahelt entered the public arena and prepared to fulfil her duty.

Hugh knelt to his father and received his blessing. Then to his mother. He embraced Mahelt again, but it was a stilted thing, performed before an audience. Little Roger squealed and held out his arms as Hugh mounted Hebon, and Hugh took him up on his saddle while the men around him made their last-minute adjustments. Then, leaning down, he returned the baby to Mahelt. "A part of you and a part of me," he said with an eloquent look. He saluted her and, reining about, led the cavalcade out of Framlingham without looking back.

Ida patted Mahelt's shoulder as the rump of the last pack pony ambled out of the castle gateway. "I know how you feel, my love," she said. "Go and lie down with a cold cloth on your brow. I'll look after the little one."

Mahelt shook her head vigorously, appalled at the notion. In truth Ida had no idea how she felt. When her mother-in-law was upset, she invariably retreated to her sewing or to her bed, but Mahelt knew she would go mad if she did that for solace. She needed to be busy—to have her mind occupied with practical matters other than the dreaded sewing.

The earl cleared his throat and said gruffly, "Daughter, the undercroft must be checked to see what needs replacing now the men have gone."

His expression was impassive and his eyes were their usual watchful flint-grey, but Mahelt detected a glimmer of something that was almost kindness. "I shall see to it, Father," she said, and although she was furious with him for sending Hugh in his stead, she felt an unwonted spark of gratitude.

Twenty-two

CROOKE, SOUTHERN IRELAND, SUMMER 1210

"WHOA THERE, STEADY, STEADY." WITH SOOTHING WORDS, Hugh coaxed his destrier down the gangplank and on to the beach. It was always a chancy business sending horses across the Irish Sea, but God had been merciful and the crossing calm; thus the animals had not suffered too much. Brunet was a young, powerful stallion from the Bigod stud herd. His hide bore the sheen of copper at twilight and his face was marked with a dazzling white blaze. He was a direct descendant of the warhorse Hugh's father had ridden into the thick of the battle at Fornham Saint Genevieve when the beleaguered royalists had brought down a rebel army four times the size of their own.

The June sun blazed like a furnace on the back of Hugh's neck as he saw Brunet safely into the hands of a groom and then turned back to disembark Hebon. The entire shoreline at Crooke was edged with the vessels of King John's transport fleet, their prows beached, their sterns sea-washed. Seven hundred ships laden with men and supplies, not just for the expected conflict, but for administering the aftermath. Over six hundred skins of parchment had been brought on one galley for writing a new constitution for Ireland that would increase John's powers and limit those of his barons.

Further down the shore, Hugh could see men and provisions being disgorged from the Marshal vessels. His father-in-law had come to the King at Cross on the Sea near Pembroke, had done him homage and promised his support. Hugh had no idea what William Marshal had said to John, but whatever it was had been enough to keep him intact, if not in favour. He had neither been cast from the court nor declared a rebel, even if the atmosphere between him and the king could have been cut with a blunt knife.

Hugh saw Longespée striding along the beach towards him from the direction of his own ships and, with a mental groan, braced himself.

"Good crossing, wasn't it?" Longespée remarked, rubbing his hands as he joined him. The sea wind snagged at his cloak and bustled his hair like a rough unseen hand.

Hugh nodded. "We had a halyard snap, but otherwise yes, and the horses travelled well."

Longespée feasted his eyes on Brunet. "Where have you been hiding that one? I didn't see him at the stables in Framlingham."

"He wasn't there," Hugh said curtly, feeling protective. "My father was grazing him with the Bungay herd." His nape prickled and he gestured to the groom to move the stallion off the beach.

Longespée's gaze lingered. "Fit for a king."

Hugh said nothing and eventually his half-brother appeared to take the hint because he turned to regard the deceptively calm and sparkling sea and changed the subject. "Once we've recovered our land legs, my brother tells me we're bringing the army to the Marshal's keep at Kilkenny."

"And at the Marshal's expense, I suppose," Hugh said.

Longespée shrugged and raised his eyes to the gulls circling over the beached fleet. "That is the nature of being a vassal-in-chief. When the king comes to your demesne, you foot the expense."

"Especially when he comes with an army."

"Especially then." Longespée moved on to speak with the Count of Aumale and Hugh returned to overseeing the unloading of his ships in a thoughtful mood. Longespée was kin to William Marshal through marriage and had always appeared to admire him, but he was also brother to the king. Who knew where Longespée's sympathies lay—perhaps not even Longespée himself.

❖❖❖

Relaxing on a cushioned bench, Hugh felt his eyes grow heavy. After a full day in the saddle commanding men, it was so good to sit in comfort in Countess Isabelle's private chamber at Kilkenny, relax his guard, and drink glorious, golden Irish mead. Curled against his side like a puppy was Eve, one of Mahelt's little sisters. The child was six years old with a plait of wavy fair hair and merry hazel eyes. A baby girl younger than his own son slept in a cradle. The Marshal might be well past three score, but his wife was still of child-bearing age and the marital bed still obviously a fruitful place. Various other Marshal offspring flitted in and out of his sight as they played. Ancel was a lively toddler. There were three little girls including Eve, and two coltish boys, one in early adolescence, the other in late childhood. He thought Isabelle looked tired, but then of late she had withstood the near destruction of her family and the loss of her two eldest sons as hostages. While her endangered husband strove to hold all together at court, she had had to maintain their estates, deal with her vassals, run a household, and cope with pregnancy. He could not imagine his own gentle mother managing such a feat, although he suspected Mahelt had it within her.

Isabelle joined him on the bench with her own cup of mead. Despite the tired lines on her face, her eyes were clear and intelligent. "Tell me of my grandson," she said, the manner of her smile informing him she was in need of distraction.

Hugh leaned back, careful not to disturb the sleeping child. "He's a fine little chap. Strong and lusty and full of curiosity. Into everything and doesn't stop while he's awake—which is most of the time." His smile was rueful. "He's very much like his mother."

Isabelle laughed. "Your hands appear to be full, my lord."

Hugh gestured agreement and regaled her with tales of the baby's antics, told her how many teeth he had, and presented her with a lock of little Roger's hair, dark like his mother's and secured with a tag of blue silk thread.

Isabelle stroked the soft keepsake. "My daughter is well?"

"Yes, indeed, madam." He wondered if she knew about the incident when Mahelt had absconded to meet her brother. It wasn't something likely to be discussed. Pretending it had never happened was the safest road. "She is anxious for her family in these troubled times and she misses you."

"As we miss her. Please reassure her that we are well and no harm has come to us."

"Of course I will." He wasn't sure if Mahelt would believe him.

"I have gifts if you will take them in your baggage."

He inclined his head. "With pleasure."

Isabelle gave him a pensive look and he wondered if she was waiting for him to speak—but what else was there to say?

Isabelle sighed. "My daughter can be difficult to deal with. She has all her father's vigour and energy—if not his tact. From being a tiny girl she always tried to match her big brothers—at everything."

Hugh chuckled. "I had noticed. She hates sewing or anything that involves sitting still, but I love her for it. She reminds me of the sky."

"Why do you say that?"

He laughed again and felt himself redden. "Because she is so different from day to day. You never know whether there will be clouds or sunshine. You bask in the sunshine and run for cover when there's a thunderstorm...but you are never bored, and sometimes you are overwhelmed that such beauty could exist."

Isabelle gave him a fond look and reached to pat his knee. "I did wonder whether we were right to match her to you—for your sake as much as hers—but your words reassure me that we made no mistake."

Hugh cleared his throat. "I cherish her," he said. "I shall love and protect her as best I can."

"You are a good man; I know you will." Isabelle smiled at him as he rose to take his leave. Disturbed from her slumber, Eve yawned like a kitten and rubbed her eyes.

"I do not know about that," Hugh said awkwardly. "I am sorry for the manner of my visit. I wish it were in happier circumstances."

"So do I," William Marshal said from the doorway.

Hugh started to bow, but the older man made a gesture to prevent him, and strode forward to clasp his shoulder. "Even as Mahelt now stands as your father's daughter in marriage, so you are my son."

"Look," said Isabelle, "a lock of our grandson's hair." She held it out on her palm. "Hugh says he is like Matty."

The seams at William's eye corners deepened as he smiled but sadness glimmered too as he looked at the silky lock. "I hope we see him one day soon." He looked at Hugh. "You were just leaving?"

"I have to check the men and the horses, sire."

William nodded. "You have a lot of responsibility in your father's absence. I hope he is not too unwell?" His tone was bland and urbane.

"His knees are troubling him, sire. His body feels the years but his mind is still sharp."

"Knowing your father, I do not doubt that," William said drily. "Nor do I doubt you will live up to his expectations."

"I hope so, sire. But I am sorry to be here."

"You do what you must to survive," William said, "as we all do, within the bounds of what is honourable and what is sworn."

Hugh bowed and took his leave. Isabelle saw him to the door, promising to send a servant with the aforementioned gifts before the army rode on from Kilkenny. As she kissed his cheek, Hugh inhaled a warm, spicy scent that reminded him of Mahelt and filled him with longing. Being here in this chamber at Kilkenny was like being at home and at the same time was something so different that it wasn't like home at all. As he left the chamber, he glanced over his shoulder and saw that Mahelt's father was sitting upon the bench he had just vacated, and was rubbing his face with his hands in the gesture of a man burdened with too many cares.

❖❖❖

Hugh strolled among the tents of his men, ensured all was in order, dealt with problems and questions, and finally went to check on the horses, because being amongst them always soothed him. Stars had begun to prick through the teal and purple sky of a long summer twilight and the air was still. The smell of horses was welcoming and pungent. The swish of their tails, their gusty breaths, and the stamp of their hooves were comforting sounds he had known since the moment of his birth.

As he reached his horse lines, he saw a figure walking towards him through the last of the light and, with a sinking heart, recognised Longespée. The latter had a costrel slung over his shoulder and was humming to himself. Somehow Hugh managed to greet him courteously.

Longespée smiled a reply and went up to Brunet to admire him again. The stallion shook himself, sending a sinuous ripple along his glossy hide.

"He's not for sale," Hugh snapped, because his half-brother reminded him of a horse-coper examining likely goods at Smithfield beast market.

Longespée flashed a hard smile. "I do not suppose you would care to wager him at dice either."

"Even given your luck at gambling, no."

The smile diminished, but Longespée shrugged off Hugh's remark and gestured to the costrel. "Do you want to share a drink? It's decent wine."

"You won't get me to drink into agreeing to part with him either," Hugh said, only half in jest, but consented to sit at the tent fire with Longespée. The flames crackled softly, spitting now and then as juices from two roasting ducks missed the drip container set beneath the spit bar. Hugh fetched two horn cups from his pavilion and the brothers toasted each other. Hugh grudgingly admitted Longespée was right. The wine was smooth and rich, tasting of grapes rather than vinegar.

A second and third cup followed the first. The men ate one of the ducks, mopping up grease and juices with bread, and licking their fingers. The atmosphere mellowed. Comfortably full, Longespée lay down on the grass, boots pointed towards the fire; pillowing his head on his clasped hands, he looked at the sky which was now as dark as a black cat's fur.

"Ever think of your wife when you're on campaign?" he asked after a while.

Hugh's mouth was full of wine and he answered by making an affirmative sound in his throat.

"I always think upon what my Ela will be doing at this time," Longespée mused. "I imagine her taking off her jewellery and combing her hair—all thick and shiny like gold water.

Then removing her gown and putting on her sleeping chemise and her bedrobe." He gave a snort of reluctant laughter. "I tell her she wears too much but my girl is modest—she doesn't even let me see her ankles if she can help it. But she will come and sit by the fire with me and we'll talk of our day, and then I'll know I am truly home."

There was a sudden tightness in Hugh's throat. He thought of his hands running through Mahelt's cool, dark tresses, and of a room flooded with light. He wondered how he was going to be greeted when he returned home. "I know what you mean."

"We are very fortunate men, are we not?"

"Indeed," Hugh replied woodenly.

Longespée settled himself into a more comfortable position. "Ela told me as I left that she is with child."

Ah, Hugh thought. So this was what all the camaraderie was about. "Congratulations!" He toasted Longespée with genuine warmth. "It is a fine thing to see one's heir in the cradle."

Longespée's smile was proud and a little anxious. "I have waited a long time for this news."

Hugh's thought processes were wine-blurred but he was sufficiently aware to realise that without the drink Longespée would not have exposed himself so candidly. "Now there will be no stopping you."

"Hah, except for wars and diplomatic voyages and attendance at court."

"Mayhap, but it gives your wife more recovery time—and absence to make the heart grow fonder." Even to himself, his words sounded hollow and uncertain.

There was a long silence followed by a fuzzy snore because Longespée had fallen asleep, and Hugh found himself feeling an unexpected glow of affection for his half-brother. Eventually, Hugh rose from his campstool to go and take a piss. On the way back, he stopped again by his horse line. Fondling Brunet's muzzle in the starlit darkness he thought about Mahelt…and wondered if she felt as empty as he did.

❖❖❖

The next evening, John sat in his chamber at Kilkenny watching his clerics assemble their writing equipment. The shutters were open to the balmy night air and assorted moths and lace-winged flies had been enticed within the room by the flicker of candle-light. An Irish harpist played softly in the background and John was toying with some small jet counters on a gaming board, although the most recent game had finished. A pile of silver coins by his elbow attested to his success. Longespée sat across from him, the sleeves of his undertunic pushed back to reveal the dark hair dusting his forearms.

"So." John gave him a calculating look. "We bring organisation to this benighted land. We pin down the vassals who have grown too powerful and who put their own interests before mine and we ensure the native Irish lords are our allies in this. We also make an example of de Braose." His eyes glittered. "We show my barons why they should remain loyal and obedient to their king."

Longespée frowned at a dark grease stain on his pushed-back sleeve—probably from the duck last night. His head was buzzing with tiredness and the effects of one too many cups of wine. He always felt alarmed when John began talking of making examples. "Speaking of the Irish lords, sire, you told me to be on the lookout for likely warhorses as fitting gifts for the men you would coax to swear for you."

John raised his eyebrows. "I take it you have found one?"

"My brother Hugh Bigod has one with him that would do well. One of those red-brown Lombard types his father breeds. Finest I've seen in a while."

"Has he indeed?"

"He won't be keen to part with it, but it's the best horse I've yet seen in any of the camps."

John gave a feline smile. "I am sure he could be persuaded," he said smoothly. "After all, he can soon obtain another one. It's not as if the Bigods are short of horseflesh."

"No, sire," Longespée said. There was a bad taste in his mouth and equal feelings of bright triumph and sordid guilt.

"Good. I shall speak with him. You have an excellent eye for horseflesh, so I'll trust to your word."

Longespée left the room to seek his bed, stumbling slightly, his belly burning. His first loyalty was to John, who was not only his brother but his king. As John had said, Hugh would easily find a replacement mount. His father had the best stud herd in England. The native Irish lords prized their horses and it was more important to win their allegiance with magnificent gifts than it was to keep Hugh's friendship—which was always a rocky channel anyway.

❖❖❖

Clad in shirt and hose, hair rumpled from sleep, Hugh was breaking his fast in the dawn when John arrived at the Bigod tents. The king was dressed and dapper, ready for the day's business. Hugh hastily swallowed his mouthful of bread and, brushing crumbs from his shirt, knelt and bowed, the men at his fire doing the same.

John gestured all to rise and resume their meal, then turned to Hugh. "Bigod, I hear you have a fine warhorse in your string. I would see him."

"Sire?" Hugh swallowed again, although there was nothing in his mouth.

"Obviously your ears are still asleep," John said with pleasant scorn. He sauntered over to the horse lines and wandered down the row, looking at the animals picketed there with feed bags and pails. Eventually he stopped in front of Brunet. "I can see my reflection in his coat," he said. "Longespée was right. A very fine animal indeed." Extending a hand, he rubbed the stallion's chalk-white blaze, and then stood back to admire its conformation.

Hugh wondered with alarm what else Longespée has been saying. There was no sign of him among the king's hangers-on this morning. "Indeed he is, sire."

John rubbed his chin. "I have need of a fitting gift to sweeten the king of Connacht. This horse is perfect for what I have in mind."

Hugh was horrified. He couldn't refuse John, but the animal was worth a fortune, not just in monetary value but in terms of how much time had been spent in his training, not to mention his abilities at stud. He licked his lips. "Sire, he is my first-string destrier."

John nodded. "Good, that is most fitting. A king should have the best. Do not make faces behind my back, Bigod. You will be able to obtain yourself another one easily enough. Ride your second string for now. There are bound to be horses taken as booty." He waved his hand. "I don't need the harness; I have better to suit. You will have recompense when we arrive in Dublin."

Tight-lipped, Hugh untied Brunet from the line and handed him to John's groom. The latter wore a smirk that Hugh was tempted to remove with a balled-up fist, but he controlled himself despite being so furious he felt sick. Once the king had gone, Hugh strode off in search of Longespée, and found him at his pavilion, donning the padded tunic he wore under his mail shirt. Hugh barged aside the squire who was helping him. Ralph, who had been sorting out equipment at the back of the pavilion, looked up in shock.

"You told him about my horse, didn't you!" Hugh snarled, kicking a stool out of the way. "You couldn't leave it alone. All that 'brotherly' talk of wives and home at the camp fire. All that sharing wine and food and being a companion in arms. It meant nothing to you, did it? It was just a means to an end!" He felt so angry and betrayed that the final words emerged as a sob.

Longespée flushed. "The king needs to sweeten the Irish kings and bring them to heel through diplomacy—you know that." His gaze darted over Hugh but would not fix in direct eye contact. "Would you rather fight them as well as our own rebellious lords? A horse is a cheap price to pay for their allegiance."

"Especially when it's not yours! What price your family blood?"

Longespée drew himself up. "I am a king's son, not a Bigod," he said icily. "You'll be well recompensed; I will see to it." A look of exasperation crossed his features. "Christ, man, it's only a horse!"

"Yes, I remember. You said that to me once before." Hugh turned on his heel and strode from the pavilion before he resorted to violence. Once he relinquished his control, he knew he would not stop until his half-brother's face was a red pulp. He was very tempted to take Longespée's destrier from the horse line, but it was only of the same calibre as Hugh's second string and he didn't know the animal.

Ralph came panting after him. "Hugh, wait! He had to do it!" he cried.

Hugh stopped and swung round. "No, he didn't," he snarled. "He chose to do it, and that is a different thing entirely."

"The king depends on him and trusts him. He feels obligated."

"Look on the other side of the coin," Hugh spat. "He depends on the king to give him position and authority. He's in love with his own royal blood and, if he could, he would tear out the part of him that is not royal."

"He is good to me," Ralph said, lifting his head.

"Because you are his servant, you fool! Because you know your place in his world as a lowly Bigod. Cease to defer to him and it would be a different matter."

"It is not like that."

"No," Hugh said curtly. "And it's only a horse."

❖ ❖ ❖

Within the hour, King Cathal of Connacht and his war band arrived at the English camp. All of the Irish lords boasted magnificent bushy beards, some of them long enough to tuck under their belts. Their legs were bare and their garments were woven in muted shades of rust, green, and blackberry that blended with the landscape. Here and there the rich yellow colour of saffron illuminated men of particular consequence who could afford to wear clothes dyed with a plant more expensive than gold.

King Cathal had a wide mouth, a short snub nose, and quick, bright eyes, seamed at the corners, as if he either laughed a great deal, or spent time in shrewd perusal of those around him. He wore a long knife at his belt and he carried a rich sword and a decorated round shield. John greeted him graciously and treated him as a valued guest. Hugh had heard tales of how as a young man John had visited Ireland and soured relations between himself and the native lords by tugging on their beards while drunk, to see if they were real. It was one mistake from which he had obviously learned, for he was charm itself to King Cathal. But then he needed the Irish lords as his allies in order to act as a balance and counteract the power of his own vassals.

John presented the Irish king with Brunet, the stallion now caparisoned in a harness glittering with silver starbursts on the breast-band. Jewels glowed on the pommel and cantle of the high war saddle. Hugh gritted his teeth as the small Irishman laid his hand to Brunet's cheek strap and spoke lovingly in his own language to the horse. He stroked the powerful arched neck and quarters and scratched Brunet under the jaw at precisely the place the horse loved to rub itself on the stable door. Then, to everyone's astonishment, he unbuckled the bridle, took off the saddle, and bade one of his attendants fetch a rope halter.

Hugh was joined by one of Mahelt's Irish relatives, a sturdy, dark-haired young man called Domnall. "Now you will see the true horsemanship of our countrymen," he said proudly. "You knights may look very fine in your mail and you ride like hammers to war so that nothing can stand against you—but can you catch the wind?"

Hugh watched Cathal grab a handful of Brunet's mane for purchase and leap nimbly across the stallion's back, which was bare except for the saddle cloth. "He rides like a child training on a pony," Hugh scoffed.

Domnall shook his head. "No, my lord; he rides like an Irishman. We do not need the heavy control of you Normans to bring our horses to our bidding. When we fight, we do so lightly armed. We are wraiths, not giants. What need have we of such trappings?"

"But you plainly like our horses," Hugh growled.

Domnall gave him a sidelong smile. "A good horse is a good horse. But your king is cunning. He knows the gift of such a beast makes the man who receives it obliged to pay him homage. He is bringing all into the fold and those who stay outside of it will be counted as wolves."

Hugh grunted. "I hardly think some of those inside it are sheep."

Domnall chuckled. "Indeed not, but they know who feeds the pack and leads the herd."

The army set out from Kilkenny on the road north in pursuit of the de Laceys and de Braose. King Cathal rode with John and directed Brunet with no more than his thighs and the rope bridle. Despite his anger and irritation, Hugh had to admit that few Norman lords would be able to control a horse in that manner. It was a method all well and good for riding an animal down to the stream or back to the stables from the field, but on a longer journey or on a campaign no Norman would consider such a thing. Hugh stored it in his memory to tell his father and try himself, and also to teach his son when he was old enough to sit a horse. His expression hardened as he thought that he would also teach the boy about loyalty and honour and to whom it was due.

Twenty-three

ITTING ON THE HEARTH BENCH IN HER OWN CHAMBER, Mahelt extended her bare feet towards the low fire and relaxed. It was late. She had dismissed her women and was taking time to drink a last cup of wine before she retired. Tripes was curled in a corner near the hearth, his nose on his paws. Now and again he whimpered in his sleep as he chased imaginary rats and mice across his dreamscape.

She had been busy throughout the day, overseeing preparations for the harvest celebration and boon work feasts. Although she had people to run errands for her, she had done much of the toing and froing herself and was pleasantly tired. During the last week she had also taken over more of the daily duties of a chatelaine because Ida had been unwell with a cold and had stayed at her hearth with her sewing, leaving Mahelt in charge, which she had relished.

There had been no word from Ireland, but she had expected none because she knew the troops would be in the field. She was missing Hugh; the rooms seemed empty without his presence and her world somehow smaller and diminished. It was like having a space at her side where the cold air could creep in and make her shiver. She wished they had not parted in so ambiguous a fashion. She feared for him and she was worried that she might not have the chance to make things right again. She feared for her father too—desperately. Hugh said he was too clever to be caught in the cross currents at play, but he had enemies who would stop at nothing to bring him down.

Suddenly Tripes lifted his head and growled; then his tail thumped the floor. The door quietly opened and Hugh tiptoed into the room. Mahelt stared at him in astonishment, half thinking him an illusion of her wandering thoughts. Yet he seemed solid enough, and when he smiled at her, she was certain. Uttering a joyful cry, she sprang to her feet and flew to his arms.

He seized her and pulled her to his body, burying his face in her neck and speaking her name against her skin.

"Hugh, dear God, Hugh!" Eventually she drew away and, wiping her eyes on her sleeve, looked him up and down. His complexion was nut-brown, and when she pushed his hat off his head, she saw his dark-gold hair was sun-bleached at the crown and tips to the white of flax. A sheep fleece was draped over his arm and she assumed he had been using it as a saddle cover.

"You should have sent word ahead and I would have prepared a fitting welcome! You must be hungry and thirsty." She hastened to pour him wine from the flagon and watched his throat ripple as he swallowed. Her joy at the sight of him was so strong that it was almost pain.

"I ate bread and cheese in the saddle," he said with a dismissive gesture. "I wanted to push on to Framlingham. I wanted to be with you tonight...I wanted to be home."

Hearing the need in his words, Mahelt threw her arms around him again. He stank of sweat and hot horse, of smoke and dirt and the battle camp. Removal of cloak, tunic, and shirt exacerbated the aroma, but she didn't care. "How broad you've grown!" Greedily she touched the curve of his bicep.

"We had to put up tents, pull them down, tend the horses, wear our armour." He made a face, but at the same time gave a smug flex of his new muscles. "It feels as if I've been carrying the weight of another man on my back for weeks on end."

Close up, Mahelt was now noticing the ingrained dirt in the creases of his skin. He was grimier than a peasant child and covered in small red marks, evidence of infestation by fleas and vermin. She had vague recollections of her father returning home like this sometimes, although never quite as bad. "You need a bath."

"Yes," he said without enthusiasm and flopped down on the bench. He gave a jaw-cracking yawn.

Gazing at him, Mahelt realised how tired he was and that "pushing on to Framlingham" had been a literal statement. He hadn't stopped for anything, not even to wash. Briefly she hesitated, considering her clothes, and then decided it was already too late. "The morning will suffice." She sat against him, and as he slipped his arm around her, the cold feeling at her side was gone.

"I saw our son when I came through the antechamber," he said, looking relieved that the palaver of a bath was being postponed. "He was sound asleep with his thumb in his mouth. He's grown."

"He can say 'horse' now and 'Mama.'"

"I wonder what he will call me." Hugh's voice was both proud and pensive.

"You can find out on the morrow." Mahelt stroked his hair. Her loins were heavy with anticipation, but she could wait. Hugh's eyes were already closing as if there were weights on his eyelids. She wanted to ask him numerous questions, but could tell she would not get proper answers. The wondrous thing was that he had ridden so hard to reach her tonight when he could have waited and arrived fresh in the morning. "Is my father all right?" she asked because it was the one thing she had to know.

Hugh grunted and forced his eyes half open. "In rude health and weathering all things well. Your mother and your brothers and sisters are all in good heart too and the babies are beautiful—but not as beautiful as our son."

There was something in his tone of voice that made Mahelt cock her head like a dog hearing an unfamiliar sound in the yard. Something was being skimmed over or else details were being omitted. However, tackling him now would be like trying to find jewels in six feet of mud.

"Come," she said. "You won't be able to move your neck in the morning if you sleep on the settle." Taking his hand she drew him to his feet and led him to the bed. The sheets would have to be changed tomorrow but they were due for that anyway. She helped him remove his boots and then rolled him into bed. He grabbed her hand and pulled her down with him. "I'm too tired to be of any use to either of us, but I still want you with me," he said. "I want to know you are more than a dream."

His words melted her and she slipped off her own shoes and got in with him. Her clothes would afford her some protection, she thought wryly, and since she had lain awake every night longing for his presence to warm the cold side of the bed, she was happy to embrace him now. Tomorrow she would deal with everything.

In the morning, Mahelt had the maids prepare a tub while Hugh was still sleeping. She fetched a narrow-tined comb from her coffer and bade one of the women bring a block of clarified fat scented with rose oil from the soap supplies. The fleabane too, and oil and ashes for removing lice. She had food and drink brought to the chamber because, although it was still early, she knew the earl would want to talk to Hugh, but she needed him to herself first. When she could leave him no longer, she went to the bed, drew the curtains, and gently shook him awake.

He gazed at her with bleary surprise. Several small dark specks bounced on the sheets and Mahelt averted her gaze. "It's morning," she said. "There's a bath waiting for you and the maids needs to put these sheets in a laundry tub."

His eyes slowly cleared and focused. "A bath?"

"I may have lain beside you last night for love, but I doubt anyone else will want to come as close," she said with asperity. "Look at you! I've seen fewer fleas on a hedge-pig and you smell like a gong farmer!"

He sat up, knuckling the sleep from his eyes. "I just wanted to get home," he said in a timbre that sent a jolt through her because the emotions went much deeper than the delight of being with her and at Framlingham after so many weeks away. There was real need and since she did not know the reason yet, it set her on edge.

"Well, now you are," she said briskly, "and your wife is scolding you because you are no longer in a battle camp or on the road and you need to be made presentable for the chamber. If you were Tripes, I'd have shut you in the stables. Come." As she tugged him from the bed, she ordered the women to strip the sheets and hang the coverlets in the air and give them a good beating. His shirt and braies she told them to boil and then cut up for clouts and privy rags.

"They're not that bad!" Hugh protested as she used finger and thumb to drop them on the laundry pile.

"They have more holes than dock leaves after a beetle attack," she retorted. "And enough dirt to grow leeks! Even the poorest beggar on the road would shun wearing these."

A smile that was not quite a grin crinkled the lines at the side of Hugh's eyes. "I missed your scolding greatly," he said.

Mahelt clucked her tongue and gestured to him to step into the tub. She noticed the gooseflesh on his arms and told the pail-maid to tip in another bucket of hot water. Then she set about the mammoth task of getting her husband clean and sweet-smelling. She anointed his body with the rose and fat mixture, then scraped it off with the comb, bringing dirt and vermin with it. The water gradually turned the colour of a river in spate, complete with debris. She ordered a second tub filled with clean water and sent a woman to fetch the shears.

"Why in God's name did you let yourself get in this state?" she demanded crossly.

Hugh shivered because his torso was out of the water and the air from the open shutters was cold. "Because we were constantly in the field and there was never enough time. Barely would I fall on my pallet before I had to be up again. It was easier to live in my clothes. Everyone was the same." His expression grew bleak. "Truth to tell, it didn't seem to matter."

Mahelt took the shears from the maid and set about cropping his hair. Beneath the sun-bleaching, it was tangled, greasy, and infested. She cut and snipped, then treated the cropped remnants with fleabane ointment. Bidding him stand, she had the maids sluice him down with buckets of clean water.

While the women were drying him and helping him don a warm loose robe, Mahelt used the fresh water in the second tub to scrub herself and comb and treat her own hair, which she had no intention of cutting off.

Hugh wandered around the room, touching this and that as if reacquainting himself with all that had once been familiar. Mahelt donned a clean chemise and joined him while the maids emptied the tubs and scattered powdered fleabane on the floors.

"There are no snakes in Ireland but I think you must have brought everything else that crawls home with you as a gift." Mahelt gave him a half-laughing, half-reproachful look. She went to put her comb down on the coffer, and then stared at the parchment scroll lying beside her jewel casket and unguent pots. A narrow strip of red ribbon secured it from unrolling, and it was attended by a scattering of pale blackberry flower petals. Frowning and smiling in mystification, Mahelt unfastened the tie and opened it out. A bundle of strung tally sticks fell from the middle and clattered on to the top of the coffer like wooden fingers. The parchment itself was an official document written in Latin. "What's this?"

Grinning, Hugh went to the hearth bench and retrieved the fleece he had draped over the back of it the previous evening. "I thought you might have a yearning to be a shepherdess, or perhaps a dealer in fleece, or cloth and parchment. They are yours to do with as you will, and this is proof of their quality."

Eyes wide with surprise, Mahelt took the fleece from him. It was white and curly with a slight shine in the twists. "You have bought me a flock of sheep?" She felt the glorious softness under her fingers, and then the suede underside, tactile and supple. This was a surprise she would never have anticipated and she was filled with laughter and warm, tearful feelings of love. These sheep were hers to do with as she chose—a source of income to manage as she saw fit.

"I thought of you when I saw them grazing in the field," he said. "We came across them in the Marches not far from Leominster when I saw them."

Mahelt smiled at him with wet eyes. Lifting the fleece she rubbed it against her cheek. "Hah, I remind you of a sheep?"

Hugh laughed and shook his head. "Not in that way. While I was riding I looked at the sky and saw clouds and the way they changed reminded me of you. And then a flock of sheep reminded me of the clouds and it seemed a natural and right thing to do—to gift my wife with the softness of a washed fleece and the wherewithal to have something for herself."

Mahelt looked at the tallies. There were five of them, and each one had ten notches. "Fifty," she guessed.

Hugh looked smug. "Times ten," he said.

She stared at him. "Five hundred?"

"I thought it was a good number with which to begin. I've arranged for them to be brought to Settrington before the winter storms begin. When they arrive, we'll go and see them."

Mahelt melted into his arms. He smelled of soap and herbs now. Clean. New. His hands went to her loose hair and then to her body under the robe and cupped her breasts. Mahelt shivered with lust and anticipation. Hugh dismissed the maids with a flick of his hand and drew Mahelt to the remade bed, where they made love in a tender, urgent, slightly damp tangle with the sheepskin under them and the morning light above.

❖ ❖ ❖

"I missed you," Hugh said. Propped on one elbow, he stroked Mahelt's hair. "I watched the stars each night as I lay on my pallet, and I thought of you."

"I watched them too," she admitted. "The maids said that night airs through open shutters would cause upset humours, but I paid them no heed. I knew somewhere you were watching the same stars in the same sky."

Hugh leaned over to kiss her. "I was. Every night."

Mahelt responded, and then drew back and cupped the side of his face with her hand. "You have said nothing about Ireland. Are there things you are not telling me again?" She sought reassurance in his expression and did not find it.

He twisted his head to kiss her palm before lying back with a sigh and folding his arms behind his head. "The king was greatly successful there. He brought the de Laceys to heel and he has bought the loyalty of most of the Irish kings with scarlet robes and gifts of jewels and horses." His jaw tightened with anger as he told her about losing Brunet. "The king reimbursed me out of his chamber in Dublin, but the money didn't take into account all the training and how much Brunet was worth at stud. I should know by now not to trust Longespée. The nut never falls far from the tree."

"John always takes," Mahelt said with a curl of her lip. "And he never gives anything either, because there is always a price to pay. What of my family?"

Hugh's expression relaxed slightly. "Your mother is well and so are your brothers and sisters. I saw them at Kilkenny. Your new baby sister has red hair like Richard, and Ancel is a sturdy little chap. Your mother sends her greeting and her love. I have a wall hanging in my baggage from her and a brooch she thinks you will like. She was very hospitable to me, and keen to hear news of how you and our son were faring."

Mahelt absorbed his words hungrily, but it was only the beginning of the meal and she was still ravenous. "And my father?"

Hugh sat up and draped his hands around his upraised knees. He looked towards the window and Mahelt studied the line of light across his shoulder and down his bicep. "Your father is well too." He gave a wondering shake of his head. "He outdoes much younger men, including me. I would be ready to drop with exhaustion while he was still giving orders and seeing to details when everyone else had been slumbering for hours. He swore allegiance to the king and he backed it up to the hilt in the campaign to bring the de Laceys to heel." Hugh dropped his gaze and picked at a knot of embroidery on the coverlet. "John captured de Braose's wife and eldest son. They're being held at Windsor until de Braose pays an indemnity of forty thousand marks."

Mahelt gasped. "No man can afford that! Holy Mary, even your father or mine could not raise such a sum!"

Hugh shook his head. "De Braose swore he would do so, then fled to France, which John took as proof he was justified in not trusting him and that de Braose had been in collusion with the French all along." He paused and Mahelt saw him gathering himself.

"Tell me," she said. "I am no milksop to faint away."

Hugh shook his head. "I am not afraid you will faint," he said.

"Then what are you afraid of?"

He sighed. "The king demanded more hostages from your father when we were in Dublin, just before we embarked for home."

"More hostages?" Mahelt sat up, her gaze beginning to spark with the indignant anger he had anticipated. "Who?" she demanded. "Who has he taken?"

"Geoffrey FitzRobert, Jordan de Saqueville, Thomas Sandford, Walter Purcel, and Jean D'Earley. Jean D'Earley has been sent to Nottingham but I do not know where the others are. He's also seized your father's castle at Dunamase."

"How dare he!" She flung the bedclothes aside like a blow and sought her chemise. "How dare he do that!"

"Your father was willing to give up the hostages and they were willing to do as he bade them," Hugh said calmly. "He is a consummate player when it comes to politics. If he had refused with the full host of England on his threshold and all the Irish kings in their new scarlet robes, then Maude de Braose wouldn't be the only one locked up in Windsor. This way he still holds the moral high ground and remains his own man. He said to me himself that it does no harm to bandage a finger that is not cut."

Mahelt thrust out her lower lip. "It is not to be borne!"

"What choice do we have? He is the king."

"I can think of a hundred better men."

"So can I," Hugh answered, "but it is not their anointed right. We should attend to our own concerns and strengthen our lands."

"So he has won. He does as he pleases and everyone lets him because it is meet and safe to do so—because he is 'the king'?"

Hugh sought his shirt and braies. The linen was clean and soft against his chafed, scrubbed skin and smelled faintly of rose petals. "I want to see my son grow to manhood. I want to play with him and show him things. I want to see him ride his first horse and court his first girl. I want him to have brothers and sisters and the kind of life in childhood that I did. One day, he will be the Earl of Norfolk and he will have to make decisions that will affect everyone in his care. He must learn to shoulder burdens and responsibilities above and beyond those of most other men. But for this moment let him have the safety of his childhood. Let him play. I will have that peace for him because all too soon he will have to grow up and face the world." He rubbed his chin. "When I go to church, I pray for all those who have been brought down, and I give thanks that we are not yet among them."

Mahelt shuddered, not knowing whether to embrace him or rage. He had frightened her and because they had so recently been lying on the bed in an intimate warm tangle, his words came as a greater shock. Her stomach was a tight knot as she left the bed and went into the antechamber where her women were going assiduously about their duties while waiting for her and Hugh to finish their private "conversation." The looks of knowing amusement dropped from their faces at the sight of Mahelt's expression as she crossed the room to the baby, who was being dandled on his nurse's knee. Lifting him in her arms, she kissed him and without a word brought him back into the bedchamber.

Hugh had donned his undergarments and was putting on indoor shoes of embroidered kidskin. Little Roger clamoured to be set down on the floor, wriggling in Mahelt's arms and shouting until he got his way. He plopped on his bottom by the side of the bed. He reached out small hands, grasped the coverlet, and hauled himself upright. "Dad-dad," he said, beaming at Hugh. Hugh laughed with pleasure and surprise. The baby let go of the coverlet and took two wobbling but determined steps towards him before plonking down again with a little grunt of expelled air. With utter determination, he pulled himself up again, wavered, and took another two steps.

Filled with pride and delight, Hugh looked from his son to Mahelt. Her face aglow, she laughed and wiped her eyes on the back of her hand. "He's been on the verge of this for days. He was just waiting for you to come home."

The baby pulled himself up a third time, and tottered the final steps to his father, grabbed his leg for support, and beamed up at him, his eyes a bright, sunny hazel. Hugh stooped and gently turned him round to face Mahelt. She crouched and held out her arms and Roger tottered towards her, plumping down, pulling himself up on the bed, walking again, determined to reach her. Hugh's heart swelled with love and pride. Moisture tingled in his eyes. He thought of sitting with Mahelt at the weaving frame, blending the colours into one harmonious pattern that would last beyond the moment. A little piece of each of them caught for ever.

"Our duty first and foremost is to him," he said, as the baby reached her and tumbled into her arms. "He is our future. John is only the now."

Twenty-four

FRAMLINGHAM, JUNE 1212

$\mathcal{M}$AHELT HAD JOINED HUGH'S SISTER MARIE AND ELA IN Ida's personal chamber and was enjoying a good gossip. Various small children played around the women's feet, although little Roger was at the stables with his father, "helping" him ready things for the next day when the Bigod troop departed for the royal muster at Nottingham, and thence to war in North Wales. Ela's son William, sixteen months old, was toddling about the chamber with a wooden horse in his hand. Ela was pregnant again and suffering nausea. Marie's eldest son Randal was off with the men too, but her three-year-old daughter played at her feet, and Marie was expecting a third child in the autumn. Mahelt herself had a second son in the cradle, named Hugh for his father.

Ida said, "When I was a young wife, I cannot remember a time when I wasn't with child or recovering from bearing one—not that I'd be without any of them," she added hastily. "They are God's gifts and I love them all." She made a face. "One of the court ladies told me that douching with vinegar before lying with a man prevented conception, but it doesn't always work."

"You tried it then, Mama?" Marie looked at her with innocently wide eyes.

"When I dwelt at court and I was..." Ida hesitated. "...when I was the king's friend, yes. But I have a son from that time, to show that God's will is not denied." For an instant she looked haunted, but then shook herself and found a smile for Ela. "And now he has a son of his own and a fine and fruitful wife, and I thank God for His mercy." She turned to Marie. "With your father I never used such wiles because we were united in righteous wedlock and I did not want to deny him heirs for Norfolk and daughters to make fine marriage alliances. It was my duty, my part of the bargain. I loved your father and I honoured and feared God."

All the women nodded with understanding, but then Mahelt said, "Even so, a woman should not wear out her body and her spirit in constant child-bearing. I know my duty to bear sons and daughters for Hugh and for Norfolk, but I will not be a brood mare—nor does Hugh wish such a thing."

Her remark elicited raised eyebrows from Ela and Ida. Marie, however, leaned forward with a glimmer of interest. "So what do you do?"

Mahelt darted a glance at her mother-in-law, and then threw caution to the wind. "The usual things. Abstinence, because the Church says it is good for the soul." She rolled her eyes as she made the remark. "A small piece of moss...Not riding all the way to London..."

"Why should not riding all the way to London..." Ela began in puzzlement and then blushed fire-red as understanding dawned. "Oh," she said.

Marie wrinkled her nose. "Someone told me to tie a weasel's testicles in a bag around my neck. I suppose that might keep Ranulf away, but everyone else too! I also heard that putting lettuce under a man's pillow makes him less amorous." Her eyes twinkled. "Or at least less able to be amorous." She made an illustrative flopping gesture with her wrist and forearm. "It doesn't work," she added. "I've tried."

The women burst out laughing. Ida took Ela's son into her lap. The child rested his head trustingly against her breast and put his thumb in his mouth.

"This will be my third," Marie said. "My heart quails at the thought that I may yet bear another dozen—more if I survive. Maude de Braose had sixteen!"

A sudden silence fell over the banter at Marie's mention of Maude de Braose. "God rest her soul," Ida said, crossing herself. Marie's daughter tripped over her smock, landed hard, and began to wail. Marie hastened to pick her up and comfort her in her arms.

Mahelt gazed upon the protective ring the women formed around the children, both the born and the unborn, and wondered how secure they really were. King John's imprisonment of Maude de Braose and her son had become murder. Everyone had been appalled by the details that had gradually emerged. John had moved Maude and her son from Windsor to Corfe, putting them in an oubliette there and abandoning them to starve in the cold and the dark. Rumours hinted that Maude had sustained herself with the flesh of her dead son until she too had perished. The news had made Ida physically sick and horrified everyone in Framlingham. How could such a man be king? Gossip was already rife that he had murdered his own nephew, and with the death of Maude de Braose, the unease was growing apace. He was an excommunicate king, a man outside of the Church. Rome had absolved the English barons of their oaths of loyalty to serve him. Each detail was akin to hard raindrops falling into a pool, causing ripple upon ripple, but contained. But one day the pool was bound to burst its banks and overflow in a murky flood because it could hold no more.

De Braose had fled to take shelter in France and King Philip was threatening invasion of England, although it was no more than a threat so far. At Framlingham, Earl Roger deliberately kept his head down and stayed out of involvement in wider political affairs, save for essential duties such as this summons to the muster in Nottingham. Her own father was pursuing a similar policy in Ireland. He had his sphere of influence there, but he was an ocean away and busy with his new port on the Barrow. But for how long could you keep looking the other way, she wondered, because if you didn't have your eye on the danger, perhaps one day it would be your turn to be seized and destroyed.

❖❖❖

Hugh lifted his son on to the back of the mischievous black and white pony he had given to Mahelt and which was now their heir's first mount. Roger giggled and smacked his small hands down on the pony's withers. Pie started and swished his floor-length black tail, but was immediately amenable to the crust of bread Hugh fed him on the palm of his hand.

"He's a greedy guts," Roger piped up. He'd heard some bigger children taunting one of their number in a repetitive sing-song way and had immediately picked up on the words because they sounded well together. "Greedy guts, greedy guts!"

"Like you then," Hugh said with a grin.

"I'm not!" Roger's hazel eyes flashed with indignation.

"Your grandsire Marshal was nicknamed that when he was a boy." Hugh eyed the child with amusement. He was a bundle of energy, never still from dawn to dusk, and it was all Hugh could do to keep up with him. He was exactly like his mother in that respect.

"Hup," said Ranulf to his own son, a year older than Roger, and heaved him across Pie's back too. Taking the pony's rein, Hugh untied him from the ring in the stable wall and led him on a circuit of the buildings, keeping his eye on the boys to make sure they were not going to fall off.

"At least we are not going to Poitou," Hugh said to Ranulf, who was pacing beside him, his gaze upon the hired carts that soldiers and servants were piling with provisions and equipment. "I fully expected to be performing my feudal service there."

Ranulf put a hand to his son's leg to stop him from bouncing up and down. "You say that as if you think Wales is going to be better," he said, grimacing. "It always rains and those forests of theirs are nothing but ambush traps."

"But we won't be stuck for days on end besieging castles; we are nearer to home, and everyone will be in agreement with a common goal," Hugh pointed out. "If Poitou were the destination, everyone would be complaining about having to fight across the sea and protesting that it's not part of their oath to do so." He gave Ranulf a sidelong look, knowing full well his brother-in-law would be one of those protesters. The insular northern barons harboured hostile feelings on the matter. Ranulf was more moderate than many, but given the choice, Hugh knew he would have stayed home at his castle of Middleham. He performed his feudal duty with punctiliousness, but no enthusiasm. "Besides," Hugh added, "if Llewelyn of Gwynedd didn't want John interfering in his rule, he should not have gone on the offensive. John's not going to stop this time until he's crushed Llewelyn once and for all. Whether Llewelyn is married to John's daughter or not won't matter—he's going for the throat."

"As he did in Ireland?" Ranulf curled his top lip. "What is going to be left for us and for our sons?"

Hugh was spared from answering as his father arrived and paused, hands on hips, to watch the bustle. His gaze fell on the pony and his grandsons and he shook his head, but he smiled nevertheless. Gathering himself, he limped over to the younger men. His knees were clearly paining him today, but he refused to use a stick. Once reaching them, he directed a groom to take over and lead Pie round the yard.

Hugh watched the boys with a pre-emptive tensing of his shoulders.

"It's not far to the ground if they fall off and they bounce at that age," Ranulf said pragmatically.

"Would that I could remember being that young." The earl's gaze was envious.

"When you do, I believe they call it dotage," Hugh quipped.

His father gave a snort of amusement. "Then I am not there just yet, nor have I quite started to dribble like a babe."

Hugh grinned. The men watched another groom bring Hugh's new warhorse out of the stall in order to check its hooves. It was a strong young beast with a brown-bronze coat and handsome chunky lines. Hugh had commented when selecting it from the available mounts amongst their stock that he was going to call this one Stott and have him slope along at the back of the remounts rather than putting him on show. The name had stuck; thus the destrier ridden by Norfolk's heir bore the name of a common plough horse.

Hugh turned his glance to his father. A messenger had arrived not long ago and Hugh knew the earl hadn't just come out here to watch his grandsons at their riding lesson. "I saw the messenger," he said. "Are there new instructions?"

His father cast a look around, ensuring no one but Hugh and Ranulf was within earshot. "Not as such," he said. "But Bened at Settrington reports hearing rumours of a plot to kill the king when we ride into Wales."

Hugh sucked in his breath. "You think it true?" He looked at Ranulf, whose expression was taut and watchful.

His father fingered the brim of his hat. "Bened is a shrewd old dog. He knows when to take heed and when not."

"Where did he hear them?"

"He says from his younger brother who serves in the household of Eustace de Vesci."

Hugh made a face. The relationship between de Vesci and John was one of hatred and distrust. There was a rumour circulating that John had dishonoured de Vesci's wife, but there was also a matter of money that de Vesci owed the Crown.

"Bened's brother sent him what could either be taken as a warning to beware, or a call to arms, depending how you read it." The earl gave Hugh and Ranulf a meaningful look. "Bened believes John de Lacey and John FitzRobert are involved too."

Hugh felt as if he had swallowed a lump of ice.

His father gave Ranulf a hard look. "Did you know anything of this?"

Ranulf recoiled with indignation. "I would not be party to such a thing! I do not keep company with these men. Grant me more sense!"

Hugh exchanged glances with his father. Ranulf had sidestepped the question. Not being a party to something was not the same thing as not knowing about it. He suspected Ranulf had heard a rumour but was feigning deafness. What really worried Hugh was that Will Marshal *did* keep company with the likes of de Lacey and FitzRobert.

"I have to know where everyone in this family stands," his father said in a steely voice. "Because the deeds of the one affect the security of us all."

Ranulf gave a curt nod. "You have nothing to fear of loyalty from me."

"I am glad to hear you say so."

"What of Will Marshal?" Hugh barely dared to enquire. "Is he named?"

His father shook his head. "Bened did not mention the younger Marshal, for which mercy we should thank God, but it wouldn't surprise me if he were implicated." His expression tightened. "Fortunately your wife has been in confinement of late and too busy to be drawn in, but I would not put it past her brother and his accomplices to embroil family members."

"Mahelt is no longer that naive," Hugh said with quiet assertion.

The earl fiddled with his hat brim. "That may or may not be to our advantage."

Ranulf was looking slightly startled. Hugh shook his head, indicating that he should not ask. "How are they planning to do it?"

"Who knows?" Roger shrugged. "Abandon him on a mountainside and hope the Welsh take care of matters, I suspect. That way the Welsh get landed with the blame."

"What do we do? Tell the king, or pretend what we have heard is no more than common rumour and await the consequences?"

His father frowned. "That needs some thought. We won't be the only ones to whom this news has been leaked and every man will be looking to use it for his own survival." He cast a glance at Ranulf, who flushed.

"And if we are approached with a view to implementing the deed?"

Ranulf choked.

Roger was suddenly decisive. "We keep our distance whatever happens, because then we can stand back and decide what to do without endangering ourselves. There will be scapegoats from this, mark my words, and they will not bear the name of Bigod. I shall burn Bened's letter and any more that come our way. Ranulf, I expect you to do the same, and not to go fraternising in private with your neighbours, especially not de Vesci. Can I trust you?"

Ranulf nodded. "You do not have to ask that."

"Yes I do." Roger fixed a hard grey gaze on the two younger men. "You must tell no one of this. Not even other family members, and that includes your wives. This goes no further than ourselves because the fewer who know, the easier it will be to control. Understood?"

Ranulf nodded again. So did Hugh, feeling slightly resentful. He did not need to be lectured; he knew what was at stake.

His father sighed and his shoulders slumped. "I swore allegiance to John at his coronation. I have served him faithfully and held to my oath. I have sent him troops when he has asked and performed my military service in person. I have travelled on the judicial circuit for him and given him my counsel. I would gladly work within the letter of the law to make him accountable." His expression was bleak. "But he has done things that are for God to judge because they are beyond judgement by man. I say let matters work as they will. I shall take no active part either way. Caution is all."

Twenty-five

HUGH SAT IN AN EMBRASURE SEAT WITH JEAN D'EARLEY, senior knight in his father-in-law's household. Jean was presently under house arrest at Nottingham as one of the hostages for William Marshal's good faith.

Jean had been playing merels with another hostage, a freckle-faced Welsh lad of about seven years old. "Sharp as an awl, this one," Jean said with a wink at the child. "Barely speaks a word outside of the Welsh but he understands the rules of the game very well, doesn't he, Richard?" He glanced over at his lord's second son, who had been given into his keeping while they both dwelt at the king's pleasure.

The mischievous sparkle in the child's dark eyes reminded Hugh of his own son, although of course, this boy was older. All told there were twenty-eight Welsh youths being held hostage here in Nottingham, each one either kin to Prince Llewelyn or the son of an important lord.

Richard Marshal looked wry. "He's an expert," he agreed. "He knows more French than he's letting on. Don't let that innocent expression fool you for a minute." His green-grey eyes were bright with good humour. "He's Welsh and we are his enemy. He might smile like an angel, but he'll always be on the lookout for ways to stick a knife in us, just like his father."

He offered the child a sip from his cup. The boy took it and drew a strong gulp. Then he wiped his mouth on his sleeve and wanted to play-fight. Richard obliged with the gentle strength of an indolent young lion. "I'm used to it with smaller brothers and sisters," he explained tolerantly to Hugh. "After Mahelt, this one is easy meat. My sister was a real fighter."

Hugh chuckled as he watched Richard fend off the Welsh lad's assault with one arm. "She still is; I have the scars to prove it."

"Hah, if scars are all, you are fortunate." He taunted his charge, calling him a scrawny rapscallion and the lad responded with a string of what were plainly rude words in his native language. Richard promptly pinned him down and tickled him until he shrieked.

Hugh glanced out of the open shutters at the close pack of tents and banners in the castle bailey. The entire feudal host was here at John's summons. A white August sun burned down on spears and armour. Cartloads of supplies were rolling in through the castle gates in a steady stream, hauled by oxen, horses, and men. The noise, the dust, and the smell mingled to form a miasma. He rubbed the back of his neck with unease as he watched the activity and thought about the letter his father had consigned to the brazier at Framlingham. The words of treason had turned to flakes of ash, but that didn't mean they had never existed. All the fire did was change them into something else, and their residue remained.

A group of Welsh youths were playing camp ball and their shouts rang out as they chased each other about the ward, all tussling for possession of the ball of fleece-stuffed leather. The sport was a combination of speed, skill, and all-out brawl. Hugh's gut surged as he contemplated joining them. As a youth he had excelled at the sport—still did, in fact, because he was fast and had kept his lithe physique, even if he was broader across the shoulders these days, although broader shoulders meant greater burdens than fighting over a ball.

❖❖❖

Sitting with Jean and Ranulf in the packed great hall, Hugh dipped his spoon into the rich marrow and barley broth. It was spiced with pepper and, for those who enjoyed the sensation, the heat in the mouth was pleasant.

Richard was serving the high table in his capacity of royal squire as well as hostage and was going about his duties with serious aplomb, although the ever-present mischievous twinkle remained in his eyes. All the talk was of the coming campaign against the Welsh. The discussion of tactics was loud and jocular. The older, experienced soldiers were exchanging tales of previous campaigns in that country and how no Welshman would stand and fight. Their ploy was to melt away into their hills and the inevitable mist and rain and then strike out from behind, picking men off one by one.

Barons looked at each other and then away, as if holding eye contact for too long would reveal some dangerous knowledge or intention. Everyone knew what no one was saying. Hugh glanced at the king. John wore a smile on his face, but it was fixed and resembled more the start of a snarl. His stares were fixed and intense, as if trying to prise thoughts out of men's heads. Hugh paid studious attention to his dinner and hoped he did not look as guilty as he felt. Ranulf was doing the same. Jean D'Earley too concentrated on his food, and the only conversation between the men was of practical matters concerned with horsemanship.

John was holding out his hands for his dapifer to pour water over them, when a messenger arrived and was conducted up the hall by an usher. A letter was produced and John wiped his knife on a piece of bread and broke the seal. As he read the contents his lips compressed. He beckoned to Longespée and his mercenary captains, and abruptly abandoned his meal and left the room.

There was silence after they had gone and then someone gave an uneasy laugh and conversation began again, but it was ragged around the edges. Hugh's appetite vanished and he pushed his bowl away. Richard came over carrying a flagon of wine and leaned to replenish their cups. "The seal is of the king of Scots," he told Hugh, Ranulf, and Jean. "Make of it what you will."

Jean picked up his cup and turned it in his hand. "It could mean a great deal, or it could mean nothing, but since he took Marc and D'Athée and my lord of Salisbury away with him, and didn't stay to finish his dinner, I would say that the news is important and he's not immediately keen to share it."

Richard put down the flagon and licked his lips. "There are rumours flying about that—" He broke off at the alarmed expression on the faces of the other men. "What have I said?"

"Listen to rumours if you will," Hugh said sharply. "Heed them if you deem you should, but keep your own counsel— even to me. Even to your father's most trusted lord and friend."

Richard's freckled complexion reddened.

"If your brother is involved in any of these 'rumours' and you are in contact with him, then tell him to be very careful."

Richard nodded, lips compressed, and moved away.

Jean D'Earley gave Hugh a shrewd look. "I suspect I do not want to know what that was about."

Hugh took a short drink from his replenished cup, and then pushed it aside too. "I imagine you already know as much as I do. From what I have seen, the Marshal household has its ear close to the ground and even members who are hostages are well informed."

"The boys are cubs," D'Earley said. "They have suffered from an absence of their father's control, but it goes no further than the fire of youth. They know the duty owed to their blood."

"There are different ways of seeing duty, my lord," Hugh answered, thinking of Mahelt's escapade at Thetford.

"Indeed, but they will not disobey their father."

Hugh's nape prickled. He had been as good as told that his father-in-law knew everything there was to know about the rumours and the situation. It came as no surprise and yet it set him on edge. D'Earley's remark was ambiguous, but then so were the entire circumstances. Glancing round, he noticed Eustace de Vesci and another northern baron, Robert FitzWalter, slipping from the hall. It might have been for no more sinister purpose than taking a piss, but given what he knew, Hugh thought not. He would confidently wager his last mark that their leaving was probably tied up with the letter that had just arrived.

John did not return to his meal and men finished eating and gathered to talk in huddles and speculate. Hugh left the hall with Jean and Ranulf. They tried to avoid the knots of conversation, but even so were pulled into a couple of them, where they listened and ventured no opinions. They had not been alone in noticing the slinking departure of de Vesci and FitzWalter.

"I had heard there was a plot to murder the king, rape the queen, kill their children, and offer Simon de Montfort the throne," declared one of the Earl of Derby's men, his eyes gleaming.

"Hah, I don't believe you. Where did you hear that?" scoffed one of his companions, but nevertheless was eager for details.

"I don't know." The knight shrugged. "An alehouse in the town. It's common knowledge."

Hugh was astonished. That was indeed wild rumour. And why de Montfort, who was a Frenchman? He had a claim to English soil, but only on the Earldom of Leicester, which John was currently holding in his own hands.

"Many are indulging themselves by inhaling wishful thinking

from the smoke of rumour," Jean said. "And as with all rumours, it has grown and changed in the telling.

"Why would they say that about the queen?" Ranulf asked uneasily.

Jean twitched his shoulders. "Because of the king's reputation for abusing the womenfolk of other men, de Vesci's wife being a case in point. He has taken his fill in the past, sometimes by force and threat. Husbands and fathers imagine what they would do, given the chance. Dishonouring a man's woman is dishonouring the man. It says he cannot take care of her or his family...that he is impotent." Jean looked at Hugh and Ranulf. "It is about power and control. It is about one dog marking another's territory and who can piss the highest up the wall."

"De Vesci and FitzWalter"—Hugh nodded his head at the men riding out of the gates with their knights and serjeants— "the king is letting them leave."

Jean rubbed his chin. "Perhaps he thinks he has no choice. What would happen if he ordered them stopped? How many of this gathering is he sure of?"

Ranulf said nothing. Hugh grimaced. He hated the murk of court life and did not understand how men like his half-brother could relish it—although for Longespée attendance on John was a validation of his royal blood and an opportunity to pose in fine clothes. "But by leaving they open themselves to accusations of either full treason or desertion."

"Then they must think they have more to lose by staying."

Hugh was still pondering a safe reply when a leather camp ball hurtled across his path, pursued by two Welsh youths and the little one who had been with Richard. In negation of all that was happening around him, Hugh launched himself after the ball and grabbed it before the boys could. "Catch me for it!" he cried, and set off at a sprint. The older ones hesitated, but the littlest one set off after Hugh with a vengeance.

Jean D'Earley shook his head as he watched Hugh become embroiled with the entire pack of the Welsh hostages, but then he began to chuckle. "That is the kind of thing my lord Marshal would have done when he was younger," he said to Ranulf.

Ranulf rubbed his thigh. "If I hadn't strained my leg yesterday I'd follow him for certain."

"He handles himself well," Jean said with approval. "My lord Marshal would only choose the best for his daughter and I'm glad to see his judgement borne out."

"Of course handling a wife bent on her own direction takes longer," Ranulf said shrewdly.

Jean gave a pained smile. "Most men don't manage that in a lifetime."

❖❖❖

"They would murder me. In cold blood and treachery they would murder me!" John glared at Longespée and threw the letter at his half-brother and the mercenary captains gathered around the trestle in his private chamber. "They are hatching a plot to kill me in Wales. To leave me exposed and let the Welsh hack me to pieces. They are poised to announce my death around the country. Men have even been told which day to proclaim it! How many here are involved? How many out there would see me dead? Is there no one I can trust?" He gestured with a clenched fist.

Longespée stared in shock at the document, which was tangible proof of the circulating rumours. Last month John had sent a troop of mercenaries north when William of Scotland had requested aid to put down a rebellion. In gratitude, and in the interests of self-preservation, the Scots king had now sent this warning acquired from his own contacts. John's death was to be accomplished and proclaimed once he reached Wales. The conspirators had covered their tracks too well for most to be known, but Robert FitzWalter and Eustace de Vesci were named.

"You cannot go to Wales, sire, not now," said Philip Marc, one of John's foremost mercenary captains. "You must look to your safety and the safety of the queen and your son."

John sat upright and Longespée saw the fury blaze in his half-brother's eyes—and the fear. Longespée was afraid too, and filled with the desire to protect this man whose royal blood he shared.

"I will not let it happen," John snarled. "They mean to bring me down, but I will tear out their livers and cast them into the abyss first." He glared round. "Whom do I trust when this letter says that no one owes allegiance to an excommunicate king and that all should seize the moment and rise against me?"

"You have loyal men, sire," said Philip Marc, his rough voice implacable. "Everyone in this room would do your bidding without hesitation."

"Because none of you would have anything without my word!" John glared round the cluster of men.

Longespée flinched. "I can vouch for the Earl of Norfolk, for Aumale and Pembroke and de Burgh."

John gave a snort of contempt. "I may trust your loyalty, brother, but dare I trust your judgement? Can you say for certain they will not conspire against me?"

"I hope so, sire."

"You 'hope' so," John mimicked, baring his teeth. "Knowing your skill as a gambler, God help us all. Pembroke could argue that his arse was the sun and people would believe him, and if the others were so trustworthy, they'd be here now, in this room." He paced up and down, the jewelled hem of his robe flaring out as he walked.

"Then surely you need Pembroke to argue on our side," Longespée said. "And his support will bring others with him."

John threw Longespée a fulminating look. "So they will listen to the Marshal and not heed me. Is that what you are saying?"

Longespée made an open gesture. "You said he could argue his arse was the sun."

"He will be useful, sire," said Gerard D'Athée. "He has shown that he will not rebel against you."

"That is because I have his sons and his best knights," John growled, but his gaze grew thoughtful as he bent his mind to dealing with the situation rather than raging against it. "De Breauté, ride to the queen and escort her and my sons to Corfe and hold them safe. I want de Vesci and FitzWalter seized. I will disband this muster immediately and I will find out just how deep this rot has gone and dig it out." His tread became heavier as if with each step he was crushing his enemies. "As to the Welsh..." His nostrils flared as he looked round at the men. "Since I cannot go into Wales to bring the Prince of Gwynedd to heel, and since my death was planned to happen on his territory, then let us have the reckoning here and now. Let Welshmen die in my stead and pay the blood debt. Let all see what happens to those who plot against the king of England."

The mercenaries exchanged looks. Longespée gazed at John. The fear was still present in his brother's eyes, but now it had thorns. There was a sheen on his face and his breathing was swift. "Hang the hostages," John said. "All of them."

Longespée's breath caught in his throat. "Sire, there are almost thirty of them."

"Then the sooner it begins the better." He snapped his fingers at Philip Marc. "See to it."

"I'll give the order," Marc said with a bow and strode for the door. The others followed him.

"But one of them is an infant—a little boy!" Longespée gagged, appalled.

John's nostrils flared. "So is my own son."

"Sire, I beg you to reconsider. Show mercy!"

"What mercy would have been shown to me in Wales?" John's eyes glittered. "What mercy would my own sons receive in the wake of my death? Hang them, each and every one, and let it be an example."

❖❖❖

Mud-streaked and laughing, stripped to his shirt and hose, Hugh avoided the leap of the Welsh youth and in the nick of time tossed the ball to his brother Ralph who had predictably seen the game and raced to join in. Welsh insults and yells mingled with similar ripostes in Norman French and English. Several more Bigod squires and retainers had attached themselves to the broil, as had Richard Marshal, and the game was proving to be a boisterous, exhilarating scrimmage.

The littlest one, Rhodri, running hard, tripped over a loose shoe thong and went sprawling. Hugh, who was nearest, picked him up, dusted him down, and set him back on his feet. A three-cornered rip showed his knee through his hose and little beads of blood were filling a graze up his sleeve. The child's eyes were liquid, but he clenched his jaw, defying his tears and anyone who dared to offer sympathy.

"Those are honourable battle wounds," Hugh said. "Have you still got all your teeth? You didn't knock any out?"

The boy shook his head and bared two neat pearly rows to prove not. As Hugh pretended to recoil, the boy's gaze widened in sudden shock. Hugh started to turn and was roughly seized by two mail-clad soldiers, who pinioned his arms, one grabbing a fistful of Hugh's fair hair to jerk back his head. An instant later, Rhodri himself was grasped by another one and borne away under his arm like a piglet, wriggling and shrieking.

"Come on, you Welsh son of a whore, the king says you've a wooden horse to ride with a rope rein," snarled one of Hugh's assailants in a heavy Flemish accent.

Hugh fought and struggled in their hard, steel grip. "I am

Hugh Bigod, lord of Settrington, heir to the Earldom of Norfolk and son-in-law to the Earl Marshal!" he gasped. "Take your filthy hands off me!"

For a moment they continued to grapple with him, as if what they were seeing and what they were hearing did not tally, but as Hugh swore at them again in their own language, they released him and stood back, licking their lips. Belatedly they bowed to him.

"I am sorry, sire," one of them said. "I surely thought you were a Welsh hostage. I did not know…" He gestured lamely to Hugh's stained, sweat-soaked shirt and muddy chausses.

Hugh's flesh burned where they had gripped him. "What do you mean about riding a wooden horse?" Looking round he saw that the Welsh boys had been herded together and were being prodded with spears towards the castle's high outer wall facing the town. Rhodri was still shrieking and pummelling at the soldier who had him tucked under his arm. Hugh's gaze widened. "Christ in heaven, you are surely not going to…" He swallowed his gorge.

"King's orders, my lord," said the second man with grisly relish. "String them up and see them kick…all of them."

Ralph rejoined Hugh, having also been briefly mistaken for one of the Welsh. "You can't!" He looked aghast as he rubbed the mark of mailed fingerprints on his neck.

"Such an act is beyond all Christian decency," Hugh said hoarsely.

The soldier shrugged. "The king's an excommunicate. What does he have to lose, except the lives of a few Welsh maggots that won't bedevil him by growing into flies?"

Hugh shoved past the soldier and ran towards the curtain wall facing the town. Philip Marc was directing operations with another mercenary, Engelard de Cigogne, and already a dozen of the Welsh youths, still hot and sweaty from their game of camp ball, had nooses round their necks and were being confessed by a chaplain. Their eyes were huge and terrified and bewildered. The other ends of the nooses were looped around the merlons of the outer wall.

Longespée was watching, his throat rigid and the veins in his neck standing out like cords. His right hand gripped his sword hilt as if to draw his long weapon from the scabbard. There was no sign of the king. Hugh strode up to his half-brother. "Make him stop!" He shook Longespée's arm. "In God's name, William, make him stop!"

Longespée turned dead eyes upon Hugh. "There is nothing I can do. He will not be moved. The die is cast. He says this is a lesson to Llewelyn and all men who would plot against him."

De Cigogne looked round at Hugh. "There are traitors in our midst, my lord Bigod, and the king is in a mood to deal with all who would defy his will. Unless you are so minded to join these wretches, have a care."

"You will imperil your souls for this!" Hugh choked.

"They are hostages for the word of their lords, a word that has been broken and defiled," Marc replied evenly. "The king is within his rights, and they are not going to their Maker unshriven."

Hugh's stomach was a void. The last thing on earth he wanted to do was watch, yet he had to, because he had to bear witness for their sake, because he could not turn his back on these boys. Dear God, dear God. What if this were his own son going to his death thus? One moment at play, the next choking on the end of a rope because of the power games of grown men. Hugh's chest tightened and his eyes blurred and stung, but he forced himself to keep looking as the youths were dragged to the crenel gaps and hurled over like sacks of flour. A few would be fortunate; their necks would snap and they would die instantly, but others would jerk and dangle there, inexorably suffocating as the sun climbed in the sky.

Rhodri was in the second group. Hugh started forward, not sure what he intended to do, but something...anything rather than let this happen. De Cigogne shot out a hauberk-clad arm and seized him. Another mercenary assisted and their grip was sure, powerful, and deliberately harsh. They seldom got to lay hands on the son of an earl with impunity, although de Cigogne had enjoyed himself on a few occasions with the older Marshal lad.

De Cigogne and his companion held Hugh fast and there was nothing he could do as each youngster was hurled over the wall. He did not see the jerk and recoil as the ropes ran taut, nor the bodies kicking, struggling and dying against the pale amber stones, but he could picture it. In the silence after the last child had been flung to his death, the mercenaries released Hugh and he wrenched away from them and, stooping over, vomited into the grass, not caring who thought him weak and soft.

Longespée said nothing, but turned and walked away towards the upper bailey, his jaw clamped and his movements stiff as if he had a rigid spear thrust down the back of his surcoat.

"Dear Christ." Ralph crossed himself. He looked towards his retreating lord and half-brother, and then at Hugh.

"Do not speak of Christ," Hugh croaked as he stood up, wiping his mouth. "He wasn't here today. This isn't His work." He shuddered and tried to pull himself together, for the sake of his whey-faced brother and because his troops needed leadership, but inside, he felt like a frightened, bewildered child himself. He swallowed another retch. "We should ask His mercy for those Welsh lads...and for ourselves, because this deed damns us all."

❖ ❖ ❖

At Framlingham, Mahelt was sorting out the undercroft and enjoying herself. The organisation brought clarity and efficiency to household processes that depended on orderly and well-stocked supplies. As a descendant of royal marshals, provisioning and organising were in her blood—and decidedly preferable to sewing! She had discovered an old barrel of meat crawling with maggots and had given some to the castle youths to go fishing in the mere; she had told them to throw the remainder on the dung pile for the poultry to peck at. The extra nourishment would fatten the hens and help with the laying too.

They were running short of honey and wax which would have to be ordered in from Ipswich, and they needed some new barrels for holding the brined meat once pig-killing began in November. She would have to tell their steward to have a word with the cooper in Thetford. Her son ran a stick along a row of barrels, counting them as he skipped. "One, two, fee, six…"

"Four," Mahelt laughed. "It's four after three." She picked up a costrel, unstoppered it, sniffed at the contents, and then took a sip. Mead, sweet, strong, and tasting of summer, flowed over her tongue. Outside she heard horses clopping into the courtyard and made a mental note that her father-in-law had returned from his daily inspection of the demesne.

"One, two, fee, four, six, tenty!" Roger declared triumphantly, whacking his stick against the last barrel in the row. He spun in circles until he was dizzy and then plopped down on the floor. Mahelt returned the mead to the shelf before a sip became two and then three.

"Dad-dad!" Roger squealed. Mahelt whirled and saw Hugh standing just inside the doorway. His clothes were dusty and travel-stained and his hat was pulled low, concealing his eyes in a manner so reminiscent of his father that she shivered. Little Roger dashed to him and Hugh swept him into his arms and buried his face against the child's neck.

Mahelt stared at her husband in surprise as she tugged her apron out of the belt of her gown. She had not thought to see him home until the end of October at the earliest. "What's happened?" she asked, because it was obvious something was wrong.

Hugh shook his head. "I rode ahead of the troop," he said hoarsely. "They'll be here soon enough."

"Dad-dad, Dad-dad, I can count to ten! One, two, fee…"

As Roger chattered in his arms, Hugh looked up and across at Mahelt and she was appalled to see that his throat was jerking and that he was fighting back tears. Hastily she took the child out of Hugh's arms and handed him to a passing maid. "Take him to the countess and tell her that my lord is home," she said. "Then tell Simon to prepare food and drink and bring it to my lord's chamber."

When the woman had gone on her errand struggling with a screaming Roger, who wanted to stay with his parents, Mahelt took her husband's arm. "Tell me!" she said firmly, doing her best to cover her fear.

Hugh made an inarticulate sound. Curling his arm around her waist, he drew her inside the musty, lantern-lit undercroft and shuddered against her. She could feel that he was indeed sobbing and her fear increased. She soothed him, one hand around his neck, stroking the hair at his nape, the other grasped in his at his breast. "Hugh, what is it?"

He continued to quiver in her embrace. It was safe in here and dark and he could vent the emotion he had been holding inside ever since Nottingham Castle. "I don't think I can tell you," he said hoarsely.

"I am strong enough to bear whatever it is. It's the not knowing that will undo me. Why are you not in Wales?"

Releasing her, he wiped his eyes on his sleeve. Mahelt went to shut the undercroft door, then she sat him on a barrel and handed him the costrel of mead. "Drink," she said. Her tone was curt because she was angry now as well as concerned. Hugh's face wore an expression she had never seen before, as if something fundamental had been broken, and she was ready to do battle with whatever had caused it.

Hugh took a swallow, lowered the costrel, and looked at her. "There was a plot uncovered against the king at Nottingham...a plot to murder him and the queen and his children."

"What?"

"It's true. The king of Scots sent him a warning, and one came from Wales too—from his daughter—but by then it was too late and it would not have changed the outcome anyway. He was set on making an example."

"What do you mean it came too late?" Mahelt stared at him, her spine tingling. Was John dead? Her thoughts flew to her oldest brother and she wondered if he had been involved or captured. She felt queasy, but told herself Hugh wouldn't be crying over Will's arrest. He would be expecting her to cry instead. Nor would he be distraught over a plot to kill the king. From the secretive way the men had been acting on their last day at home, she suspected he had known something even before he set out. Her father-in-law had been on edge since they had been gone too, limping out of his chamber to intercept every messenger who rode in.

"Since we could not ride into Wales as the king intended and since Wales had been planned as the place to kill him, the king hanged the hostages Prince Llewelyn gave to him last year." His eyes were wide with remembered horror. "All twenty-eight of them. Threw them off the ramparts one at a time while those waiting the same fate watched it happen, and John's mercenaries counted them over the edge like our son counts his numbers. Some of them...some of them were little boys who should still have been at their mother's skirts. One was called Rhodri; I don't know who his father was, except Llewelyn's vassal. I was in the midst of playing camp ball with him and the others when John's mercenaries came to take them. One minute he was chasing me for the ball, the next he was throttling on a rope. Philip Marc said we should rejoice, that it was one less nit to grow into a louse, but I say we are damned for this."

Mahelt dropped to her knees before him and took her hands in his. "No, Hugh, not you," she said fiercely. "Dear God."

"Do not talk to me of God; I have been supping with the Devil." His mouth contorted. "I thought I had a long enough spoon, but I was wrong. There is not a spoon long enough in this land." He looked down at her hands, folded over his. "But I have no choice, because if I do not sup, I shall be eaten and my family will be eaten too, or starved or…or hanged. I am ashamed that I did nothing, but there was nothing I could do, and in truth, the king was within his rights. In law, it could be well argued that it was a just move—but it was not merciful and it was not moral…"

Mahelt gazed at him, feeling numb. She wanted to give him words of wisdom and restore everything to its rightful place, but her mind's eye filled with the image of corpses swinging from a castle wall, each one of them a member of her family, and the closest one to her was her child, struggling to count his numbers as his throat mottled and turned blue around the rope cutting into his neck, and her own throat was so tight she could not speak.

"Two of the plotters were discovered," Hugh added hoarsely. "Eustace de Vesci and Robert FitzWalter. They fled before they could be arrested but the king has ridden north with his hell-hound mercenaries and is replacing the castellans and sheriffs he suspects of conspiring to murder him."

Mahelt bit her lip. "What of Will?"

Hugh disengaged from her and rose to his feet. "He is close to de Lacey and FitzRobert and both are suspects." He gave her a warning look. "If Will is involved, I hope to God he has had the wisdom to cover his tracks."

She whitened. "I have heard nothing, I swear it."

He nodded stiffly. "We must be careful. The king suspects everyone, and the mercenaries and sycophants with whom he surrounds himself will do whatever he bids because he pays their wages and gives them their power."

There was a sudden loud thump on the door and both of them leaped with tension. "Dad-dad, Dad-dad, come out!" little Roger bellowed. They heard his nurse trying to shush him and his indignant yell of refusal, followed by another thud.

Mahelt started forward, but Hugh pre-empted her. "It's all right." He put her gently to one side and going to the door, opened it on his furious, red-faced son, who was trying to fight off the nurse. Hugh held up his hand to her, then he stooped and swung Roger into his arms. He was a solid, warm weight for his years, but light too. Sturdy as oak, fragile as gossamer, and buzzing like an angry little wasp. Alive. Hugh had never seen anything more alive in his life. "I'm here," he said. "I'll always be here." He wiped the tears of fury from his son's cheeks, and then those of raw heartache and guilt from his own with the same hand.

"What happens now?" Mahelt asked.

He kissed Roger's salty cheek. "We draw breath and count to ten."

"One, two, fee..." said Roger, laboriously holding up one finger at a time. "Four, fi..." He bounced in his father's arms.

Hugh took him out into the yard to watch the rest of his troop riding in.

"And after that?"

"Then we find a way through," he said wearily, "because for all our sakes, we must."

Twenty-six

*M*AHELT WAS ON TENTERHOOKS FOR SEVERAL WEEKS WAITING to see if anything happened to Will, but nothing was said and for once she preferred not to know. No news was like throwing a blanket over an untidy corner. It didn't clear the problem but it made matters look better on the surface. The king had spent more than a thousand pounds fortifying his castles in the North; various castellans had been replaced and others had been forced to yield hostages—and after what had happened at Nottingham Castle, no one was in any doubt as to the consequences of rebellion.

At Martinmas in the second week of November it was time to slaughter the hogs that had been fattening on beech and acorn mast in the park. The males, saving the stud boar and his deputy, were destined to become bacon, salt pork, sausages, hams, brawn, blood puddings, and lard to feed the household through the dark days of winter, while the sows were kept for breeding. The swine were herded into the lower bailey and one by one slaughtered with an axe blow between the eyes and a knife smartly stuck into the jugular, one person to do the sticking, another to catch the blood in big shallow bowls. Then the dead hogs were scalded to remove the bristles before being hoisted up on ropes and eviscerated.

The yard and the slaughter sheds were a hive of bloody industry and Mahelt was engaged in the thick of things, an apron at her waist and her hair bundled in a linen kerchief. Organising such toil and taking part in it was to her taste because the rewards came far more swiftly than with something like sewing, where a project might take weeks of work to accomplish. Tonight in the hall there would be roast pork crowned with crisp golden fat and accompanied by sour baked apples and sharp sauces to cut through the richness of the meat, and plenty of bread to mop up the gravy. Amid a communal spirit of feasting there would be songs, poetry, and merriment, including a performance by one of the earl's serjeants, Roland le Pettour, a jester who held his land for the service of tumbling, juggling, and performing musical tunes from his anus when the occasion demanded.

The castle women jested with each other as they stirred great vats of pig blood to prevent it from clotting, and boiled cauldrons of lard to fill the cleaned-out bladders. Brine-pickling solutions had been made from the salt brought in by pack pony from Earl Roger's coastal villages. Spices had travelled from the family's wharf at Ipswich and all the knives had been sharpened on the whetstone until they gleamed with blue fire.

Agatha, one of the kitchen maids, eyed the pig parts on the slick bloody board in front of her. "My husband says he never wants to see another pig's trotter on the table for dinner as long as he lives," she declared, "but I say he gets what I put in front of him and be thankful. Pickled, or sauced or stewed in honey, pig's trotters he will have and like it!"

The other women cackled and nudged each other and Mahelt laughed with them, enjoying the camaraderie.

Hugh came to the kitchen door and beckoned to her. He had been busy in his father's chamber and was clutching a roll of parchment. His breath was white vapour in the raw November air and his hat was pulled down low over his ears. Seeing the portent in his gaze, Mahelt wiped her hands, removed her apron, and, having bid the women to keep at their stirring, joined him in the yard.

The slaughter was finished and the ground was being swilled down and brooms energetically applied. Hogs were still being scalded by the fire and men were busy with knives, hauling the carcasses up on rope tackles to gut them. Little Roger watched with interest, a floppy pig's ear clutched in one hand. Tripes, despite his advancing years, had managed to dart in and grab a chunk of offal and now lurked under a cart, devouring his prize.

Hugh drew Mahelt away from the noise and mess and sat her on a bench outside the new hall. "A letter's come from your father to mine," he said. "I thought you'd want to know. Your father has offered his support to the king. He says he will bring five hundred knights from Ireland and he and de Grey have managed to swing the support of the Irish lords behind John." Hugh's expression was eloquently blank. "Your father has advised the king to treat with the pope and bring the excommunication to an end, because until John has the protection of the Church, all men have sanction to act against him."

"I wish my father did not owe his loyalty to a creature like John," she said vehemently.

Hugh rubbed the back of his neck. "So do I, but your father does what he must according to his oath. The king has thanked him for his support but wants him to stay in Ireland for the time being to help the justiciar, and return in the spring when the crossings are better." He handed her the parchment. "Read for yourself." His voice warmed. "There's some good news too."

Mahelt scanned the lines and then, giving a joyful shriek, flung her arms around Hugh and kissed him hard. "My brothers are to be released and all the men who stand hostage for my father!"

Smiling, Hugh returned her embrace. "Your father is restored to favour. The king needs loyal men of wisdom to advise him what to do about the pope and King Philip."

Mahelt released him to reread the message. Her delight at the news about her brothers and the hostages did not alter her feelings towards the king. "When John is in trouble, he needs help from men willing to stand by him, but when times are favourable, he turns on them," she said with contempt.

"I doubt he will tangle with your father again. He knows how popular the lord Marshal is and I think he has come to realise it is better to have him working for the Crown than being neutral or driven into opposition."

Mahelt stood up, but could not resist reading the words one more time because, although written by a scribe, they were of her father's will and intent. Finally, reluctantly, she kissed the parchment and returned it to Hugh, who rolled it up and pushed it through his belt.

"At least with your father advising the king we might see some sense and decency brought into affairs of state," he said. "I may not trust John, but I do trust your father to do what is best for all."

Twenty-seven

A HARD FROST COVERED THE GRASS IN FEATHERY SILVER RIME and the December air was knife-cold to breathe. Dusk was falling and the sky was a luminous turquoise over the gleaming white buildings of Salisbury Palace. The cathedral shone beside it, the magnificent west front a confection of masons' work rising in glory to God. Standing on the palisade with Hugh, Mahelt gazed skywards and inhaled the frozen purity of the first stars, her breath short with anticipation.

She and her marital family were spending the Christmas celebration at Salisbury. Hugh said they had only been invited because Longespée wanted to show off the gold plate on his sideboard and lord it over everyone. Mahelt had nudged him and told him to be more charitable and tolerant, which had made Hugh raise his brows, although in the interests of self-preservation he had not commented on her own reputation where those virtues were concerned.

"There," said Hugh, pointing outward over the palisade. "Listen."

Mahelt strained her ears and eyes. Hugh had the sharp senses of a fox. Then she heard it: the jingle of harness bells and the sound of voices. Narrowing her eyes, she made out shapes moving in the darkness towards the hill. Someone at the head of the party bore a lantern and others, carried by retainers, glowed along the edges of the cavalcade, creating a bobbing snake of light in the deepening dusk. As they came closer, the blue and gold banners of Salisbury were just visible and the jingling grew louder.

Hugh lifted his son on to his shoulders to watch the procession. "See," said Mahelt. "See, it's your uncle Will and your uncle Richard." Her voice shook.

"Not forgetting your uncle Longespée," Hugh added neutrally. The Bigod party had arrived a day ahead of the illustrious Earl of Salisbury and his vast entourage.

"Uncle Will, Uncle Richard," little Roger repeated and pointed eagerly at the lanterns. Mahelt left the palisade and hurried down to the bailey where Ela was already waiting. Hugh followed more sedately, but joined Mahelt and set one hand to her shoulder in a gesture of affectionate support. He knew how much this meant to his wife and could feel her quivering under the palm of his hand. His mother arrived, breathless from her dash from the cathedral where she had lingered to pray when everyone had gone. She was robed in her best mulberry-coloured cloak and her eyes were sparkling as she anticipated the arrival of her firstborn son.

The horses clopped across the ditch, through the gatehouse arch, and entered the bailey in clouds of lantern-lit steam from breath and hide. Longespée dismounted and Ela went forward to curtsey to him in greeting. He stooped and raised her up and kissed her on either cheek. Then he greeted his Bigod relatives and exchanged formal words of welcome.

Mahelt smiled and curtseyed and kissed him in a distracted fashion, but her attention was all for her brothers, and the instant she had finished her formal greeting to Longespée, she abandoned propriety and flew to embrace Will and Richard.

Richard engulfed her in a massive bear hug that took her

breath. It had been six years since she had last seen him at Striguil. Now, a grown man of twenty-one years old, he towered over her, being at least the size of their father, and broad across the shoulders. Will looked as insubstantial as a youth against him, and even Hugh, who was well muscled and tall, might have been a squire.

"Perhaps you'll learn to value us now, instead of treating us as nuisances." Richard's voice was a deep rumble.

Mahelt ceased wiping her eyes to make a face at him. "I've always valued you," she retorted, "but it doesn't prevent you from being a nuisance!"

"Well, we're here to bedevil you for a while now." Richard clasped Hugh's arm and bestowed a mutual kiss of peace.

The gathering repaired to the private apartments where food waited on laden trestles and the fire gave out a roaring heat. Standing near the flames was rather like being near a smith's furnace, but the rest of the room was pleasantly warm.

Will gazed at his three-year-old nephew in astonishment. "I cannot envisage you a mother"—he shook his head at Mahelt in bemusement—"but who else's could he be? He looks just like you."

"He is certainly his mother's son," Hugh said drily as he handed a cup of wine to Mahelt and gently ruffled his son's dark hair.

"What of your other one?" Richard asked.

"He's in the nursery," Mahelt replied. "He's more like Hugh."

"Keep him satisfied with food and attention and he doesn't shout," Hugh said, tongue firmly in cheek, and earned himself a dig in the ribs from his wife. Rubbing his sore side with one hand, he raised his cup in toast to Mahelt's brothers with the other. "Now you are no longer obliged to dwell in the royal household, where will you go?"

Will studied his shoes, suddenly seeming to find the

embroidery on them of great import. "I haven't decided yet. Striguil or Pembroke, most likely." He avoided their eyes. "Or perhaps I'll stay for a while at my father's manor at Caversham." He raised his head to slant Hugh a challenging look. "You need not fear. I shall not go anywhere north of the Trent."

Hugh returned his gaze. "I do not fear, brother," he said. "I know you will always have the greater good of your family at heart—and your father's honour."

Will did not answer, but Richard took up the slack of the momentary silence and said, "I'm going to Longueville in the spring. Our father wants me to assume governance there."

Hugh eyed Richard keenly. The young man was heir to his family's estates across the Narrow Sea, but only had an inheritance there because his father had managed by some very rapid footwork to hold on to it when King John had lost Normandy. Richard's allegiance would be to King Philip, not to John. He would also be well placed to keep his family informed about what was happening at the French court. "You are going to have much to do."

Richard shrugged his wide shoulders. "I was born to this duty and I have trained for it. I spent my childhood at Longueville and Orbec. Those places are the homes of my heart." An irrepressible grin brightened his face. "There's good tourneying to be had there in the summer too."

Hugh received the impression that Richard was deliberately making light of matters. His smile was genuine, but it was also a mask, and beyond the humour in his eyes, there were shadows. Like Hugh, he had not emerged unscathed from Nottingham. At least he was going to be safely out of John's way in Normandy, and Philip of France was a reasonable overlord.

"You will stay a little while though?" Mahelt said anxiously.

"Of course, little sister, and I shall visit often. Do not expect to be rid of me so easily."

Mahelt wagged her finger at him. "You had better keep your word. I'm not going to give you up again."

"I wouldn't dare renege," he said wryly.

"I suppose you have heard the rumours about the king being deposed before Ascension Day?" Will said.

A servant replenished the cups. Hugh shook his head and looked uneasy.

"I thought you might have done with having lands in the North."

"I've been at Framlingham of late," Hugh said shortly, "and I do not listen to rumours."

Will ignored the hint not to pursue the subject. "Some religious hermit accosted the king when he was hunting rebels up past Doncaster. Told him that by Ascension Day he would no longer be sovereign of the realm."

"It is probably what the Church wishes since its revenues are going into John's coffers," Hugh said dismissively. "There are always men with strange notions in their heads."

"Yes, but this one has been spreading the word in the towns and villages, and raising so much unrest that John has had him committed to prison until Ascension Day has passed. Perhaps he knows something."

"If he does, he's more foolish than wise to spread it abroad— even for pay." For once Hugh was relieved to see Longespée join the gathering, because while he would have been glad to have John no longer king come next Ascension Day, he was not going to endanger himself or his family with foolish talk. Anyone might be listening, and the Longespée household was a loyal one.

Longespée was eager to talk about the warship John was having built for his command at Portsmouth. "It'll have capacity for a hundred and twenty fighting men as well as crew and horses," he said.

"Won't she be unwieldy and slow to manoeuvre?" Richard asked. "She'll be a cog, not a fighting ship."

"Oh, she'll not be as fast as a nef, but she'll have speed enough, and what she lacks in pace, she will make up for in strength," Longespée said confidently. "I'll be manning her with the best crossbowmen silver can buy, and she'll have fighting castles built fore and aft." He proceeded to elaborate in a loud voice with many flourishes. Hugh was irritated by such affectation, but nevertheless listened with interest, because he was familiar around ships himself and an accomplished sailor.

Ships were being built and commandeered because of the threat of invasion from France. Everyone knew King Philip was preparing an army to invade England with the intention of overthrowing John and putting Prince Louis on the throne. John was using the winter to make preparations and arm the south coast with vessels and troops to repulse that invasion with Longespée as his intended fleet commander. And, of course, Hugh thought with amused irritation, it meant Longespée had to have the best ship.

❖❖❖

Growing bored with Longespée's boasting talk, Mahelt left the men to their strakes, steerboards, and tides, and joined the women gathered round the fire, including Ida and Ela. Ela had recently been churched following the birth of her second son, Richard. The baby's hair had a coppery tinge, reminiscent of his royal grandsire. Ida kept leaning over the crib to coo at the infant and stroke his cheek. "I am blessed to have my children and my grandchildren here," she said with a smile. "God in His mercy is bountiful, and I thank Him dearly."

"I thank Him too," Ela said. In the firelight she glowed like a young Madonna. She had grown in confidence now that she had secured two sons to her marriage and fulfilled her duty. Her glance rested on Longespée with affection and pride. "I thought my husband might have to spend Christmas at court, but he has managed to escape for a short while."

"It is always difficult," Ida said a little sadly. She had accompanied Mahelt and Hugh to Salisbury, but the earl had stayed with the king. "There are so many demands made on our men and as wives we are often forgotten. Our children are our consolation—and our grandchildren."

"Their households wouldn't run without us," Mahelt said forthrightly. "Who gives the orders to the stewards and chamberlains? Who cares for the welfare of the retainers and feeds and entertains their guests? Who bears their children? We are only taken for granted if we let it happen."

Ida sighed and lifted little Roger on to her knee as he took a brief respite from his play. "I used to think like that. I used to blame myself, and think it was my fault for not being a good enough wife. Sometimes I still do because I know I do not fulfil what the earl wants of me."

Mahelt bristled. "From what I have seen, the earl doesn't—"

"Hush, hush." Ida held up her hand in warning. "I will not have you speak against him. You are young and impatient and swift to judge." Her lips set in a stubborn line. "The earl is what he is. We are both what time has wrought of us. Even if I laid the blame at his feet, what would it change? Sometimes we have no choice. A rock can only stand so long against the sea before it is rendered to sand, and in the same wise, the needs of a king and a country will always overrule the needs of a wife." She cuddled her grandson and kissed his cheek. "And to a woman, the needs of a child will always overrule the needs of a husband. That is the way of the world." She paused and took a deep breath. "In the end we all leave each other, do we not? In the end we all sleep alone."

Mahelt looked away, not wanting to receive such wisdom. Ela said to Ida with concern, "Would you like some more wine, my lady mother?"

Ida smiled and shook her head. "I think from what I have just heard myself say and from the look on your faces that I have already drunk more than I should."

Roger wriggled down off Ida's knee and dashed off again to join the men. He pressed himself against Hugh's leg and Hugh absently tousled his son's hair and set a protective arm on his narrow shoulder. Glancing across at the women, he smiled at Mahelt and drooped his right eyelid in a half-wink. Mahelt returned him a provocative look and reached for the flagon warming on the hearth. "Perhaps Ela and I haven't," she said.

The moment passed and Ida's mood lightened, but still, what she had said left its impression on Mahelt like a footprint in damp sand. That night she lay with Hugh in their curtained bed and made love to him fiercely while the winter wind rattled at the shutters. When it was over, she held him yet within her, craving the contact of their flesh as one, her ribs heaving as if she had been running for miles. Hugh tenderly pushed her hair away from her face, and then rolled over with her, curling his body around hers like a sheltering cave.

"Your mother's wrong," Mahelt said as their breathing calmed and settled into a new mutual rhythm.

"What?" he mumbled sleepily against her ear.

She didn't answer him, but gripped his hand and secured his arm against her side as if gripping a shield.

❖ ❖ ❖

In the morning when Mahelt woke, there was no sign of Hugh, but he had left a scrap of rolled parchment on the pillow, tied with a scarlet silk hair ribbon on which two lines of a poem were written in his swift, elegant hand.

Bele amie, si est de nus
Ne vus sanz mei, ne mei sanz vus.

Mahelt read the words with a tender smile. "Sweet love, so it is with us. No you without me, nor I without you." She combed her rich, dark hair, plaited it with the red ribbon, and then covered it decently with her wimple so that no one would know.

There was no sign of Hugh in the hall, but she heard the sound of masculine voices and, following them outside, found her husband, her brothers, Longespée, and a cluster of fascinated knights, soldiers, and small boys inspecting Longespée's new trebuchet. The siege machine had obviously just arrived, to judge from the attendant carter and the craftsman carpenter. The day was raw with cold but no one seemed to notice except her. Longespée wanted to set up a target to try out his new toy's range and capabilities. Ralph went running to see to it, and performed a deliberate cartwheel on the way, making everyone laugh. Little Roger was perched on Hugh's shoulders, clapping his hands with glee. Mahelt watched for a moment thoughtfully; then she turned and went back inside, but only to fetch her warmest cloak.

When she returned, chin jutting and stride determined, Hugh eyed her with quizzical amusement. "I thought you would still be warm abed," he said with a suggestive arch of his brows and a languorous edge to his voice. He tumbled Roger to the ground and the little boy whizzed off to look at the round ammunition stones that the knights were piling beside the trebuchet.

"I thought the same of you when I woke up," Mahelt retorted, "but I was wrong."

"I had to use the piss-pot, and so did Roger, and then Ralph came running like a dog with two tails to tell me the trebuchet had arrived, so I left you to sleep."

Mahelt relaxed a little. "Thank you for what you left in your stead." She lifted her veil to show him a glimpse of the ribbon binding her braid. "And the verse."

"I meant what I wrote."

"Despite abandoning me in favour of a siege machine," she jested, not quite prepared to let him off the hook. Then she nodded at the trebuchet. "What's this all about?"

Hugh's expression contorted. "Ach, you know Longespée and his need to have the newest and best of everything. He's had this commissioned for Salisbury lest the French invade, and also to give his men target practice over the slack winter period."

Mahelt cocked her head, considering. "I am told my maternal grandmother was a fine shot with one—so the stories go."

Hugh looked startled.

"It was in the war between the empress and King Stephen. My grandmother Sybilla learned before her marriage. My grandsire Marshal apparently always boasted with pride that she was capable of manning one." She extended one foot beyond the hem of her gown and examined the dainty toe of her shoe. "Supposedly she was taught in this very courtyard because she lived here as a girl. I think I should follow her example."

Hugh palmed his hand over his face. "You know what my father would say about that."

"Yes." Their eyes met and a frisson ran through Mahelt, reminding her of the illicit moments of intimacy she and Hugh had been wont to snatch from under the earl's nose in the days before they were permitted a bed.

Hugh lowered his hand and she knew that although his mouth was straight, inside he was laughing. "Then you had better join us. Christmas is a time for family tradition, after all. I bow to your grandsire's wisdom and your grandmother's skills."

"Amen." Mahelt lifted her chin. "They survived, did they not?"

Mahelt spent the rest of the morning enjoying herself outside with the trebuchet. The men got to do most of the loading and launching at the targets, for they were all big and eager and this was important business. Nevertheless, Mahelt swiftly learned the basic skills of juggling counterweight versus missile weight versus position in order to have a chance of hitting the target, in this case a large straw shield set up in the bailey. The men enjoyed showing off their knowledge to her.

Mahelt was in her element. She was happiest when active, added to which the skills attained made her feel as if she were doing something to protect herself and her family. She was entering into Hugh's world and her father's, a world from which women were mostly excluded, just as men were excluded from the bower, and she was exhilarated. By the time they finished their practice and repaired indoors to hot wine and pastries, she was glowing and happy and felt almost as satisfied as she did after making love.

Ida and Ela were sitting by the fire and Ida was holding a piece of parchment. The seal tag attached was the equestrian seal of the Earl of Norfolk. As the trebuchet party trooped to the fire to drink and warm their hands, she rose and came over to Hugh and Mahelt.

"The earl has sent news from court," she said with troubled eyes. "The king is coming to Framlingham."

Twenty-eight

STANDING IN THE DAIRY, STARING AT THE CHEESE WHEELS lined up in rows on the shelves, Mahelt seriously considered taking her mare from the stables and absconding. Bungay or Thetford or Ipswich. The nunnery at Colne. Anywhere but here. The king was due in three days' time as he made his way southwards from his campaign to set the northern shires in order. She could think of nothing worse than entertaining the man who had done so much wrong to her family and committed, in her eyes, evil beyond redemption. She had already decided she would find excuses to stay in her chamber and keep out of his way, because she could not imagine being civil to him. Each time she mentally rehearsed interacting with John, she always found herself spitting in his face before sticking a knife in him and tossing him in the mere with stones tied to his ankles. She intended keeping her sons as far away from him as possible. She did not even want him looking at her children. They would have to be present for the formal greeting in the bailey, but after that, they would be hustled out of sight.

Hugh and his father were in the park with the huntsmen marking game and checking the rides in case the king wished to hunt while he was their guest. Neither Hugh nor his father were particularly sanguine about playing host to John, but the earl had shrugged it off, saying there were some advantages. There were men in the royal entourage with whom he could talk business, and it was proof of John's trust and the earldom's stability that he chose to pay a visit. Of course it might also be interpreted as a statement that John had his eye on them and wanted to assess their defences for himself.

Ida had been struggling to prepare for the visit. She was overwhelmed by the responsibility. Never before had royalty come to Framlingham. Once she would have coped with fortitude, but age and uncertain health had taken their toll. She wasn't sure where everything was, except for the textiles, of which she knew the location of every hanging, every bolster, and embroidered cloth. She worried and twittered about having the right sort of curtains in the guest chamber and agonised over whether the red cushions or the green should be used and if the king's bed should have two or three mattresses. Mahelt was anxious too. Even while hating John, she knew this was a grand occasion and it was necessary to make a good impression, but Ida was obviously not herself.

"Which cheeses?" Mahelt asked her now. "Those on the top? They've been there the longest, so they'll have the strongest flavour."

Ida nodded. "They'll need to be checked for weevils though…I don't know how much the king and his household will eat. And what about the butter? What if there aren't enough crocks…" She put a hand to her forehead and Mahelt noticed that she was shivering. It was always cold in the dairy. In the winter the dairy maids had permanently red noses and blue, chapped hands, even when they wore fingerless mittens. Ida was better outfitted for cold than the servants, for she was wearing a fur-lined gown and a hood over her wimple, but in the pallid February daylight, she looked peaky and drained.

"Go to your chamber, Mother," Mahelt said, touching her shoulder. "I shall see to the cheeses. We can always bring in more from the manor at Acle, and butter too if needs must. They always have a surplus and there's time."

Ida shook her head. "I cannot let you do all this yourself. There's still the wine to inspect." She straightened up. "Let me…let me check on that furthest cheese."

Mahelt summoned a servant to fetch a stool and bring down the required wheel. Mahelt released it from its paste and linen binding and looked at the crumbly honey-gold result of what had been laid down in the late summer from cows grazed on the lush water meadows around the mere. Unsheathing her belt knife, she cut a sliver from the side. Not too small, because where was the point in having just one mouthful of something so delicious? "No weevils," she said, giving a nugget to Ida, and then, because she was feeling very generous, the servant.

Rich flavours of salt, cream, and summer greenery embraced her palate and she gave a pleasurable moan. "Far too fine for the court," she said. "Let's give the king one of the others."

Ida stared at the morsel of cheese between her forefinger and thumb. She swallowed convulsively and compressed her lips.

Mahelt licked her fingers. "Mother?"

Ida made a mewling sound and dashed out of the dairy; doubling over, she was violently sick.

Mahelt stared at her in shock, and then whirled round to the servant. "Put that cheese away and fetch help!" she commanded. "The countess is unwell." She stooped to Ida and put her arm around her shoulders. Ida's hands were icy, but her forehead was like a brazier.

"I'm all right," Ida gasped between retches. "It will pass."

Mahelt said nothing because her mother-in-law was patently not all right. People came running and Mahelt overrode Ida's gagging protests and had her borne to her chamber. Ida wasn't in time to reach the privy as her bowels voided themselves. She had to be stripped and washed, all the time shuddering as if her entire body was disintegrating.

"I'm sorry," she wept wretchedly as she was helped into bed. "I'll be all right in a while and as soon as I can, I'll help. I—" She was taken with another fit of retching and her maid hastily held a bronze bowl under her chin.

"Yes, Mother, of course you will," Mahelt agreed, although to look at Ida, she doubted that "soon" was likely. "Just rest here awhile and I shall attend to matters until you are well enough."

As the spasm subsided, Ida flopped back against the bolster and sent Mahelt a look compounded of gratitude and guilt. "Thank you. I do not mean to be a burden."

"You are not." Mahelt gave Ida's hand a brief, hard squeeze. "Never think that." Leaving the room, Mahelt's perspective shifted. She had been deeply resenting John's imminent arrival and had been caught up in her own antipathy, but things had changed. She would not prepare Framlingham for John because he was not worth it. But she would prepare it to honour Ida. As this thought took root, it gave her strength. She felt her confidence growing: she could fulfil the role of chatelaine, and do it justice, as befitted her upbringing and her position.

❖ ❖ ❖

Ida's condition worsened and by the following day she had a raging fever and was out of her wits, babbling about events in the past that only she could see. Taking her turn at the sickbed, Mahelt was a witness to the unhealing grief in Ida's soul caused by having to give up her baby son when she left court to marry Roger of Norfolk. "Please, please don't do this, sire, give him to me!" Ida wept, beside herself, her eyes fogged and murky. "I beg you. I shall die!"

Mahelt laid a soothing hand on Ida's brow. "Hush, it's all

right." She swallowed a tight lump in her throat. "He is a fine grown man with children of his own—your grandsons."

"But my baby is lost..." Ida struggled to sit up. "I have to see the king. I have to take William with me; I'm his mother!"

Mahelt murmured gentle words over and over in a shushing tide. "Don't worry. He's coming to you; all will be well, all will be well."

Ida fell weakly back against the pillows and closed her eyes. Tears leached from under her lids. Moments later she began to speak instead of a loving moment she imagined she was sharing with her husband—sitting in his lap, feeding him morsels of toasted bread. Mahelt couldn't envisage Ida and the earl in such an intimate scene. It was the kind of thing that she and Hugh would do and that her father-in-law would frown upon if he saw them. Her own eyes stung with grief.

Hugh put his head round the door. "How is she?"

Mahelt shook her head. "She has a high fever and is rambling. The physician has bled her and says to moisten her lips with honey and water and let her sleep. Father Richard is saying prayers for her and has asked for the intercession of Saint Adelard."

Hugh came to the bedside. "We take her too much for granted," he said, looking at his mother with concern. He stooped and gently pushed back the grey frizz at Ida's temples. "When I was little, her hair was dark and shiny and scented with nutmeg," he said. "I remember playing with her braids when she held me on her knee."

Ida turned her head towards him and licked her dry lips. "My love," she croaked, "my dear, dear love."

"Your father should be here," Mahelt said crossly.

Hugh looked uncomfortable. "He has been busy holding all together."

"He has been busy avoiding her," Mahelt retorted. "He

expects us to run the household and see to matters and not disturb him. Your mother is his wife, not a chair or a table existing for his convenience."

Hugh looked appalled. "He doesn't feel like that. Indeed, he does not!"

"Then where is he? I have not seen him in here beyond a passing glance, and your mother is very sick indeed."

Hugh went very still. "Is she...Will she...?" He left out the portentous word as if by not saying it he could fend off its shadow.

"I do not know." Tears pricked Mahelt's eyes. "She is like canvas that can withstand the rigours of the weather, but will rot if stored away and neglected. I will do what I can for her; she is a second mother to me."

"I'll speak with my father."

She cast him an angry look. "You should not have to. He should be here of his own accord."

"Perhaps he thinks she is in good hands and does not realise how sick she is."

"That is what I mean; he has not noticed." Mahelt wasn't just indignant for Ida; she was afraid of what the future might hold for herself and Hugh. *Ne vus sanz mei, ne mei sanz vus.* What if it wasn't true?

"I am not so sure. It is just that he has a different way of dealing with matters." He sat down on the coffer at the bedside. "I will stay with her awhile if you have things to attend to."

Mahelt hesitated, but there was indeed still far too much to arrange for the king's arrival—because it wasn't only the king, it was his full entourage and everyone would have to be found sleeping places suitable to their rank. She stood up and pointed to the bowl and spoon by the bedside. "Moisten her lips with honey and water and call the women if you have need."

Hugh looked slightly pained. "I think I can manage," he said.

Mahelt kissed the top of his head and departed to her business, the first item being a word with her father-in-law, whatever his manner of dealing with matters was. She found him in his chamber, busy with his constable, William Lenveise, discussing matters pertaining to the security of the castle. He broke off to look at her, his expression one of impatient enquiry.

"The countess has been asking for you, my lord father," Mahelt said, curtseying and adopting a modest demeanour, although she felt like stamping her feet.

The earl waved a dismissive hand. "I have matters more pressing than attending a sickbed just now."

Mahelt kept her voice at a reasonable pitch. "I know you are busy, sire, but surely you could spare a minute before or after dinner. The countess would be much cheered to see you."

He gave her a warning look from weathered sea-grey eyes. "Do you tell me my business, daughter?"

Mahelt dug her fingernails into her palms. "No, Father. I came to you without expectation."

He fiddled with the brim of his hat and drew it down over his brows. "I doubt she will know me if she is raving with fever."

"She will feel your presence, sire, and I think she knows you very well."

He gave a grunt. "I shall see," he said, "but I make no promises."

Mahelt curtseyed and went on her way. She had done what she could; the rest was upon his conscience. She would have been angry with him for his indifference, save that just for a moment she had glimpsed something unutterably sad and lost in his gaze before he drew his hat brim low and turned back to his business.

❖ ❖ ❖

Roger hesitated outside his wife's chamber. Damn the girl, damn her. He had better things to do than visit a sickroom.

He had been placating his conscience by ensuring Ida had the best nursing care from her women, the best treatment from a renowned physician, and the spiritual comfort of their chaplain. Keeping an eye on her welfare from a distance meant he did not have to burden himself with worrying about her on top of everything else. But now Mahelt had pricked him through the barriers he had built up. "I do not have the time," he muttered to himself, and realised that these words had dogged his marriage down more than thirty years.

Drawing a deep breath, he opened the door. Hugh looked up at him from the bedside.

"That troublesome wife of yours said your mother was asking for me," Roger growled like an accusation as he reluctantly approached Ida's supine form.

"I was going to tell you, but obviously Mahelt reached you first," Hugh said with a rueful look. "Mother is sleeping now and she seems a little cooler than she was."

"What did she want of me?"

Hugh gave his father a steady stare. "Just you," he said.

Roger sat on a stool opposite Hugh and, for the first time in several days, really looked at his wife. The fight with fever had stripped her face of flesh and it was like staring at a delicate bird skeleton lying there against the bolsters. Once she had been a bright little robin, busy with all of her babies, nurturing and caring for them. Now she was as fragile as last year's bones in an empty nest. And her mate? Her mate no longer existed because he had not remained a robin, but become an eagle. He steeled himself to take her hand in his and felt how thin and frail it was. Like a claw. She stirred and a frown crossed her brow.

"I am here," he said. "You have me."

Her eyes remained closed, but she squeezed his hand and whispered his name. In a while her breathing deepened and she slipped into her first proper sleep since falling ill. He watched the light rise and fall of the covers, then he carefully withdrew his hand from beneath hers. "I will come and see you again," he said. "When you are awake."

He left the room, forcing himself to maintain a measured tread when all he wanted to do was flee. Once outside, he leaned against the wall, his eyes closed and his breathing ragged. Hugh followed him out and touched his arm. "Sire?"

"I did not know she was so sick," Roger said numbly. "She has often been ill in the past when a crisis strikes and I thought some of her ailment was crying wolf...you know how she can be."

Hugh nodded because he did, but he knew too that this time it was more than a fit of the vapours. "Mahelt says she is a little improved."

Roger grimaced. "I shall pray for her and have prayers said in vigil." He turned towards the stairs, each step away from the chamber a small relief, but also filled with guilt. "She will not be well enough to greet the king," he said to Hugh, who was following on his heels. "That much is obvious, even if she does improve over the next two days." He removed his hat and ran his hand around the felted brim. "Is your wife capable of all that is required? I need to know that I can rely on her."

Hugh drew himself up. "She will not let you down," he said. "I know she will not."

His father frowned. "She is of Marshal stock, ordering and organising are in her blood; but she is unpredictable, and I do not want any untoward behaviour while the king is here. He will be looking for anything that he might consider insurrection."

"She knows what is at stake," Hugh said. "Just as much as we do."

Roger gave his son a dark look. "Let us hope she does," he said.

❖ ❖ ❖

By the time John's arrival drew nigh, Ida was beginning to recover. She was as weak as a kitten but her fever had abated and she was able to sit up and take light nourishment. Mahelt visited her soon after dawn on the day the king was due and watched her drink a cup of buttermilk and eat a small piece of soft white bread. A warm shawl of fringed green silk was tucked around her shoulders over her chemise and her combed and braided hair lay in a neat, thin plait on her breast.

"I am sorry," Ida said. "It was my place to do all that has been laid upon you. It should be my burden."

"You have nothing to be sorry for," Mahelt replied stoutly. "Sickness strikes where it will. You are in the best place here. I have managed all that has been asked and I can fend for myself."

"You are a good daughter to me"—Ida gave a tired smile—"even if you are sometimes hard to hold. But your spirit is one of your best qualities." She reached her free hand and took Mahelt's. "I am proud of you and what you are becoming... what you will become, even if I am not here to see it."

Her throat tight, Mahelt leaned to kiss Ida's temple. "You will see it," she said fiercely.

"Ah, well, that is as God will decide." Ida sipped the buttermilk and watched the maids build up the fire and open the shutters to let the weak winter light filter in through the thick window glass. "The earl is fond of you too, you know," she said. "In his own way."

Mahelt smoothed the bolster under her hand and diplomatically said nothing. She didn't think "fond" was the right word. They tolerated each other. She knew he had been to visit his wife after her prompting, because Hugh had told her, but the earl himself had not spoken of it, and since then had kept his distance even more than usual. If there were any warm feelings at all between them, then they were bound up in the children; in the fact that she had borne two healthy, bright little boys to guarantee the earldom's future. It was only with them that she saw his softer side. He would sit his namesake grandson in his lap and patiently teach him to tie a particular kind of knot, or show him how to feed a treat to a horse with his palm flat so that his small fingers wouldn't be nipped. Her sons were where they met on common ground. But Hugh was a battlefield, as were their different notions of what constituted moral and appropriate behaviour.

Mahelt rose to her feet. "I should go and change my gown," she said, making a face. Before leaving, she fetched Ida's sewing basket to the bed and plumped up the bolsters and pillows.

Ida delved in the basket and brought out the small pair of socks on which she had been working before she took ill. Fashioned in two shades of green silk, they were intended for her youngest grandson and the task did not take much concentration, being just a repetition of loops with needle and thick thread. "Good fortune, my daughter," she said. "And keep your wits about you."

"Oh, my wits are going to stick closer than my shadow today, I promise you," Mahelt replied with steely resolution. "He won't get the better of me."

As she left Ida to her sewing in her warm, light chamber, Mahelt felt the weight of responsibility drop on to her shoulders like a lead cope. She was both Bigod and Marshal and had the reputations of the two families to uphold. It didn't prevent her from imagining putting poison in John's dinner. To have him enter here and not leave. To rid everyone of this tyrant. She had to make a concerted mental effort to push such notions to one side and focus instead on being the perfect hostess to a man she loathed.

Her best gown was of a ruby silk damask that enhanced the lithe lines of her body whilst still being demure. She didn't favour the low necks of the French court, and great dangling sleeves just got in the way, so hers were a modest length, and trimmed without fuss in a contrasting shade of rich blue entwined with garnet beads and gold thread.

"The colour won't show blood," Mahelt said to Hugh only half in jest as she smoothed the dress over her body and turned to him. As Ida's proxy, she was wearing the jewelled coronet of the Countess of Norfolk, and she could almost feel the power flowing down through her body from the filigreed goldwork and sapphires.

Hugh snorted and shook his head. "He won't tarry beyond a night unless we have heavy snow. Just pray the weather holds good for travelling." He glanced towards the open shutters where the sky showed plenty of blue between grubby fleeces of cloud.

Mahelt tried to bite her tongue but there was too much pressure. "I know it is our duty to play host, and that there are important matters to discuss. I know we should consider ourselves honoured, but he will pick fault with everything, and I cannot bear to think of him running his eyes over our possessions, judging how much we have and what he can seize— assessing our defences too and imagining how he could take us. I don't want him here looking at us—looking at our boys."

"I don't want him here either, but it is a necessary evil—a matter of policy," Hugh replied, his blue eyes quenched with shadows. He pulled her into his embrace and kissed her. "Don't worry. I intend to keep our children well away from his sight and out of his mind. He'll be gone soon." He touched the coronet with his fingertips. "You look magnificent."

"I need to," she replied darkly.

❖ ❖ ❖

Standing on the wall walk overlooking the mere, Mahelt watched the royal cavalcade approach the barbican. Banners flapped in the bitter winter wind as the horses, two by two, jingled along the path. Spears pointed at the sky and silver sparks glanced off their tips. John's mercenaries glittered in their mail shirts and scarlet surcoats. Mahelt breathed deeply and tried not to think how much this parade looked like an invading army rather than a visit by guests seeking hospitality on the road. She imagined how her parents would deal with the situation; she envisaged the calm expression on her father's face and made an effort to compose the same look on her own. She must don a mask and conceal herself behind a gracious façade.

The gates heaved open to admit the troop: the heralds first, in red and gold livery, blowing a fanfare on trumpets and horns. Then came an escort of household knights, again in the royal red and gold, with John well protected on all sides, and behind, a long train of mounted troops like a fat silver snake. Mahelt knelt in the courtyard with the rest of the Bigod household and bent her head. Her mouth was so dry, she could not have spat in John's face had she tried. She concentrated on the feel of the bailey floor under her knee, the sensation of individual bits of grit, and thought that each moment that elapsed was a moment closer to John leaving.

John greeted the earl with the kiss of peace, then Hugh. Mahelt was next and, as he raised her to her feet, she steeled herself for the feel of his lips against her skin. It was closer than she had ever wanted to get to him. She half expected him to use his tongue in the deed, but he didn't. His eyes were filled with mocking amusement, as if he could read her thoughts. Mahelt was determined not to let him invade that particular sanctuary and solidified her expression until her smile was of stone.

"So you send out your young beauty to make the greeting." John addressed Earl Roger with raised brows and a smile.

"The countess is unwell, sire," the earl replied, "but my

daughter-in-law has made all ready and will do everything that is fitting to make you comfortable at Framlingham."

"I am sorry to hear the countess is ill," John said. "I have always enjoyed her company." His voice was a smooth glide that could either be taken for courtliness or a very slick insult. "She is not too sick, I hope."

"Confined to her chamber, but recovering, sire."

"Then I shall keep her in my prayers and hope she is soon well."

Longespée, who was among the royal party, kissed Mahelt and as they walked towards the domestic lodgings said anxiously, "What is wrong with my mother?"

"Sickness and a high fever, but she is improving. She will want to see you."

Mahelt escorted John to the prepared guest chamber and showed his body servants where to stow his baggage. Although she knew everything was in order, she checked again that her own servants had done their jobs. There were sweet-smelling candles of beeswax in the sconces with bundles to spare in a wall cupboard, and clean olive oil burned in the hanging lamps. She had put Ida's costly tapis rug across the back of the settle. Luxuriant fleeces from some of her own sheep covered a couple of stools and were placed either side of the bed. There was a chessboard and pieces by the window together with a harp, a lute, and a psaltery should the king feel inclined to music. A flagon and matching cups stood on a small, napery-clad trestle. There were also several books for the king to read.

John picked up one of the latter and unfastened the clasp to flick through the pages. "*Ars Tactica*," he said. "It's a pity your father doesn't read. He would enjoy this and learn a lot."

Mahelt dug her fingernails into her palms, smiled sweetly, and thought about escape. "Would you like to rest awhile, sire?"

John glanced towards the bed. "That depends on the company." He looked her slowly up and down, as if his stare was a hand with busy fingers. Mahelt swallowed her gorge, relieved that she wasn't alone with him. Servants were carrying items of baggage into the chamber and various household officials were in the room. A mercenary gave her a sly smirk from the corner of his eyes. Hugh was talking to one of John's chamberlains just outside the door. She could hear his voice and see the edge of his tunic and folded arm. "If you will excuse me, I have matters to attend to."

"Oh, don't go," John entreated with a glint in his eyes. "I have never spoken with the daughter of William Marshal before. His sons, often, but not his eldest girl. Stay and entertain me awhile…" He ran his tongue around the inside of his mouth. "You have your father's eyes, but your mother's way of looking—did you know that? A fair and beautiful woman, your mother."

"Sire, by your leave, with the countess so ill, I have many extra duties. I crave your indulgence." Her words emerged as a polite monotone and she felt them grate in the saying. How did her father manage to be civil to this man? She wanted to pick up the flagon and tip it over his head.

John's gaze was vulpine. "My indulgence…" he mused, stroking his dark and silver beard. "Very well then, I grant it. I like pleasing women, and they are keen to please me when they realise the rewards that may be reaped. We shall speak later."

Mahelt curtseyed, thinking the only thing she was keen to do to John was tackle him with a gelding knife. Making a swift exit, she flashed Hugh a furious look as she swept from the chamber, then compressed her lips because what could she say? John's words had been suggestive, but he could easily claim she had misconstrued them, or that he had been teasing. If she made a fuss, there would be repercussions for herself and both her families. What she had to do was ensure she was never alone with him and not give him a single opportunity to play his game of cat and mouse to its conclusion.

She marched into the kitchens, which were bustling with mad activity as the cooks and their assistants toiled to prepare a feast fit for a king—difficult at this time of year with so little fresh food and everything in short supply. Over the last weeks by ingenuity, force of will, and formidable organisation, Mahelt had succeeded in planning food and entertainment that would not disgrace the name of Bigod and Marshal, but just now she did not care if all John received was burned horse bread and sour ale. After a single cursory glance at the bubbling cauldrons of spicy beef stew, she stalked from the kitchens and headed for the musty darkness of the undercroft in order to have some peace for a moment and draw herself together.

Sitting on a barrel, swinging her legs and drinking mead straight from the costrel, she remembered Hugh hiding in here a few months ago, telling her about the hanging of the hostages. She thought about Maude de Braose and her son. She thought about Arthur of Brittany. She thought about her brothers. "Rewards, indeed!" she spat, and swore she would not allow herself or her family to become victims of this man. After a final swallow of the mead, she forced the bung back into the hole. She had to keep her wits about her until John had departed. She stood up, smoothed her gown, adjusted the coronet, drawing strength from its symbolic power, and left the sanctuary of the undercroft for the dangers of the open castle.

❖❖❖

The feast Mahelt had prepared occupied most of the short winter afternoon and continued into dusk and evening. As the hostess and in Ida's absence, she had to endure sitting at John's side and behave as if he were a thoroughly welcome guest. She pretended she was her mother and sent the real Mahelt away to the secret dark peace of the undercroft and a nice fat costrel of mead. Her smiles were gracious; she made polite conversation and acted with decorum and courtesy, behaviour which both acknowledged John and kept him at a distance. She watched time burn down the wicks of the numerous candles blazing in candelabra and sconce, and told herself that soon he would be gone from here—please God—and life could resume its usual course.

John set out to be a charming, affable guest. He talked horses and hunting with the earl and Hugh, and cheerfully argued points of law with them. He was suave and urbane and well mannered. He praised Mahelt for the delicious beef and cumin dish her cooks had prepared and said that she should tell his own cook how it was made.

Sipping spiced morap wine at the end of the meal, John leaned back to give himself stomach room and smiled at Mahelt like a well-fed cat. "I am sure you are pleased, Lady Bigod, that your father is returning to England in the spring as soon as the weather permits a sea crossing."

"It is good news indeed, sire." Mahelt's heart quickened; she sensed danger. If John was being pleasant, there was bound to be an ulterior motive. "I shall be glad to see my family again, and my new brother and sister."

"Indeed, your parents have been well blessed with offspring," John said. "Let me see, there must be ten of you now. God grant I am as vigorous when I reach your father's mature years, even if my wife might not appreciate such energy." There was the hint of a smirk in his tone; he'd said nothing that could be pinned down as an insult, but nevertheless managed to conjure an image of her father as an old goat. "You come from strong stock, my lady."

"I am proud to do so, sire."

"I value the counsel and the support of my Marshal and Bigod vassals—especially when they are so easy on the eye. Your good health, Lady Bigod." He toasted her; then he returned his attention to her father-in-law. Mahelt put down the cup with which she had answered him, her wine untouched.

The king's mercenaries and household knights were swilling their fill of Framlingham's wine, and the noise levels rose as the drink sank in the barrels. As small savouries, tarts, and spices were served to finish the meal, several vassals and knights clamoured to be entertained by Roland le Pettour. The latter held his lands of the Bigods by dint of his ability to fart tunes through his braies, perform acrobatics, and tell scurrilous and risqué stories involving nuns, monks, and indefatigable privy members of stupendous proportions. Men in their cups generally found him hilarious. Sometimes women did too, but Mahelt had witnessed his performances on several occasions and tonight she was not disposed to laughter. Before he could commence his opening barrage of notes, Mahelt begged leave to withdraw and make sure her mother-in-law was comfortable and well attended.

John was amused. "You do not stay to listen to music and poetry?" he said.

"Sire, I leave such entertainments to more discerning tastes," Mahelt replied, and made her escape.

❖ ❖ ❖

When she arrived at Ida's chamber door, Longespée was just taking his leave, leaning over the bed to kiss his mother's cheek.

"It has been so good to see you, my son." Ida's voice was animated and her eyes were bright. "I am glad God has given me the opportunity."

"Just rest and get better," Longespée said.

"I am doing my best. I want to see your fame grow. My blessings to Ela and the children. Kiss them for me."

Longespée said that he would and made way for Mahelt. "Sister," he said in acknowledgement.

She inclined her head. "If you go to the hall now, you will be just in time for Roland le Pettour's repertoire."

Longespée rubbed the back of his neck. "Ah, it's reached that stage, has it?"

"Unfortunately so."

He heaved a sigh, hitched his belt, and, grimacing, left the room.

Ida gave Mahelt a guilty look as she readjusted her shawl. "Has it been so terrible playing host to the king?"

"It is true I would rather beat myself with thistles." Mahelt screwed up her face and, removing the coronet, wrapped it in its silk cloths and placed it reverently in its coffer. "But I have managed to be civil thus far—we all have. She sat down on the coverlet. I'll be glad to see the tail of his horse tomorrow though." She did not add that she was afraid of the way John kept looking round the chamber as if assessing and tallying all they owned. She had hidden the children from him, but still she did not feel safe.

Ida looked sad. "John always resented those who came between him and his sire. His father loved him dearly, but it was never enough for him. When the need is so great, no matter how much love you pour into a bowl, it will never be full. Or sometimes it is damaged, and the love all runs out through the hole in the bottom. I…" She stopped and her eyes were suddenly swimming with tears. "Ah, I am a foolish old woman."

"No, Mother, you're not!" Mahelt declared vehemently. "I wish I could pour out love as generously as you do."

Ida blew her nose and laughed. "It is kind of you to say so, but you flatter me too much." She blinked hard and sniffed. "My son tells me his ship will be finished by the end of the month and that he is to lead a campaign in Poitou this summer. He is one of the king's most trusted advisers." Pride shone in her eyes and Mahelt thought that in a way it was a blessing Ida was so ill. If John had always disliked anyone coming between him and his father, he must have resented Ida when she was at court, and probably still did because of her emotional bond with Longespée.

Mahelt stayed with Ida a while longer, then set off to retire to her own chamber across the ward. Descending the outer stairs from Ida's room, she drew her fur-lined mantle more closely around her body and shivered. The sky was filled with ragged clouds patched with stars and she felt the light, cold spatter of sleet against her face.

"Ah, Lady Bigod, well met."

She almost leaped out of her skin and stifled a scream as John appeared soft-footed out of the darkness from the direction of the latrine.

"Sire." She curtseyed and straightened, thinking that this was not well met at all. From the direction of the hall she could hear roars of merriment and the sound of cups thumping on trestles. She prayed that someone else would come to use the privy.

"How is the countess?"

"She is a little improved, sire. If you will excuse me..."

John tilted his head to one side. "No, Lady Bigod, I will not. Every time I try to talk with you, you find a convenient reason to rush off, and you interest me far more than a man farting 'Sing Cuckoo' through his arsehole."

"Sire, it is cold..."

"Indeed, but we have warm cloaks, and there are other ways and means of generating heat."

Shock blazed through her and she felt the façade she had built beginning to crumble. "Sire, by all means let us talk, but come within to the hall."

"I would rather talk to William Marshal's daughter alone," John said, lowering his voice and stroking the edge of her cloak. "Without distractions."

"Sire, you ask something that is improper and inappropriate."

John gave a soft chuckle. "'Improper'?" he mimicked. "Come now, you are hardly a shrinking flower or an unknowing virgin, are you, girl? And from what I have heard, propriety has not always concerned you."

Mahelt wasn't sure if it was the way he called her "girl," or the fact that he obviously had spies in the Bigod household, and even her father's, but suddenly she was on fire with rage. "I am an honourable and faithful wife to my husband," she said through clenched teeth. "People will be wondering where you are. For the king to go missing in these uncertain times must surely be a matter for concern."

"I dare say they'll search for me by and by, but we have a little leeway, and surely I have nothing to fear in so loyal a household. Let us talk a little about honour and faith, shall we?" In a sudden swift move, he pushed her against the wall, crushing her spine against the stones. He pinned her with his body, groin to groin. "What would you give to see your husband and sons kept safe, my lady? What would you pay? How highly do you value your honour?"

Mahelt struggled. "More highly than you can afford to despoil it!" she spat. John's face was in hers. She could smell wine on his breath and feel that breath invading her mouth as she was forced to draw it into her own lungs.

"Is that so?"

"You need my father. You need Norfolk!"

"Do you think they'd turn traitor for the word of a chit?" John hissed. "A silly spoiled girl? What do you think would happen? How much you think you are worth and your true value are different matters!"

Mahelt gasped in outrage. However, he was right about one thing. She was indeed no shrinking flower or unknowing virgin. Having grown up with brothers, and from Hugh's occasional trepidation in the bedchamber when she was being intimately playful, she knew how sensitive men were when it came to their cods. She went limp, allowing John to think she had yielded, pushed her hand down between them, grabbed his genitals and twisted as if wringing a cloth one-handed.

The reaction was gratifying and instantaneous as John doubled over with a strangled sound of agony. Mahelt heaved him off and fled, but not to her chamber. That was her sanctum and where her children were. She would not lead him to them. Instead she made for the safety of numbers. Towards light and noise and affable bonhomie.

Now came the greatest test of her control and courage. She had to act as if she had just come from Ida's bedside and nothing had happened. If she made an outcry here and now there would be no going back. And what if John were right? What if she was dismissed as a chit? What if she discovered that her value was indeed that of a "spoiled girl" and not a future countess? Yet if they took the opposite view, what could they do? John's mercenaries were here inside their walls, and they were outnumbered.

Roland le Pettour was still capering about breaking musical wind and everyone was roaring at his antics. He was juggling apples and every now and again raising one leg and throwing an apple under it in time to a loud report. Mahelt took her place at Hugh's side and signalled a squire to pour a cup of mead. She rinsed her mouth, filling it with the taste of honey. Her hands were shaking and as she set the cup down, she tipped it over. A squire moved swiftly to blot the liquid on his dapifer's towel.

She had thought Hugh thoroughly engrossed in the entertainment, but he turned to her, immediately alert and sober. "What's wrong?"

Mahelt shook her head. "Nothing," she said in a tight voice. "I wasn't looking properly."

He set his hand over hers. "You are shaking."

Her lips barely moved: "It was cold in the privy." She swept her gaze around the hall. Although men were still laughing at Roland's antics, restive glances were being cast towards the king's empty place. Two of John's household knights left the gathering and went outside. Longespée followed.

The squire refilled her cup and Mahelt drank. Her neck and jaw were so tense that a headache had begun to rage at her temples.

Moments later, Longespée returned to his place at the high table, and the household knights to their seats at a lower trestle. "The king has retired," Longespée announced to those on the dais. "He intends to leave at first light and desires to be fresh for the journey."

Mahelt exhaled on a sigh of relief because it looked as if the matter was going to blow over. She silently hoped that John was going to lie in agony all night.

She heard her father-in-law saying he bade the king good rest but expressing surprise because he had been under the impression that John had only gone to the latrine.

Longespée shrugged. "The king is feeling the strain of long days in the saddle and does not wish to be disturbed until the morning."

Mahelt finished her mead and excused herself. Hugh immediately rose to attend her, and although she would have preferred her own company, she was grateful of his presence across the ward from one dwelling to the other.

As they reached the foot of the steps leading to their solar and bedchamber, he took her arm and drew her round to him. "I know something happened between you and the king," he said. "I am not a fool."

"Then do not act like one," she hissed. "The king is saddle-weary. Leave it at that."

"If he has despoiled you—"

"Hah! Do you think he would have retired if he had?" Yanking away from him, she started up the stairs. "He made an offer I declined to accept."

"What sort of offer?"

Mahelt swallowed her impatience. "Oh, in Christ's name, Hugh, what do you think!" She flung open the door and entered their chamber. The warmth from the fire and the comfortable surroundings enveloped her in welcome familiarity. Roger sat on his nurse's knee listening to an adventure story about a knight and his magnificent white horse but when he saw his parents, he scrambled off the woman's lap and ran to them. Mahelt swept him up in her arms and absorbed the wholesome smell of him: fire-warmed linen and rose water and sleep-ready child. Her voice trembled with revulsion and fury. "He thought that I would yield and keep quiet, because of my honour and yours, but he does not know me." She looked at Hugh. "A man who does such things to prove he has power over women is a weak reed indeed."

Roger held out his arms and swapped parents, wrapping himself around Hugh and clinging like a limpet.

"He does it to prove his power over men. To prove he can take what he wants," Hugh said grimly.

"Then he hasn't succeeded in proving anything tonight—for his pains. He will harbour a grudge because of my refusal, but that is nothing new. My family has lived with his grudges for almost ten years."

"Grudges cut both ways." Hugh's eyes were dark with anger and disgust.

Mahelt gazed at his hands holding their son, the span of his fingers against the small body, the tenderness and strength. And then she thought of John's grip on her, forcing her against the wall. Would her son's hands cup life and revere it, or would they spill and rip and tear?

"He must be stopped," Hugh said.

A frisson ran through her as she imagined John dead in his bed with a sword through his breast. Dead at Framlingham. She began to shiver at the enormity of the vision. "Hugh?" Her voice was a mere breath.

A shudder ran through him too and he took a step backwards and shook his head. "It must be done in clean daylight, not in a dark corner with a bloody knife, otherwise there is no difference between us and him. It must be embraced by all, not just the few. He has to be bound by the law and that law has to be enforced by all."

Going to the fire, Mahelt sat down and extended her hands to the warmth. She sought the heat, trying to dissolve the cold lump at her core. "It is easy to say these things," she said, "but how will it be accomplished?"

Hugh returned Roger to his nurse and joined Mahelt at the fire, setting his arm around her shoulders and drawing her close. "The barons and the bishops need to come together and decide upon what must change, and then make it law," he said.

Mahelt gazed into the flames. "In the spring, the French may invade," she said softly so that her voice did not carry beyond the curve of the firelight. "What of the prophecy that John will no longer be king by Ascension Day?" It felt good to say the words, to speculate and imagine a time without John's presence brooding over their lives.

"If the French do come, we must decide what to do. Louis of France does not have John's vices and we may find it no hardship to accept his rule, but he will be looking to promote his own men. Not everyone will desert the king. Your father will not for a certainty, and neither will Longespée. Many others will not kneel to a Frenchman in the pay of Rome, but it does also mean that those who stand loyal for John will have more leverage on him."

"Longer spoons than before, you mean," she said.

Hugh conceded the point with an uncomfortable shrug. "There is a deal of thinking as well as talking to be done and it will depend upon the will of all and not just the word of a single mad soothsayer."

Mahelt sighed and leaned her head on his shoulder. In the warmth, the bruises where John had grabbed her were beginning to throb in poisoned reminder. Tomorrow he would be gone, although, like a snail, his trail would linger behind him. She suddenly felt exhausted and tears were not far away, although she refused to give in to them. "The tale of tonight's happening must not go beyond these chamber walls. Neither to your father, nor to mine, and especially not to Will—for his sake, not the king's."

"It won't." Hugh kissed her temple. His voice hardened. "But even if the matter goes unspoken, it will not go forgotten. If the will of all is to be known and directed, then more than the sword, those who desire change will need a lawyer's pen and a lawyer's mind."

❖ ❖ ❖

Longespée stood in his mother's chamber and prepared to make his farewells. The dawn had opened a narrow crack of oyster-shell gold on the horizon and he had a few moments of free time while the servants finished harnessing the horses and securing the baggage. The king had broken his fast in his chamber and was in a sour mood and some pain. A strained muscle in his groin, he said, caused when dismounting from his horse the previous day. Longespée suspected there had been some kind of altercation last night between the king and one of the women of the household—probably Mahelt—but had chosen not to delve. It was easier to turn a blind eye. Mahelt was present in Ida's chamber but tight-lipped and silent. Hugh was in a similar mood and it was plain to Longespée that welcomes had been outstayed—if there had ever been welcomes in the first place.

His mother had risen from her bed to bid the royal party Godspeed and she seemed improved upon yesterday. She was swathed in furs to ward off the cold and because she had been standing near the fire there was a flush of colour in her cheeks. She was insisting on personally offering the king the stirrup cup to send him on his way and, to that end, wine and herbs were steaming in a cauldron ready to be ladled out at the last minute.

The children were unaffected by the strain in the atmosphere. His oldest Bigod nephew flew around the room brandishing his toy sword, darting between the adults, and fighting imaginary enemies with gusto. Longespée chuckled to see him because it reminded him there was still innocence in the world and joy in small things. The lad's baby brother was just about a year old and had very recently begun walking. The infant had a mop of golden curls, scarlet cheeks, and vivid sea-blue eyes. It was wearing a beautifully embroidered white smock and all it needed was a set of fluffy little wings to complete the angelic resemblance. Charmed, Longespée squatted down to be on a level with the baby. "Come, little Bigod," he said, holding out his arms. "Come to Uncle FitzHenry."

The baby giggled at him, revealing two perfect rows of milk teeth. Longespée was fascinated. He had never really engaged with a child of this tender age before. Long absences from home had left gaps in witnessing his own son's development, and the times he did see him, it was always in the arms of his wife or a nurse, and he wouldn't have felt manly holding an infant so small.

He gave this one a poke with his forefinger. The baby plopped down on its bottom with such a look of surprise in its big, round eyes that Longespée chuckled. "Let's test your mettle, little Bigod, eh?"

The child put out its chubby hands and laboriously regained its feet, almost tripping on the hem of its smock. Longespée grinned and poked it a second time. Amused and fascinated, he watched it plump down and once more struggle to a standing position. Somewhere inside him, buried so deeply he did not even acknowledge it existed, there was a sense of a hunter with its prey. This was a pup from his own pack, but a lesser member, and it should know its place, or at the very least show that it was strong enough to fight for a higher one. The infant certainly proved tenacious, toiling to its feet again with an expression of absolute concentration. Longespée let it take two steps, and then, laughing, prodded it. As the baby tumbled over like a soft ball, Longespée looked up to share his mirth with everyone else and instead met Hugh's thunderous expression, which was so filled with fury and revulsion that Longespée felt as if he were the one who had been poked.

Hugh strode forward, stooped to his baby son, and lifted him in his arms. "How dare you," he said, his voice husky with rage.

Longespée stared at him open-mouthed with astonishment. "What have I done?" Laughing at the ridiculousness of Hugh's outburst, he spread his hands. "I was only playing with the babe. Is he harmed in any way?"

Hugh glared at him. "Pushing over a child just learning to walk and whom you have encouraged to come to you is no game," he said with cold fury. "You are no better than your royal brother. Even if your actions are less extreme, they still have the same intent." He kissed the baby's tender, pale neck. "I will not have you near my children again—ever, do you hear me?"

"Are you mad?" Longespée stared round at the others who were all watching the exchange with frozen faces. No one moved to intervene.

Hugh fixed him with a stare as blue as his son's. "If you do not see, if you do not understand, then that is your madness, not mine."

"Christ, man, you are making a fuss over nothing."

"I do not call it nothing. I do not want you near my children—ever again."

Longespée snorted with contempt. "You are not lord here. You cannot prevent me from visiting when I choose."

"But I can choose not to be in your company," Hugh retorted. Turning on his heel, he strode from the chamber, calling his older son to him and carrying the baby on his shoulder.

Mahelt hesitated, started to follow, and then paused before her brother-in-law. "You should think on this," she said. "Hugh is overset, but not without reason. Would you have done such a thing to your own child?"

"I do intend to think on this," Longespée answered tightly, "but I shall be pleased to do as my brother Bigod suggests—more than pleased." His heart rammed inside his chest as if he were fighting a battle. He was still astonished; he could not believe this was happening. He needed to return the strike and recover his balance, but there was nothing to hit.

Ida made a distressed sound. "You mustn't quarrel with each other!" she cried. "You must mend it, I implore you."

Longespée bowed to her. "Mother, when Hugh apologises to me for his words, I shall do so, but I will not be treated like this. He has ever hated me for being the firstborn and of royal blood. I was only playing with the babe. In the name of Christ, he's my nephew. Does he think I would harm my own kin?" Hitching his cloak at the shoulder, adjusting the large round brooch, he strode from the room, feeling both guilty and aggrieved. It was always the same when he came to Framlingham. The pieces of the relationship were all there but somehow they either failed to fit, or else they broke into small sharp splinters that left someone bleeding.

Ida cried his name and extended her hand, but he was already gone. Ralph pinned his own cloak. "I have to go." He gave his mother a swift peck on the cheek. "I'll do what I can." He embraced Mahelt. "My lord does not understand small children," he said. "What he did was from ignorance. Hugh shouldn't have taken such umbrage." With a swift nod, he hurried after Longespée.

Ida sat down on the bench and rocked back and forth with tears in her eyes. "I try and I try to bring them together," she sniffed, "but always they quarrel. Why can't they befriend each other? Ralph has no trouble, nor do the other boys. They will be the death of me."

"Don't say that," Mahelt said sharply. "It will blow over. You cannot live your life through them or you will indeed make yourself unwell." She stayed to comfort Ida a moment longer, then went in search of Hugh and found him sitting in an embrasure off the hall, still holding their youngest son.

"I do not know why you let him bother you," she said with exasperation. "What he did was foolish and stupid, but there was no malice intended."

Hugh curled his arm around his namesake. "He thinks we are made of coarser stuff than he is," he said furiously. "He thinks that pushing over my son is fair game because he's just another Bigod, to be put in his place and that means subordinate to him. I won't stand for it any more. Enough is enough."

Mahelt frowned at him. She knew he was on the defensive and behaving like this because he had had to swallow his rage at what John had tried to do to her. This was yet another threat to his family from the royal side—from a man who rode with the king and shared his blood. Longespée had been a fool, but surely not enough of one to cause this kind of rift.

"Your quarrel will break your mother," she said.

Hugh kissed his son's fluffy curls. "There is nothing to

stop her having contact with him if that is her wish," he said frostily. "When he comes to Framlingham, I can arrange to be away in the North, or at Thetford or Ipswich. If we are not in each other's company, there can be no quarrel—and that is my last word."

Mahelt sighed. She thought him too stiff-necked on the matter, but knew that if she pushed him now, she would only drive him further into a corner. Hugh was flexible, but he had a stubborn streak too and there were certain matters upon which he would not bend.

"You must go and bid farewell to the king for the sake of formality," she said, taking the baby from him.

Hugh stood up and straightened his tunic. "You are right." His mouth twisted "I shall do my duty and I shall see the hellspawn lot of them out of our gates…and then I shall go and wash my hands."

❖❖❖

Riding out of Framlingham, Longespée felt a terrible sense of loss settle over him. His mother had handed up the stirrup cup with shaking hands and eyes full of anguish, but even for her he would not relent, especially with Hugh standing behind her, his posture and expression carved from stone.

"It will be all right," Ralph told him in a jocular voice, riding up beside him. "Hugh's never angry for long."

Longespée bestowed a withering look on his half-brother. "I care not. Hugh is nothing to me. Even if he apologised now for his behaviour, I would not accept it. I have finished trying with him."

"I am sorry." Ralph's tone was curt.

Longespée grunted. "If you want to ride back to Framlingham and join him, I will not stop you."

Ralph hesitated and even glanced over his shoulder towards the towers coroneting the horizon; then he looked at the shield strapped to his packhorse. Not the red and yellow of Bigod, but the blue and gold of Salisbury. "But you would mind," he said. "Wouldn't you?"

Longespée said nothing, but Ralph saw a muscle crease in his half-brother's cheek. He would mind, and dearly. "You are my lord," Ralph said. "My fealty is to you, but I shall not cease speaking to Hugh because he is my brother too."

"As you wish," Longespée replied, but he relaxed in the saddle and Ralph saw him exhale the breath he had been holding. The young man shook his head and wondered why family ties had to be so bitter and complicated.

Twenty-nine

CANTERBURY, KENT, JUNE 1213

*H*UGH ROSE FROM MAKING HIS OBEISANCE AT THE TOMB OF the martyr Thomas Becket, who, forty years ago, had been slain on the spot where Hugh and his brother-in-law Ranulf now worshipped, his brains spilled from his skull and spread abroad on the sword blade of King Henry's knight Reginald Fitzurse. An archbishop, murdered on the order of the king. It had been unthinkable, but it had happened, and might do so again. Hugh had put his hand into the hole that gave access to Becket's coffin and touched the smooth wood as countless others had before him. He wondered how long it would take to wear through and if one day, someone would reach in and touch the saint's bones instead.

Hugh had not made the pilgrimage to Becket's tomb before. The shrine of Saint Edmund was closer to Framlingham and it was better to patronise a martyred king with a special interest in East Anglia than a former archbishop of Canterbury but recently elevated to sainthood. Hugh's father said with a sardonic lift to his brow that Becket hadn't been much of a saint in his lifetime anyway—just a quarrelsome, proud, and stubborn man, and in the end those qualities had killed him. However, his Church had made him a martyr, miracles had happened at his tomb, and before King Henry knew it, he had a saint to deal with rather than a formerly contumacious and now deceased priest.

Hugh would not have made a special pilgrimage to the shrine, but since the court and the royal army were camped nearby and he had time to kill, he had undertaken to visit the cathedral, accompanied by his brother-in-law. Ranulf genuflected and rose too. "They say that before he was archbishop, he went to France on a diplomatic mission, and so great was his display of wealth that the French mistook him for King Henry himself. I can well believe it." Ranulf's clear green eyes roved the bejewelled opulence of the shrine and the rainbow glitter of the painted windows. "He may not have been able to take it with him, but he is certainly entombed in riches."

"Even so, he is of greater value than anything surrounding him," Hugh said. "Without his martyrdom, none of this would be here. In the year before the interdict, he was worth more than three hundred and seventy pounds of silver a year in offerings from pilgrims."

Ranulf pursed his lips in a silent whistle. "They don't really need our offering of two marks and five pounds of wax then, do they?"

Hugh smiled. "You are turning into a careful Yorkshireman."

"I'm insulted," Ranulf said loftily. "I've never been anything else."

The two men walked amiably up the nave, examining the painted columns, the gilded sconces, the hangings and decorations. Hugh immersed himself in the magnificence of the shapes, textures, and colours. Ranulf's eye was not artistic and his interest less deep, but he was good-humoured and patient, content when he had looked his fill to wait for Hugh.

The outer part of the nave bustled with pedlars doing a roaring trade in votive candles, lead badges featuring the saint, and ampullae containing holy water in which the garments Becket had been wearing at his martyrdom had been steeped. There were even some rock-crystal phials of Becket's blood, the latter purportedly collected at the time of the murder by some monk more enterprising than horrified, if one was gullible enough to believe the tale. As the men emerged through the west door into the early June sunshine, they were set upon by yet more tradesmen selling signed writs confirming that a pilgrimage had been undertaken. There were prayer beads in assorted stones, types of wood, ivory, and bone to suit all pockets. Trinkets and tokens. Chaplets of flowers both real and artificial. Belts, horse mounts, brooches, buckles, crosses, reliquaries.

"I'll warrant that this trade continued throughout the interdict," Ranulf said. "They wouldn't want to lose all this, would they?" He paused to contemplate a coil of prayer beads at one of the stalls.

"It certainly carried on at Bury from what I saw, and at Norwich." Hugh eyed him askance. "You're not going to... Good God, Ranulf!"

Ranulf waved his hand. "I have a wife who will give me a sweeter welcome home if I return from campaign bearing gifts as well as dirty laundry. If she discovers I have been to Canterbury and not brought her a token, there will be hell to pay at home rather than a few shillings here. What do you think of these blue ones? You're the one with a talent for colour."

Hugh considered. The beads were attractive and looked as if they might be lapis. "Do they match her eyes?"

Ranulf frowned; then he peered into Hugh's face. "Well, they match yours, so that's close enough since she's your sister."

Having negotiated a price, Ranulf tied the purchased beads through his belt. Business accomplished, the men repaired to the nearest alehouse, ordered a jug of wine, and sat beneath the shade of an oak tree.

Other men from the royal camp were taking the opportunity

to visit the shrine and the crowds coming and going from the cathedral were peppered with soldiers and servants of varying ranks and stations. Ranulf stretched out his legs. "If this is what it's like before the interdict's officially ended, how much custom will they have once it's been ratified?"

Hugh rubbed fingers and thumb together to show what he thought about the financial side of matters and drank his wine.

Ranulf shook his head. "I still cannot believe what the king did. He certainly pulled the ground out from under everyone's feet...I thought John was finished..." His tone contained admiration without pleasure.

Hugh shrugged. "I suspect my father-in-law had a lot to do with persuading him to bow to the pope's wishes and make peace."

Ranulf exhaled down his nose, the sound expressing his thoughts on that notion. "Why would he want to do that? After the way the king behaved towards him over Ireland, you would think he'd want to see him go down."

Hugh gestured with his cup. "My father-in-law plays the game with subtlety and balance. Besides, he gave his fealty to King John and his oath is his honour. It's the reason men follow him and trust him. If the French had invaded, how many would have gone over to Prince Louis?"

Without answering, Ranulf busied himself pouring a fresh cup of wine.

"There was no other choice but to make peace with the pope."

"Mayhap not, but there was no reason to give England to him as well. We're a papal state now—hah!" There was disgust in Ranulf's tone as he referred to the fact that, in a complete volte-face, John had knelt to the papal envoy, agreed to accept Stephen Langton as archbishop of Canterbury, and in one fell swoop made England a vassal state of Rome. The hermit who had predicted John would no longer rule England by Ascension

Day had been right, if not in the way folk expected. The hermit himself had been hanged.

"But at a distance, and since John has sworn fealty to the pope, it protects us from France and it means Stephen Langton can set foot in England as archbishop of Canterbury...and that in turn means we can begin the work of binding John through due process of law. We need both Church and barons for that."

"You think John is going to tamely agree to be bound?" Ranulf's gaze was cynical.

"Not tamely, no, but he will have no choice when the archbishop of Canterbury and the senior earls give it their backing."

"I've always admired your optimism," Ranulf said. "Personally, I foresee stormy weather."

There was a brief but comfortable silence as each man digested his thoughts. Hugh had been in the field with the Bigod troops for just over a month, awaiting the French invasion. Over the past few weeks spies had been reporting daily on the state of the gathering French fleet. King Philip had invested sixty thousand pounds on his planned bid to take England from John, claiming that an excommunicate king was outside the pale of society. Philip said it was his Christian duty to rid England of such a monarch. However, John had rallied support behind his banner. He might be unpopular, but not everyone wanted to see French rule in England. William Marshal had come from Ireland with five hundred knights and John's Flemish mercenaries were standing firm. Their loyalty depended on pay, not hereditary oaths. William Longespée was staunch too. Hugh tried to avoid thinking about his half-brother but was often forced to do so because they dwelt in proximity in the camp and sat at the same board in counsel.

Hugh finished his wine and called for another flagon. Once John had yielded to Pandulf, the papal legate, the latter had hastened to the French and informed King Philip that the invasion was off because England was now a papal state and John had undertaken to accept Stephen Langton as archbishop of Canterbury, welcome back all the churchmen who had gone into exile during the interdict, and pay reparations. Rebellious barons such as de Vesci and FitzWalter who had gone into exile were to be restored to their lands and granted the kiss of peace.

With an army prepared and no invasion to pursue, King Philip had been justifiably furious and had turned his attention on John's ally, the Count of Flanders, bringing his full force to bear on Ghent. The count had begged John for help and John had responded by despatching Longespée at the head of the English fleet with seven hundred men under his command. The ships had sailed five days ago for Flanders and as yet there was no news.

"I'll just be glad to go home," Ranulf said. "I left a newborn son in the cradle. At this rate, by the time I return he's going to be walking and his sisters will be ready for marriage!"

Hugh thought briefly of his own sons. With Roger the rate of growth and change had slowed down, but his namesake was at the fleeting stage between baby and toddler where one month or two made a vast difference. Except this might not be one month or two; it might be all summer, fighting to protect the rule of a man who made his flesh crawl.

"That is an ominous silence, brother," Ranulf said, and now there was no amusement in his eyes.

"Once Langton has returned and depending on what happens in Flanders, the king may well cross to Poitou and strike north to try and catch King Philip between two fires," Hugh said.

Ranulf pushed his hands through his fringe, leaving deep finger tracks in the silvered brown. "Well, he's not doing the catching with me and mine," he said shortly. "Even if it weren't for my wife and babes, I have a harvest to bring in and affairs to attend to at home. I won't stay beyond the terms of

my service and I am not prepared to set one foot off this shore."
He finished his wine and banged his cup down. "I won't pay
for him to hire men overseas either. I've done my service and in
person. Once the term is complete I am quit—until next year."
He looked at Hugh. "What about you? Will you go if he asks?"

"I would have to think about it." Hugh rubbed the back of
his neck.

"I'm surprised you would even consider it."

"It's for the whole family to discuss and for my father to decide."

"But you are the one who has to go and perform the service."

Hugh sighed and spread his hands. "Yes, but what would I
gain in rebelling against my father? I will not let John divide us.
I have seen him dig his knife into the mortar that holds families
together, prise it apart, and then wait to see everything tumble
down. When the time comes, we will act for the good of all."

"Well, wassail to the good of all," Ranulf said sourly. He
poured another drink and raised a toast. Hugh responded to the
gesture by raising his own cup and wondered whether to make
this his last one. *In vino veritas.* He wasn't certain that he wanted
to start talking truth should they hit a third flagon.

A pilgrim entered the alehouse laden down with lead ampullae,
crosses, prayer beads, and an ornate parchment scroll tied with
red ribbon. "No wonder the pope wants a few of Saint Thomas's
bones for Rome," Hugh muttered to change the subject. "They
must be worth more than their weight in gold."

Ranulf's eyes gleamed sardonically. "I wonder which bits
they'll decide to…" He paused and cocked his head towards
the street where someone was shouting in wild excitement.
Leaving their mugs, Hugh and Ranulf raced outside. Several
folk had linked arms and were dancing a carole. Two soldiers
were whooping at the tops of their voices in between blowing
on hunting horns. Beyond them another man was waving and
gesticulating and being embraced by yet more people.

Hugh and Ranulf hurried over to that particular group. "What news?" Hugh demanded.

The messenger at the centre turned to them, his face glowing. His hat had been knocked askew and hung at a precarious angle on his sweat-flattened curls. "Great news, messires!" He clenched his fist. "The Earl of Salisbury, my lord Longespée, has won a great victory against the French! Their fleet's been destroyed and enough booty taken to fill the cathedral fifty times over! God is smiling on England again. It is a sign, a true sign!"

He was lifted up on the shoulders of his companions and borne on towards the cathedral, still crying his tune to the noise of bells and horns and hoarse cheers. Hugh and Ranulf repaired to the alehouse to finish their wine but did so swiftly and standing up. The news would already be all over the camp if it had arrived in Canterbury.

"Well, that answers the question about the French and puts them out of the reckoning," Ranulf said. It was a forthright statement and the inflection difficult to tell, as was the manner in which he raised his cup. "Here's to our brother by marriage, the Earl of Salisbury."

Hugh raised and drained his cup. "To justice," he said.

❖❖❖

Hugh unfolded the protective bundle of grey cloth that Ralph had just flourished at him and discovered inside a cloak made of thick scarlet wool, lined with the fur of Russian squirrels. The breast clasp consisted of a silk cord, attached to two round brooches of solid gold, and the edging was of gold brocade set with gemstones.

Hugh stared in amazement. "This is fit for a king!"

Ralph flushed with pleasure. "I thought you'd like it. Who knows, it might even belong to Philip or Louis. I found a chest with three cloaks and five silk tunics!" He pressed his hand to his breast, indicating one of the latter: a magnificent affair of red damask that set off his dark hair and made his eyes shine. An ornate dagger in a gilded sheath weighed down his right hip and his hands glittered with gold rings. He was strutting like a barnyard cockerel, but his open pleasure and his delight in being able to extend largesse for once, instead of receiving it, saved him from being smug. "I have a bolt of silk for our mother and a gold cup for my lord father…as well as two hats."

"Oh, he'll like the hats." Hugh chuckled. He shook his head at his brother. "You've moved on from wolfskins, I grant you that."

Ralph laughed and made a rude gesture at Hugh. "Are you not pleased?"

"Oh, certainly!" Hugh said and opened out the cloak to try it on.

"You have never seen such plunder!" Ralph enthused, and settled down to tell his story as the June evening darkened and the sparks rose from the camp fire in dragon flashes of orange and gold. "We couldn't believe it!" His eyes shone. "The entire French invasion fleet anchored in the harbour at Damme, and hardly any guards because all the crew and soldiers were away from their ships besieging Ghent! We had the pick of five hundred cogs and galleys! We seized what we wanted and cut the rest adrift. We'd have had more if King Philip hadn't got wise to us, but by the time he reached Damme there was nothing he could do. He didn't want what was left of his fleet falling into our hands so he sent in fireships and burned them to the water. We sank some for him in the right place to block the harbour." Ralph rubbed his hands. "It was glorious! There'll be no invasion now lest we are the invaders! Our brother Longespée's new ship has proven its worth ten times over, and so have English sailors! Never have I seen so much booty so easily seized. We barely had to strike a blow. The weather was on our side too and we're safe home and laden with French spoils!" A mischievous smile curled his lips. "You see what happens when you have the backing of the pope?"

Wry looks were exchanged around the fire and someone cuffed him good-naturedly. "I am not sure that God has had His hand in any of this, whoever the players are," Hugh said, fastening the cloak, "but at least for the moment we are safe and we have a breathing space to consider our next move."

"Reclaiming Normandy, of course!" Ralph said without hesitation. "We have the men and the means. We should strike while we have the advantage."

"It's also a matter of having the will," Hugh said with a glance at Ranulf. "There are issues at home just as pressing."

Ranulf nodded. "Not everyone is as eager as Longespée to do the king's bidding, nor have the excommunication and interdict been officially lifted yet."

"But they will be—very soon they will be," Ralph said.

Ranulf rose to his feet and stretched. Ralph had given him a silk purse for Marie with a rope of pearls inside it and he held it with diffident courtesy, as if he was accepting it because he had to, not from sincere choice. "I'm for my bed," he said. "If I drink any more I'll be nursing my skull in the morning." He saluted the men on the bench and walked off to his own pavilion.

Ralph stared after him. "What's wrong with him?"

"He has a lot to think about," Hugh said. "We all have." To distract Ralph, he tossed one edge of the cloak over his shoulder to show the patterned grey and white lining and opened his hands in a gesture that invited comment.

Ralph grinned. "I'm regretting not keeping it for myself." He refilled his cup and said anxiously, "You're pleased for our brother Longespée, aren't you?"

"Of course I am." Hugh tried to sound wholehearted. "It's a great victory and one to be proud of." Which was true. The politics of the situation might be murky and the future uncertain, but it didn't detract from what Longespée had achieved. Such expeditions were what he had been born for—dashing enterprises that risked all. "But I am just as proud of you." He squeezed Ralph's shoulder. "A good commander is nothing without his men."

Later, lying on his camp bed, Hugh pillowed his hands behind his head and listened to the champing of the nearby horses and the sounds of movement and soft conversation from the men on duty. He was tired but his mind was churning. Longespée had won a great victory for them, and the impetus should be maintained by taking the gathered army to Poitou, but it wasn't going to happen. The loyalty and commitment were not there and men who had affairs at home had already been kept in the field for too long. There were other issues to be faced, and until that happened, John's army, whatever the successes on its periphery, was merely going to march on the spot.

Thirty

WINCHESTER CATHEDRAL, JULY 1213

A CLOUD OF INCENSE GHOSTED WITHIN THE ILLUMINATED rays of sunlight streaming through the arched cathedral windows, and rainbow motes sparkled upon the crowd standing in the great nave. Mahelt stood with her mother and her brothers and sisters to witness King John being formally absolved of his excommunication and welcomed back into the bosom of the Church by Stephen Langton, restored archbishop of Canterbury.

John swore upon the gospels to love and defend the Church, uphold the laws of his ancestors, and abolish bad governance. Mahelt listened and thought that it was all very well, but really the words meant nothing, because John would not keep such vows unless pinned down and nailed to them. He was swearing with fervent sincerity just now because he wanted to take his army across the Narrow Sea and strike at the French while they were still reeling. Longespée was already back in Flanders with a brief to aid its count and keep Philip's army occupied.

Langton leaned to bestow the kiss of peace on the king. He had already done so on the steps of the cathedral, but now he performed the act again before God and the Holy Saint Swithun. Langton's face was that of a didactic with pursed lips that could by turns be pedantic and primly amused. He liked to guide, direct, and educate; he saw himself as a man of reason and balance with much to set in order.

The mass celebrated, the king, the archbishop, and attendant bishops exited the cathedral by the west door and, a third time, John and Langton exchanged the kiss of peace before a throng of witnesses so that no one could be in doubt that a full reconciliation had taken place.

Mahelt walked with her mother from the cool dark of the cathedral into the full blaze of the late July sun and had to shade her eyes with her hand. Her father stood close to the king, as did her father-in-law who had come from Framlingham for the occasion. His complexion was a livid scarlet in the day's heat because he had insisted on wearing his ermine-lined mantle. Ida was absent because her health remained uncertain and the journey would have exhausted her reserves. For the moment Mahelt was the acting Countess of Norfolk.

Will joined her from the huddle of young bloods and older knights with whom he had been standing, including Mahelt's brother-in-law Ranulf FitzRobert, and former rebel Eustace de Vesci who had been pardoned and reinstated. "The king should take up the life of a travelling minstrel," Will muttered scornfully. "Those promises are just falsehoods to get him off the hook and persuade us to go to Poitou. It won't do him any good."

"Peace will do us all good, my son," his mother said, her gaze sharp with warning.

"Not all of us," Will sneered, "because it won't extend to all, will it?"

"Be glad that the interdict is over and that we have a sound archbishop at the helm," she replied with disciplined serenity.

"And a rotten king. How can I be glad for that? How can you, Mother?"

"I did not say you should be glad for such a thing. What I said was that Archbishop Langton is sound. He will bring a balance that has been lacking. Your father is here too and that is all to the good of the country and our lands."

"But not to his own, I warrant, even if he won't see it. He never does."

"He has been gone a long time from England. He is pleased to be back. Ireland for him has always been a place to mark time."

Will glowered. "Better Ireland," he said and, seeing someone else he knew, excused himself and strode away to talk to them.

Isabelle sighed and gazed after him with a lined brow. "I fear his time as a hostage has corroded his good nature."

"I'm not sure he had a good nature to begin with," Mahelt replied, and held her tongue on the other things she knew; the things that had put bitter iron in her brother's soul. She loved and trusted her mother but some matters were private between herself and Will.

Isabelle gave her a perceptive smile. "You neither, my daughter. I feared for the Bigods when you went to them, as much as I feared for you."

Mahelt flushed. She was unsure how much her mother knew about her own clandestine activities on Will's behalf in the early days of her marriage. It was probably a subject best left unbroached. She gave a reluctant laugh. "Hugh treats me well and I love him dearly. With his father...I have come to understandings or truces, mostly truces." She glanced ruefully at her boiled crab of a father-in-law. "I adore Hugh's mother, but I worry about her. She was very ill in the winter and we thought she might die. She's a little better now, but not well enough to undertake more than light duties."

"I am sorry to hear that; I hope she soon recovers."

Mahelt nodded agreement. "She became ill just before the king came to Framlingham, and I had to take the part of chatelaine." She glanced round to make sure no one was within hearing distance. Lowering her voice, she said, "The king...

when he visited…He suggested I might want to open my legs for him."

Her mother inhaled sharply. "He didn't—?"

"No!" Mahelt said with angry contempt. "I put my hand to his jewels and almost wrenched them off his body."

Isabelle put one hand to her mouth and stifled a gasp.

"He thought he had me alone, you see, and that I would be his victim, but he became mine instead."

"It is well that you defend yourself from him, but have a care because he will look to ways of getting his revenge." Isabelle frowned in concern. "Does Hugh know?"

"Yes, but we have told no one, not even his father, and I do not think the king has spoken of the matter to any of his cronies. He claimed his discomfort was caused by saddle sores." Mahelt's eyes sparked with remembered anger. "Hugh would have finished the gelding were it not for the fact that the king was under our roof at Framlingham and all of his knights and hirelings were camped in our ward. Hugh says we must play a reasoned game and not be fools."

"He has a wise head on his shoulders."

Despite the heat of the day, Mahelt shivered. "I hate John," she said.

Isabelle raised an index finger in warning. "He is the anointed king, and while you may not want to sit by him at dinner or spend time in his company, he is wily and intelligent. We must play the game with astuteness and caution—as Hugh and your father both know."

"Mama…"

"I understand." Isabelle squeezed her arm. "But you must separate your heart from your head in this. No more, here comes the archbishop." She dropped a reverent curtsey.

Mahelt didn't answer as she did the same. She was not sure she could find it in her to separate heart and head. If the price of diplomacy was swallowing her hatred for John, she didn't think she had the right currency in her purse.

❖ ❖ ❖

Mahelt curled her forefinger around a lock of her hair and extended her feet towards the residual warmth from the hearth. It was late and apart from starlight and the occasional glimmer of a watch fire or guard's lantern, Winchester was humped in darkness. The household had retired long since, but she was waiting up for Hugh who had gone to talk matters of state with his father and other barons, including her brother and the archbishop of Canterbury. Her father was elsewhere, attending on the king. It was the mark of a good and attentive wife to wait up for her husband, but Mahelt's vigil wasn't entirely the result of duty. She was curious.

She and her mother had spent the early evening together, catching up on general gossip while their children played. Ancel and Joanna were similar ages to Mahelt's sons. Her other sisters had either joined in the play or the gossip, as the whim took them. When Mahelt had last seen them, they had been infants and small children. Now, Belle at thirteen was starting to develop a figure and bid to be the beauty of the family with her waist-length flaxen hair and dark blue eyes. Sybire was twelve, and baby Eve was a long-legged eight year old. Gilbert and Walter were no longer mischievous boys, but adolescents with breaking voices and little interest in the domesticity of the bower. Gilbert was in training for the Church and already had his focus fixed on a bishopric, and Walter was as restless as a colt in springtime.

The men had still not returned by the time her mother left, and it was well after midnight when Mahelt was roused from a doze by sounds in the yard and the barking of dogs mingled with sharp low-voiced commands. Rubbing her eyes, she went to the open shutters. By the light of a lantern borne by a squire, she saw Hugh bidding goodnight to his father, while Tripes and a couple of other house dogs milled around their feet.

As Hugh started up the outer stairs to the chamber, Mahelt hurriedly returned to the bench so she would not be caught gazing out of the window like an over-anxious wife.

"Still awake?" Hugh asked as he opened the door. "I thought you would be long abed by now." Wagging his tail almost fit to knock himself off his own three legs, Tripes bustled around Mahelt and Hugh before flopping down in front of the embers.

Mahelt rose from the bench. "I wasn't tired." She removed his hat and kissed his cheek, noting as she did so that he was holding a piece of parchment.

"Naturally your curiosity had nothing to do with it?" His eyelids creased with amusement.

Mahelt made a face at him. "Of course not. Do you want some wine?"

He shook his head. "My back teeth will be awash. I've already drunk too much as it is." He sat down on the bed and Mahelt knelt to remove his boots.

"Are you going to tell me what happened then? What's that in your hand?"

Hugh glanced round to check that no servants were lurking and handed her the parchment. "The future," he said.

Mahelt gazed down at the words. The writing was not that of a scribe; indeed she suspected it belonged to her father-in-law. There were a few scorings out on the parchment and places where the wording had been scratched away and changed, but although the document was not a best copy, it was still clear. Mahelt's complexion began to flush as she read the points. "'King John concedes he will not take men without judgement, nor accept anything for doing justice, nor perform injustice.'" She glanced sharply at her husband and then back to the parchment. "'We will appoint as justices, constables, sheriffs, or other officials, only men that know the law of the realm and are minded to keep it well. I concede that my men should not serve in the army outside England save in Normandy or Brittany and this properly; and if anyone owes thence the service of ten knights, it shall be alleviated by the advice of my barons. We will entirely remove from their bailiwicks the relations of Gerard D'Athée so that in future they shall have no place in England, namely Engelard de Cigogne, Peter, Guy, and Andrew de Chanceaux, Guy de Cigogne, Geoffrey de Martigny, Philip Marc, his brothers, and his nephew Geoffrey and the whole brood of the same. We will at once return the son of Llewelyn, all Welsh hostages, and the charters delivered to us as security for the peace.'" She had to raise her eyes and wipe away tears, but at the same time she was nodding vigorously and aglow with pride. Of course this was the simple part. Getting John to accept it was going to be more difficult.

"Put it in the strongbox in the weapon chest," Hugh said. "As you can see, we didn't just sit down tonight to drink and indulge in idle talk. Now Langton is back we can begin in earnest. This is only a rough draft; there's a lot more to do, but when it is finished, we shall have our charter and, come hell or high water, we will bind the king to its terms." His colour was high as he spoke. "It is neither rebellion nor treason. John swore today in that cathedral to mend his ways, and these points are to be the manner of his mending."

Mahelt took the parchment and stowed it away in a wooden coffer inside the weapon chest. The latter was kept double-locked because of sharp weapons and mischievous little hands. Returning to the bed, she knelt over Hugh. If she had been awake and restless before, now she was effervescent with anticipation and excitement. "Does my father know?"

"We have asked Will to tell him when he returns from attending on the king. John will need men of balance around him to bring him to the table. Better that your father has knowledge, but is involved from the other side, so to speak."

Mahelt reached forwards to unpin the gold brooch at the top of his tunic and then unlace the ties of his shirt. "And will John agree?"

Hugh threaded his hands through her long brunette hair and, pulling her down to him, kissed her. His mouth was warm and tasted of wine and Mahelt gave a delicious little shudder. She hoped he hadn't drunk too much.

"Not at first," he said between kisses, arching his spine and gasping, "but we will bring him to do so. He won't be allowed to make empty promises."

Her busy hand discovered that her hopes concerning his condition were all delightfully confirmed. He was as hard as a lance. "Neither will you," she said with a breathless laugh as she straddled him.

❖ ❖ ❖

Will looked at his father and drew a deep breath. He was navigating a fraught channel. "You have said before the king must be curbed. You yourself have been a victim of his abuses—we have all suffered."

It was late and there were only the two of them in the small screened-off room beyond the hall of the Marshal lodging in Winchester. Everyone else had gone to bed long ago. Will's eyes burned with tiredness and he could tell from the pouches beneath his father's eyes that he too had had a long, difficult day. However, neither man was going to be able to sleep with the draft of this charter lying between them. Will was irritated that he had been chosen to speak with his sire. In his opinion it would have been better for someone outside the family to do it because now the issue of father and son was muddying the waters. He was having to ask his father to listen, and that was a reversal of the roles.

"But holding clandestine meetings involving men who have been in rebellion against the king is not the way to go about it," his father replied, and his voice had a biting edge.

"Langton was presiding. Roger and Hugh Bigod were there. Just because de Vesci and FitzWalter and de Quincy are among the group, that doesn't make this a document of rebellion. It's based on a charter of the first King Henry." Will fixed his father with a solid, determined stare, impressing on him that he was not for backing down. He was twenty-three years old and his own man. "These men are not going to melt away, sire."

"I wouldn't be so sure of that. Saer de Quincy is not a man to trust in a storm, nor one with whom I would keep company."

"Neither is John," Will retorted.

A crease appeared in his father's cheek. Abruptly he turned away to the flagon and poured them each a cup of wine. "You do not have to be a part of this," he said. "You can return to my household and take time to recoup and settle down."

Will accepted the wine to show willing, but his expression was as fixed as his father's. "With respect, it is too late for that. Sire, you must listen. If it…if it comes to the crux, what happens if you go down?" The words were out and he felt sick for saying them, but it had to be done.

"I never thought to see my own son align with rebels," his father said with weary distaste. "It is like looking in a cracked mirror."

Inwardly Will flinched, but kept the recoil from expression and body. "All we want is a just rule."

His father shook his head and held out his hand for the scroll. While he might not be able to read words, he was capable of reading seals and knew each one by heart. Will watched him with trepidation. His father had a superb memory—he only needed to hear or see something once to fix it in his mind. If Will had read him the wrong way, everything would come crashing down. All his father need do was take this document to John and forewarn him. "Are you willing to stand against such men?" Will asked, trying to keep the trepidation from his voice.

"I would stand against each one individually if I had to," his father said, "but this isn't a matter of that. It is a matter of standing against treachery. I have always striven to protect our family. I have devised strategies and sought intelligence, but I have never plotted in corners—never!"

Will swallowed. "So are you willing to stand against me as a traitor too?"

"Should I bless you that you will go behind the king's back? You are no better than that which you seek to overthrow."

Will blenched but held his ground. "God forgive you and God forgive me. Do you not see?" He extended his hand in a pleading gesture. "You cannot stand against this. It's not just these names. There are others without number. I came to you tonight to ask you to smooth the path and help make the king see reason. Do his actions not violate your heart and your honour? What will happen if it comes to war? Where will you stand when the country is covered in ashes? Will you be a puppet of this tyrant king, or will you use your foresight to see the right way forward?"

His father said nothing, but turned away and, pacing to the wall, stared unseeingly at a hanging, his fists clenched. Will knew he had hurt him, but then he had hurt himself too. He felt raw and mangled, and the root cause of it yet again was John.

His father turned round and if he had looked tired before, now his expression was utterly exhausted. "What is the right way forward?" he asked. "For I scarcely believe that Eustace de Vesci or Saer de Quincy have it—or even my lord of Norfolk, although I suppose his skills as a lawyer are proving indispensable."

Will gathered himself. "Sire, I have told you, it is not just de

Vesci and FitzWalter. Your skills are indispensable too. Look at the terms on the charter. Can you truly say you object to them? Do you not want to see the back of de Cigogne and his ilk?" Will gave an involuntary shudder. "Do you not want to see the protection of women and an end to false arrest?"

His father pinched the bridge of his nose and sighed. "Yes, of course I do, and yes, the terms are worth debate, but in the open. I do not deny there are men of good name on that list, but there are others who intend nothing but mischief. They do not see this as a means of curbing John's excesses, they see it as a step to replacing him with the king of France or his son and furthering their own petty interests, and that, however you dress it up, my son, is treason."

"That is why I came to you, sire. You are one of the few to whom John will listen. You can persuade him to agree to this charter and it will set men's minds at rest and give us a code to work by."

His father shook his head again. "Even as you believe I am a stubborn old man, I think you are a naive young fool. Since this thing is already in motion, it should be declared in public where all can hear the terms. I am the king's marshal. It is my duty to give him impartial advice and to stand by him. Through thick and thin. Think on it, Will. Think hard, because one day that same duty is going to be yours."

"You should think too, my father." Will looked at the door. "I should go; it's very late." Turning, he knelt before the older man in duty and respect.

"There is a bed here. You can stay...It is your home."

Will hesitated for a moment, so badly tempted that it was a physical ache. To sink into a soft mattress, inhale the scent of clean sheets, and make believe he was home and tomorrow all would be fine. But he shook off the weakness and stood up. "No, I have a lodging in the town and it is better if I go."

Because under this roof he was a subordinate, not an adult in his own right, and for now he needed to know he was the latter.

His father nodded and clasped him in a brief, hard embrace that was half affection and half reprimand. When they parted, Will strode from the room and, although he was tempted to do so, he did not look back. He knew his father thought all this was part of a young man's wildness, but it wasn't. It was a grown man's conviction.

Thirty-one

SOUTH COAST, SUMMER 1213

*H*UGH WATCHED THE KING GRIP THE FINIALS AT THE END of his great chair and squeeze. The powerful movement, the rigidity of John's body within the jewel-crusted robes, the slight quiver he was giving off like a heat haze, told its own story of rage. His campaign tent was packed with knights and barons.

At Hugh's side, Ranulf was also rigid, but with stubborn determination rather than fury. "Sire," he said, "I have kept myself and my men in the field as long as I can afford. My coffers are empty. I have come at your summons. I have stood firm against the threat of a French invasion, but unless you provide me with funds, I cannot follow you across the sea to Poitou. I have no money to feed my horses or my men."

"You want me to pay you to perform your feudal duty?" John asked with dangerous softness.

"Sire, I have fulfilled my obligation to you. Next year I shall do so again, but for now I am quit—unless you provide me with the wherewithal to stay in the field."

Murmurs of approbation followed his speech. Ranulf was not going out on a limb, nor was he particularly the spokesman, only this time his voice had been the one the king had chosen to hear and pick upon.

"I will do no such thing," John snarled. "You are bound to obey me and follow where I command."

Ranulf folded his fingers around his belt and stood firm. "Sire, I am not bound to serve you overseas lest it be in Normandy or the Breton lands. The oath I have sworn to you does not include Poitou."

There were more mutters of agreement and restless shuffling of feet as if men were adjusting their stance to the deck of a ship heaving in uncertain seas. No one was willing to sail with the king to take on the French by striking upwards from Poitou. As Ranulf had pointed out, everyone had been on alert the summer long and the men were jaded. Feeding horses, paying wages, keeping all up to scratch had emptied the coffers. Matters needed attending to at home. John's foreign war could wait.

"Sire," Hugh said, speaking out in support of his brother-in-law, "it is near the end of the season and any campaign will have to be squashed into two months instead of six. We are not prepared."

"I am not wet behind the ears, Bigod," John growled.

"Neither are any of these men, sire," Hugh replied in an even voice, although his heart was pounding. "Most of us are seasoned campaigners."

"Seasoned in perfidy and out for your own gain." John bared his teeth. "I curse the day I agreed to make peace with the pope and allowed men who had conspired against me to return from exile and receive the kiss of peace. When the tide is full and begins the ebb, I will embark, and all of you will follow within two days. See to your weapons and horses and make yourselves ready. Any man who does not, I will count a traitor. Get out, all of you!"

Once outside the royal tent, Hugh stood in the sunshine breathing deeply and regaining his equilibrium.

"The whoreson!" Ranulf was incensed. "All those words

of contrition, all the oath-taking. He meant none of it. All he wanted was to remove the pressure put on him by the pope and France and ship us all to Poitou! Well, you can set sail for a foreign war if you want, but I'm going home." Throwing up his hands, he stalked in the direction of his pavilion.

Hugh followed more slowly. He had not expected any other reply from John, but unlike Ranulf he had more than one option. He had no intention of following the king, but did have the handy excuse of requiring his father's sanction to take the Bigod men overseas. He also had a contingent of Ipswich and Yarmouth sailors with him, and even if he did not embark himself, he could give the men to the king to crew the mercenaries across to Poitou.

Ranulf was already shouting orders to strike camp and load the sumpter beasts. Hugh instructed his servants to dismantle his own pavilion and then sought his brother-in-law. "Have a care to yourself," he said, "and to Marie and the children."

Ranulf clasped Hugh's arm. "The same to you."

The men exchanged looks in which much was said but nothing articulated. They both knew the dangers of the path they were treading.

❖ ❖ ❖

In the Friday Street house in London, Mahelt leaned over Ela's four-month-old baby girl, Isabella, who was gurgling in her cradle. She chucked the baby under the chin, making her giggle, and quashed feelings of broodiness. This would be Ela's third infant in as many years and Mahelt had no intention of emulating her. The bearing of children in rapid succession took its toll on a woman's body and since Hugo was not yet two years old, she could afford to wait a while yet.

Ela sat in the embrasure, sewing a small smock while a nurse cared for her two sons. She was visiting Mahelt in London, and due to return to Salisbury on the morrow. Longespée was in Flanders and not expected home until the autumn. King's business. War business. But it seemed to Mahelt that war business and peace business were often the same thing. Her father was occupied in Wales dealing with an uprising. Hugh was attending a council at Saint Paul's in the company of the archbishop of Canterbury. The king was sulking at Wallingford and threatening to take his mercenaries and punish those who had refused to sail to Poitou with him. His expedition had failed. None of the barons had answered the summons and the only men prepared to go had been his household knights and hired soldiers. He had sailed to Guernsey and returned in a white rage, claiming that he was a gazing stock and reiterating that he would never have agreed to peace if he had known the insubordination of his ingrate barons and clergy would continue.

"Do you know how Hugh's sister and her husband are faring?" Ela looked up from her needle to ask.

"Hugh's mother wrote from Framlingham to say Ranulf has sent Marie and the children there for safety," Mahelt said. "Ranulf's still at Middleham but keeping his head down."

Ela sighed "These are such worrying times. I pray to the Blessed Virgin Mary that all will come to peace."

It was on the tip of Mahelt's tongue to say that actions that accompanied prayers were usually of more benefit than prayer alone, but she kept quiet. Ela must know it too and while she was gentle, she was no mouse. Autumn would be upon them soon, then winter, and perhaps there would indeed be peace. Only extremists fought in the frozen months when there was no forage for the horses, and surely it had not come to that just yet.

Looking out of the window, Mahelt saw Hugh hurrying towards the house from the direction of the stables. Her stomach jolted because it was not the manner in which she was expecting him to return from the debate at Saint Paul's. Something had happened. Leaving the window, she hastened to open the door.

Hugh gave her a perfunctory kiss on the cheek, strode to his coffer, and rummaged out his heavy travelling cloak. "We've heard that John's left Wallingford and he's heading for York to punish the northern lords. He must be stopped before there is open war. The archbishop's preparing to leave now and I have said I'll ride with him."

Mahelt was alarmed but not surprised. Whether or not John would strike had always hung in the balance. "Can he prevent him?"

Hugh grabbed his saddlebag and stuffed a fresh shirt and tunic into it. Arriving on his lord's heels, a squire was ordered to take the leather bag containing Hugh's mail shirt and coif and load it on the packhorse. "We're all hoping so. He has a gift for oratory and debate. He also has the teeth and grip of a baiting dog, thank Christ. John will be passing through Northampton. We'll try and stop him there. Langton will tell the king he is bringing down contempt upon the oath he swore at his absolution and that he has no legal grounds to persecute these men." He closed the coffer and turned round, his chest still heaving and his complexion flushed. "Langton says he will excommunicate anyone who goes to war before the interdict is lifted—and that won't happen until the agreement over compensation has been settled. It'll be midwinter at least."

"And what about the meeting?" Mahelt asked.

A dour smile flitted across his face. "Langton read out the charter of liberties before all in the cathedral. It's public now. I don't expect it to change matters immediately, but now it's out in the open, the debate can begin in earnest."

"What charter?" Ela asked in bafflement.

"One to curb the king's excesses and make him accountable," Mahelt said, and swiftly explained the situation to her cousin.

Ela nodded in judicious agreement. "It is more than time it was done. I am sure even my William would say so if he were here."

"It's probably a good thing he isn't," Hugh replied, "because he'd still have to side with the king, wouldn't he? A charter is one thing; getting John to accept it and abide by it is a different matter. It is the same for my father-in-law. Whatever he thinks of the merits of this charter, his oath to John comes before all else. It is no wonder he was glad to go to Wales." He embraced Mahelt. "I have to go. Speed is of the essence. I'll eat in the saddle."

He was gone in a flurry. Mahelt's lips tingled from the pressure of his kiss. "Thank Christ that Marie and her children are at Framlingham," she said.

"You don't think John would..." Ela began, but did not finish the sentence.

"Even with all the charters in the world, no one is safe from that man," Mahelt replied, and felt a sudden need to go and cuddle her sons.

Thirty-two

FRAMLINGHAM, SPRING 1214

MAHELT SET HER FINGERS TO THE FRETS OF THE LUTE AND plucked out a gentle, melancholy tune on the strings. Pale spring light shone on the instrument's swollen yew-wood belly and glinted on the red silk ribbons tied at its neck. The tune was one Mahelt had learned as a tiny girl at her father's knee and the words were all about the joys of springtime and the renewal of life.

Ida had requested Mahelt to play and sing rather than sew, and Mahelt had been delighted to oblige because music was a hundred times better than needlework. Her mind was not entirely on her craft though. Hugh was going away on the morrow to serve the king in Poitou and she was distracted.

Last summer's aborted campaign had only been postponed, not abandoned. Another year meant that once again men owed military service or taxes in lieu. Since the autumn, an uneasy peace had settled over the country like a scratchy blanket upon a restless sleeper. Langton had managed to persuade the king not to take punitive measures in the North, but John had still headed up to Durham in a demonstration of force, claiming it was diplomatic business. There had been threats but no fighting, and discussion on the charter had taken place but with no progress beyond talk. The interdict had finally been lifted in December and John had begun preparing for his long-delayed expedition to Poitou. Ralph and Longespée were already in Flanders, liaising with England's allies there and recruiting troops.

Mahelt understood that Hugh's service was an obligatory part of his position, but she was displeased to be parting from him for the greater part of the summer, especially when he would be in John's service. She knew what to expect. Her childhood had consisted of her father leaving home in the late spring and not returning until the nights were long, dark, and cold.

The first piece finished, she sought a different key and experimented with notes heard on the Irish harp in her mother's solar. Then she sang a song of Leinster, one she had heard as a girl, although she didn't know its meaning, save that it was about the span of a woman's life. It was a poignant, sad song, the words of which she did not understand but that tugged at her heartstrings nevertheless. She had heard it again recently when visiting her mother for Will's betrothal to Alais de Béthune. The couple's marriage was to be celebrated later in the year. Mahelt had found Alais something of a difficult project, for the girl was sulky and quiet in company, but she positively lit up for Will, who seemed mutually smitten. In some strange way, Alais seemed to soothe the sore spots in her brother's soul and make him more amenable; thus Mahelt was prepared to grant the girl some leeway.

As she coaxed the final, fading notes from the lute and let her voice die with them, she realised that Ida was sniffing and wiping her eyes on her sleeve.

"Mother?" Mahelt set the lute aside in consternation. Ida had recovered considerably from her illness the previous winter, but it had left a permanent residue of frailty and she was often weepy.

"That music," Ida sniffed. "It is so sad."

"I am sorry; I should not have sung it."

344

"No, no, it is beautiful too. I am glad you did."

"I do not know what it means, save that it is about a woman thinking upon her life."

"It sounds like a woman's song." Ida bent over her sewing once more, but had to stop again as tears splashed on to the fabric. "My sons," she said in a grief-stricken voice. "I bore them from the travail of my body. I bathed and tended and watched over them and soothed their hurts with love and ointments. Now again and again they ride to war. Their father spent so many months away serving the king that our good years were wasted and in our twilight, there is only long familiarity like two stones rubbing together with the harder one wearing away at the softer until the softer one is dust. I watch my boys leaving their wives and children—leaving me—and the pattern repeats itself all over again." She fixed a drenched gaze on Mahelt. "The first thing a man asks of his newborn son is: 'Will he be a good soldier? Will he have a strong fist?' Never do they ask: 'Will he be a good husband and father?' And as mothers, we never ask that question. That is what makes me weep."

"Unless our sons become monks, they are bound to be soldiers," Mahelt replied pragmatically. "It is their station in life. The first thing I would ask is: 'Will he be honourable? Will he be strong—not of fist, but of principle?' We should change what we can and make the best of what we cannot."

Ida wiped her eyes again and forced a smile. "That sounds like your great father talking."

Mahelt flushed. "It was what we were taught from the cradle." She gave a self-deprecating laugh. "I am too impatient; I want to change everything."

"Patience will come with age," Ida said. "Just do not let it roll over into resignation as I have done." She looked towards the open window where the first swallows were diving and swooping in the arch of air. "I shall pray for my sons every day they are gone and beg God in His mercy to return them unharmed. But I wonder sometimes if God hears my prayers."

"I am certain He does." Mahelt knew she was uttering a platitude.

"I have prayed for reconciliation between my two oldest sons, but to no avail."

"Surely it will come given time." More platitudes.

"Sometimes I fear that I do not have the time," Ida said sadly. "Play something else, will you? Something happy."

Mahelt obliged with "Sumer Is Icumen In," a firm favourite in the Bigod household. It was simple, repetitive, childlike—and optimistic.

❖❖❖

Lying on their bed, Mahelt propped her head on her bent arm and watched Hugh dress. Her hair cloaked her body in a glossy dark skein and she had arranged it with a few deft touches so that as Hugh prepared to leave for Poitou, he would carry the vision of her thus clad, lying on sheets thrown back in invitation, the warm scent of her body reaching towards him. It was the pose of a mistress as much as a wife and she intended it thus. "Make sure you take proper care of yourself this time," she said. "I want you to come home to me whole and well and not in the kind of state you returned from Ireland."

He smiled at her and her chest fell full and hollow at the same time. Fine weather lines had begun to seam his eye corners and she thought him devastatingly handsome. A man in his early prime with whom she had just made love and whom she was not going to see again for most of the summer.

"Don't worry about me." His smile became a grin as he looked her up and down. "If you are trying to tempt me not to leave, you are making a fine job of it." Returning to the bed, he leaned over to kiss her. Mahelt pulled him down for a moment, tasting him again, feeling his skin under her fingertips.

He drew back after a moment and pulling on his hose, began tying them to his braies. Tossing back her hair, making a show of the gesture so that it drew attention to the length of her bare arm and the curve of her breast, she moved to help him. The service was intimate, and despite appetite having recently been sated, it was intensely erotic too.

"I want you to remember this moment," Mahelt said with a breathless little laugh. "Keep it with you as extra warmth when you're lying on a lumpy pallet in your tent."

Hugh made a sound that was half laugh and half groan. "Such a memory will surely set me on fire," he said. "I do not know whether you are an angel or a very wicked woman."

"Neither do I." Giving him a sultry look, Mahelt rose from her knees and fetched a belt of blue braid that had been lying on her coffer. "All the pearls were stitched on by me, and I used my hair for thread. Wise women say that a wife can bind her man to her if she girds it upon him herself. And see." She showed him the reverse of the belt. Worked along the centre of the length in gold thread were the words that were inscribed on the parchment scroll he had left on her pillow: *Ne vus sanz mei, ne mei sanz vus.*

Hugh's throat was tight with emotion as she passed the belt around his waist and latched the buckle. He recognised the pattern and the colours. It was the piece they had woven together when Hugh was a baby.

They would have wound up in bed again—except there was no time for the slow, tender loving that the moment required. The men and the laden sumpter horses were already assembling in the courtyard and the rumble of the slow-moving baggage came through the window as they set out ahead of the main troop. Such noise was always a marker on the path to a long farewell. With huge reluctance, Hugh drew away from her and, with a final stroke of her hair, strode from the room, leaving her to dress.

There was a second, formal leave-taking in the courtyard. Little Roger was upset because he wanted to go to war with his papa and was utterly disgusted at having to stay behind. As far as he was concerned he was almost five years old and a "big boy," grown enough to serve as his father's page. Being told it was his responsibility and his duty to care for the womenfolk and help his grandfather protect Framlingham was small consolation. However, he was steadied by his grandsire's grip on his shoulder, and proud of the gold ring his papa gave him to wear on a cord round his neck in token of his responsibility.

Mahelt held Hugo in her arms. Unaware of the solemnity of the occasion or that the Bigod men were headed for a hard battle campaign far away, the infant waved his arms and shouted joyfully, "Bye-bye, bye-bye!" The moment was poignant and funny at the same time and cause for tears and laughter among the adults. The outriders heeled their mounts and trotted forth in a blaze of red and gold banners. Then came the household knights with Hugh in their midst, followed by more knights, serjeants, and footsoldiers. Michael the chaplain rode his mule with the portable chapel packed into baskets on his sumpter nag. The rumble of wheels, the clop of hooves, and clank of accoutrements filled the yard like thunder, and then, like a storm, rolled on and faded into the distance. Muddy water plinked in the bailey puddles and grew still. With the rest of the household, Mahelt climbed to the battlements to watch the cavalcade grow smaller and smaller and eventually vanish from sight.

"Dada gone?" said Hugo. "Dada gone now."

Mahelt's chin quivered. It was the first time her second son had strung his words together, and Hugh, even while being the catalyst, had missed it. "Yes, Dada gone," she said and, with Hugo on her hip, she placed her free hand on her other son's head. "Your brother's the man of the castle now."

Thirty-three

NANTES, POITOU, SUMMER 1214

*H*UGH CLASHED BLADES WITH A FRENCH SOLDIER, FORCED him backwards, and struck with the hilt of his sword. The soldier fell away and Hugh pressed his stallion forwards, barging and cutting a path amidst the heave and sway of heavy battle. The midsummer heat blazed down on his mail and his skull felt as if it were encased in a hot lead cauldron. He was breathing hard through his mouth and his throat was a fiery tunnel. Blood dripped from his right wrist where he had taken a wound earlier in the skirmish. Stott's implacable, solid strength came into its own as Hugh strove to gain advantage. "*À moi!*" he bellowed to the knights churning up the dust around him. "*Bigod, à moi!*"

King John was pressing the advance and intent on seizing the port town of Nantes from the French. Hugh and the Bigod contingent were immersed in the full thick of the broil. The town militia, composed of ordinary folk, could not withstand the onslaught and were melting back into Nantes, but the garrison had more backbone and there was a sudden surge as they rallied under one of their commanders, and hurled forwards again. The area surrounding the Bigod red and yellow standard became a mêlée of hacking, slashing men. A footsoldier grabbed for Hugh and tried to drag him from the saddle, but Hugh cut him down and applied the spurs. Stott reared and sprang forward on his hind legs. Hugh hacked his way free of the knot of French, turned the destrier in a tight arc, and came back at them. The sound of fighting was like the roar of a great sea and he felt like a stone caught in the surf.

Another knight rode at him, his raised shield displaying the blue and gold chequered blazon of Dreux, his matching silk surcoat torn and blood-splashed. Royalty, Hugh realised. King Philip's own cousin, no less. Hugh turned to meet him, presenting his shield to the first blow of Dreux's sword. The assault gouged splinters from Hugh's shield and pressed him back against his saddle. He attacked with a counter-blow and spurred forwards. Stott snapped at Dreux's horse, which lashed out, and the fight became one of hooves and teeth and stallion muscle as well as sword and shield. Hugh was aware of Hamo Lenveise fighting to his right, using the Bigod banner as a lance, and his brothers Roger and William fighting hard on the left. The sight of the Bigod colours spurred him on and he redoubled his efforts. Dreux was a hard fighter, but that very fact had left him isolated from his troops. As the Bigod soldiers closed around him, Dreux realised the danger, but it was too late to retreat because he was already encircled. "I yield!" he cried. "I am the king's cousin, Robert de Dreux, and I yield!" He lowered his guard, exposing his breast, and presented to Hugh the sword with which he had just been trying to kill him.

Hugh gave Dreux his own credentials and accepted the surrender. More French knights were throwing down their weapons or fleeing as it became plain that the battle was lost. The inhabitants either shut themselves in their homes or ran for safety as the garrison yielded. Nantes was John's and the English were within striking distance of Angers. Once again an Angevin king had entered his heartlands.

Hugh deployed his men to secure their position and Lenveise

found them a billet close to the river. The previous owners had left in a hurry and a cauldron of stew still simmered on the hearth. Hens in the yard meant a good dinner tonight and fresh eggs on the morrow. Albram, the troop chirurgeon, bathed and bandaged the wound to Hugh's wrist, shaking his head and insisting it be sutured before Hugh left for a council with the king and the other battle commanders. There hadn't been any pain from the injury in the heat of the conflict, but as Hugh changed his tunic, he felt as if he'd plunged his forearm into a nest of wasps.

The king was restless with impatience. He had split his forces and the other half were in the North, commanded by Longespée and supposed to be closing southwards in a pincer movement to trap the French between the two lines. However, Longespée's division had not started out yet because their German allies under Otto of Saxony were still arriving and Otto was not ready to march. John was eager to move while he had the advantage.

"Tomorrow we strike at Angers," he said, his eyes glittering with impatience. "The French are on the defensive. We captured twenty of their best knights today, including the king's own cousin." His gaze slid briefly over Hugh in acknowledgement. "Within the week, I will hold court in the capital of my forefathers."

John's words were greeted with murmurs of approbation and gestures of accord. "From there, we'll seize La Roche-aux-Moines."

"Sire, the men have to rest," spoke up Poitevin baron, Aimery of Thouars. "We should have a day at least for the sake of the horses."

"No." John shook his head and gave him a hard look. "If we slack, the French will take advantage. You can have your day's rest in Angers, my lord. We are here to perform a task, not sit on our backsides."

De Thouars flushed and his gaze slid around the chamber,

seeking supporters, daring anyone to laugh or mock. Without a word he turned and shouldered from the room.

"Does anyone else think we should stay behind, or are the men of England made of stronger stuff?" John enquired, arching a scornful eyebrow.

❖❖❖

By the end of the week they had taken Angers and for two nights the king presided over a city that had been the cradle from which his forefathers, the counts of Anjou, had begun their rise to power through marriage and conquest.

Hugh's wound was proving slow to heal and he had a low fever that made him tired and grumpy, but did not prevent him from fulfilling his duties. While in Angers he had the horses checked over and reshod. He replaced two jaded sumpters with new beasts and refurbished his hauberk, mending broken links and rolling the mail shirt in a barrel of sand and vinegar to remove the rust. With Mahelt's strictures in mind, he also found time to take a bath, delouse himself, and have a barber crop his hair.

On the third day, John's army rode out of Angers at dawn and headed south-east towards the recently built fortress at La Roche-aux-Moines. Their arrival before the walls was greeted with sangfroid by the defenders, who responded with showers of slingshot and a token flicker of arrows to show defiance without profligate waste of ammunition. John pitched camp, ordered the siege machines to be brought up, and set about assaulting the castle.

❖❖❖

A fortnight later, Hugh stood beside one of the trebuchet teams as they prepared to launch another stone at the keep walls. Blotting his brow on his sleeve, he thought of Mahelt. He suspected she would be capable of scoring a direct strike. For a moment he could almost see her standing at his side, clad in a hauberk, a sword girded at her hip. Sweat stung his eyes and he blinked hard, nearly losing his balance.

"Careful, my lord," said the captain of the trebuchet crew.

Hugh knew they were wondering if he'd imbibed too freely the previous night. He certainly felt as if he had, but the malaise was caused by tiredness and the wound in his hand, which continued to fester and was slowly worsening. "How soon do you think?" he asked.

"Me and the lads are taking bets on later today or early tomorrow," the man said. "That section of wall yonder won't take much more to breach it."

"That's what I thought." What he hoped too. And then to have cool respite and a decent bed.

One of John's squires ran up to him. "Sire, you are summoned to the king's tent!"

"Now?" Hugh rubbed his forehead.

"Yes, sire." The youth licked dry lips. "Prince Louis's army has been sighted by the foragers. He's coming to relieve the castle, and he's issued a challenge to meet us in battle!"

Hugh exchanged glances with the trebuchet team. "Best make haste," he told them. The squire ran off to summon other men from their billets and duties and Hugh set off for the royal pavilion. On his way, he noticed a French herald being escorted out of the siege camp under a banner of truce.

By the time everyone was assembled, more foragers had returned with confirmation that French forces were approaching from the direction of Chinon and that if John chose to accept the challenge to battle, he would have one on his hands by the morrow dawn.

"We have twice their numbers," John told the gathered barons fiercely. "We can shake them like a dog shakes a rat and put an end to them here and now."

Murmurs of agreement rose from his mercenary captains

and household knights. The English barons were stoical. The Poitevins shuffled uneasily and exchanged glances. Once more Aimery of Thouars stepped forward as their spokesman, his head raised in defiance. "I am not prepared to face the French in open battle," he said forcefully. "Such a thing is madness. You would kill us all."

John stared at the count of Thouars with rage and disbelief. "You traitor!" he snarled. "You spineless cur! You will not do this to me!"

De Thouars turned scarlet but held his ground. "I am no coward, but I will not risk all on a single fight. It is not my battle. I am telling you this to your face because I am an honourable man. If the French army is so close, I must go and defend my own lands because the French will ravage them!"

"Hah!" John scoffed. "You have as much honour as a whore's bawd!"

"Then I am in good company—sire." De Thouars bowed and marched from the tent, followed by his captains. John's jaw worked and the veins in his neck bulged as if they would burst through his skin.

"Shall I go after him, sire?" asked Gerard D'Athée.

John took a deep breath that shook his frame. "No, it will further split the troops and the coward isn't worth chasing. I'll deal with him later." His eyes narrowed. "I will not forget this betrayal. May he not have a sound night's sleep from this day forth."

Knowing John, most men did not doubt that de Thouars would suffer from insomnia for a long time to come and be forever looking over his shoulder and fearing to eat any meal without the services of a taster.

Abruptly John rose from his chair and retired behind the awning into the back of the tent. Moments later he sent an aide out to announce that they were pulling back to La Rochelle.

Bile burned Hugh's throat. They couldn't fight without the Poitevins. They needed the numbers. Given the Poitevin tendency to change sides as swiftly as the weather changed in April, they might be on their way to Louis even now. It was all for nothing, unless Longespée succeeded in the North.

Thirty-four

*H*UGH SAT ON A JETTY WITH HIS LEGS DANGLING OVER THE water. Two fat herring, ruby-gilled and silver-scaled, gleamed at his side, purchased on impulse from one of the fishing boats mooring up and landing its catch. Below his boots, the water was a murky green as the tide washed against the harbour walls. A host of small nefs, galleys, and cogs rocked at anchor and supply boats were unloading at the wharves. Galleys were being loaded with casks of wine bound for England, and a group of Templar knights waited to embark on a ship flying the cross of their order. Hugh watched all the activity with idle curiosity and listened to the scream of the gulls. The sound had permeated his fevered sleep as he lay in his chamber overlooking the harbour, the shutters open to let the sea breeze cool his burning body.

He had been very sick during the retreat from La Roche-aux-Moines, barely able to sit a horse, but refusing a litter. Once back in the port, his worried men had brought a Spanish physician to attend him, Spaniards having a reputation for being the best doctors. Amid much muttering, the man had opened up the festering, swollen wound and, in cleaning it out with salt water, had discovered a fragment of rusting blade within the gash. He told Hugh he was lucky to have a strong constitution and even luckier to have such as himself on hand to find the splinter, otherwise the poison would have spread throughout Hugh's body and eventually killed him, no matter how strong he was. The physician's services had cost Hugh as much as a palfrey, but the wound was finally healing; his fever and debilitation were gone, and he judged it a small price to pay for his life.

John had sent to England for troops to replace the Poitevins. A desultory trickle had arrived, but not enough to engage with Louis. The second English army in Flanders, under Longespée, however, had started out for Paris and was threatening King Philip's army in the field.

Feeling the sun begin to burn the back of his neck, Hugh picked up his silver dinner, rose to his feet, and turned back towards his lodging, stepping carefully on the warped boards of the jetty. As he reached the end, he saw Hamo Lenveise running towards him. "Sire, there is news from the North." Lenveise halted and pressed his hand to the stitch in his side. "There's been a battle…on the road to Paris at Bouvines…The French have carried the day!"

Hugh stared at the knight while the words made their impact. He could feel the string securing the fish he held cutting into his index and middle fingers. "My brothers. What of my brothers?"

Lenveise shook his head. "I do not know, sire. The messenger has gone. He said it was a disaster though. Emperor Otto has fled; there are nine thousand dead on the field."

Hugh suddenly felt weak and sick, as if he still had the wound fever. All the money, all the striving, all the expenditure of life and limb, and for what? Ralph might be a crow-pecked corpse on the battlefield, or just another jumble of arms and legs shovelled into a mass grave. And Longespée…His throat closed. He had thought not to care what happened to him, yet the notion of him no longer in the world was impossible to contemplate. When you had measured yourself against someone for so long, even in enmity, how did you cope with them no longer being there?

He walked on to the lodging and handed the herring to the silent cook. They were still stiff and fresh. Ralph and Longespée; Longespée and Ralph. He washed his hands, sluiced his face, and headed for the royal lodgings at the castle to find out what he could.

❖❖❖

The open cart jolted over yet another rut in the road. Ralph squeezed his gummy lids together and stifled a groan. Every bone in his body ached as if someone had pulled him apart and then jumbled him back together with rough abandon. He was covered in abrasions and bruises—both from battle and from the beating he had received afterwards. He knew he might yet be killed, or die from the vicious and neglectful treatment meted to the prisoners. He could not recall the last time he had eaten or drunk. His sword was gone and his mail shirt. His horse and equipment. Even his cloak. All he had were the torn, stained clothes he was wearing and they were no protection from the drizzle that had been falling steadily all morning. He raised his hands to wipe his face and the iron fetters chafing his wrists clanked at their chain fastening.

He felt sick at how easily he had surrendered when the moment came. He should have fought on; he had let Longespée down, but he also knew that in the thick of the fight he could not have done more. They had been defeated by better luck and manoeuvre. The only sensible thing to do was surrender, but it still left a bitter taste in his mouth. After the battle the men not rich enough to be worth a ransom had been killed there and then rather than being held prisoner. Ralph had been spared having his throat cut, but he still felt vulnerable. After what he'd witnessed on the battlefield and afterwards, he knew men were capable of any atrocity. The French might hang him in Paris for the entertainment and satisfaction of the citizens. Being Longespée's brother and the Earl of Norfolk's son might not be enough to save him. Younger sons did not always merit good treatment and he knew his survival was unimportant in the schemes of kings. Whoever you were, you could still die.

He shifted, trying to make himself comfortable, but to no avail. A group of mounted soldiers trotted towards the cart from the rear of the troop, and Ralph's stomach lurched as he saw Longespée among them, riding a fine bay horse. Although Longespée had no weapons, he was still in possession of his fancy cloak with the miniver lining and he looked his usual polished self. Ralph put his head down, trying to make himself inconspicuous, feeling it should be his punishment to share a dark dungeon with the other men in the cart after his failure on the battlefield. Longespée was jesting with one of his captors, remarking that if only they would return him his longsword, he would show them a few manoeuvres. They laughed with him, and the sound rang hollowly in Ralph's ears. Longespée seemed to be taking a long time to pass. He risked glancing up and saw his half-brother peering into the cart, seeking among the prisoners and the wounded. Ralph hastily dropped his head again, but it was too late.

"That man there, that man in the torn hose is my kin and the son of the Earl of Norfolk," Longespée suddenly called out, the jesting note gone. "Whoever takes him up and sees that he lives will be assured of a fine ransom."

Ralph tried to swallow but his throat was so parched that all he could do was cough and choke. Black spots marred his vision. Distantly he heard Longespée asking someone to give him water. A hard rim was pushed against his lips and liquid sloshed into his mouth. He gulped and spluttered. Then he was plucked from the cart and given a mount—an elderly rouncy with spavined knees and a bumping gait that jarred him almost as much as the cart had done. He welcomed the pain as if it were a penance and mumbled his thanks to Longespée. "I let you down," he said.

The latter gave him a stern look. "Never say that. Fate let us both down. It's a setback, that's all. The greater failure is to give up. The ransom will be paid and we'll both soon be free. Until that time, we will show our captors only our bravery and our pride."

Ralph didn't know how much bravery and pride he had left, but if Longespée demanded it of him, he would try. He suspected that underneath the confident exterior, Longespée was uncertain of the future too. What was going to happen once the ransom was paid? Their defeat at Bouvines was a disaster for King John because it sank all hopes of him ever regaining Normandy and Anjou. All the land and money and human life—lost. The ransom was going to be paid in blood.

❖❖❖

Mahelt was supervising the cheese-making. There had been a good surplus of milk this season and she enjoyed dairying. Her father said it was in her blood because her grandmother Sybilla had been an expert. Barons and bishops had detoured to Hamstead just to sample her famous cheeses, and Mahelt's grandsire John had always been expected to bring a wheel of mature Hamstead cheese to Westminster for his fellow barons when serving at the exchequer.

She watched the maid fleeting the cream off the top of the milk and, satisfied that all was in order for the moment, emerged from the dairy to watch her eldest son being given a riding lesson by his grandsire. She smiled as she watched the earl on his solid grey palfrey and the child on Pie. The pony had a mind of his own and was not always the easiest mount to master. The earl was showing Roger how to squeeze with his knees and make Pie step sideways, and for once Pie was obliging. Whatever differences she had with her father-in-law, Mahelt acknowledged that he was a good and patient teacher. She turned back into the dairy to give the maid instructions, and when she looked back to the courtyard, a messenger had arrived on a sweating horse and was presenting the earl with a parchment and speaking rapidly. Her father-in-law stiffened and the messenger shook his head in a doleful manner.

"My lady, shall I put this—"

Fear blazed through her. "Not now," she snapped at the maid and, removing her apron, hurried to join the men, uncaring if her presence irked her father-in-law. If there was news, she had a right to know.

A green tassel bearing a wax impression of Hugh's seal dangled from the parchment in the earl's hand.

"What has happened?" Mahelt suppressed the urge to snatch it from him.

The messenger licked his lips and looked apprehensively at his lord.

"There has been a battle between our forces and the French," said the earl, shaking his head. "A disaster…"

"Hugh," Mahelt said in a strained voice. "Not Hugh…"

"Hugh is safe. He was with the king in Poitou and not involved in the fighting…but Ralph is taken for ransom and the Earl of Salisbury too." His eyes were bleak. "Nine thousand dead on the battlefield."

"Holy God." Mahelt crossed herself.

"Hugh is on his way home," the earl said in a voice steely with control. "Go to," he told the messenger. "Find food and take rest. I shall need you to ride again in a while."

Mahelt gestured to a groom to take care of Roger and followed her father-in-law into his solar. He dropped into his cushioned chair and rubbed his face. "It is a disaster for the king," he said, "a disaster for us all."

"At least Hugh was not involved and even if Ralph and Longespée are prisoners, they are not among the dead." She spoke bravely even while her stomach was hollow.

Roger gave her a jaundiced look. "Yes, God is merciful; he has spared my sons, but many soldiers of my affinity are among the dead. There will be empty saddles and widowed women and orphaned children. There will be ransoms to pay, and they will cost more than a bag of beans."

"What about the countess?"

Roger's mouth tightened and turned down at the corners. "You tell her," he said with a brusque gesture. "I have too much to deal with here. She will take it better from you than from me."

Mahelt compressed her lips. Had it been her own family in this situation, she knew her father would make the time to tell her mother, and they would face the problem together. "Sire, I think you should be the one—"

His eyes flashed. "For once can you not do as you are told without kicking in the shafts?"

Mahelt's cheeks scorched. She wanted to retort that someone had to if this matter was to be dealt with decently, but knew it would provoke a full-blown quarrel on the subject of what was and was not decent, and she would lose because his word was law. Lips tightly folded, she flourished him an elaborate curtsey, putting all of her anger into it, and stalked from the room. She was so agitated, she knew she could not go straight to Ida. She wanted to saddle her mare and gallop through the hunting park at full pelt. Since this wasn't feasible she marched into the pleasance and, to the surprise and trepidation of the gardeners, spent several minutes pulling up weeds and flinging them as far as her strength would allow. Finally, she felt sufficiently calm to go to

Ida, although she had to lean against the door and summon her courage before entering the room.

Her mother-in-law was sewing by the hearth, which was all she seemed to do these days, apart from look after her grand-children and tell them stories. Her age-spotted hand moved over the linen stretched on the frame. Front to back, back to front, in a swift, steady repetition.

Ida looked up with the beginning of a smile, saw Mahelt's expression, and ceased sewing. Her face fell. "Whatever's wrong?"

Mahelt crossed the room, knelt at Ida's feet, and told her the news, trying to break it gently, stressing the detail that Hugh was safe and Ralph and Longespée, although hostages, were not among the dead.

Ida's wide brown gaze fixed on Mahelt all the time she was speaking. "No," she whispered. "Not my boys, not my babies!"

"They're safe; the messenger said they were safe." Mahelt folded an arm around her mother-in-law. "The king will help to pay the ransom of the Earl of Salisbury, and we can raise the silver for Ralph. We'll have them home soon, you'll see. The earl is already writing the letters." At least Mahelt hoped he was. "I shall write to my father too; he will bring his influence to bear."

Ida rose unsteadily to her feet and crossed the room to her jewel coffer. "These are mine to sell." She lifted a handful of rings, brooches, and jewelled buckles. "I never wear them and I would give them all to see my sons safely home. When I think of them as prisoners—in fetters...I cannot bear it. I would give my lifeblood to save them. I would take my gold and my jewels and I would walk barefoot to put them in the hands of their captors and beg on my knees with my hair unbound if it would free them." Her eyes filled with desolation. "Kings are cruel," she said. "And often so are men..."

"Mother…" Mahelt started towards her, one hand extended in a pleading gesture, but Ida fended her off.

"No," she said. "I want no comfort while they have none."

Mahelt chewed her lip. "Then what about the comfort of the divine? Ask the Holy Virgin Mary for her intercession. She is a mother and will surely listen."

Tears glittered in Ida's eyes. "You are right," she said. "Will you come with me to the chapel now?"

"Of course." Mahelt fetched Ida's cloak from the pole and placed it tenderly around her mother-in-law's frail shoulders.

As the women crossed the ward, they saw little Roger and his brother chasing the poultry with loud yells. The boys were being scolded by their nurse, who had lifted her skirts above her ankles, the better to run after the younger one, who had a twinkling turn of speed. Ida caught back a sob as she watched them. "My sons," she whispered again with anguish. "No matter that they are grown men, I still hold the memory of them as children."

Although the day was warm, Mahelt shivered and wished that she too had her cloak.

❖❖❖

A week later Hugh returned from Poitou. Mahelt was in the bailey to greet him with the rest of the household and was shocked to see how thin he was. The horses were out of condition after a summer on campaign, their hipbones prominent and their flanks showing a hint of rib. Although Hugh had raised a fine trot when he arrived, the impetus did not last. The troop was missing men and horses and there were wounded in the baggage cart, which was devoid of supplies. Hugh dismounted and clasped his father man to man before turning to Mahelt. She curtseyed, and then rose and flung herself into his arms and gripped him tightly. For a moment he held on to her and buried his face in her neck; then with an effort he pulled himself together and went to embrace his mother with gentle tenderness. Watching him, Mahelt felt an overwhelming burst of love and pride and grief.

Ida clung to him, touching his face and hair, weeping and calling him "my son, my son." And Mahelt understood that to Ida, Hugh represented hope and survival, while at the same time pointing up her anguish because the other two had not returned.

Gently he disengaged from her. "Mother, I am all right. I wasn't in the North. Ralph and Longespée are alive and well. I have letters from them in my pack. Dry your tears; we are all safe."

"Dad-dad, Dad-dad!" Unable to contain himself any longer, little Roger tore from his nurse's arms and flew to his father. Hugh swept him up and his son immediately seized the advantage and swarmed to sit on his shoulders. "I've got a new sword! Do you want to see it? Will you play with me?"

Hugh never wanted to see a sword again, but he couldn't say so. In his own childhood, a new sword had always been something of a special event; he had so often imagined himself a man dignified with the real thing, and an accomplished warrior. And when he finally got one, he had practised with it every day until he could juggle with it and make a spinning blur of blade and hilt. Foolish tumbler's tricks.

"Yes, let me have a look at this wondrous thing," he said, "but later, when I have talked to your grandsire and your mother." He swung Roger down so he could dash off to fetch his sword and picked up Hugo, who was beaming up at him, waiting his turn with a patience lacking in his big brother. Hugh was thankful to be home, but the embrace of his family and the high walls of Framlingham burdened him with guilt that he was here and his brothers were not.

❖ ❖ ❖

Lying on the bed, Hugh tumbled with his youngest son. Roger was off with his new wooden sword, playing with other castle children, and for a moment there was peace. As the last of the bath maids closed the door behind her, Mahelt turned to her husband. His hair was still damp but drying in fronds around the edges. This time there had been no fleas and lice to deal with beyond the usual, and only a customary accumulation of sweat and grime. Now he was clean and a faint scent of rose water clung to him, mingling with the aroma of dried lavender from the chest in which his fresh shirt and hose had been stored. The sight of the livid scar on his wrist had shocked her. She was used to seeing men with such marks, but seldom those so close to her. Her father had very few, apart from an old white one on his thigh, sustained long before she was born, but to see the blemishes of war on Hugh made her realise how easily she might have lost him and that the news entering Framlingham could have been so much worse.

"Longespée is to be ransomed in exchange for King Philip's cousin," he told her. "It's ironic that Robert of Dreux was captured by me and my men at the fight for Nantes. It's going to irritate Longespée like a burr under his shirt to have to thank me for his rescue. It galls me too because I would rather the exchange were made for Ralph."

"But at least one of them will be set free."

"The wrong one."

Mahelt felt a glimmer of impatience. "Your father will do his best to raise the money and have Ralph returned as soon as he can. Surely Longespée, once he is free, will do the same? It is his obligation." She unpinned her wimple and draped it over a coffer.

"We'll see, won't we?" Hugh looked down at his son. "I did not tell my mother, but I fear for Ralph's situation."

"Why?" Mahelt was suddenly concerned.

"While Longespée is a prisoner too, Ralph has the protection of an influential brother. Once Longespée is ransomed, Ralph's importance diminishes. He becomes not the kin of the king of England's half-brother, but just the minor son of an earl. There will be no one to look out for his welfare. I wrote to his gaolers from La Rochelle and sent all the money I had with me to pay for his keep but it will not last long."

"Do you know how much they are demanding for him?"

"Not yet, but it will be steep because of his tie with Longespée. If Longespée is worth Robert of Dreux, then Ralph's price will not come cheaply."

"So it behoves them to keep him alive and in good condition."

"Depending upon how patient they are, yes, but once Longespée goes it will grow more difficult."

"How much is a lot?"

He rubbed his forehead. "Perhaps a thousand marks."

Mahelt gasped. "That's as much as the relief on an earldom!"

"The French are not fools. They calculate how much men have in their coffers and what will be a serious inconvenience. It increases the resentment against the king and it drains yet more of England's silver." Hugo wriggled away from him and went to fetch his wooden animals. "It's a total ruin and it should never have happened. It doesn't matter how brave and dashing men are in the thick of the fight if they cannot coordinate their actions. If all had come together at the same time, we would have wiped the French from the field, but they had the better control and command. John will have to agree humiliating terms with King Philip, and there will be anger and dissatisfaction on all sides. These are bitter and difficult times." He beckoned to her and she came to lie down beside him. "I dreamed of your hair," he said in a cracking voice. Reaching out to stroke it, he began unfastening her braid.

"Just my hair?" she teased.

"Well, no, other parts too—frequently."

She gave a splutter and nudged him, but the glint in his eyes made her breath grow short. Hugh cupped the side of her face and kissed her and she set her hands to his shirt where the laces were untied and she could feel his skin, still with the dampness of the bath upon it.

Little Hugo rejoined them on the bed with his collection of wooden animals and, in the true light of sharing, gave the sheep to Mahelt, the cow to his father, and kept the horse for himself. Then nothing would satisfy him but that everyone should make the noises pertaining to each animal. By the time Hugh and Mahelt had finished baaing, mooing, and neighing, they were helpless with laughter, part of it release, and part of it the sheer incongruity of such foolish play when set against the backdrop of what had happened and the uncertainty of the future.

Thirty-five

MARLBOROUGH, WILTSHIRE, FEBRUARY 1215

*E*LA, COUNTESS OF SALISBURY, CAUGHT HERSELF SMOOTHING her gown yet again and immediately clasped her hands together, gripping her right over her left, using the pressure as an anchor. Beyond the shutters, a wet February dusk was encroaching on the last of the daylight. She had set out soon after dawn from Salisbury, but the journey had been interminable—the roads had been muddy and the side-saddle precarious, although necessary for her dignity. She would rather not have come to court, but was determined to talk to the king and press him to make haste with arrangements for her husband's release. Negotiations had been dragging on for six months and there was still no sign of an agreement. Ela could not understand why John was trailing his heels when his half-brother was so needed here in England and had sacrificed so much for him.

Trestles draped with embroidered white cloths had been set up in the royal apartment to provide food for the guests, but informally, and the king was mingling with his barons and bishops. He reminded Ela of a wolf who would devour her if the chance arose. She hated being in his presence because it was difficult keeping her distance without transgressing the rules of courtesy. However, for the sake of her husband and children, she was prepared to brave that wolf in his lair.

"Sire." She curtseyed to him.

Resplendent in a jewelled mantle lined with ermine and sable, John raised her to her feet. "Sister." He kissed her on either cheek; then he set his forefinger under her jaw and applied pressure. "Chin up. Matters are progressing well. We'll soon have Longespée home—which is why I assume you have come?" He gestured around. "Everyone in this chamber wants something from me. If they had nothing to ask, they would not be here. That's another reason to miss sweet William. At least he'd keep me company and lose to me at dice and not begrudge it." He eyed her with bright speculation like a hawk considering its prey in the grass.

Ela's throat was so tight she felt as if she were being strangled. "Yes, sire, I am indeed here on my husband's behalf."

"At least you are honest, which is more than the rest can claim." John curled his lip. "Or are you?"

Ela said nothing but stood very straight, pretending there was a steel rod down her back assisting her to face him.

"Will's not in chains, you know," John continued. "He is held in honourable imprisonment."

"For which I thank God and His mother daily, but it is still a great grief to me that I do not have him with me," Ela said stiffly. "The children need their father."

John's gaze was cynical. "Surely you must find ways to solace yourself and your infants. You are a resourceful woman. I am sure you are not yet at your wits' end."

Ela drew herself up. "I find comfort in prayer and in God."

He looked pained. "Indeed."

"I pray too for Ralph Bigod," she said, aware of her duty to kin.

John's lip curled as he glanced across the room towards the Norfolk contingent. "His family will deal with that matter."

"But you could help. He is half-brother to my husband."

Ela glanced across too. Mahelt was here, in the company of some other baronial wives. At least she would have a haven in a moment. There was safety in numbers.

"And almost my kin because the Countess of Norfolk used to be my father's poppet?" John looked contemptuous. "I think not. The Bigods are scarcely impoverished, are they?" He had spoken in a raised voice so that those nearby could hear. There was a certain amount of sniggering and knowing looks were exchanged.

"The countess is unwell and she frets for both her sons," Ela replied with dignity.

Still smiling, John turned to the food-laden trestle behind them and picked up a small hard-boiled egg, mottled bright yellow from being cooked in saffron. "Your gentle heart commends you, sister. It's a rare delicacy—like this dish. Have you tried one yet?"

Ela shook her head. "No, sire."

"You should. Eggs are hard to come by at this time of year and the cook has impregnated the yolk with grains of paradise, no less." He raised and lowered his brows suggestively and held it out towards her.

Knowing full well that grains of paradise had a reputation as an aphrodisiac, and revolted by his tone as he said the word "impregnated," Ela shook her head. "Sire, I thank you, but I am not hungry."

"Oh, but you must try it, I insist!" John smiled wolfishly. "We don't want you to pine away to nothing in my brother's absence, do we? He doesn't want to return to skin and bones; that would be a terrible sin. Open your mouth, there's a good girl."

She was cornered. To others it would just look as if John were jollying her along. It was a compliment of the highest order to be given food by the king and since they were not sitting to share a trencher, this was but a variation of the favour.

But she couldn't bear the thought. She felt as if she was going to gag as he put the egg against her lips. She had to part them and John parted his at the same time. Eyes brimming with delight, he began pushing it into her mouth. It was too big to eat in one go and Ela had to bite down, and then chew and swallow. And then the other half. The spices were pungent and stung the roof of her mouth and the back of her throat.

"Is it not wonderful?" John asked, licking his lips with sensual pleasure as if he was savouring the food himself.

Ela couldn't answer. She put her hand to her mouth to cover the motion of her jaw. He was waiting for her to swallow it; so she couldn't spit it out into a kerchief. Somehow she succeeded, but the taste lingered in her mouth and little morsels clung to her teeth and tongue. "Sire, by your leave…" She curtseyed to him and without waiting for his dismissal clapped her hand to her mouth and fled the room. At the first latrine she reached, she was violently sick down the evil-smelling hole until her stomach was sore. She wiped her mouth and pressed her forehead against the cold stone wall while she tried to stop shuddering. At a sound behind her, she spun round and then cried out, for John was standing in the entrance, blocking her way.

She tried to scream, but all that emerged was a wordless croak. He stepped forwards, took her by the tops of the arms, and pushed her against the wall. He ran one hand down her body from breast to crotch. "You didn't like what I gave you?" he said hoarsely. "What a shame, when it was an item so perfect."

Ela twisted her head aside and struggled, but he held her fast.

"Think on this," he said. "A brother's wife becomes the other brother's property when her husband is not there to defend her. You must rely on me now to keep you safe— hmm?" He forced himself against her. "Always remember that I am here to defend your honour, my sweet as honey sister." He kissed her cheekbone hard with his mouth parted so that she could feel his teeth and then he licked the side of her face before pulling away and playfully tweaking her nose. "That's my brave girl. Your husband will be home before you know it."

When he had gone, Ela propped herself against the wall to prevent her knees from buckling. Her breath was stuck in her chest and she had to fight to draw it into her lungs. She couldn't scream for help; she felt as if he had ripped her inside out and thrown away a vital, private part of her.

"Sister?"

Her knees did give way with relief as she saw Mahelt and Hugh, the latter with one hand on his knife hilt.

"Dear God, Ela..." Mahelt hastened to put her arms around her.

"I'm all right," Ela gasped.

"No you're not. I've had my eye on you ever since John forced that egg on you. Did he harm you?"

"No," Ela said, but her shuddering increased.

"Come." Mahelt beckoned to Hugh. "We'll take you to your pavilion."

They bore Ela to her round blue and gold tent standing in a corner of the bailey. Mahelt dismissed Ela's women and seated her cousin on her fur-covered travelling bed while Hugh poured her a cup of wine.

"He would dishonour his own brother." Ela's voice shook with loathing.

"What did he do?"

"He...he touched me and he said I had to rely on him for my safety because in my husband's absence, I am his property."

Hugh's mouth curled with revulsion. "The whoreson."

Ela flashed him a panic-filled look. "You mustn't say or do

anything. My husband and Ralph are still prisoners. I want them both home and safe. If you speak out, I shall be dishonoured and so will my William. He is a proud man and it would overset him."

"You are not the first he has intimidated in this way," Mahelt said grimly. "He attempted de Vesci's wife, and he offered insult to me when he came to Framlingham. He seems to think that everything he sees should be his."

Ela stared at Mahelt in renewed shock. "Dear God…"

Mahelt smiled with sour satisfaction. "I twisted his jewels hard enough to make sitting a saddle a harsh discomfort. It wasn't punishment enough, but I knew I couldn't take it further with his mercenaries in our ward and him as our guest. None of us could."

Ela swallowed. "I want my husband home," she said and, putting her face in her hands, began to sob. "I want William."

Mahelt enfolded Ela in her arms. "You can sleep in our pavilion tonight, and we shall escort you back to Salisbury on the morrow."

Ela nodded. A shudder ran through her as she straightened up and controlled herself. "Thank you."

Hugh summoned Ela's ladies and told them to gather together what their mistress deemed necessary and bring it to the Bigod pavilion. Then, in a group, the women crossed the sward with Hugh walking protectively beside them. On the way, they encountered Mahelt's oldest brother returning to his own lodging in the company of several other young knights. Mahelt had no intention of telling him what had happened to Ela. Instead, she asked after Will's young wife Alais and behaved as if she and Ela were just socialising in the way women did at such gatherings.

"She is well," Will replied, and his expression was more cheerful and satisfied than Mahelt had seen in a long while.

"The baby is due soon." He looked at Hugh. "An heir for the heir. You must know how that feels."

"Indeed." Hugh smiled. "To have a part of yourself to bear your name into the future is a true gift from God. I am happy for you."

Will returned the smile. "You must come to the christening and wet the baby's head!"

"Oh, you can take that for granted," Hugh said with another grin.

The young men went loudly on their way, and the smile dropped from Hugh's face. Ela was hiding herself against Mahelt's cloak. When they arrived at the Bigod pavilion, Hugh set a double guard around it and bade the men keep the camp fire burning and the torches lit all night.

Thirty-six

*H*UGH LAY ON THE BED IN HIS CHAMBER, HANDS TUCKED behind his head and legs crossed at the ankles. He had discarded tunic, belt, and shoes and was glad of the luxury of a soft feather mattress under him rather than a hard saddle, and before that a splintered wooden bench at Northampton Castle, from which he and his father had recently returned. More than eighteen months after its first drafting, the charter of liberties was finally on the trestle being discussed by all parties.

"The king has rejected the charter," Hugh told Mahelt. "He says he will listen to grievances on a case-by-case basis but he refuses to consider a document that will bind him for all time."

"Of course he has rejected it!" she scoffed. "It's not in his interests to agree."

Hugh raised his elbows behind his head and gripped his hair in a frustrated gesture. "We thought there was a chance of negotiation, since it's based on a charter agreed by the first King Henry, but he's refused outright. Now we must decide if we should openly renounce our fealty. It will come to a confrontation, no doubt about that." He looked pensive. "Your father stands by John and so does Langton. He says agreement must come through sanction and negotiation. John's asked the pope for his backing. FitzWalter and de Vesci want to force John to negotiate by defying him and inviting the French to intervene, but FitzWalter and de Vesci are hardly the stuff of leadership."

Mahelt felt as if she was caught between two rooms and being squeezed in the doorway. Her father would hold firm for John whatever happened, because his honour demanded it. He had given his allegiance for better or worse. She had been taught that a promise was a promise and you stayed true, but what if the other person was a perjured oath-breaker and a despoiler of all? What was right and what was wrong? She no longer knew, and neither, she thought, did anyone else. "If you renounce John, you will be at war with my father." She knew Will would be among the rebels too. Although he and their father were on speaking terms, they still stood on opposite sides of the divide.

Hugh sighed. "If we can get John to at least consider some compromises, there might be hope. No man wants open war."

"Lest he be a mercenary, or lest he can gain power from it." Mahelt moved to close the shutters against a chill evening breeze and lit more candles.

"Then we must make sure that men gain more from peace. That is the ambition of your father and mine, and the archbishop, but we must wait and see what the pope has to say." Hugh looked at his fingernails. "I heard today that Longespée is to be freed at last. The exchange is to take place this week."

Mahelt brightened. "Oh, that is great news for Ela and for your mother."

Hugh did not look particularly overjoyed. "Indeed, but Ralph is still a prisoner and it has been nine months now. Being the half-brother of the king's half-brother plainly carries no weight except in terms of the demand. That I helped capture Dreux goes ignored. Once Longespée is home, I hope he sees fit to contribute towards Ralph's release, but I won't hold my breath. I also suspect Longespée is being ransomed now because John needs his support against the threat of armed defiance."

Mahelt turned from lighting the candles and joined him on the bed. "You should not let Longespée trouble your soul. God knows, we have enough worries without you brooding on him."

"He doesn't trouble my soul," Hugh snapped. "It just is not right that he goes free and Ralph does not." He looked thoughtful. "I wonder what Longespée will do when he discovers what John did to Ela."

She looked alarmed. "You wouldn't tell him…"

Hugh made an irritated sound. "Of course not. It is not my place and even if it were, he would not listen to me. I am just his rustic Bigod brother who doesn't understand noblesse oblige and has no idea of a proper man's behaviour." He started to leave the bed because the thought of Longespée had agitated him into motion, but Mahelt pushed him back down.

"I have some news for you of my own." She took his hand and laid it against her waist. "I am with child again."

As she had hoped, his focus immediately changed. A slow smile spread across his face and he angled his fingers downwards over her womb. She was tall and taut-muscled, never showing her pregnancies until well into her fifth month, so there was no telling how far along she was. They had not been taking precautions since Christmas time. "That is good news indeed. Do you know when?"

"Before November, I think."

He pulled her down to him and kissed her tenderly and for a brief while lost his cares and concerns in paying thorough attention to his wife.

❖❖❖

In the morning, Mahelt visited Ida, who was dozing by the fire as usual. These days she barely ate enough to keep a sparrow alive, but now she was animated and her eyes were sparkling.

"Have you heard the news about my son, my William?" she cried. "He's to be released!"

Mahelt embraced her. "Yes, Mother, I have heard."

"I hope he comes to visit soon. I'm longing to see him."

"I am sure he will," Mahelt said diplomatically.

"Of course he must see his wife first, and the king."

Mahelt said nothing.

"Men and their foolish politics," Ida sniffed. "Fighting like cockerels over who is to be on top of the midden." She picked up her embroidery and began to sew. Mahelt watched Ida's dextrous fingers. Sometimes she thought that her mother-in-law's wits had disappeared into her sewing and it was the only thing these days she could make a positive decision about.

"Ralph must surely be freed soon." Mahelt began sorting through the silks in Ida's work basket, looking to see if she was running short of any colours. "They cannot keep him for much longer."

Ida paused her stitching. "I had not forgotten Ralph," she said, her voice suddenly sharp. "I pray for him as I pray for all of my children. I wish with all my heart that my sons had been freed together, but since it was not to be, surely it is better to rejoice for the one than weep for the other—at least today."

"Indeed so, Mother, I am sorry," Mahelt agreed, but wondered what would have happened if it had been the other way around and Ralph released while Longespée remained a captive.

Ida fell asleep over her embroidery and Mahelt went to look out of the window at the garden. She wanted to talk to the gardener about planting some roses like the ones at her father's manor at Caversham with their wonderful scent and petals the colour of wild strawberries and clotted cream. Her ruminations were interrupted by Orlotia, Ida's chamber lady, who crossed the room on tiptoe and spoke to her in a low voice. "Madam, your brother is here."

Mahelt frowned. She wasn't expecting visitors. "Which one?"

"The lord William, madam."

Mahelt was nonplussed. What was Will doing here at Framlingham when he should be with their father or about the business of the earldom? His wife was due to give birth any day now as well—perhaps had already done so. "Where is he?"

"In your solar, madam."

The note in Orlotia's voice made Mahelt certain that something terrible had happened. Without waking Ida, she hurried from the chamber.

She found Will sitting on the smaller hearth bench with his back to the fire, his face in his hands.

"Will?" She was suddenly very frightened and, because of it, almost angry. Her brother shouldn't behave like this. It wasn't right.

He sat up and lowered his hands. "Close the door and make sure no one is listening," he said in a cracking voice.

Feeling queasy, Mahelt did so, then went to the curtain between solar and bedchamber to make sure no maids were lurking in there. "What is it?" she repeated. "Tell me!"

He swallowed and swallowed again and shook his head.

"Look, I'll go and get you a draught." Mahelt turned towards the door but he put out his hand to stop her.

"No, just...just let me get my breath."

She retraced her steps and sat beside him on the bench, feeling really scared. What if her father had been taken ill again? What if something had happened to her mother or one of her siblings? "Take your time," she said, as much for her benefit as his.

"It's..." Will shook his head and almost retched. "It is the life of my unborn child and my wife...the light of my life."

"What?" Mahelt stared at him in dumbfounded shock.

"Alais is dead!" Will began to sob in a harsh, breaking voice.

Appalled at the way her imperious brother was disintegrating before her eyes, Mahelt tried to embrace him, but he thrust her off, and she had to be content with running her hand up and down his spine instead. Dear God, Alais must have died in childbirth. She tried not to think about the new life growing in her own womb as if she would do harm by association.

Will washed his palms over his face. "My wife, my son, my future," he said in a sick voice. "Murdered by John's assassins at the heart of where they should have been safe."

Mahelt stared at him open-mouthed with disbelief. "Murdered?"

"They were left dying in their own blood. Someone killed them, and vigilance was so slack at Pembroke that the murderer made good his escape. Alais was in our parents' care and they didn't protect her. They ignored the threat. John is out to destroy us, from inside out and outside in." His spine shuddered under her palm.

"What do you mean?" She was shocked that he was talking of their mother and father like this. The entire situation was unreal and unbelievable. "Mama and Papa are always on their guard. You are overset and mistaken."

"There is no mistake. I have seen their bodies." He opened his clenched fist and showed her the small embroidered flower he had been gripping. "From Alais's wedding dress," he said hoarsely. "They were not on their guard that day. However you defend them, you cannot defend this!"

Mahelt felt hollow inside. "How do you know an assassin was sent by John?"

"Who else?" he said with bared teeth. "Who else would do such a thing or want to harm our family in such a way? He has never forgiven or forgotten how my father humiliated him in Ireland. You do not know the half of what happened at court when Richard and I were in his clutches. He will bring us all down. Richard is out of his way in Normandy, but the rest of us are not."

His words, their tone, what he had told her, caused Mahelt to press her hand to her womb. She wanted to run and find her sons and make sure they were safe. If someone could do this to Alais in the heart of the family's protection, then nowhere was out of harm's way. "You cannot blame our mother and father," she repeated.

Will ignored her. "They were my pride and joy," he said in a shattered voice. "They made my life bearable. Now I have to live with this evil and eke out my existence until I join them in the dust." His shoulders shook and he started to sob again.

This time he did let Mahelt fold him in her arms: her big brother with whom she had fought tooth and nail as a child. Neither of them had ever backed down or yielded an inch, but now she felt a great wash of maternal, tender pity. She let him weep until the storm abated enough for him to raise his head. Then she found him a napkin to mop his face and fetched a cup of wine from the bedside flagon. It was little enough, but she felt as if she was helping.

"What will you do now?" she asked as she returned with the cup.

"I do not know," he said numbly. "Only let me stay here a few days to gather my wits and think, then I shall go elsewhere. I have friends." His gaze sharpened. "I don't want you telling our parents where I am...swear to me."

Mahelt's heart turned over. "They have to know, Will."

"I forbid it," he snarled. "I've severed my ties and I won't go back—not while my father supports that tyrant. You must promise me, you must!"

Mahelt was not sure that she should, but the anguish in his eyes, the twist of his mouth, made her acquiesce. "Hugh and my father by marriage will have to be told. I cannot keep such a thing secret from them, and they will know you are here."

Will knuckled his eyes again. "It doesn't matter. It might even make them willing to listen, and alter their minds. Our sire is set on his course to support the king whatever happens. He would rather keep to his precious honour than deviate by so much as a step. He's like a sheep on a well-worn track who won't change because that is how it has always been."

Mahelt gasped at the bitterness in his remark. "You mustn't say that!"

"Then what am I allowed to say?" He bared his teeth. "Is it not true? Have we not from infancy been force-fed the fact that honour is sacred? No matter what it costs, we must keep it. But what if the cost of honour is supporting another's dishonour? What then?"

Mahelt said nothing because if there was an answer, she did not know what it was.

"I came to you because I could think of nowhere else," Will said, his shoulders slumping. "Earl Roger dislikes me, but he is a fair man of sound judgement, and I thought he might just be willing to listen. Is there...is there somewhere I can sleep?"

"There's a guest chamber in one of the towers that I'll have aired and a mattress put on the bed."

"Thank you. And a bolt on the inside of the door." He pressed his lips together.

Mahelt almost said that there was no need: he was utterly safe at Framlingham; but then Alais should have been utterly safe at Pembroke. "Wait here," she said. "I will have it seen to."

"No...don't go." He caught her sleeve. "Please."

Once more she was assailed by anger and outrage that her strong, steady brother should be brought to this. A lost child. "Just to instruct the maids," she said in a soothing voice. "I won't leave. I promise you that."

❖❖❖

The men of the Bigod household sat around the trestle table in the earl's chamber and listened as Will haltingly told his story. Mahelt was present too, sitting beside him, lending her silent support, with Hugh at her other side. Will warded off the exclamations of revulsion and the tendering of appalled sympathy as if fending blows with a splintered shield.

The earl leaned back. "Whether John perpetrated this deed or not, this is no way for a country to be governed. The king's mercenaries do as they please and he puts them in positions of authority which they abuse. No one is safe. There are spies in every household. What the king cannot achieve by legitimate means, he digs from the underbelly. He has secret signs and countersigns and his men act according to their dictates no matter what they may say in public. People are tortured and murdered and killed. Demands are made and made again. Promises are broken. Enough is enough. I say that unless the king not only agrees to the terms in that charter but carries them out, we must stand against him."

"Others have already risen," Will said, "and not just in the North. Mowbray, de Bohun, de Vere, and Albini have all declared against him and more will come."

The earl eyed him from beneath the long brim of his hat. "But not your father." He shifted position in his high-backed chair. "I am not without information. De Vere and Albini are my kin. I do not undertake this lightly because if I defy the king, I must be prepared to fight both his hirelings and those barons who do not rebel against him—likely with sword and shield as well as with a lawyer's pen. I have no fire in my belly for that kind of conflict, but we have reached a point where we must choose." He sent a weighty gaze around the people gathered at the trestle.

Mahelt looked down, rubbing her thumb over her wedding

ring. Her stomach was hollow; she felt trapped. If defiance were chosen, it would set her husband and brother against her father. Her adopted marital family against the kin of her birth. She hated John, but defying him also meant defying her father, and that was almost too painful to bear.

"So how do we go forward in this?" Hugh asked. "It is one thing to say we will defy the king, another to do it. We need leverage, and for the moment we have nothing."

"I agree," the earl replied. "We know who will support us among our peers, but we must cast our net wider and look beyond our own walls to the towns...and perhaps to Paris as well."

A deep silence ensued as everyone considered the enormity of the words because having them out in the open made them real. "You mean London and Louis?" Hugh said after taking a deep breath.

His father nodded. "If we hold London, then we have the heart of England's commerce. And if John still refuses to negotiate, Louis of France has been waiting his opportunity..."

❖❖❖

When the conference was over, Mahelt stood in the yard, waiting for Hugh to bid his father goodnight. Her brother had already retired to his own chamber and barred the door. Framlingham's wall walk bristled with soldiers; the guard had been doubled and security tightened. Mahelt shivered and laid her hand protectively over her womb and the unborn baby.

Hugh emerged from the chamber and, opening his cloak, enfolded her within its fur-lined wings.

She bit her lip. "What has happened to Will—what is happening now—makes me realise how easily everything can be taken away."

"Everyone is safe here." He pulled her against him so she could feel the upright strength of his body. "There are guards at every chamber door—loyal men."

"But there should not have to be. We should be able to sleep in security, without the fear of being murdered in our beds."

"I agree. John must be brought to account and his creatures banished."

"And when that happens, my father will fall too. But if John survives, we go down. It's an impossible state of affairs."

Hugh traced her cheek with his fingertip. "Your father is well versed in politics and he will endure, even if it means retiring to Ireland. If John does prevail...well then, he will not harm the daughter and grandson of the man who is his mainstay."

"Even if he saw to the killing of my brother's wife?"

"There is no proof of that, only your brother's opinion, and that is not entirely trustworthy. You know how much he hates the king."

"Because he has lived with him," she said in a voice filled with repugnance.

"Yes, but it still does not prove John did the deed."

"He's behind it. You only need to look at his reputation. Who else would it be?" Mahelt pushed out of his arms and walked briskly towards their chamber. On reaching their rooms, she passed the guard on the outer door and found another one of Hugh's most trusted men sitting outside the curtained-off portion of the chamber where their sons were asleep. The man silently rose, bowed, and moved away to give her space. Mahelt parted the curtain to look in at the boys. Never had the potential for disaster and the destruction of everything she held dear been clearer to her. The rumours about Arthur, the truth about Maude de Braose and her son, John's predatory intimidation of women, and now the suspicion and speculation over the death of her brother's wife and unborn baby. What more proof did Hugh or anyone need? She pushed the awareness of her father's loyalty to John from her mind and sealed it away because it was too painful and complicated to think about.

Roger was surrendered on his back, cheeks rosy with sleep, his dark hair slightly damp. His little brother had his thumb in his mouth and was sucking on it in slumber, his lashes and brows dusted with gold. Oh God, oh God. She pressed the back of her hand to her mouth and her vision blurred.

Hugh arrived in her wake and curled his arm around her shoulders while he too looked at their sleeping sons. "Whatever happens, I swear on my soul that I will keep you and them safe," he said.

Roger muttered in his sleep and tossed. His parents withdrew so as not to waken him. At their own bed, Hugh lit the canopy lamp. Mahelt fixed her gaze on him like a warrior focusing on a field where battle was soon to be joined. "On your soul," she repeated.

"Yes," he replied, his jaw set. "On my soul."

She had to drop her gaze. Either he was taking matters too lightly and uttering the oath as a placebo, or he meant every word, and if she held him to that oath and he failed her, he would be damned—and so would she. "Then keep your word," she said as a scent of incense from the perfumed oil began to fill the bed space.

"May I be damned if I do not." Hugh placed his hands either side of her face and sealed the moment with a long, intense kiss. Mahelt hesitated briefly, then she set her arms around him and committed her trust.

Thirty-seven

*L*ONGESPÉE CHECKED HIS SWORDBELT AND ADJUSTED THE latch. He had lost weight during his imprisonment and the customary notch hole was too slack. He had to grow used to wearing weaponry again too. There was comfort in having his famous long sword at his hip once more, but nothing fitted as it had once done and it bothered him. The taint of defeat and imprisonment needed time and prayer before it could be fully healed.

Looking out of the chamber window, he watched a groom add his destrier to the warhorse string—not one of the Bigod mounts, but a sturdy dun stallion from the king's own stable. Flemish soldiers milled in the yard, making last-minute preparations for the imminent march to London.

Longespée drew a deep breath to steady himself. He had not been home yet, had not even seen Ela or his children. John had been at Sandwich to greet his landing when he was finally exchanged for Robert of Dreux, and had immediately put him back in harness saying there was time for all else later. For now he was needed to deal with the rebellion of various barons before it could gain strength and support. Northampton had withstood a fortnight's siege, but Bedford had fallen and the rebels were en route to London. Those rebels included many good friends and his own kin. His Bigod half-brothers; his mother's husband. He tightened his lips. Perhaps Ralph, still a prisoner in Paris, was in the best place.

"Are you ready?"

Longespée turned to John, whom he had not heard enter the room. His brother looked older. His eyes were bloodshot and pouched. New lines dragged at his mouth corners. There was also something hiding within him that Longespée could not quite grasp—an element of watchfulness pertaining to Longespée himself that had not been there before, and which he assumed was caused by his closeness to the Bigods, or perhaps even guilt at the months of captivity following Bouvines. August to May had been a long time. "Yes, sire," he said. "I am ready." He pinned his cloak with the round gold brooch that was as much his signature as the long sword at his hip.

"Do not delay on the road," John warned. "I want London secured and then I want you and de Melun to encircle the whoresons and bring them down."

"I shall make all haste." Longespée donned his spurs.

John's mouth twisted. "At least I can count on you. Men whom I have thought allies have deserted me and reneged on the oaths they swore to me at my coronation."

Longespée heard an odd note in his half-brother's voice. There was anxiety and sadness, and almost a hint of accusation, as if Longespée himself were being measured for his loyalty.

"I will never desert you, sire." He paused to kneel to John, who raised him up and gave him the kiss of peace on either cheek.

"It gladdens me to hear you say so. Go to your business. I am trusting you and de Melun not to fail me." He didn't say *this time* but he might as well have done.

❖❖❖

Hugh dusted the board with his hat, sat down on the trestle table in the main room of the family's London house on Friday

Street, and accepted a cup of wine from the flustered porter who had not been expecting the sudden arrival of the earl, his heir, and their knights. His wife was hastily concocting a pottage out of what they had in the stores and various underlings had been sent running to the cookshops to see what could be procured.

"Easier than Northampton," Ranulf FitzRobert said as he directed a squire to place his baggage roll in a corner, took a cup from Hugh, and joined him. Hugh agreed that it was. Being a Sunday, the citizens of London were all at church, having conveniently left the gates wide open for the rebels. While there had been no tumultuous welcome, there was subdued approval. "Now the king will be forced to negotiate."

The earl walked into the hall and glanced with amused irritation at his son and his son-in-law sitting on the table together. "The effort spent on your upbringing all went to waste, I see," he said.

Hugh shrugged. "We're rebels now."

"That doesn't mean we should relax our manners—to the contrary," his father replied sharply, but when Ranulf started to get up, he waved his hand. "Ah, let be. We're not likely to be eating off this thing until vespers at least. How's the wine?" He took the cup Hugh poured for him.

"Musty but drinkable."

"King Henry's used to have the taste and consistency of mud." The earl took a sip, wrinkled his mouth, but didn't comment. "I've heard that we arrived here first by the skin of our teeth. The Earl of Salisbury and Savaric de Melun were hard on our heels."

"The skin of our teeth is good enough," Hugh said. "There is nothing they can do to us. Providing we do not upset the citizens we have a safe haven."

His father nodded agreement. "Possession of London

and the support of the Londoners give us a strong bargaining counter. I shall not deny it was a blow not to take Northampton, but we have Bedford."

Ranulf swirled the wine in his cup. "Some might think it less of a bargaining counter and more of an acquisition. A base from which to offer the French rule of England."

"Indeed," Roger replied, "but we wait and see how John responds. I am not overjoyed at the notion of a French prince on England's throne—John is our anointed sovereign, but he must be reined back and brought to account." He looked sombrely at Hugh and Ranulf. "My father rebelled against the rule of what he saw as a tyrant, but he was defeated and Framlingham was taken away from us and razed to the ground. After my father died I spent the next twelve years trying to regain our lands and obtaining permission to rebuild Framlingham. I have ever played a cautious game because I know that what has taken years to build up can be destroyed in a single day. One false move is all it takes."

"And is this a false move?" Hugh asked.

"You tell me, my son," Roger said wearily. "Is it?"

❖ ❖ ❖

Longespée compressed his lips as the scout drew rein in a puff of dust. Even before the man spoke, he knew it was bad news. "Sire, the rebels have entered London! The gates were opened to them by the citizens."

Longespée turned his gaze to the distant smudge of the city walls. He had ridden like hell to cut off the rebels' path and sent envoys to the city to plead his cause, all to no avail. He had been outmanoeuvred and out-distanced by faster men.

"What now?" John's mercenary captain Savaric de Melun joined him. He was thickset, broad across the shoulders, and battle-scarred like a seasoned bear-baiting dog. His mail shirt gleamed like snakeskin with each breath.

Longespée gnawed his thumb knuckle. "Leave a contingent

to watch their movements and harry any messengers coming in and out. No point in us all remaining here. We'll return to the king and let him decide what to do next."

"He will be enraged," de Melun warned.

"What else can we do?" Longespée shrugged. "We can hardly lay siege to the place the size it is and with what we have."

De Melun gave him a sidelong look. "Then you tell him," he said. "You are his blood kin after all."

❖ ❖ ❖

Mahelt gasped as Hugh pulled her into his embrace and gave her an intense, scratchy kiss. He was hard-muscled and tanned from days spent outdoors on campaign and Mahelt's heart turned over with love and desire. She had received occasional letters from him, but had had no idea when he would return to Framlingham. During her childhood, her father had often been away all summer, and she had resigned herself to similar from Hugh, so to see him now was a wonderful surprise—and a relief.

He broke from her to fend off Roger who wanted to show him the sword skills he had been developing as the summer advanced. Laughing, Hugh dodged and ducked and then allowed himself to be caught and slaughtered. "I yield, I yield!" he cried as his sons pummelled him. He made a face of mock-worry at Mahelt. "God save me when I have three of them leaping on me!"

Laughing, Mahelt placed her hand on her ripening womb. "That won't be for a while," she said. "You have a few years' grace at least." When he had finally extricated himself from his heirs' murderous intentions and sent them off to attack his squires instead, Mahelt asked where his father was.

"Still in London, busy with legal matters." Hugh's expression grew serious as the initial pleasure of coming home subsided. He removed his tunic and, pushing back his shirtsleeves, sat down on the bed. "Ranulf's gone home to Middleham to prepare for conflict."

"Conflict? Why?" Mahelt's sense of pleasure and wellbeing dissipated and she looked at him in alarm.

"The king has signed the charter of liberties. He met us in a meadow just outside Windsor and he put his seal to the terms. I was a witness; so was my father, and yours, and Will and Longespée."

"Is that not good news? Is it not what you were all hoping for?"

He sighed deeply. "It should be, but it's worthless. The moment after he signed it, John was writing to the pope, begging to be absolved of his vow to keep the terms. He considers the charter something to be circumvented, or trampled on from behind and thrown in the midden. He might as well not have signed it at all. The quarrel has only escalated."

"So what happens now?"

Hugh shook his head and said without enthusiasm, "Prince Louis has agreed to send us French reinforcements while he deliberates whether or not to come himself. Your father and Archbishop Langton are doing what they can from their side of the fence too because we need a workable peace—but for the moment it seems unlikely to happen. John has signed without intention of keeping his word and the moderates have lost ground on our side. The likes of de Vesci say that if we cannot contain him, then we must bring him down."

"And if Louis does come in person?"

"Then he will be offered the throne."

"And that will mean war..."

"War is already a fact," he replied bleakly. "It is happening now. I am not home to rest, but, like Ranulf, to prepare us for what is to come."

❖ ❖ ❖

For the first time in over a year, Longespée stood in his own chamber at Salisbury Palace and feasted his gaze upon his wife. He did not think he had ever seen a sight more beautiful. Ela wore a close-fitting gown of kitten-soft green wool. A wimple of gossamer-thin linen hinted at the glossy dark gold hair beneath. The sun streaming in through the window gilded her, so that she almost seemed to be fashioned from rare illuminated glass.

A flick of his fingers sent his chamberlain bowing from the room. Longespée waited until he heard the latch drop before he put his arms around her, kissing her on the forehead, both cheeks, and finally on her warm, pink lips. Then he held her away for the pleasure of looking at her all over again. "I dreamed of you every day I was a prisoner. I thought of you and our children and it raised my spirits when I was at my lowest ebb." Raising her hand, he rubbed his thumb over her wedding ring, and then kissed the gold, enjoying the moment to the full, enhancing it for himself by playing a game of courtly love. "I come to you remade, my mistress and my wife, to ask your favour and acceptance again."

Ela gazed at him numbly, a forlorn expression on her face. He saw her slender throat move as she swallowed and he began to feel anxious. "What is it, beloved? Have I changed so much? Am I not still pleasing to you?" He grew more alarmed as she covered her face with her other hand and began to sob.

"It's not that, husband," she whispered. "It's because I am no longer worthy of you; indeed, I shall never be worthy again."

Longespée began to feel sick. "What is this?" Seizing her arm, he shook her. "Have you played me false? Have you been unfaithful?" He would never have imagined his Ela looking at another man, but he had been gone a long time and he could think of no other reason for her reaction.

"Not by my choice," Ela sobbed, "upon my honour, not by my choice, but a certain one has disgraced the name of brother."

Longespée reeled. His brain swirled with so much agitation that it might as well have been blank. "What has that Bigod peasant done to you?" he snarled. He closed his fist around his sword hilt. "I will know it all."

"Bigod?" Her drenched gaze filled with shock. "You mean Hugh? Oh not him, no! He and Mahelt rescued me and kept me safe. Rather look to your brother the king..." Making an effort, she steadied herself and told him everything.

Shocked, Longespée slumped down on a bench. "So you tell me that John has dishonoured us both by his wantonness? That he touched you and checked himself only within an inch of the act itself?"

Ela nodded. "I am afraid it is true, my lord." She wrung her hands. "I would never lie to you. He...he said that in your absence I was his property."

Longespée clenched his fists and his eyes were dark with anger. "Then he can be my brother no more. He has defiled that bond."

She gave him a wide, frightened look. "What will you do?"

"Nothing as yet. I need time to think." Now that the initial shock was wearing off, his mind was working again. He felt a prickle of guilt at having thought Hugh responsible. There was humiliation and chagrin that Hugh had protected Ela when he could not. There was Ralph too, his Bigod brother who had ridden and fought alongside him, and still languished in a Paris prison. And then he thought of John. His royal kin with whom he had stuck through thick and thin and for what false reward? Yet he knew he must tread very carefully. He was one of John's mainstays, but he was not a man of independent wealth who could easily go his own way. He only commanded sixty-four knights' fees and the rest of his wealth came from the royal coffers. For now he would have to remain as he was, but he would make plans and when the time was right, he would act.

Turning to Ela, he knelt as if he were a baron doing homage to his lord, and put his hands between her thin, white fingers. "I swear liege homage to you, my wife. I no longer owe my brother first loyalty. That crown is now yours. Whatever I do, it will be for you and your honour and glory."

Ela hesitated and then stooped over him. Their lips met again and this time it sealed the pact of a new direction in their relationship. Rising, he took her hands in his. "Let us go to mass in the cathedral," he said, "and we will be cleansed of this unholy thing. And after that we will not speak of it again."

Thirty-eight

FRAMLINGHAM, NOVEMBER 1215

*H*UGH LOOKED UP AS ONE OF THE MIDWIVES EMERGED FROM the bedchamber. Moments ago he had heard the unsteady wails of a newborn infant amid a mélange of women's voices. "Your lady wife has been safely delivered of a daughter, sire," the woman announced with a smile. "The babe is strong and well limbed."

Hugh rose to his feet. "And my wife?"

Before the midwife could reply, Mahelt answered for herself, shouting from the room that she was well.

Her reply made him smile because it was so like Mahelt to break with decorum. "I am glad to hear it, my love!" he called back. "I'll see you presently. Bring my daughter out to me," he told the midwife.

She curtseyed most properly, thereby restoring without words a certain correctness to the proceedings, and went back into the room, returning moments later with a lambskin bundle of newborn baby. Hugh's daughter was squawking like an angry little crow. Her few damp wisps of hair were gilt-blond and her eyes were the misty blue of all infants. Somehow he had been expecting another son and she was a surprise, albeit a welcome one. He felt protective towards his sons, but looking at his daughter, just minutes old, he experienced a deep and ancient feeling running in a different channel. He kissed her forehead and was comforted by a sensation of peace and continuity in a dangerous world. She almost seemed to be looking back at him and her concentrated regard reminded him of Mahelt when she was deciding whether to accept his word or not.

His mother emerged from the birthing chamber bringing with her the scent of herbs and incense. Her over-gown sleeves were hooked back and she was drying her hands on a towel. "Is she not beautiful?"

"Indeed she is." Hugh's smile of agreement continued until it became a broad grin. He stooped to kiss his mother, who was as flushed and lively as a girl today, her eyes glowing with the twin pleasures of being a nurturer and of having a new grandchild.

"You have a baby sister," Hugh said to his heir, who was running around with a toy banner pretending to be a standard-bearer.

"Let me see, let me see!" Roger ran to his father and hopped up and down, one foot after the other, trying to peer into the bundle of sheepskins.

"Me too, me too!" Hugo stood on tiptoe, craning because his father was holding the new baby too high up. Hugh stooped and gently parted the swaddling to show them the baby's little face. Roger immediately drew back, wrinkling his nose. "Why's she got those marks on her?" he demanded.

"Being born isn't easy. You had them too."

"She doesn't have any teeth!"

"They grow later."

Roger grimaced and, clearly unimpressed, ran back to his play. His brother peeped, touched the baby's cheek, and then dashed after Roger. Hugh chuckled and, with a laughing glance at his mother and a shake of his head, took the baby back in to Mahelt. The midwives were bustling around like swallows at nesting time. Mahelt was sitting up, decently covered, her hair combed and braided.

"Let me hold her." She reached for the baby and Hugh watched with tender amusement as his wife checked her over, making sure she had all her fingers and toes, filling her eyes with the sight and scent of her. "Isabelle," she said. "I want her named Isabelle for my mother."

"As you wish, my love. The boys have Bigod names. It is only fair you should have the naming of the first daughter, and she is indeed *très belle*. I pray she has your sweet nature."

Mahelt eyed him. He was biting the inside of his lip. "That is a given," she said loftily.

"I…" He looked up as a servant poked her head round the door and whispered urgently to one of the chamber ladies. The woman nodded and hastened over to the bed. "Countess, my lord, my lady, Messire Ralph is here."

Ida gasped and, gathering up her skirts, left the room at a run. Hugh hastily retrieved his daughter. "I won't be gone long." He kissed Mahelt again and hurried after his mother.

Ralph was standing by the hearth, staring round as if imprinting the walls, the hangings, and furniture on his memory. He was gaunt, haggard, and travel-stained. Ida threw herself upon him and burst into tears, sobbing his name. Ralph curled his arms around her and squeezed his eyes tightly shut, but still the tears came and his shoulders shook with sobs. After a moment, still weeping, he disengaged to embrace Hugh, but awkwardly because of the baby.

"Your new niece," Hugh said, a quiver in his own voice. "Born this very morning."

Ralph gazed upon the baby and, having wiped his eyes on his sleeve, gently stroked her face. The boys charged into the hall, chasing each other, shouting, waving their toy weapons. Roger's cloak flew from his shoulders and his legs galloped as he pretended he was on a horse. Hugo surged in his big brother's wake. "Wearing clothes now, the little one," Ralph said in a quavering voice. "Last I saw him, still in smocks...and the baby...Jesu, she was not even conceived..." Emotion choked him and fresh tears spilled down his face.

Hugh handed his daughter to a maidservant with instructions to return her to Mahelt. Then he embraced Ralph again, properly, and in so doing noticed the deep red weal abrading his brother's wrist. "Dear Christ!"

Ralph snatched his hand away and looked round in alarm, but their mother was at the other end of the hall, calling for a warm bath, hot food, and fresh raiment. "Don't let her see," he whispered fiercely. "They put the fetters back on me when Longespée left and they thought the ransom might not be forthcoming."

Hugh shook his head. "I did not realise our father had paid."

"My gaolers told me he sent half the money and pledged to deliver the rest over the next two years. Longespée went surety." Ralph's mouth twisted. "I may only be a younger son, but it seems to the French that I am as valuable as an earl."

"Longespée didn't pay anything towards your release?"

Ralph shrugged. "He cannot afford to."

"No?" Hugh raised a contemptuous brow. "He could try selling some of his fancy cloaks."

"He saved my life," Ralph said curtly. "If not for him, I might have been hanged."

Hugh bit his tongue. He didn't want to quarrel on the day his daughter was born and his brother returned to him. "Then I thank him, and I thank God to have you safely home," he said, finding diplomacy.

"Where's our father?"

"In London..."

"Ah." Ralph's brow puckered. "They told me very little

while I was a prisoner, but even so you hear things and I talked to the ship's master on the voyage home. I heard we had defied the king. I think that too was part of the reason they let me go. The French will want support when Prince Louis invades England."

The brothers looked at each other. Despite their antipathy for John, it was a disquieting thought: the prospect of swearing allegiance to a French overlord.

"Longespée is still with John," Hugh said. "God knows why after—" Again he bit his tongue. It was not his to reason. "It is your decision, of course, and you may feel beholden to him."

Ralph heaved a deep sigh. "I fought the French at Bouvines... and to change and fight for them now..." He rumpled his hand through his hair. "I do not know where I stand."

"Neither do any of us," Hugh said, and added, "but I do know it is good to have you home."

Ralph smiled wanly. "I don't suppose you've kept my wolfskins?

Hugh shook his head. "That would have been asking too much."

Thirty-nine

YORKSHIRE, JANUARY 1216

*M*AHELT RODE BESIDE HUGH ON HER BLACK MARE AS THEY made their way home down the great north road from their visit to Yorkshire. Although it was full winter, the sun was bright and sharp, and the sky was a fine blue with clouds that reminded Mahelt of her flock of sheep grazing on the upland hills. She was enjoying the ride and it was good to be out in the fresh air. Ten weeks on from the birth of her daughter, she felt well and full of energy, and she always enjoyed travelling on horseback.

A covered cart pulled by two sturdy cobs followed behind. Cocooned in furs, Mahelt's women, the nurse, and the baby were keeping warm inside whilst young Roger proudly rode his own pony. He considered himself very much the man now that he was allowed to ride on his own—for a few miles anyway—and thus far he was keeping up the pace, helped by friendly encouragement from his uncle Ralph who was accompanying them. Hugo was having a turn on his father's saddle and looking around as if he was lord of all he surveyed.

"Clippety clop, clippety clop," sang Hugo, clapping his hands.

Roger dug his heels into his pony's sides and urged him to a faster pace. Hugh chuckled with pleasure at his son's daring, but when Roger galloped too far in front and disappeared from sight, he handed Hugo to Mahelt and cantered after him to return him to the fold.

Rounding a turn in the road, Hugh saw that Roger had drawn rein and was staring at something at the roadside. Expecting to find a dead animal, Hugh rode up to the boy and pulled Hebon round in a tight arc. Three bodies sprawled in the grass: a man, a woman, and a child, their clothes torn and bloody. With a horrified jolt, Hugh recognised Matthew, his wife, and son. The gem pedlar lay on his side, his legs bent and his arms raised, a huge rusty patch saturating the left side of his tunic.

"Are they dead, Papa?" Roger stared at him with wide eyes, seeking reassurance.

"Yes, son." Hugh took Roger's reins and turned the pony around. He could feel his throat closing. He wanted to heave. The little boy had shining golden hair just like Hugo's.

Mahelt arrived, looked and covered her mouth. "Dear Christ!"

Ralph spurred ahead, his sword drawn and his shield high.

Hugh gestured brusquely to his knights as they joined the scene. "Keep your eyes peeled," he snapped. He told Roger to get in the cart with the nurse in such a way that the white-faced child obeyed without question or protest. Mahelt handed Hugo to a knight.

Hugh's skin crawled as if there were ants under the surface as he dismounted to inspect the bodies. All of them had spear wounds. Their packs were missing and the woman had been raped. Hugh fought the urge to retch. "Get these people put across a horse and covered up," he ordered harshly. "In God's name let us have decency here, even though there be none. Be quick about it; there is danger." He cursed to himself, wishing they had stayed at Settrington.

Hooves pounded on the track ahead as Ralph came galloping back, yelling a warning. "Beware! Armed men!"

Hugh sprang back into the saddle and thanked God he was

wearing his gambeson. It had been as much for warmth as protection, but it would serve him now. He was able to grab his helm off the packhorse and his shield. Hastily he directed his knights to form a protective barrier around Mahelt and the travelling cart.

The soldiers pursuing Ralph consisted of half a dozen mercenaries, their pack beasts laden with booty. The leader's shield was plain red, but his saddle cloth was fringed blue and gold. "It's our brother Longespée's men!" Ralph panted. "That's Girard of Hesdin!"

"What?" Hugh's revulsion increased. His own brother's hirelings desecrating his territory? How much deeper in filth could Longespée sink! "I want him taken alive," he snapped.

The mercenaries swiftly realised that in pursuing Ralph they had ridden upon a party four times their size and well armed. They reined around and tried to scatter into the winter forest, but Hugh's crossbowmen brought down two as they rode for the trees and another three were chased down and caught before Hugh blew on his hunting horn to regroup the men at the cart, not wanting to divide his own troops. The slower, loot-crammed pack ponies were seized and Hugh recognised Matthew's pack on one of them, still laden with its pieces of garnet, jet, and amber. There was a new iron cooking pot among the booty too, a bacon flitch obviously purloined from someone's smoke house, strings of onions, and a bag containing small items of cheap copper, bronze, and silver jewellery, some of it bloodstained. Hugh was rigid with shock and fury. When he had mentioned hunting wolves to Ralph, he had not realised they would be of the two-legged kind. The mercenaries they had caught reeked of smoke and their clothes were battle-splashed. Now that smoke had been called to mind, there was a distant whiff of it in the wind too. Somewhere a homestead was burning.

Hugh ordered three nooses strung from the bough of a

sturdy oak tree. Seeing what he was about, Hesdin knelt at his feet and craved mercy. Hugh stepped back from the man so that the hem of his robe would not be sullied by the grasping fingers. "What were you doing riding *chevauchée* on my land?" he snarled. "By God, tell me or I will slit your belly and spin you round that tree by your entrails! Did Longespée send you to do this?"

Hesdin shot a wild glance at his companions.

"You can die the hard way, or the easy way—all of you."

"Rochester has fallen to the king," Hesdin said, sweat dewing his brow. "He sent us north to punish the rebels and we were ordered to raid the lands of his enemies."

"Ordered by whom?" Hugh kicked Hesdin in the stomach. The news that the keep of Rochester had fallen filled him with dismay, for it was a major castle held for their cause. "I ask again, who sent you to do this?"

"Lambert of Allemain," Hesdin choked, his hands clasped at his midriff.

Who rode with Longespée and had been in his employ in Ireland. "And is Lambert of Allemain working for the Earl of Salisbury?" Hugh demanded. "Is William Longespée part of this?"

Hesdin shook his head. "The earl is still in the south. This is by the king's order."

"How many?"

"I don't know...I..."

Hugh kicked him again. "How many?"

"As many as the king can afford to pay. I know not...but he is coming here soon himself." Hesdin held up one hand in supplication, the other clutching his belly. "I was doing as I was bidden. I beg your mercy, sire."

"As they did?" Hugh indicated the corpses. "As that child did? As you would have done with me and my wife and my sons?"

"No, my lord. I swear…"

"Hang them," Hugh said implacably.

"A priest, God's mercy a priest!"

Hugh beckoned to his chaplain. "Shrive them," he snarled.

"I demand fair trial and judgement!"

"I am a judge," Hugh said ruthlessly. "And I condemn you as guilty for the murder of these innocents. Make your confession."

He stayed to witness the execution, hardening himself to watch the men swing and kick and finally hang limp. Inevitably thoughts of what had happened at Nottingham came to mind, but he remained steely. He wasn't hanging children; he was meting out justice to their murderers. Mahelt watched too, with rigid spine and clenched jaw.

As they rode from the scene, leaving the mercenaries to twist and dangle in the raw wind, Hugh took Matthew's pack on to his saddle and began rechecking it. "Rochester's fall is a hard blow," he said to Mahelt. "If only your father would change his allegiance…"

"He won't," she said with certainty. "Will has pleaded with him until he is hoarse, but he will stand by his oath of fealty until he drops. Perhaps it is a good thing to have someone of integrity on the other side to prevent the ravages of the worst of the faction…"

"It doesn't seem to be having much effect, does it?" Hugh delved further into Matthew's satchel, fumbling down to the base.

Mahelt stared at him. "What are you doing?"

"There's a false lining." A moment later, following several tugs and a curse, he withdrew a long strip of parchment, covered in what at first sight seemed like random lettering. Mahelt recognised it as a code strip. She had seen them enough times in her father's household. Reaching to his saddle pack, Hugh withdrew a slender beechwood rod. He drew rein for a moment and with meticulous precision rolled the parchment strip around the rod until certain rows of letters aligned.

"What does it say?" Mahelt's breath puffed in the air. Ralph nudged his mount closer and craned his neck.

Hugh's finger moved along the rod and his lips silently formed the words. "The French have landed seven thousand troops at the mouth of the Orwell where my father's writ runs, and are marching to London to help us. More are coming, and Louis himself is making preparations. Matthew must have been on his way to give me this."

Mahelt frowned, unsure if this was good news or not. The more entrenched each side became, the more atrocities that were committed, the harder it would be to make peace. "It's escalating, isn't it?"

"It was bound to," Hugh said grimly. "John has agreed to the treaty with one hand and denied it with the other. It is bad news that Rochester has fallen, but at least we have French troops to shore us up." He tucked the parchment in his purse and returned the rod to his saddle pack. "We must make all haste to Framlingham. With the king headed north and his mercenaries plundering the land, it's not safe. The wolves are out in packs and it's a hunter's moon."

Forty

FRAMLINGHAM, MARCH 1216

ONCE, STILL HALF IN GIRLHOOD, MAHELT HAD GIGGLED AS SHE helped Hugh pile a cart with valuables as they set out to thwart the demands of King John's tax gatherers. Now, in the blustery cold of a March morning, she refused to lift a finger to assist as the wealth of Framlingham was slung across packhorses and loaded into carts. There were barrels and sacks of silver pennies, and even a few pouches of precious gold bezants. Bolts of silk, reels of gold thread wound on ivory dowels. Boxes filled with the gleam of gold rings and precious stones. Silver cups and plate. Flemish wall hangings. Ida's gold and sapphire coronet. All the moveable wealth of Framlingham was being piled into carts to be dispersed at sundry religious houses where the Bigods were patrons. One lot was headed for London to supply the earl. Another sizeable portion was going to the nunnery at Colne where it could easily be transported overseas if it came to the worst. Yet more was bound for Thetford, Hickling, and Sibton.

Mahelt felt queasy as Hugh came from their chamber carrying his personal jewel box. He was taking that too? Sweet Virgin. Having ravaged Yorkshire and Lincolnshire, the king had turned southwards again. Castle after castle had capitulated. Men seemed to think because Rochester had fallen no fortress could withstand the royal forces, and it had become a self-fulfilling prophecy. But Framlingham was well fortified. It had a trained garrison and enough supplies to hold out for months. The defences had never been tested but they were strong and of the latest design. Why was everyone acting as if they thought it was going to fall?

"Why do you have to go now?" she demanded as he strapped the box to his packhorse. "I don't understand."

Hugh tightened the buckles and faced her, but even though he met her gaze, she knew he was deliberately not seeing her. "It's just a precaution. Only a fool keeps his eggs in one basket. My father says it will be better if we split our wealth and put it in several different places as we did before."

"And take it all from Framlingham?" she asked on a rising note. "Every last piece?"

"I told you, it's just a safeguard. My father is short of funds in London and he thinks it better to hold the reserves there. I won't be gone long. I'll be back within four days, I promise you."

Mahelt persisted because she knew he was not dealing honestly with her. "If matters are so urgent that you have to move our reserves, then you must take me and your mother and the children with you."

Hugh shook his head. "Then I would have to see to your protection as well as that of the goods. I would not be able to move as swiftly—my mother is too frail to keep to the pace." He stepped forward to rub her arm. "You are safer here behind our walls until I return."

She shrugged him off. "So the treasure is not safe to stay here, but your family can take their chance. Is that it?" Her voice was loud now and people were beginning to look, but she didn't care.

Hugh firmed his lips. "I cannot perform two tasks at once. I don't have the men to escort you and the treasure both. You are safer at Framlingham for the time being." He reached for her again. "Lenveise is here to command the garrison. You have nothing to fear."

"So you say," Mahelt said with scorn in her eyes. She had no love for William Lenveise, nor he for her.

"As soon as I return, we'll decide whether to move to London."

Mahelt said nothing because there was no more to be said. He was putting his duty to all these barrels and sacks of glittering dross before the most precious treasure of all.

Hugh kissed her and she neither moved her lips under his nor raised her arms to embrace him. "You might as well be gone," she said stonily, knowing that if she gave her feelings full rein she would scream at him like a fishwife and to no avail because he would go whatever she did.

His jaw tightened. "I'll say farewell to my mother and our sons," he said. "And then I'll arm up."

"As you will." Mahelt dug her fingernails into her palms while the words "Don't leave me!" crashed through her like a storm. The words of the love song he had left on her pillow were as worthless as if the ink had dried in the horn, unwritten.

❖❖❖

"What other cloth do we have?" Ida pointed to the back of the cupboard. "What's that?"

Mahelt tugged out a bolt of mid-blue wool. All the silk had been taken, and the better twill weaves, but there were still a few ells of linen and some tunic lengths of wool. A chambermaid had a son who was getting married and Ida had promised him some cloth for a good pair of chausses.

"This would suit." Ida tested the fabric between forefinger and thumb.

Mahelt put the bolt to one side and checked it herself to make sure the moths had not eaten any holes in the fabric. Nearby she could hear her sons playing a game of knights and squires with Roger ordering Hugo about in an imperious voice. She found the will to smile a little. Hugh had been gone for two nights and this was the morning of the third day. She was still on edge, but by keeping herself occupied was able to stave off the worst of her anxiety. She remained angry with him that he wasn't here to watch the defences, but kept repeating to herself that he would be home soon. She had been tempted to take the boys and the few horses remaining in the stables and make her own way to her father's manor at Caversham, but she couldn't leave Ida in her fragile condition, and she knew how dangerous the roads were without a fitting escort. She was as good as a prisoner here. She wouldn't think about that either.

She was carrying the cloth to the cutting trestle when Michael the chaplain ran into the chamber. "Countess, my lady, you must come quickly," he panted. "There's an army sighted approaching our walls!"

"What?" Ida gave him a startled look.

"Madam, it is the king and Savaric de Melun!"

Mahelt's blood froze. She shook her head. "It can't be."

Michael moistened his lips. "I wish it were not so, madam, but the sentry is certain about the shields and the banners."

Mahelt dropped her armful of cloth on to the trestle. It struck a pot of pins, scattering them across the board like tiny gleaming daggers. She stared at them and fought a nauseous feeling of panic. "I knew this would happen."

Ida pressed her hand to her throat. "What are we going to do?"

"Not open the gates, that's for certain," Mahelt snapped and, rallying, hurried from the chamber and out on to the wall walk. A bitter March wind beat around the defences and cut through her gown and chemise like iced steel. A crowd had gathered to watch the approach of the troops. Mahelt stared at the banners fluttering on spear and pole, most prominently the leopards of England in their snarling, burnished gold. The mercenaries bore that blazon on their shields too, rank upon rank of them under the command of mercenary captain Savaric de Melun. Dear Holy Virgin!

William Lenveise arrived on the battlements wearing his armour. Having run up the steps, his chest was heaving as he rested one hand on his sword hilt and with a set jaw gazed towards the force advancing on them at a steady tramp. Some of the footsoldiers were beating their spears on their shields and others were chanting out a rhythm as they marched. Towards the back, sturdy cobs hauled carts piled with siege equipment and in their rear smudges of smoke showed where hayricks and farmsteads had been set alight.

"Let me see, let me see!" Roger was hopping up and down. One of the knights obligingly picked him up to show him the view from the battlements and his eyes grew as round as goblet rims. Ida joined Mahelt on the wall walk, gasping from her climb. Her hands went to her mouth and she cried out at the sight of the army surging around their towers like an incoming sea. Mahelt briefly closed her eyes. *Hugh, what have you done to us? Why didn't you listen?*

As John's army started to spread out and pitch camp, two men detached from the throng and rode towards the gatehouse, one of them cantering ahead bearing a banner of truce while the other stayed off the pace. Mahelt recognised the latter as Savaric de Melun himself and cold prickles shuddered up her spine. The herald shouted up on behalf of the mercenary, demanding those inside the castle to surrender in order to prevent bloodshed, and spare lives.

"Tell them no," Mahelt said through clenched teeth. "Tell John to go and boil his head."

Lenveise gave her a swift glower. "We should at least listen to what they have to say, my lady."

"Why?" Her lip curled. "It will all be lies and falsehood. I won't give them so much as an inch of ground unless it be for their graves."

Lenveise shook his head. "With respect, my lady, in the absence of the earl and Lord Hugh, I have the command of this keep. I shall do as I judge fit for its defence and protection."

Mahelt stared at him and he stared back in a way that went through her as if she had no more substance than a shadow.

"My lady, we should listen to what they have to say, even if we reject it." He gestured brusquely. "I need to clear the wall of all but my men. I cannot have women and children cluttering the fighting platforms."

Mahelt knew she could not stand against him—that he would go his own way whatever she said. Wordlessly she turned away and, with her head carried high, left the battlements.

The postern gate was unbarred to admit de Melun and send out two senior garrison knights as guarantors for his safety. When he entered the great hall in the company of Lenveise, Mahelt stood with her arms protectively around her sons, Ida trembling but resolute at her side. Roger tugged at his mother's gown. "Look, Mama, look at his sword!" He pointed to de Melun's decorated scabbard.

Mahelt squeezed his shoulder. "It is not the sword that makes the man, remember that," she said in a voice loud enough to carry. De Melun glanced in her direction and gave her a look that was amused, calculating, and wolfish. Mahelt responded with an icy glare. Seeing him cast his gaze round the chamber, taking stock, she wanted to rake out his eyes.

Lenveise gestured and a squire poured wine for de Melun. The latter hesitated to taste it. "No offence, my lord, but caution has more than once kept me alive."

"Understandable." Lenveise poured himself a drink from the same flagon and took a long swallow. "If you will come to the earl's solar, we can discuss matters in comfort." He gestured with an open hand, and de Melun walked towards the door. Leaving the children with Ida, Mahelt followed the men, and when de Melun looked at her with a raised eyebrow and Lenveise scowled, she stood her ground. "I will not be excluded," she said icily. "I am the daughter of the Earl of Pembroke and my son is a future Earl of Norfolk. I speak in right of him and my husband."

A vein throbbed in Lenveise's neck. "As you will, madam," he replied with a stilted bow. De Melun narrowed his eyes, but said nothing.

Once they had reached the earl's solar and closed the door, de Melun put his wine down on a small trestle table. He eyed a hat sitting on top of a pile of parchment, several pheasant feathers pinned to the side by an amber jewel. "The lord king demands that you open Framlingham's gates to him and yield the castle and its garrison to his mercy," he said.

"And we have all seen that 'mercy' many times over!" Mahelt spat, eyes flashing. "We will never open the gates—never!"

De Melun smiled sourly. "You have courage, my lady, but little sense. You would be wise to cooperate with the king."

Lenveise said, "I cannot surrender Framlingham without the earl's consent. I must seek his permission and he is not here."

"But you would do so if he commanded?"

Lenveise inclined his head. "I obey the earl's will and when last I spoke to him, he gave me no such instruction. The castle is well defended, as you can see for yourself, and as any of your men will discover if they come within range of our crossbows."

"That may be so, my lord, but any castle can be broken, as well you know. Even the great keep at Rochester was no proof against the lord king's sappers. Every stronghold he has invested has fallen to his onslaught."

"London holds out," Lenveise said.

"Indeed, but soon it will be isolated…"

"The French…"

"…are not coming." De Melun made a dismissive gesture. "I am authorised to give you a choice. Yield Framlingham and go from here in the peace of God with your lives and your lands intact, or see all wasted and destroyed. The Isle of Ely is in flames. It would take little enough to do the same to Framlingham."

"Do you think my father will stand by and let you do this to us?" Mahelt demanded with frozen rage.

De Melun shrugged. His eyes were as hard as clear brown glass. "The Earl Marshal knows what is at stake and where to give due loyalty. As his daughter you might think yourself worthy of special consideration, but as the wife of a traitor, your fate is tied to that of your marriage family. Yield and all will be well. The king is willing to offer his peace even now to the Earl of Norfolk and his son if they will only return to their allegiance."

"We will never yield, never!" Mahelt spat. "We will withstand whatever you send against us. Let your men come and let them die." She was the child picking up handfuls of salve to sling at her brothers. Defending the castle with whatever she had to hand, determined to win.

"Madam, this is not woman's work," Lenveise said brusquely. "The earl left the defence of this castle in my hands. It is my task to make the decisions."

She stiffened. "In my father's household, it was women's work if the lord was not by. My mother faced down the Irish lords when my father was absent, and she was heavy with child at the time."

"But you are not in your father's household, my lady. You are a Bigod wife now and different rules apply. I pray you retire and leave this business to men."

Mahelt glared at Lenveise, hating him with every iota of her being because he made her powerless, and the only threat she had to offer was the power of another man. Whatever words she threw at him, she would be like a spitting cat outnumbered by dogs. "I may be a Bigod by marriage," she said as she went to the door, "but I am all Marshal by blood, and you will know it before I am done."

❖❖❖

Once Mahelt had gone, de Melun looked at Lenveise. By mutual agreement, neither man mentioned her. Her leaving was like shutting a window on a cold draught and made it more comfortable to get down to business.

"You will make it much easier on yourselves if you surrender the castle," de Melun said.

Lenveise shook his head. "I cannot do that without my lord's permission."

"If you do not yield, the king will be savage. You have seen what he is capable of. He would order the destruction of the demesne lands, hang the garrison, and if men such as yourself survived it would be to the humiliation of fetters and a ransom that would beggar your kin to pay." De Melun leaned forward for emphasis. "You know he can take you. Rochester was reckoned impregnable, but it wasn't. The French won't come."

Lenveise gave him a hard stare. "We can hold you off these walls with our archers for as long as you choose to be slaughtered."

"I appreciate your fighting talk." De Melun gave a judicious nod. "I know you have to say such things. But would you see your lands confiscated or destroyed? Your barns razed? The king can send his mercenaries out to ravage at will while you are shut in here. Slaughter runs both ways."

"And if I agree to yield, how do I know that such punishments will be spared?"

"You have the word of the king."

Lenveise arched his brows. "In that case, I prefer to take my chance with my life and that of everyone else within my care."

"You will be given letters patent." De Melun gestured brusquely. "Your knights will be asked for hostages for their good word, and in exchange they will receive the king's peace and be given full seisin of their lands. If not...I have told you the alternative."

Lenveise chewed on his thumbnail. "What of the countess and Lady Bigod?" he asked after a moment.

"That can be negotiated. The king has no quarrel with the countess, and the other lady is the Earl Marshal's daughter. Since he is one of the king's mainstays, I am certain we can come to mutual agreement."

Lenveise finished his wine and eyed the feathers in his lord's hat as they quivered in a movement of air. "I shall need a day to consider my decision..."

De Melun drank up and made to leave. "I shall convey your reply to the king. Make no mistake, he will win this fight, and those who do not bow to him will be destroyed."

When de Melun had gone, Lenveise rubbed his hands over his face, and then, squaring his shoulders, sent his oldest squire to summon the knights to the guardroom. He bit the inside of his cheek as he saw Mahelt advancing on him, her stride as bold as a man's. The countess knew her niche but the young mistress was imperious and lacked any sense of the natural order.

"My lady." He gave an infinitesimal dip of his head.

She afforded him no similar courtesy. "What did you say to him?"

"I said we needed time to consider," he replied woodenly.

"There is nothing to consider," she snapped.

"On the contrary, madam, there is a great deal to consider, not least the lives of everyone within this castle."

"Then you will keep the gates shut. You must send word to Lord Hugh and the Earl of Norfolk."

Lenveise struggled with his patience. "They do not have the resources to relieve the siege, my lady. If they come to us, they will only be captured themselves."

"We can hold out. We have the men and the supplies." Her eyes blazed. "I will not yield to that man."

"My lady, I will do my best for all concerned. Do you think I want to give in to tyranny? You will excuse me." Without waiting her leave, he bowed again to terminate the encounter and strode away.

Mahelt clenched her fists. She sensed this was not going to end well because Lenveise did not have the stomach for a fight. She had been right, and the price of Hugh's refusal to heed her was going to beggar everyone.

❖❖❖

In the morning, the king's heralds returned to demand the surrender of the castle. Mahelt was praying in the chapel with Ida when the summons came and the first she knew was when a frightened servant interrupted her prayers to whisper that the royal army was entering Framlingham.

"No!" she cried, rising from her knees and running to the door to stare at the mercenaries and soldiers streaming through the gateway. The king rode a white palfrey, the horse turning its head to one side as it paced, high-stepping, into the heart of her home. The garrison was kneeling to him, their weapons tossed in a surrendered pile in the middle of the yard. "Holy Christ, no!"

Ida joined Mahelt at the chapel door and crossed herself. "So be it," she murmured.

Mahelt flung her an aghast look. "Lenveise wasn't to give in!"

Ida shook her head. "If Lenveise deems it for the best, we must trust his judgement. Be calm, daughter, or you will make the situation much worse than it is."

Mahelt compressed her lips and strove to control her rage and her terror. Images of a starving Maude de Braose and Will's murdered wife and baby flashed through her mind. Was this what it had come to? Were they all going to die of hunger and thirst in a dungeon? Or on the edge of a knife? John must be gloating now.

Ida turned to Mahelt with the composure of someone weary beyond caring. "I will go out to him," she said. "I am the countess, and it is my duty. You stay here." She started forward, a diminutive, fragile figure in her gown of green silk.

"No, I won't hide." Mahelt lifted her chin and drew herself together, knowing she could not let her mother-in-law shoulder this alone.

As the women emerged from the chapel, Mahelt's blood froze as she saw that her eldest son had escaped his nurse and was standing fearlessly in front of John, brandishing his toy sword. No thought in her mind but saving her child, Mahelt rushed forward, grabbed Roger, and pushed him behind her.

John dismounted at his leisure, the very indolence of his movements a threat. "Lady Bigod," he said pleasantly. "Countess Ida."

"Sire." Ida knelt.

John's lips curved and he said smoothly, "You will be glad I have not damaged the castle defences. It would have been a pity to do so." His tone insinuated that the walls of Framlingham were no more than fancy gilding on a marchpane subtlety. He removed his riding gauntlets. "Your constable is wise and more fortunate than he knows. His prudence has saved you—as has your father's loyalty, Lady Bigod. I would not treat harshly with the favourite daughter of so faithful a man, even if she is allied to those who would do us harm." He stepped forward and around Mahelt and pulled Roger forwards. "Hah, you're a fine little knight, aren't you, my boy?"

Roger jutted his chin with pride. Mahelt dug her fingernails into her palms. "Leave him alone," she said in a burning voice.

Keeping his hand on Roger's shoulder, John eyed the women with triumphant scorn. "Countess, Lady Bigod, you have my leave to go from here and seek succour where you will. You may take two knights for escort and the earl's huntsmen and grooms. Let him feed those men rather than I. The younger child and the infant may accompany you, I care not, but I have a mind to have this one as surety."

"No!" Mahelt felt as if a stone had been dropped on her from a height. "Never!"

John's gaze narrowed. "I could keep all of you; think on that. I expect you to inform the earl and his son that I dearly wish them to return to my peace. If they do, I shall treat them as leniently as I do yourselves now. They have a month to comply and in the meantime I shall take the boy into my service…He will do well for me, I think."

Mahelt couldn't think for the raw pain and terror. All she knew was that she wasn't going to let him take away her son as he had taken away her brothers. Seizing Roger from the king, she caged her arms around him. "No," she hissed through bared teeth. "You shall not have him!"

John gestured and de Melun moved to separate mother from child. Mahelt fastened herself yet more tightly to Roger, protecting him like armour. "You shall not take him!" she shrieked. "You will have to hack me to death first!" She bit de Melun and managed to twist free. Cursing, he grabbed her again. One of his men seized her from the other side. Mahelt fought them with the strength of hysteria, but eventually her muscles weakened and she was overpowered. Four of them prised her off Roger, threw her to the ground, and a fifth pinned her down while she writhed and struggled.

"It is the king's will," de Melun panted. His hand dribbled

blood where she had bitten him. "And you will yield to it, madam!"

"Kill me!" Mahelt sobbed, blind with tears. "Because if you take him, I might as well be dead!"

Roger stared at her, his face white with shock, but he was still gripping his wooden sword. He turned now to attack de Melun, but the mercenary picked him up by the scruff, wrenched the sword out of his hand, and cast it across the ward. "You will learn your manners, brat," he said, shaking him like a terrier with a rat. "Whether you be the Marshal's grandson or not!"

John had stepped aside from the fray. "Madam, you are a harridan," he said with contempt, flicking his fingers at de Melun. "See that she is confined for her own good. Bring the boy."

"Sire."

Still fighting and screaming, Mahelt was hauled to her feet, dragged to a guardroom cell in one of the towers, and flung inside. She struck the wall, rebounded, and fell to the floor where she lay winded and bruised; defeated, but refusing to admit that defeat. She scrambled to her feet and hurled herself at the door, kicking and screaming, throwing herself against the solid oak planks. There was a grille in the door but as she tried to peer through it, the soldier on the other side slammed it shut and put her in darkness.

Eventually, worn out, Mahelt collapsed on the floor, weeping with rage and despair. Hugh had left them inadequately protected, knowing this might happen. He was free and clear with his chests of money while she and the children paid the price. Her brothers had been taken hostage and she couldn't prevent it, and now it had happened to her son and still she was powerless. It was as if her family's past was a great loop, repeating and repeating itself. Would Roger grow up to have sons and in his turn see them taken away? Would he live to grow up at all?

Would any of her children? She would not put it past John to have them thrown down the castle well and claim their deaths as unfortunate accidents. The thought jolted her to her feet and once more she battered at the door and screamed for her babies, but no one came. Finally, exhausted, she curled herself into a ball of misery in the corner and stared numbly at the wall.

❖❖❖

It was morning when they let her out to an overcast day with sleet in the wind and a bitter chill in the air. Bruised, dishevelled, tear-stained, Mahelt staggered from her confinement and glared at William Lenveise who was standing several wary paces away. "You traitorous whoreson!" she hissed. "May you burn in hell! What have you done with my children? Where are they? I want to see them. If they have been harmed..."

Lenveise recoiled. "They are safe with their grandmother, I promise you." He caught her arm to steady her and in warning. "Best make yourself presentable first, my lady. If you walk in upon them looking as you do, you will terrify them."

"And whose fault would that be?" Mahelt wrenched away. "Do not touch me! I despise you!" In the courtyard she could see carts being laden and horses harnessed.

"My lady, I did as I saw fit." He would not meet her eyes.

"Then you are not 'fit' to command."

"My own son is a hostage too," Lenveise said wearily. "I did not take the decision lightly."

"May it burden your conscience for the rest of your life!"

"Doubtless it will do so," he said, tight-lipped. "You are to be escorted from the castle this morning as soon as all is made ready."

Mahelt became aware of the stares of servants and soldiers and glared back at them until they dropped their eyes in shame. "So you will not have to look on me and be reminded of your perfidy?" She struck him across the face like a soldier making a battle challenge. His head snapped back, but he took the blow. It didn't make her feel any better. Turning her back on him, she stalked away to her chamber.

Her women were waiting, twittering like a flock of disturbed sparrows. But she wasn't a sparrow; she was a lioness, even if her claws had been ripped out. The room, previously bare of its hangings because the valuables had been stripped, resembled an empty barn. The chests were packed and the bed dismantled. Cloaks hung ready. She thrust off the wails of dismay, and the shocked exclamations, and ordered one of her ladies to bring her a comb and a bowl of scented water. She had them open a packed chest and find her a fresh chemise and gown. When the water arrived, Mahelt undressed and scrubbed herself with the washcloth from head to toe, and then towelled herself vigorously, as if by doing so she would strip herself of the night and day that had just been. She made it clear she did not want to talk to her women, neither to give them reassurance nor to be reassured herself. The only way she could endure these moments and go forward was by shutting the door on her emotions. It was another form of prison, self-imposed, but it was also her fortress against all comers.

Her ablutions complete, her garments fresh, she felt better able to stand straight and lift her head. She knew from the tenderness on the side of her face that she must be showing bruises to the world, but there was no help for that. Let that same world see what John was capable of.

Carrying herself like a queen, she crossed the ward to Ida's solar. As she entered the room, Hugo flung from his grandmother's side and ran to her, shouting, "Mama! Mama!"

Mahelt seized him and held him fiercely against her body. "I love you so much!" she gasped. "Never leave me, never!"

Ida, who was cuddling the baby, rose from her chair. "Oh my

dear, what have they done to you?" she asked, her eyes filled with distress.

"They have torn out half of my heart," Mahelt replied bitterly. "But even if they take it all and wring it dry, I will not yield. Where's Roger? What have they done with him?"

Ida's chin wobbled. "Oh my love, he has gone already. They took him yesterday just after they put you in that cell. The king had him sent to Norwich Castle. I am sorry, I am so sorry." Tears spilled down Ida's face and she kissed the baby and held her close. "He was very brave. He said you were not to worry, that he would do his duty."

Mahelt gave a great gasp, but held herself together because she knew that if she broke, she would shatter beyond repair.

Ida closed her eyes. "I would have put my body over his too, but I was not strong enough."

"No, you were wise." Mahelt's voice threatened to crack. "The little ones needed you. Who else would look to their welfare with me locked up?" She hugged Hugo again, and then set him down before it became impossible to let him go.

Ida swallowed. "I had to help Roger pack his chest. I had to separate his clothes from his brother's and I kept thinking back to when I was a girl at court and I was made to give up my son at the king's will...I fought too on that day, but to no avail. Kings always win. They always take away." She stopped speaking, her eyes glassy with tears.

At the door, the knight Enguerard de Longueville cleared his throat. "It is time to leave, my ladies," he said.

Mahelt nodded. The sooner she was away from this place the better. There was nothing to hold her here now. No cause to defend it. All of that had been swept away. She donned her cloak and knelt to help her remaining son with his. "Fasten tightly," she said. "It's cold outside." Tenderly she drew up his hood and stroked his flushed cheek and tried not to think about

Roger and whether anyone would have the care or consideration to do the same for him.

Hugo studied her from solemn bright blue eyes. "Where are
we going?"

"To London...to your grandfather's house."

"Will Dad-dad be there?"

Mahelt's stomach clenched. "I don't know." She wanted to
add that she didn't care either, but she did. Too much. And
most of what she felt was rage and blame.

Ida had picked up the piece of sewing she had been most
recently working on and that had not been packed with the rest
of her belongings. "I need to take this," she said. "Then it will
be finished for our return. We must keep busy. There is always
so much mending. How shall we ever do it all? How shall we
repair what is torn?" She stared into space and seemed to lose
the thread of what she was saying.

"Perhaps we won't," Mahelt said. "Some things can't be
mended."

Their escort was waiting in the courtyard. A small cart stood
ready for Ida, the women, and children. Tripes too, for he was
too old and unsound to run behind the horses. For Mahelt
there was her black mare. The bailey was full of strange knights
and mercenaries, and of men who would not meet her eye.
Lenveise was conspicuous by his absence. But John was present,
watching from an upper window, saying nothing, but wearing
his triumph like a gold chain.

"I want Roger," Hugo said as Orlotia settled him in the cart
and tucked a rug around him. His bottom lip was pushed out
and threatening to tremble.

"You'll see him in a few days," Mahelt said in a tight voice,
knowing she was probably telling a lie. "He's had to go to
Norwich just now."

"Why?"

"Because the king said he had to."

"Why?"

Because the sky is falling upon us. Because this king is a tyrant. Because your father and your grandfather have allowed this to happen to those they should have protected the most. "Because there is a price to pay for everything," she said.

Ida rallied and distracted Hugo's attention by giving him some wool to wind into a ball for her, and telling him a nonsense story. As they left Framlingham, Mahelt concentrated on riding and refused to think. It was as if there was a wild storm blowing outside but she had shut herself away from it. At some point she would have to emerge and deal with the damage, but not now, not yet. Perhaps never while she walked this earth.

Forty-one

TOWARDS DUSK OF THEIR THIRD DAY ON THE ROAD, MAHELT and Ida reached the Bigod house on Friday Street. A heavy drizzle had been falling since noon and there was a creeping chill in the air. Ida was coughing and flushed; Hugo was wan and shivering; the baby was teething and had been wailing fractiously all day. Mahelt was aware of all this misery, but she watched it pass by from the refuge of her internal castle. Nothing was going to broach her walls.

As they turned into the yard, she saw that Hebon was tethered outside the stables being briskly rubbed down by Hugh's groom. The stallion's back bore the imprint of the saddle and tendrils of steam curled from his black hide. Other grooms were busy with horses and the stables were packed to overflowing.

As Mahelt dismounted from her mare, Hugh emerged from the building looking harassed and desperately worried. His travelling cloak was mud-spattered from hem to knee and he was white with exhaustion. Mahelt saw him and she saw none of him. All she knew was that he had allowed her and the children to become John's victims when he had promised he would hold them safe. Her stomach muscles were knotted to her spine with the effort not to scream at him, because she knew if she started, she would never stop.

"Dada, Dada!" Hugo scrambled from the cart and ran to his father.

Hugh seized him in his arms and, lifting him up, kissed him hard. "You're all right! Thank God you are all right!"

"The king's taken Roger away!" Hugo said.

"I know…We'll get him back. I promise we will."

Mahelt clenched her fists as Hugh approached, and stepped back because she didn't want him touching her. "Is that like all your other promises?"

"I was doing my duty…" He reached one hand towards her cheek. "Dear God, Mahelt, your face…What have they…?

"Duty?" she spat. "Do not speak to me of duty. You abandoned me and our children to the hands of weak traitors. You put gold and silver above our very lives!" Her temples pounded as she fought to stanch her fury.

His eyes darkened. "That is neither true nor fair."

"How dare you talk of truth and fairness? You weren't there when the king rode in and took Roger. When they dragged him out of my arms and threw me in a cell!" Her voice tore. "You weren't there, Hugh. You weren't there!"

Ida was helped from the cart, staggering slightly as she gained her feet after the long journey. "Please," she implored, looking stricken, "you must not argue, please, not here. Let us go within out of the cold and the rain."

Mahelt closed her eyes and summoned the last of her reserves. For the sake of her children. For the sake of Ida and the refugees from Framlingham, she had to keep her balance.

"Is your father here?" Ida took a few steps towards the house and swayed on her feet. Hugh set his son down and took her arm to support her.

"I'm all right," Ida said, although she plainly was not. "It's the journey. I just need to rest and see your father—and make sure he is well."

A red mist veiled Mahelt's eyes. They wouldn't be in this position if the earl had put his family first and his precious treasure second. "I'm sure he is," she muttered. "Let us worry about you first."

Hugh lifted Ida in his arms and carried her up to the private chamber. He issued rapid orders to the servants to draw back the bed covers, and sent one of them to find his father.

They had put a warm stone at Ida's feet and were tucking the blankets around her when the earl arrived from his business, his eyes red-rimmed and his face grey and weary. He looked at his wife and pinched the bridge of his nose between forefinger and thumb.

"Husband," Ida said with a dry swallow. Mahelt directed a servant to fetch her a drink.

The earl approached the bedside hesitantly, as if trying to remember something he had forgotten how to do. Reaching down, he took her hand. "You've had a long journey," he said. "Rest now."

Ida took a few sips from the cup and lay back against the bolsters. "I just need to sleep," she whispered. "I am so tired."

The earl held her hand until she closed her eyes, then he gently disengaged and, without looking at anyone else, shouldered from the room. Hugh went after him. Drained and exhausted herself, but knowing she would be unable to sleep even if she did lie down, Mahelt bade the servants keep watch on Ida, and followed the men.

De Longueville was reporting on what had happened at Framlingham and the earl was looking grim.

"Lenveise should have fought," Mahelt said, joining them without invitation, treating her inclusion as her right. "We had the garrison; we had the military resources. I told him to fight."

"My constable surely knows more of military matters since

it has been his training since birth," her father-in-law said in a reproving tone.

Mahelt tossed her head. "And I am William Marshal's daughter and my mother held Kilkenny against all who would have seized it."

"Your mother's constable held Kilkenny," the earl retorted. "Your father may be a great soldier, but even you would grant that you have neither his skills nor his training, and for that matter he has never held a castle against siege. There is more than just soldiering at stake here, madam."

Mahelt was seething. "Indeed so, and now the king has seized my son, your grandson. What kind of stakes would you call those?"

"It is unfortunate, I agree."

"Unfortunate?" Mahelt was so enraged, she gagged on the word.

"Had there been more time we would have evacuated the castle. As it is, the younger ones are free. You and Hugh are both safe, and whole."

Mahelt was swift to pick up the implication that she and Hugh were out of harm's way and at liberty to breed more children and was incensed. "But it's hardly a victory," she spat. "Does your grandson count for nothing?"

The earl's brows puckered. "Daughter, you speak out of turn."

"I speak as I find," she said contemptuously.

"Mahelt—" Hugh began but his father cut across him.

"Madam, I suggest you go and tend to your children and take some rest because you are clearly overset. We shall speak when you are in your senses."

"If I have lost my senses, at least I still have my honour. Think on that!" Mahelt retorted and, without affording him either curtsey or obeisance, turned on her heel and stalked back to the bedchamber.

Appalled, Hugh gazed in her wake. He was exhausted; reeling from what had overtaken them. The foundations underpinning his life were crumbling away at a rapid rate, leaving him hanging over a very dark chasm indeed.

His father palmed his face and sighed. "There is no peace to be had anywhere," he said. "Not in the kingdom, not in my household." He looked wearily at Hugh. "That boy is my grandson and I love him whatever his mother thinks. That I could not protect him is a heavy burden."

"But a lesser one than being his father," Hugh said tautly. "Mahelt is right. I wasn't there either. I should have brought them with me as she desired, but I thought they would be better off at Framlingham. I thought they would be safe. I thought I had time..."

"The boy's Marshal kinship will protect him," his father said sharply. "It is pointless crying over spilled milk."

Hugh gave his father a hard look. "But it helps to know why the milk was spilled in the first place. Roger is my son and he is only six years old and worth more than platitudes. I know what this king is capable of."

"I repeat to you, the lad will be protected because his grandsire is the king's backbone. My father lost our earldom for rebelling against the king and Framlingham was razed to the ground. It took me twelve years of solid toil to regain our inheritance and our title. I rebuilt our home from the ashes and I will not see it reduced to ashes again or end my life in exile. We are opposed to the king, but we must leave doors open too. John offers us a month's grace to come to him and sue for peace."

"On what terms?" Hugh asked huskily. A terrible notion was growing in his mind.

His father opened his hands. "Probably the kind we'd not accept; John triumphant will be twice as bad as John on the back foot. We must have a peace that will bind both sides. We have French knights in London and Louis will come, but the immediate future is like a sea mist, swirling and changing. We must hug the shore to stay safe, even if we stay off the land."

"Just tell me, did you give Lenveise orders to yield if the king fetched up beneath our walls? Is that part of your 'hugging the shoreline' policy?"

His father lowered his head so that all Hugh could see was the brim of his hat. "The king moved faster than I thought," he said. "I expected Framlingham to be empty."

Hugh swallowed bile. "You gave the order to yield even though you knew they were in there."

"I bade Lenveise use his judgement. Don't be naive. It was a risk we ran and we miscalculated our timing. That is all."

"That is all?" Hugh shuddered. "What of the consequences?"

"We deal with them." Now his father did look up, and his grey eyes were implacable.

Hugh exhaled hard and, with clenched fists, walked away from him.

He found Mahelt in a chamber off the hall that was used for hosting guests. She was lying on the bed with her back to him and her arms around Hugo and the baby. Her breathing was slow and deep but Hugh could not tell if she was feigning sleep or not. He sat down on the edge of the bed and looked at the three of them, knowing there should be four. "I am sorry," he said and reached to stroke her lustrous braid. "I know I have made a damned mess of everything. We'll get him back, I promise you. I know you set my oaths at naught, and I do not blame you, but I will keep this one with my life."

She made no reply and he did not know if he was relieved or disappointed. The angle she was lying at exposed the bruise on her cheek, and seeing it, he felt as if he had struck her himself.

Forty-two

*E*LA AT HER SIDE, MAHELT KNELT BEFORE THE TOMBS OF HER grandparents within the church of the Augustinian priory at Bradenstoke, and paid her respects. John FitzGilbert and his wife Sybilla lay beneath engraved slabs of Purbeck stone, with their eldest son beside them. Mahelt and Ela's great-grandparents, Walter of Salisbury and Sybire de Chaworth, rested here too, with others of their kin.

Mahelt paid particular attention to the tomb of her grandmother Sybilla, who had also been forced to give up her small son as a hostage. The child had survived his ordeal and grown up to become Mahelt's own father. But what had Sybilla thought as her boy was taken by the enemy? Had her heart died inside her too? Her father seldom spoke of the ordeal from his perspective, although other men did, relating the tale of his near-hanging with relish. Mahelt tried not to dwell on that aspect, but it still haunted her dreams.

In the month since Framlingham had been taken, nothing had been decided. Hugh and his father had been garnering resources from the parts of their lands that had not been occupied or plundered. They had sent messages to John playing for time, saying they were considering their position. Roger was still a hostage at Norwich, but Mahelt was honing ideas, and had come to Bradenstoke to ponder them at her grandmother's grave. She had brought an offering of a mark of silver to be given in alms and had paid for fourteen pounds of beeswax for candles. As a personal supplication, she kissed the garland of spring flowers in her hand and laid it reverently on her grandmother's tomb. A few damp mayflowers shed pale petals on the engraved stone. Crossing herself, Mahelt rose and went from the church into the pale April sunshine. Ela followed her out, and the women stood for a moment, enjoying the gentle warmth and gazing across the views afforded by the priory's raised elevation.

"How is the countess?" asked Ela after a moment.

Mahelt shook her head. "A little better but still unwell—upset and confused mainly."

"I am sorry to hear it," Ela said with concern. "She is a good and gentle lady."

"She is indeed." Mahelt thought of her mother-in-law. The spark she had possessed when Mahelt had first known her was all but extinguished, replaced by a dull weariness. It was clearly an effort to drag herself through each day. She was at her best with her grandchildren, dandling Isabelle on her knee, telling stories to Hugo and feeding him sweetmeats. She still sewed too, but in the repetitive way that was a comfort mechanism, in much the same manner as Hugo sucked his thumb. Mahelt bit her lip. "I have something to ask of you—a boon."

"Of course, if I can help." Ela squeezed Mahelt's arm. "You know that."

Mahelt drew a deep breath. "You know my son is still a prisoner in Norwich. It has been a month now that the constable has had him."

"Yes," Ela said with sympathy in her eyes, but caution too. "I am sorry for that. I would not like to think of my William or Richard in such custody."

Mahelt hesitated because this was no small thing she was asking of her cousin. "Would your husband be prepared to petition the king for custody of Roger and have him brought to his cousins at Salisbury?"

Ela looked briefly taken aback, but swiftly rallied. "I do not know." Her brow creased. "I was under the impression that William and Hugh had quarrelled badly."

"They have, but this goes deeper than their quarrel."

Ela narrowed her eyes, suddenly suspicious. "You do ask me this with Hugh's agreement, don't you?"

Mahelt thrust out her jaw. "Hugh knows I have come to you," she said stonily.

"To do other than visit and pay respects to our ancestors?"

Mahelt watched fleecy clouds roll across the sky like a flock of migrating sheep. Then she turned to Ela and said on a pleading note, "You are a mother and my kin. If my son was with you, I know you would treat him well. I am afraid of what might be happening to him. I know what my brother suffered at the hands of the king—more than he will ever tell my parents—and I know what John did to those Welsh boys at Nottingham. I dare not think what sights my son is seeing and what he is hearing while in the custody of men who think nothing of robbing and torturing others. Ida said I should come to you. Usually she has no opinion on matters of policy, but she was keen to have me broach this."

Ela looked troubled, but eventually she nodded. "I will see what I can do," she said and embraced Mahelt with compassion.

"Thank you!" Mahelt felt hope surge through her, but held it down before it could take hold. Once she would have been certain that to ask was to receive, but no longer. That particular expectation lay in ruins.

Drawing back, Ela said, "I told William about what John did to me at Marlborough."

Mahelt had been longing to ask, but had deemed it best to wait for Ela to speak in her own time. "What did he say?"

"He was furious and upset, but once he'd thought about it, he said it was pointless charging like an enraged bull and making matters worse for all of us." Her head came up and pride shone in her hazel-grey eyes. "He says his allegiance is to me and to God, no longer to his brother—that I am his sovereign lady." She set her lips. "People think me gentle and quiet. But they do not realise how strong I am when I make up my mind. My faith in my husband, in God and His Holy Mother sustains me."

Lacking such faith just now, Mahelt said nothing. She had taken her own strength from kneeling at the tombs of female ancestors who in their lives had had to find within themselves a place beyond courage. She had vowed to honour that lineage and find the fortitude within herself to survive.

❖❖❖

Roger's teeth chattered and he was shivering so hard that he thought his bones must be clacking together inside his flesh too. He didn't have a decent cloak to protect him from the cold spring rain that was sheeting down. His best one with the warm lining had been left at Framlingham when they brought him to Norwich. He hadn't liked Norwich's constable, Hervey Beleset, who had handled him roughly and kept him locked up except when he was making him do chores like clean harness or shovel ordure. Once he had been dragged from his confinement and Beleset had made him watch rebels being hanged on a gibbet whilst implying that this might happen to him or his family if the king so willed. He wanted his mother and grandmother and Hugo, and baby Isabelle even though she cried and belched milk almost every time she was picked up. He wanted smiles and praise and reassurance. He desperately missed his father, who would have recognised his fears and immediately banished them or helped him understand. He was always hungry and thirsty. Beleset made sure he received food, but it was mostly gristle and gruel—enough to sustain him, nothing to enjoy. Roger had endured the disgusting slop by telling himself that these were a soldier's rations and the kind of treatment he was receiving was the sort meted to real men. It was just like the stories his uncle Ralph had told him about being a prisoner in France.

Yesterday afternoon, a man had come with orders to take him from Norwich to a place in the south called Sandwich. He had been collected by a powerful, grey-bearded mercenary called Faulkes de Breauté, who had picked him up by the arms and held him up to his eye level, his grip as solid and bruising as the man himself. "One word out of place from you, brat, one whine, and you'll swing on a rope, understood?" he'd said.

Roger had refused to be intimidated and had nodded and looked boldly back into the mercenary's black eyes. After de Breauté had set him back down with a sour grunt, Roger had not rubbed his sore arms until the man had turned his back.

They had been travelling for a day and a half. The previous night they had pitched tents by the roadside. Roger had helped to unfold the canvas and fetched firewood. In some ways he rather enjoyed being with the men and pretending he was grown up. He had helped see to the horses, tended the fire, and stirred the pottage. De Breauté had growled at him from a distance and given him a half-hearted kick in passing, but other than that left him alone, for which Roger was grateful. He had heard the mercenary grumbling to one of the other men that he wasn't a nursemaid and that escorting a lordling whelp was beneath him. Roger considered it an affront to his own standing to be in the care of such an uncouth man, and made shrift to avoid him where possible and be aloof when he could not.

Now, as he rode along, he began to recognise familiar terri-tory. The path that branched off to the camp-ball ground, the hazel coppice where his dog had chased a fox to earth, the hollow tree where he had made a den last summer. Despite being chilled to the bone, Roger had an excited feeling in his tummy as they approached Framlingham. Perhaps he was being returned to his mother and Hugo and his baby sister? Perhaps his father would be there? He considered asking de Breauté, but decided against it after one look at the mercenary's dour mouth, ringed in blue stubble.

The rain continued to pour, trickling down the back of Roger's neck, dripping off his hair and over his face. Feeling thirsty, he sucked moisture out of his sleeve. As they squelched into sight of the castle, he could see numerous men on the battlements, busy as ants. De Breauté, who had been riding ahead on his great dappled stallion, reined about and joined him. "Little drowned rat," he said with a smirk. "Hardly the Bigod heir now, are you, boy? You put me in mind of an urchin off a herring boat."

Roger rather liked sailing on herring boats but he knew he was being insulted and kept quiet. He was chilled and tired. His legs were frozen and yet they burned from chafing against the saddle. Knowing de Breauté was watching him, he put his chin up and pretended he was entering Framlingham as its lord and master. The mercenary grunted and looked sourly amused.

The castle gates were open but well guarded and they entered a courtyard full of purposeful activity. De Breauté turned in his saddle to study the packed courtyard. Roger sensed that something had annoyed him. Surreptitiously he looked round at all the coming and going, and was filled with a strange, unsettled feeling to see so many strangers in his home. Heavy-eyed with cold and hunger, he watched a man crossing the courtyard and vaguely recognised him. He had glossy dark hair and was wearing a magnificent green cloak with a big gold brooch at the shoulder. De Breauté muttered something under his breath as he dismounted, and then bent his knee. "My lord," he said reluctantly.

The man gestured him to his feet, then cast a bright, hazel-brown stare in Roger's direction. Anger clouded his features. "Good Christ, man, why does the child not have a decent cloak?"

De Breauté shrugged. "A bit of rain won't hurt him. Never hurt me when I was his age. Breeds toughness."

"It can breed a chill in the lungs too. You know how important he is."

"Ah, don't fuss," de Breauté growled. "The boy's all right—more than I can say for my arse." Rubbing his backside, he gestured a groom to take his horse.

Roger dismounted from his pony and almost fell because his legs were so stiff and numb with cold. He clung to the bridle and bit his lips and squeezed his lids on a shaming heat of tears. The man with the beautiful cloak beckoned to a minion and Roger found himself folded in a thick, scratchy blanket and hustled away to a chamber in the guard tower. Glancing over his shoulder, he saw de Breauté and the lord in the cloak having a heated conversation. He couldn't tell what they were saying, but the words were accompanied by several choppy, vigorous hand gestures.

The soldier who had charge of Roger set him down on the bench before a hearth filled with glowing peat turves, and ladled out a bowl of chicken broth from the cauldron hanging over the fire. Roger cupped his hands around the heat and felt his fingers begin to burn as sensation returned. He had just taken his first scalding sip of the wonderful greasy soup when the dark-haired man entered the room. A faint smell of incense clung to his cloak. "Do you know who I am?" he asked curtly.

Frowning, Roger was about to shake his head, but then his

eyes lit on the very long scabbard at the man's belt and a dim memory surfaced. "My uncle FitzHenry," he said slowly. "My uncle Longespée."

The man's eye corners crinkled. "Clever lad. And you are my nephew."

Roger eyed him with a mingling of suspicion and curiosity. "What are you doing at Framlingham?" The feeling was returning to his limbs with a vengeance and the pain made him want to screw up his face, but he knew that brave knights did not show their weakness.

"It is a place to stay on my way to the king, and I have men here with whom I need to speak."

"I'm going to the king too," Roger said.

"I know." Longespée turned to a squire who had entered the room. "Find the lad some dry clothes, and look sharp about it."

"Sire."

Roger took another sip of the broth and then looked steadily at Longespée. "Do you know where my mama is?"

"In London with the rest of your family," his uncle said, adding as a curt afterthought, "They're all safe."

"Have you seen them?"

"No, but trust me, they are safe."

Roger wanted to be safe with them. It was all very well being told to be brave and a knight, and his own vivid imagination and tenacity had carried him far. But just now he was almost at the end of his tether. He wanted the softness of a loving arm, and there wasn't one. Holding his head up, refusing to cry, he put all of his pride into the look he gave his uncle.

Longespée's stomach jolted because the boy had the gaze of his grandsire, the great William Marshal. Steady, measuring. The squire returned with clothing and Longespée watched Roger put down his half-drunk broth and begin stripping his wet garments. The clothes clung to his body and he was trembling so much that he was making very little progress, but Longespée recognised and approved the pride and determination in his efforts. He gestured to the squire. "A gentleman should always have assistance to dress," he said. "That is the correct way."

Roger gave him a suspicious look to see if he were being patronised, but then nodded and allowed the youth to help him don a clean shirt, tunic, and hose. The clothes were much too big for him, but they were warm and dry and would do for the moment. Seeing his nephew's narrow white body sent a pang through Longespée. Whatever the conflicts between himself and Hugh, the child was still kin, still a vulnerable little boy. And too many vulnerable little boys had died of late. Watching Roger sit and finish his soup by the fire, Longespée drank a cup of wine and contemplated his new charge. The boy had beautiful manners and charm. Much as it pained him to do so, Longespée had to admit that Hugh had done a good job with him thus far.

"De Breauté has handed you into my custody for the rest of the journey to the king," he said as Roger put down his bowl. "After that you will be sent to live with your cousins until you can be with your family again."

A spark kindled in Roger's eyes. "My cousins Ranulf and Marie?"

Longespée shook his head. "No, my children. My boy William is five years old and he has a brother about the same age as Hugo." His mind's eye filled with the image of Hugh's fair-haired second son and the incident that had led to estrangement. He still thought it ridiculous. He wouldn't have harmed his nephew for the world. A game, it had been no more than a game. He knew where to stop—unlike John. His mouth tightened. The old bridges still stood, but they were rotten, and if he was to enjoy the future, he had to destroy them and build new ones.

Roger's head began to droop. Longespée told the squire to make up a pallet for him in his own chamber and put a hot stone in the bed first.

Roger blinked at Longespée like a little owl. "Does your son like playing at knights?"

Longespée smiled. "It is his favourite game," he said, and felt sad, because he had seen so little of his children that he didn't really know whether William liked playing knights or not.

❖❖❖

Ela raised her eyes from the altar cloth she was working on to look out of the window and watch the children at play in the ward. They had made boats out of bark and straw and were sailing them in the horse trough, thoroughly absorbed in their play. It was a warm spring day, the sun hot in the sheltered spots; impossible to believe that a violent storm had ravaged the hilltop a week ago, flattening one of the bailey buildings and tearing oak shingles from the stable roof to leave moth-eaten holes. That same storm had scattered the English fleet defending the coastline against French invasion. William had written to her saying he had not been aboard ship on the night of the storm, for which she thanked God, but she was still worried because she had read the tension in her husband's words. Their defences were open and if the French did land, Salisbury lay directly in their path and it was a fortified palace, not a mighty fortress.

The children abandoned their boats to play a game of romp and chase. Roger was skilled at turning cartwheels and his cousin tried to copy him, but did not have Roger's advantage of age and muscular development. Ela was finding her young nephew hard work. He was like a whirlwind and possessed prodigious levels of energy and curiosity. It was as if he had to experience everything at once. In many ways he reminded Ela of Mahelt. He had his mother's restless vitality and he could be imperious. There was no spite or pettiness in him though, and he never sulked or whined. He had courage and a good heart. He was proud too, but when she had ignored protocol and cuddled him, he had not pulled back, but rested within the security and comfort of her embrace, blinking back tears.

Ela picked up her sewing again, but had barely taken half a dozen stitches when she heard horses and looked up to see her husband and his entourage pounding into the bailey at a sweated gallop. Her heart started to thump. Folding her needlework aside, she gave brisk commands to her women and hurried downstairs to greet him.

He came striding towards her and she saw from the look on his face—intense, bright, and anxious—that something of vast import had happened. "My lord." She dipped him a curtsey.

"My lady wife." He raised her to her feet and kissed both her hands and then her mouth. "Louis has landed and the king has drawn off to Winchester. The Marshal advised him against risking all in a pitched battle. Canterbury has yielded to the French, and now Louis is besieging Rochester with the London barons."

Ela searched his face. "So what is to do?"

William continued to hold her hands. "I cannot stand against the might of the French," he said. "Unlike the Marshal I do not have lands in the Welsh Marches or Ireland where I can retreat or keep my family safe should we be overrun. I have no choice but to surrender to Louis." He tightened his grip and looked into her eyes. "When I knelt to you and gave my fealty, I meant it. I will serve you first and above all, saving God. I want you to pack what you need and take yourself and the children to London. That at least is safe for now."

Ela raised one hand, still clasped in his, and stroked his cheek with concern. "I know this is difficult for you." He had always been intense about his royal position and to be closing the door on it was no small thing. She could see the pulse beating fast in his neck and his tension was palpable.

He gave a pained smile. "De Warenne, Arundel, Aumale, and Albini are of the same mind. We shall go en masse and tender our swords." He shook his head. "It is not difficult, my love. The difficult part has been the time until now, and will be in severing allegiance with certain honourable men who will still follow my brother. I know I have done the right thing for us, and that makes it very simple indeed."

❖❖❖

Hugh emerged from his tent and, with hands on hips, studied the walls of Winchester Castle. Defenders paced the battlements and sent sling stones and quarrels raining down on anyone who approached within range. Clods of dung and ordure too. Yesterday one of the Bigod knights had received a direct hit on the shoulder from a turd. It could have been worse; Thomas could have been dead, but removing human excrement from the links of a mail shirt was a salutary lesson.

Louis had taken Rochester with little difficulty and had moved to London where he had been formally offered the crown amid great rejoicing. There had been a grand procession in St. Paul's Cathedral and the barons in rebellion against John had knelt in homage to Louis, who had sworn to restore all their good laws and lost heritages. From there they had ridden out to the hinterlands. Reigate, Guildford, and Farnham had all surrendered and now they were encamped at Winchester. John had fled before them, having first fired the suburbs. The flames had spread to the town, leaving it in smoking ruins, but the castle and the bishop's fortress at Wolvesey still held out under the command of Savaric de Melun. Louis had brought up his siege machines and this was the tenth morning that the walls had received a pounding. The word was that de Melun had sent to ask John for permission to surrender.

444

"Won't be long now," Ralph said as he joined Hugh. He was breakfasting on a chunk of bread wrapped around a hunk of blue-veined cheese. "Want some?"

Hugh accepted the portion Ralph tore off. "You think today's the day?"

"Could be. We've pounded them to within an inch of surrender. Might be a bit bloody on the walls though." Ralph chewed and swallowed. "I remember when I was with Longespée at one castle in Poitou, we piled stones into a fishing net and dropped them on the attackers. Not pretty."

"Let us hope they're not up for such tricks." Hugh eyed his brother. Having recovered from his time as a prisoner, Ralph had also rediscovered his optimism, even in the face of hard danger, and his honest relish for life. He made Hugh shake his head, but smile despite himself.

"What do you think of Louis thus far?" Ralph stuffed the last bite of bread in his mouth and dusted his hands.

Hugh shrugged. "In terms of being able to do the task, he is fit enough. He's no saviour, but he is far better than the alternative. But we must watch our lands and privileges and make sure he does not erode them in favour of his own French lords."

Ralph smiled. "Since you and Papa are so well versed in the law, I doubt we'll be fleeced."

"No, but we daren't relax our vigilance."

The first boulder of the day hurled from a siege machine and crashed against the castle's already damaged and ragged defences. A puff of dust rose from the impact and shards of broken stone flew like missiles.

"Good aim," Ralph said. "Needs to be a bit higher. They'll get it next time around."

Hugh agreed, and then turned at a commotion near the entrance to the camp. He narrowed his eyes the better to focus. "Flags of truce," he said.

"Dear God, it's…look at the shields!" Ralph's complexion flushed as he pointed. "It's Longespée and de Warenne."

Hugh's stomach plummeted as he stared at the men riding in.

"Looks as if they've come to yield to Louis," Ralph said cheerfully. "That's good news, isn't it? God's lance—Arundel and Albini too!" He craned his neck. "I'd never have thought it of Longespée."

"Salisbury lies in Louis's path," Hugh said, recovering himself. "He's yielding before we put him under siege. This way he will get to keep his lands intact. Besides, he has a score to settle with John."

"Doesn't everyone? What's Longespée's?"

"His wife," Hugh said.

"You mean John and Ela?" Ralph looked stunned.

"It went as far as threat and assault while Longespée was a prisoner."

Ralph's mouth curled with revulsion. "Why would he do that? Longespée fought his heart out for John at Bouvines."

"Jealousy," Hugh replied, watching his half-brother on his powerful dappled palfrey. "He wanted Longespée to himself, and Ela was a distraction."

"Sometimes I wonder if we are doing the right thing," Ralph said, "and then I hear something like this and I know for sure we are."

"It is about power too. About being able to break something that belongs to someone else. I'm surprised Longespée has lasted this long, but then I suppose he had to calculate his moment for Ela's sake." He compressed his lips because his words reminded him that his own calculations had gone awry and had caused devastation to his life, both the political and the domestic. Mahelt was still barely speaking to him. "We shall be wanted in council," he said abruptly and shouted for his squire to fetch his swordbelt.

❖❖❖

Hugh stood amongst the barons who were already fighting for Louis and watched the French prince accept the surrender and homage of the four lords who had come to him for terms. Louis knew exactly how to play them. He wore a sympathetic smile and he was gracious. He smoothed the path with courtesy and Hugh watched the supplicants begin to relax. Longespée in particular seemed to find Louis's courtliness reassuring. Here was familiar territory and a language that he spoke. It was not a case of how were the mighty fallen, but more one of allies welcomed late to the meet. Louis bade them bring up their baggage and their men, and pitch camp in camaraderie. Longespée caught Hugh's eye as he turned from making his obeisance to Louis and for a moment they examined each other, before both looked away. Hugh knew they were going to have to speak at some point, but whatever was said would be forced and unnatural. Someone would have to make the first move. Hugh bit the inside of his lip. After the incident with Hugo, he had vowed to have no more to do with his half-brother, but he couldn't ignore him if he were here in Louis's camp.

Pondering the matter, he returned to his pavilion, and then paused and looked at the space beside it. Before he could change his mind he sent Ralph to go and tell Longespée that there was room to pitch a tent alongside the Bigod camp. "God knows he won't find lodging with half the city burned to a cinder," he said.

Ralph's expression brightened and he ran off to the task with alacrity. Hugh rubbed his temples and sighed.

Longespée's knights began arriving, followed by his pack-horses and baggage carts. Hugh directed them towards the space and had a quick word with Longespée's chamberlain. In the periphery of his vision, he caught sight of a stocky black and white pony, and turned round in surprise and shock.

"Roger?" he said, disbelieving.

His son dismounted with an accomplished leap and ran to him with a whoop of delight. Hugh seized him and swept him into his arms and Roger half throttled him in a stranglehold embrace. "Uncle Longespée said we were coming to see you!" Roger cried, his voice high-pitched with excitement. His face was rosy and bright with life; his dark hair gleamed like his mother's and he smelled faintly and cleanly of herbs.

"Did he?" Hugh could barely speak. Knowing that Roger was the king's hostage had been a constant ache inside him, exacerbated by the guilt of his own part in the matter. To have him here now, so vibrant and full of life, almost unmanned him with joy, relief, and remorse. "What are you doing with your uncle?" He set Roger on the ground.

"I'm his page," Roger said stoutly.

"I mean how do you come to be in his care?" Looking up, he saw Longespée coming towards him, the familiar green cloak thrown back from his shoulders and the light flashing on the chappe of the long scabbard at his hip.

"He came for me," Roger said.

"I see you've been reunited." Longespée halted a few feet away from Hugh and folded his arms. "You'll observe he's still in one piece and full of spark."

Hugh noticed the new lines graven at Longespée's eye corners and between nose and mouth, and the gaunt cheekbone shadows that spoke of insufficient sleep. "Indeed he is, but I would have you tell me how he comes to be in your custody."

"You don't know?" There was wary surprise in Longespée's dark hazel stare.

"Obviously, or I wouldn't be asking you," Hugh said tersely.

Longespée rubbed the back of his neck. "It was arranged between the women," he said. "Your wife asked mine to take him into our care and make sure he came to no harm." His mouth curled in a bitter smile. "At least your wife thinks I can be trusted with his welfare. I can see why she might not see fit to ask you."

Hugh's stomach lurched at the betrayal. "Mahelt asked you to take him?"

"She asked Ela when she came to Bradenstoke and Ela said yes and wrote to me. I agreed because Ela is my beloved wife—and my sovereign lady. I owe her my fealty and my loyalty and I would do anything she asked."

"As you do not owe your loyalty to your brother the king?"

Longespée gave him a hard look. "No," he said, "not any more—and I think you know the reason why."

Still reeling from the shock that Mahelt had gone to Ela without consulting him, Hugh managed a mute nod.

Longespée flushed. "Ela says you cared for her at that time, and I am grateful."

"I did not do it for your sake, but for Ela's."

"I realise that, but even so, you have my thanks."

Hugh made a gesture of negation. "Bestow them if you must, but they are not necessary." He cleared his throat. "You have mine for keeping my boy whole."

A gleam kindled in Longespée's eyes. "So I take it that for now we have a truce."

Hugh gave a curt nod. "It would be foolish not to."

The brothers embraced and gave each other the kiss of peace, and even if the gesture was stilted, it was in public and genuine. Longespée turned to see to his affairs, and in the act of departing ruffled Roger's dark hair. "You've been a fine squireling, nephew," he said. "I've much enjoyed your company."

Roger smiled and flourished him a courtly, perfect bow. Longespée chuckled at Hugh. "He was very fast to learn his manners once shown the way."

Hugh narrowed his eyes. "My son had his manners before he

came to you, but then stitching gauds on to garments already suited to their purpose has ever been one of your whims."

Longespée looked surprised and a little hurt. "I meant it as praise."

Hugh exhaled his irritation. "Yes," he said. "Of course you did."

Forty-three

London, July 1216

MAHELT SAT AT IDA'S BEDSIDE, HOLDING HER HAND. HER mother-in-law was becoming increasingly frail. Her appetite was poor and she had to be coaxed to eat. She slept a great deal, and when she was awake, often wandered in her wits. The chaplain and physician were frequent visitors, but the latter declared that matters had gone beyond his skill and the Countess of Norfolk would either recover by God's grace, or be taken by Him in His great mercy.

Just now, Ida was awake and aware. Her gaze on the open shutters, she said in a desolate whisper, "I won't see my son again. It is too late."

"Of course you will!" Mahelt replied with false heartiness. "By the autumn you'll be home at Framlingham, you'll see."

Ida shook her head. "It does not matter," she said wearily. "Framlingham has always been the earl's more than mine. I would have been content to dwell with him in the old stone hall before the towers went up, and want nothing more than a quiet life. Oh, I enjoyed the court when I was a girl...the games and the dancing, but it is a long time since my lord has danced with me...and we were different then."

Mahelt looked at the hand clasped in hers. It was small and capable, and bore the marks of the years like mottles on an autumn leaf. The nails were clipped short because Ida didn't want them interfering with her sewing. She wore no rings save her wedding band. Mahelt rubbed her thumb over the bright circle of gold on Ida's finger, then looked at her own and thought of Hugh and the distance that had sprung up between them since the loss of Framlingham. Hugh had said he thought he was keeping her safe, and that there would be time, but he had been wrong on both counts. Was she going to condemn him for ever for that misjudgement? Every time he smiled or made a jest, she wondered how he could do so when their son was a hostage. Each time he approached her to make love, her response was frozen because she could not bear to think of begetting more sons to become pawns in the power games of men. She was aware of still being very angry, but in some ways anger was a good thing, because it kept her strong, and God knew, they needed their strength just now.

With great tenderness, Mahelt unplaited her mother-in-law's thin rope of grey hair and combed a scented lotion of rose and nutmeg through it, remembering the times when Ida had done the same for her while she was in confinement with the children. Then she fetched her a shawl of soft rose-coloured silk to fold around her shoulders. The hue of the fabric put the illusion of colour into Ida's cheeks.

"You are a good girl," Ida said.

Mahelt shook her head. "I am not sure that I am."

"Tush, I know what I speak of." Ida fiddled with the shawl for a moment and then gestured with a languid hand to a small gold and red enamelled box on her coffer. "The key is on my belt."

Mahelt brought both to the bedside. Ida took the little box in her hands and unlocked it; then she withdrew a tiny pair of shoes fashioned from delicate kidskin. A lock of fine, dark hair tied with a piece of faded scarlet thread was tucked down into the toe of one of them.

"These were his first shoes," Ida said. "My William's, my Longespée. I have kept them all these years, ever since the day I had to let him go." Her voice quivered. "I lost a child and never got him back. This is all I have."

Mahelt almost choked on her emotion. The sight of the little shoes was heartbreaking because they were so fragile and minute. To have kept them for so long, such a precious treasure locked in that box like a heart…dear God.

Ida stroked the thin-grained kidskin. "Promise me you will give them to him. Tell him it is a part of him I have kept all of my life. Always my burden, my grief…and my solace. Promise me."

"I promise," Mahelt whispered. It was more than she could bear, and as soon as she could make her escape without obviously running away, she did so. Once in her own chamber, she dismissed the servants, drew her bed curtains, and had a good cry. Somewhere in one of the coffers was a tunic belonging to Roger. Was she going to keep it down all the days of her life as an item of worship, imagining her son's body fleshing its folds? What of the items from her own curtailed childhood? Sniffing on tears, she went to a wooden chest in the corner of the room and pushed back the lid. Beneath folded-up chemises strewn with lavender, beneath old hawking gauntlets, bone skates, various pieces of fabric, and scraps of leather, was a drawstring bag made from blue wool with white silk cords. Mahelt took it from the coffer, tugged open the drawstrings, and tipped out the wooden *poupées* with which she had played as a little girl: small wooden pegs carved into human shape and clothed to represent members of her family. A man in a green and yellow surcoat with an exquisite red lion stitched on the breast and a fur-lined cloak. A woman with fat golden braids of yellow silk thread. Children…four of her brothers, herself, and three sisters. And there they stopped. There was no Ancel, no Joanna because they had not been born. There was no record of herself in her wedding gown, no Hugh, no Ida, no Roger, Hugo, or Isabelle. Their history was not carved here.

The sound of horses in the yard and men's voices rose up to the window. Mahelt scrubbed her eyes on her sleeve and, having hastily returned the *poupées* to their cloth home, looked out of the open shutters to see knights and soldiers dismounting amid a cloud of summer dust.

"Mama, Mama!" Roger burst into the room wild with excitement, his face alight. Then he checked himself, a slight frown between his brows as if he were remembering something. Slowly, he drew his wooden sword from his belt and, bending one knee, proffered the toy on his outstretched hands, and suddenly it wasn't a toy at all. "My lady mother," he said.

All Mahelt wanted to do was seize him in her arms and press him against her to heal the great empty hole she had been carrying around since March, but she knew she could not—at least until this scene had been played out. Her heart swelled with pride and elation and she had to clench her fists to rein back the emotions threatening to overwhelm her. "You may rise, my lord Bigod," she said to him, and somehow kept her voice from quivering.

Roger stood up and smiled at her. He had lost a front tooth and he had grown. His skin bore the golden tinge of outdoor summer and his eyes were alive with sunshine. "I've been practising with my sword," he said. "Don't worry; I'll be able to protect you now. My uncle Longespée has been teaching me."

Mahelt swallowed. "You have returned as a man and a true knight of your house," she said. "Words cannot tell how proud I am of you." And then the dam burst and she did throw her arms around her beautiful child and cry.

A servant arrived bearing a jug of buttermilk and a platter of honey cakes, put them down, and bowed from the room, leaving the door open for Hugh to enter. Mahelt looked at him and felt tension strain the atmosphere. There was a storm coming and she was both apprehensive and glad. A storm to tear down; a storm to wash clean. But one that would not break while there was a child between them, even if he was the lightning. "How?" she asked.

Hugh answered carefully, measuring his words as if balancing on a high rope in a gale. "Longespée decided Louis was getting too close to Salisbury and that it was time to make his move and renounce his fealty. When he arrived in Winchester, he brought Roger with him."

"That is fortunate," she said, her words like knives. "Had he still been in de Melun's or Beleset's custody, we would not have him home, would we?"

Hugh inhaled to reply but was forestalled as Hugo came running into the room, shouting his brother's name and leaping on him like an exuberant puppy. A bout of rough and tumble ensued and Roger turned from mannerly knight into excited little boy in the space of a heartbeat.

"Go," Hugh said. "Go play with your brother while I talk to your mama."

Roger was only too keen to run outside and show Hugo his new play sword with its red and gold binding. Their voices clamoured in the doorway and left a fading trail to the bright outdoors. The room settled to silence and Mahelt's heart began to pound.

"You should have told me you had asked Ela to take him in," he said. "Do you know what a shock it was to see Roger in Winchester with Longespée? To know that you had gone behind my back?"

Mahelt faced him with her chin up. "Perhaps I had grown accustomed to using my own wits and fending for myself. If you depend on other people, they let you down, don't they?"

His complexion reddened. "Are you going to belabour me with that club for ever and a day? You knew what Longespée had done to me and to our dependants in the past, and you still went to him."

"Would you rather have had him in the tender custody of the king's mercenaries?" she snapped. "Of men like Engelard de Cigogne and Gerard D'Athée? William Longespée is a thousand times better than the alternative. Ask your mother. She gave me her blessing."

"She would. She thinks the sun shines out of Longespée's backside—always has done."

"Oh, in the name of the Virgin!" Mahelt tossed her head. "Longespée is neither a saint nor a monster. He's a man, Hugh, and he was my best hope for Roger. We wouldn't have been in this position if you hadn't abandoned us in the first place. I had to think and scrabble and claw to protect him because you, his own father, could not see his way clear to that duty!"

"Christ, woman, I did not abandon him and I did not abandon you or Hugo or Isabelle. You might as well say your father abandoned your mother in Ireland—but of course, that wouldn't be the same thing, would it? It's one rule for ordinary mortals and another for the Marshals!" His voice was raw and breaking with pain. "I am a man too, trying to find a way through this morass. Yes, I make mistakes and I stumble in the mire, but in God's name, Mahelt, why can you overlook it when others fall down, and not have the same compassion for me? Or am I the one who has to take the blame for everyone else who has let you down in your life? Am I your scapegoat? Is that the truth of it?" His eyes glittered like sapphire chips. "If I abandoned you, then you betrayed me! Or would you have the grace and humility to see that perhaps it is neither."

Mahelt's throat was painfully obstructed by a bolus of grief and anger. At Hugh, at herself, at the world. "How dare you," she mouthed.

Roger burst back into the room, still busy play-fighting with Hugo. Two other small boys had joined in, and a daughter of one of the knights.

Hugh exhaled and looked at Mahelt and she returned his scrutiny, feeling as if they were two fighters disengaging to reassess one another, both bleeding hard, but both with swords at the ready. The space between them was taut with the potential for renewed assault.

The children swooped around the room like a flock of sparrows, assaulted the honey cakes, and darted out again, their voices bright across the courtyard.

"Ah God," Hugh said in a cracking voice. "I am your husband, not your enemy. Think on it." He strode out, but left the door open behind him. She watched him walking away through a wide bar of light that trapped the gold in his hair and brought out the bluebell shade of his mantle, and then she closed her eyes.

Forty-four

FRIDAY STREET, LONDON, SEPTEMBER 1216

STANDING IN THE COURTYARD, HUGH INHALED THE SCENT OF the autumn night. It was too early in the season for a frost, but the air carried a cold warning and the smell of woodsmoke and damp were prevalent and he was glad he had grabbed his thick cloak from the peg on his way outside.

From the house there came different varieties of silence: that of sleepers lost in oblivion; the taut silence of breath being held so as to make no sound that would carry emotion; and that where each breath drawn was a victory. London was quiet under curfew but he could feel the life of the city heaving beyond the walls like a stealthy giant.

He was making preparations to leave London in order to protect Lincolnshire and the North from further depredations by the king. Longespée and Ralph were with Louis besieging Dover and his father was remaining in London with Ida, Mahelt, and the children.

There was a sour taste in Hugh's mouth. John had ripped their family apart. He had winkled his way into the mortar with a sword point and brought all the good things tumbling down and Hugh did not know if they could be rebuilt, as his father had once rebuilt Framlingham.

He did the rounds of the stables, checking the horses, taking comfort from the sound of their stamping, the warm gusts of their hay-scented breath. He fed Hebon a crust of bread from the flat of his palm. Pie kicked in his stall and played up as he always did when he knew there were titbits around. Smiling ruefully, Hugh went to him with two apple cores he had saved from earlier. The pony crunched them greedily and sought more. Hugh thought about the day Pie had tried to eat Mahelt's wimple, remembered the stomach-gripping laughter, the mutual spark. First he smiled, and then he squeezed his eyes shut and cursed under his breath. Mahelt had kept him at arm's length since Roger's return. She was civil, courteous, attentive, and she was not Mahelt. It was like having a fine wax candle that refused to light by his hand, and it would have been unbearable had he thought about it too often. He kept himself busy—there was plenty to do—and sustained his emotional life at a superficial level. Mostly it worked, but sometimes, like tonight, the pain would heave up from the depths and attempt to swallow him whole.

Returning indoors, he tiptoed to the curtained alcove off the hall where the children were asleep under a coverlet of pale, fluffy sheepskins. The shutters were open and he gazed on his boys, washed in blue moonlight and curled up like puppies. Their little sister slept in her cradle, close by the string-framed bed of the nurse. Hugh felt a pang of heart-searing love and the burden settled across his shoulders with increased weight. How could he be all things to all people?

With dragging steps he turned bedwards, although he had wondered about sleeping in the hall tonight with the men. It would be easier, but it would be admitting defeat and, given the state of the country, he might never see Mahelt again. Heartsick and apprehensive, he entered the chamber, intending to join her and see whether she turned towards him or not. However, the bed was empty and there was no sign of her maid. His chest tightened as he wondered if she had run away—put a ladder over the wall and galloped off as she had done before. Then he shook his head and told himself he was being foolish. She might leave him, but she would not forsake the children.

A light still burned in his mother's chamber and he found Mahelt there, sitting in vigil at the bedside. She wore her cloak over her chemise and her long, dark braid hung over her shoulder, although the top of her head was covered by a loose scarf in respect. Father Michael was present at the other side of the bed, his hands clasped in silent prayer.

She looked up at the doorway. "It will not be long," she said quietly. "Those who are going to make their farewells had best come soon."

❖❖❖

Morning light poured through the shutters, gilding the woven matting on the floor and shining on the red silk coverlet. Outside the children were playing in the orchard, the sound of their laughter vivid and joyous.

Ida opened her eyes. A faded smile curved her dry lips. "I am glad to hear my grandsons at play," she whispered. "It is balm on a sore place."

"Try to rest," Mahelt replied. Her mother-in-law had survived the night and had rallied with the dawn, but she was very feeble.

"Time enough for that later," Ida said. "A long, long time." But her eyes closed and for a moment she drifted into sleep. The shouts of the children grew loud as they ran past the window, and then they ceased.

Apart from the priest, Mahelt was alone in her vigil. Hugh had left briefly to give orders to the men in preparation for riding north, and the earl had yet to put in an appearance at all. A message had been sent to Longespée and Ralph, but they

were four days' ride away and, even with fast horses, Mahelt
knew they would not arrive in time.

Ida's eyes were open again and she said weakly but with
clarity, "Daughter, you must forgive Hugh and move on from
all this blame. It does no one any good, least of all you and
the children."

Mahelt said nothing and sat up, which gave the effect of
drawing back.

"I ask it as a boon to a dying woman," Ida said huskily. "I
want you and my son to live in harmony, not as enemies. You
must not let the king drag apart this family because then he will
have won." She gave a dry swallow and Mahelt helped her take
a sip from the cup of watered wine. "You are stronger than
that." Ida laid her head back on the pillows, the wine shining
on her lips, most of it unswallowed. "Stronger than I was...
so much stronger." Her voice faded. Mahelt looked at her in
sudden fear, but Ida was only gathering herself. "Promise me."
Her grip on Mahelt tightened.

There was a dragging sensation in Mahelt's stomach. What
Ida asked was impossible; yet how could Mahelt refuse? "I
promise," she said, and squeezed Ida's hand.

"Good." Ida nodded. "Now bring Hugh to me."

Mahelt went in search of him, but it was the earl she came
across first, seated at the far end of the hall, busy dictating
messages to a scribe. Mahelt felt sick. This was the man she had
to call father. The man who sat composing letters while his wife
lay dying. The man who was ultimately responsible for what
had happened at Framlingham. Did he not care for anyone?

Roger and Hugo were sitting beside him and the earl was
allowing them to press the seal into the warmed green wax,
watching them carefully and showing them what to do. There
was gruff tenderness in the old man's voice and manner and the
boys were being touchingly serious.

"Sire," Mahelt said and dropped a stilted curtsey.

"Daughter," the earl said without looking at her.

"The countess..." She raised her chin. "Will you come to her?"

He continued to be busy. "She knows I have things to do. All is being done for her that can be done. She lacks for nothing."

"Save your presence, sire."

The earl's jaw made a chewing motion. He waved away the scribe and rose to his feet. "You still do not know when to hold your tongue."

Mahelt glared at him, thinking him uncaring and vile. And then, as before, she saw the glint of fear in his eyes and realised that they were not just wet with rheum, but glittering with tears, and that his jaw, sprouting with an old man's silver stubble, was trembling. "Sire, I do," she replied. "The countess thinks herself of little consequence to you, but I say she is of great consequence and if that is not knowing when to hold my tongue, I will not apologise."

The earl told Hugo to return the seal to its box and without a word strode from the room.

"Why is Grandpa cross?" Roger asked.

"Because I reminded him of a duty he would rather avoid," Mahelt said, putting her hands on his shoulders. "He's not cross with you."

"I've been helping him seal things," Roger said importantly. "A charter to a nunnery. He said it was for Grandmother's soul."

"Did he?" Charters were all very well, she thought, but making pacts with God, sending physicians, paying for prayers, such measures were not the same as being there. It was running away. Had the situations been reversed, she knew Ida would not have left the earl's side. She sent Roger and Hugo to their nurse and then continued in search of Hugh. Rounding the corner of the stables, she stopped abruptly, for her father-in-law was leaning against the wall, crying deep wrenching sobs as if he were weeping his heart blood. Hastily Mahelt backed away and changed direction, knowing that her presence would be met with a snarl, and that she would never be forgiven for seeing him thus. She doubled back and took the long route to the garden, intending to pick some late-blooming roses and greenery to take to Ida's chamber. Then she stopped, because Hugh was emerging from the wattle-surrounded garth with a gathering of flowers already in his hands.

They stopped and looked awkwardly at each other.

"For my mother," he said. "I thought they would give her ease and pleasure."

"I was going to do that myself." She decided not to tell him about his father.

"Then we can both take them to her." He didn't move, but squared his shoulders as if bracing himself to fight. "I have been doing a deal of thinking."

Mahelt raised her brows. "About what?"

He let out a long breath. "I have done everything I can think of to set matters right between us. Some of those things may have been wrong, but I have no more remedies and I am losing the will to keep trying. Perhaps I cannot bear to dwell in a garden that once flourished but is now choked with briars, knowing I have not been a diligent gardener and that the one for whom I made it no longer comes there."

Mahelt's eyes stung and her throat was so tight that it ached.

He lowered his voice. "If you do not want me...if you want a separate household...I can arrange it."

The enormity of his suggestion hung between them like a heavy, dark cloud and Mahelt could almost feel her body tensing against the imminent deluge. "I am a Bigod wife," she said stiffly. "My responsibilities are here, to this household and these people. What would such an action say to the world? To our children? That you have sent me away? Again, that you do not value me?"

He looked appalled. "Dear God, no! Why must you twist everything?"

"I don't. It was twisted from the start."

"Then let it unwind...I beg you."

"Is that what you want? To separate?"

He shook his head. "Never! I thought it was your wish, and I wanted to give you that choice in honour. You would not be disparaged."

"You expect me to thank you or think well of you for this?"

Hugh gave her a desolate look. "No," he said. "I don't expect that at all, but I hope, perhaps in vain. Just think on it. I shall ask you again when I return from the North." He turned towards the hall and Mahelt fell into step beside him and they were silent with each other. Her life was indeed twisted, she thought, but instead of unwinding, it was unravelling.

❖❖❖

Ida's breath scarcely stirred the covers and her hands were as cold and fragile as the claws of a winter sparrow. Hugh held them and remembered their dexterity with a needle. He remembered all the embraces, all the times when she had drawn him close, or else sent him forth with strong, unconditional love, and now it was something he would never have again. Beyond the open window, the autumn day was as bright as an illumination. The flowers from the garden stood in a jug in the embrasure and a fresh breeze wafted an outdoor scent above the aromas of incense and sickness.

Father Michael knelt at the bedside, his rosary beads woven between his fingers, his rich voice strong but subdued as he led the prayers for the dying. Hugh's other brothers had quietly entered the room, but there was still no sign of his father. Roger and Hugo were ushered within the chamber by Orlotia and joined their parents, their eyes wide and solemn. Hugo started to pipe a question, but then remembered and shushed himself with a finger to his lips. Ida's head moved on the pillow and it was plain that she was still aware but too tired and faded to open her eyes. But she did whisper a word.

"She wants Grandpa," Hugo said loudly.

Mahelt had been sitting at Hugh's side, saying prayers, occasionally murmuring words of comfort. Now she rose and left the room.

She found her father-in-law in his own chamber, sitting in his chair and holding the most recent piece of embroidery Ida had been working on before she became too sick to sew. It was a band for a hat with a design of green foliage. A rabbit peeped out cheekily from behind one of the leaves.

"Sire," Mahelt said. "You have to come now." When he did not reply, she added, "It is your duty. You have often told me what is mine. Now I tell you yours."

She saw his jaw clench. "I cannot," he said.

"She asks for you. Will you let her down?"

For a moment she thought he was going to snarl at her again, but he rose to his feet and drew a deep breath. "You are right, daughter. I do owe her this duty. I may not love you for it, but you are correct to persist in reminding me." On dragging, stumbling feet, he left his sanctuary and made his way to his wife's chamber. Mahelt walked at his side as escort and support, and in that brief journey, felt as if she had grown while he had diminished.

When the earl entered the room, Hugh immediately vacated his place at the bedside and ushered his father to take his place. The earl tripped as he sat on the folding stool, but recovered himself. Slowly he raised his hands and removed his hat, exposing his sparse silver hair. Leaning forward, he took one of Ida's hands in his own. "Wife," he said. "Would you leave me

465

with your sewing unfinished?" He set under her other hand the band he had been clutching.

Ida made a slight sound and turned her head towards him. Her hand gripped the cloth. "I don't want to go," she whispered, "but when the thread is cut, a thing comes to an end whether it be done or not. You should know that. I am sorry I have not fulfilled my duty…"

"Ida, you always have, and more."

She gave a faint, sad smile. "I have loved you since I saw you," she said, and after that, she did not speak again.

❖ ❖ ❖

There was silence in the moment after Ida died, in the infinitesimal time between the knowledge and the welling of grief. Mahelt controlled her own anguish, knowing that she was now the mistress of the household and its functioning and stability depended on her and her direction. Ida would have to be washed and laid out; sewn into a shroud, borne to church, and a vigil kept.

Her father-in-law still sat at the bedside, holding his wife's hand, watching her still face with a desperate, desolate look on his own, as if willing her to wake up. Going to him, Mahelt set an arm across his shoulders in a comforting gesture. He pinched tears from his eyes, the embroidered band still woven through his fingers. "I loved her," he said in a choked voice.

Mahelt wondered how far back that past tense went. It was too late to be sorry now. But then other things so often got in the way of love, as she had cause to know, this man being part of that obstruction. All she felt for him now was sorrow and pity. He might strut in his furs, he might hold greatness in his hands, but just now he was defenceless and naked, and she was the one with the strength. "Come," she said. "Let the women have her. We shall wash and prepare her fittingly and you can visit her again in a while."

He rose like a sleepwalker and Mahelt handed him into Hugh's care. Hugh's face was lined with grief too, but, like her, he was composed and in command of his faculties. Their eyes met in a moment of cooperation and understanding, and even if it was only on a practical level, it was a stepping stone.

❖❖❖

Preparations began to remove Ida's body to Thetford for burial. That first night they held a vigil for her in the church of Saint Margaret, close to the house. The earl insisted that her bier be draped with the richest silk cloth they could find, and set upon it with his own hand the banners of Tosney and Bigod, and the half-embroidered band with the needle still tucked neatly into the back of the stitchwork as if its owner had just stepped out of the room for a moment.

At dawn, bleary-eyed, they broke fast after mass and the men donned their armour. It was a subdued party that rode out from London to escort Ida's coffin the eighty miles to Thetford. Rain was spitting in the wind and the overcast sky threatened more to come. The silks upon the coffin had been covered with grey woollen cloth for protection and then by waxed tent canvas. Mahelt kissed farewell to her sons and the baby, who were staying in London with their nurses and the servants, and mounted her mare. The earl had retreated into an oblivious, stricken silence and those around him had to guide his every move. She had half wondered if Hugh or his father would try and make her stay behind, but no one had spoken to deny her and she had been ready to fight them if they dared—certain that this time she would win.

Forty-five

*I*DA WAS BURIED IN THE CHOIR AT THETFORD PRIORY WITH all due ceremony, if not the great pomp associated with the laying to rest of a countess. In a way, it reflected her life, Mahelt thought. Ida had never wielded power beyond the domestic circle, nor had any interest in doing so. It was fitting that she should lie here, one day to be joined by her husband, who would then sleep at her side for eternity. Her death had sent the earl into a vague, lost world of his own as if he walked his own twilight between life and death. For the moment at least, his mind was not at the helm. Hugh had taken command, made the decisions about where to stop for the night, and seen to all matters pertaining to the security of the entourage.

They stayed in the priory guest house and were given cautious hospitality by Father Vincent. Thus far Thetford had escaped a mauling from the various armies criss-crossing the region and he had no desire to attract attention to Saint Mary's from whatever faction. He warmly welcomed his patrons, but at the same time made polite enquiries as to when they would be leaving.

"The morrow," Hugh reassured him. "At first light."

The prior relaxed after that and set out in his turn to promise that he would keep the countess safe and have masses said daily for her soul.

"It is terrible to see the country tearing itself apart again," Prior Vincent said. "My grandsire told me dreadful stories of the war between the Empress Matilda and her cousin Stephen over the right to rule England. They say Christ and His saints slept. Now it has come again. The fields burn and men kill each other for power. I pray daily for peace."

"As we all do," said Hugh. "But until we have justice, peace will not come."

"Then I pray for justice too."

"Amen to that."

"And mercy."

Hugh nodded in polite agreement. He had seen precious little of that of late, although he still believed somewhere in a corner of his mind that God was merciful. All the ruthless cruelty belonged to man.

He spent another night in vigil at his mother's tomb, supporting his father, who was a husk of his former self, as if Ida had been the part that nourished his soul. The earl refused to remove his armour and insisted on standing guard in his mail hauberk, coif, and chausses.

"I was always leaving her," he said, his frame bowed by the weight of his mail. "Throughout her life I had to go away and she hated it. I suppose you remember those times—the headaches and the tears. There was no help for it; I had to do my duty, but she never understood. And now…" He closed his eyes. "God help me, she is the one to leave me, and I do not know how I shall bear it…but bear it I must, because like her I have no choice." And he bent his head and wept.

❖ ❖ ❖

In the morning, Mahelt came to bid a final farewell to her mother-in-law as their party prepared to return to London. "Be at peace," she said, laying a garland of evergreen on the tomb. "I shall come again—often. You will not be forgotten, that I swear."

Her only answer was the soft patter of the rain on the roof shingles, the scuff of a monk's soles on the tiled floor, and a feeling of deep melancholy.

Five miles along their road home, they began to smell smoke in the wind, and then to see dark billows rising from the direction of a nearby farmstead. Hugh ordered close formation and sent scouts to investigate.

"It's not a fire from a charcoal clamp or from any ordinary sort of burning," he said, looking worried. He placed his hand to his sword hilt.

Mahelt's mare tossed her head and sidled, disturbed by the smell. "It can't be the king, surely," Mahelt said.

"It could be a foraging party."

One of the scouts that Hugh had sent ahead returned at a gallop. "Burned-out farmstead, my lord," said Gervase de Bradefield. "Slaughtered animals and a couple of bodies. Reckon everyone else managed to flee. The horse dung is fresh. I would say they came through soon after dawn. About thirty I'd guess from the tracks, but the ground's well churned."

Which was about their own strength, excluding the earl and Mahelt. A troop of such numbers suggested foragers stringing out from a larger army within striking distance, but where that army was, Hugh did not know. Heading for Cambridge perhaps, or Peterborough, but there was no telling for sure. He hoped not Thetford, for wherever they came, destruction would follow.

As they picked up the pace, a church bell from a distant village started to toll a warning. Mahelt shuddered and was glad she was riding astride and able to keep up with their increased speed. She was thankful too that the children were safe in London. It began to rain harder. Hugh rode at her side, his gaze constantly checking their surroundings and his hand close to his sword hilt. They spoke little and kept their mounts to a rapid trot.

Suddenly, ahead of them, a band of mounted men, armed to the hilt, rode out of the rain and blocked their path. Mahelt gripped the knife at her belt. Around her the Bigod knights and serjeants reached for their weapons. "Be still," Hugh cautioned, holding up his right hand. "These are allies. Look at their shields. They bear the device of Perche. They serve Louis—and is not the count of Perche your kin?"

"My father's distant cousin," she said, trying not to show her anxiety.

Hugh nudged Hebon forward and greeted their leader, a hard-eyed man with a broken nose and a missing front tooth. "We have no quarrel with you," Hugh said, "unless you make it so."

"Nor we with you, my lord Bigod," the man replied, displaying his own knowledge of heraldic blazons. His gaze lit on Mahelt with jaunty impertinence. "Or my lord's kin. You let us go about our business, and we shall let you go about yours."

"And your business is?" Hugh enquired.

"The erstwhile king of England. Our scouts say he is in Cambridge, my lord. We ride to take him."

"You will need more men than you have."

"There are more," the soldier said. "We're an advance party. Others are following behind."

"Then beware. There's a raided farm about three miles back to the east; you may run into the king's foragers."

"Thank you for the warning, sire; we'll be on our guard."

The soldiers drew aside on the road to let them past. Hugh noted that their pack beasts were laden with cooking pots, strings of onions, crocks of honey, and several necked hens, one of them dripping dark beads of blood from its beak. His feeling of unease grew. When he looked over his shoulder, it was to meet the hard gaze of the knight upon him in speculation.

The next homestead they came to had been raided too. An old woman sat on a stump in her garth, wailing and cursing, while behind her flames roared through her cottage and animal shed. A dead guard dog sprawled in her yard, entrails spilling from a gaping slash in its side. At the sight of armed men, the woman tried to run, but stumbled and sprawled full length in the dirt. Hugh started to dismount, but his father was faster, suddenly shaking off his grey mood to ride over to the woman and block her escape.

"Bastards, bastards!" she screamed in English, shaking her gnarled, clenched fists at him. "French sons of whores!"

"Dame, we are not French, we are English," the earl replied in her own tongue, which he spoke tolerably well.

"English, French, you are all the same," she spat. "You care nothing—nothing for us! My home gone, my hens necked, my stores raided. Kill me now, because I won't survive the winter. I might as well be dead!"

Her story emerged in incoherent bursts. The day before soldiers had come through, demanding food and provisions. They had taken her goats and the pig she had been fattening for slaughter, her sacks of flour, and even the mushrooms she had picked that morning. Her hens had been foraging and they hadn't bothered to catch them, but she had lost her goose and gander. Then this morning another band had arrived and taken what the others had not—her cooking pot, the hens, the honey. They had demanded money and when she said she had none, they had set fire to her house as a parting "gift."

It was an ordinary tale of *chevauchée*. Soldiers passed through. They took, they burned, they destroyed so that their enemies could not have the spoils or live off the land.

Hugh offered to bring her to the next town, but she spat a refusal. However, she took the handful of silver pennies he gave her, and the blankets and bread Mahelt provided from their own supplies.

"You should keep off the road and go to the priory at Thetford," Hugh said. "Tell them that you were sent by the Earl of Norfolk and that you are to be given alms in the name of Countess Ida."

She gave him a contemptuous look. "In whose name was I given this?" she asked, indicating her wasted homestead.

❖ ❖ ❖

Hugh made the decision to take the troop off the road and travel by little-known byways too, because although it increased the journey time, it made them less likely to encounter marauding groups of whatever faction. Nevertheless, the stench of smoke continued to lie heavy on the air and they came across people hiding in copses and hollows with their goods and animals. Sometimes there were corpses: men swinging from trees with swollen throats and broken necks. At the roadside they passed bodies of the elderly and the infirm, cut down as they fled. Once they came across the heartbreaking sight of a dead elderly woman clutching a small baby that was evidently her grandchild. Mahelt made herself look because she knew she had to bear witness and to turn away would be cowardice. Hugh looked too, his mouth tight with unspoken revulsion. Everywhere, they heard the same story: King John's men had come through burning and looting and the French were following on his heels doing the same. As the old woman said, there was nothing to choose between them. The world was burning.

The party stopped at dusk to water the horses and spend the night at Bishop's Stortford, which Hugh judged to be reasonably safe since they were within a day's ride of London. There were no king's men here and the French who had gone north to harry had already passed through.

They claimed hospitality at the manor and were provided

with stabling and sleeping space in the hall by the bishop of London's steward. Food was in short supply and they made do with their own provisions augmented by locally brewed ale, which tasted weak and sour. The servants watched them with the whites of their eyes.

Hugh's father huddled in his furs and brooded over his cup. "That old woman," he said, "what justice has she had? All those farms put to the torch. All those burning fields and dead animals and people. We husband and nurture, and then either we watch it be destroyed or we take torches and destroy it ourselves. Once I had a lovely young wife and I built a castle for us from the ashes of the one the king burned down. Now I have no wife and no castle and all I have seen today are burned-out homes, courtesy of more kings. I have lived too long."

"You are tired and road-weary and grieving." Hugh was shocked that his father would speak of giving up. Always he had been there, meeting each new challenge with steady, stoical calm. "You will feel different when we get to London."

His father raised exhausted, red-rimmed eyes. "Do not presume to tell me what I shall feel." He sought the straw pallet that his squire had laid out for him and, without another word, rolled himself in his cloak and turned his back.

Hugh sat on the hearth bench and drew his own cloak around his body. Mahelt joined him and he handed her his cup. She took a swallow and he watched her throat ripple. She had said very little on the road and had withdrawn further into herself as they came across each new sight of rapine and atrocity, the torched farms, the destruction and waste of life. "Your father is right," she said dully. "It is all the same. Louis and John. There's not a penny to choose between them, is there?"

"Between them in a time of peace there is a great deal," Hugh said, "but between them in war—no. Not for ordinary folk." He took the cup from her, drank, and replenished it, because even though the ale was foul, it was something to do that was commonplace. Glancing towards his father's huddled form beneath the blanket, he couldn't believe he had turned his face to the wall.

"You must take up the reins," Mahelt said. "Even if your father recovers, he is certainly not capable of making decisions."

He laughed without humour. "And you think I am capable?"

She was silent for a while, and then she said quietly, "Yes, I do."

Hugh exhaled shallowly. Mahelt was brave and true and strong, but she never admitted to being wrong. Even to compromise was a struggle for her. He felt as if a door that had been slammed in his face had now reopened to show a thin wedge of light. "And of making the right judgement?"

"Is anyone?" Her jaw suddenly trembled. "I know why you wanted me and the children to stay at Framlingham. You are just a man, as you said. And I am not only a Marshal daughter, but a Bigod wife, and I have to go forward or I shall be forever stuck in this terrible, lonely place."

Hugh's chest was painful with all the emotion swelling there; with all the hope he dared not show. He drew her against him and kissed her hesitantly and she responded in the same way, their embrace a question mutually asked, and as yet without certain answer. They retired to the straw pallets that the squires had laid out and slept bundled up in each other's arms, closer than they had been in an age, Hugh's hand claiming Mahelt's long, dark braid, and hers upon his chest, over the solid rhythm of his heart.

And the earl slept alone, as he had done for a long time, tears seaming the age tracks at his eye corners.

Forty-six

*M*AHELT WAS BUSY SUPERVISING THE HANGING OF A NEW SET of bed curtains on the great bed at the Friday Street house. They were deep red and the Flemish-spun cloth was good and heavy, ready for winter, but putting them up made everyone's arms burn like fire. Eventually she stood back, studied the drape, checked the length, and, with relief, nodded to her women to hook the curtains out of the way until it was time to draw them for sleep.

They had been back in London for ten days and she was gradually settling into a routine. The first thing she had done on her return was embrace her children and for a while had not let them out of her sight.

Hugh had had to leave almost straight away on the business of the earldom: collecting funds from the treasure deposited at Colne Abbey. The mention of the place, the knowledge he was going there, had renewed the friction between them, but she had made an effort to avoid opening up wounds that had scarcely begun to heal. They had to have funds and they had to live on their surplus because they had little access to revenues from their demesne estates.

Since their return her father-in-law had spent most of his time sitting by the fire, at first gazing into it, conjuring pictures of the past and holding to his breast the band of embroidery Ida had been working on. However, during the last few days he had begun emerging from his numbness and had started work on documents and charters concerned with the legal aspects of Louis's rule. He seemed to find comfort in the study and use of measured words and cerebral matters requiring no emotion. For comfort he turned to his grandsons and while Roger was too energetic to be still for long, Hugo loved to sit beside his grandfather and watch him write. Both boys were fascinated by the sand sprinkler and the process of melting wax and pressing the seal into the malleable substance. Mahelt could remember doing the same when her father sealed documents handed to him by his scribe, and how important she had felt. A pang of sadness flickered through her. She had barely seen her father since his return to England. The current state of hostilities meant that she was unable to visit her family because it wasn't safe. While Hugh's father sat by the fire and pored over legal documents, hers was riding hither and yon in John's service, still active and energetic, still in the saddle, but in his seventieth year, he should be at home too with his grandsons at his feet.

"Madam, your brother is here," announced Orlotia from the doorway.

"My brother?" Mahelt looked round.

"The lord William."

Mahelt's gut clenched. The last time her brother had arrived unannounced, he had brought catastrophic news. "Send him up," she said, keeping her voice level. "And bring wine and honey bread."

Orlotia departed. Moments later, Will strode into the room. Mahelt hastened to embrace him with a glad cry of welcome, although she was shocked at how haggard he looked. "It is so good to see you!" she said. "How are you faring?"

He made a short, open-handed gesture. "Well enough, sister," he replied, with more courtesy than truth. "And you?"

She grimaced. "Well enough in my turn. I thought to make this room ready for winter because it seems as if we shall be spending it in London."

Orlotia returned with the wine; Mahelt bade her leave it and then poured for Will herself. "We hear that all of Lincolnshire has been burned under John's hand and that he set some of the fires himself." She shivered, remembering her own ordeal. "Reports say that when de Melun accepted a bribe from the monks of Crowland Abbey to leave their lands alone, John struck the silver out of his hand and went to do the deed himself. They say he torched hayricks and buildings and ran up and down laughing like a madman."

Will nodded. "I am afraid it is all true. I would not put anything past this excuse for a king we have." He curled his lip. "He's at Lynn now, soliciting support from the merchants, but there is news and that's why I'm here." He gave her a look glittering with impatience. "De Burgh is in difficult straits at Dover and has requested a truce while he asks John's permission to yield the castle. If Dover falls, then Louis has control of the South and we're a step closer. Where's Hugh?"

"Gone to the abbey at Colne," she said, "but I expect him back soon. Have you seen our father?"

Will shook his head and turned his mouth down at the corners. "Not since Gloucester. I withdrew from there because I had to—I had no choice."

Mahelt nodded. "You couldn't have fought each other." Will had seized Gloucester, but their father and the Earl of Chester had arrived to relieve it. Had Will not backed down, there would have been a pitched battle with father against son, and no way back.

Will shuddered. "I am weary of warfare. No matter how

many times I chop myself free with my sword, I wind up entangled again, and each time it is harder to cut loose. I shall never stop fighting John, but sometimes I wonder what it's for. What kind of peace are we going to have even if Louis prevails? The peace of the grave, I sometimes think, and then at least I could sleep beside Alais." He looked at his little niece who had toddled into the room, pursued by her nurse. "My son would just be finding his feet by now, had he been allowed to live."

"Will, don't." Mahelt clasped his shoulder, hating to see her vibrant, imperious brother so downcast and feeling his grief crack her own heart.

He raised his hand and placed it over hers in silent acceptance of compassion.

The sound of horses in the yard floated through the window. Mahelt hastened to peer out. "Hugh's back," she said with a surge of relief. She saw him glance up at the window and then walk briskly to the stairs. "Something's happened."

Will stood up and instinctively put his hand to his sword hilt.

Hugh flung into the chamber, the wild October wind at his back. "Have you heard?" he panted, his eyes as bright as speedwells and his chest heaving. "John is dead!"

Mahelt and Will both stared at him.

"Of the flux. He took sick at Lynn, but pushed on to Newark and died there. I heard the news on my way here. I thought you might already know. It'll be all over London by noon."

"John is dead?" Will blinked like a sleeper being shaken awake from an intense dream. "You are certain?"

Hugh nodded. "He was borne into Newark on a litter, crying out in agony every step of the way. The abbot of Croxton was at his deathbed. He has appointed your father one of the executors of his will and given him particular care of his eldest son."

"My father?" Mahelt repeated with a quickening heart.

"With supervision from the papal legate. The king is to be buried at Worcester and young Henry is to be crowned at Gloucester Abbey. It looks as if either your father or Ranulf of Chester will be appointed regent until the boy is of age."

Mahelt looked between her brother and her husband and saw similar expressions on their faces. They were all like swimmers who had been battling against a tide for so long that they were exhausted and had finally been tossed upon an unknown shore with no idea of what lay beyond the strand. The relief still to be breathing was not as yet euphoric because it was a struggle to draw the breath.

Will inhaled shakily. "For all of my youth and manhood I have suffered at the hands of that man. He has cost me my wife, my family, my honour. And now he is gone…It's as if I have raised my sword to strike and cloven nothing but mist." Scraping his hands through his hair, he rose to his feet. "I have to go away and think about this—about what to do."

"We all do," Hugh said, his tone more grim than joyful.

❖ ❖ ❖

Sitting beside Mahelt on their newly curtained bed, Hugh took the comb she had been about to run through her hair. It was very late but folk were only now retiring. All of London was agog with the news of the king's death. The alehouses and cookshops had been packed with customers discussing the news and speculating on what would happen now. People had been reluctant to go home. There had been several drunken disturbances and there were going to be some sore heads in the morning—not all the result of too much wine.

Hugh took a handful of Mahelt's heavy dark hair and drew the comb through its thick sheen. "If I had no other task than to do this for the rest of my days, I would be content," he murmured.

"Your arm would soon grow tired," she replied, but she was smiling.

"I would bear it. The pleasure would outweigh the pain."

She laughed with her mouth closed. "Indeed?"

"I would hope so." The sense of easiness with each other was tentative, but it was there, like the first day of spring after a long, hard winter. The ground could easily freeze over again. He combed and smoothed until her hair was a gleaming, lustrous skein, crackling with life. Eventually she turned to him and slipped her arms around his neck.

"Then let us see about hope," she said.

Their lovemaking was a blend of the wild and the tender. Of fierceness in which residues of anger and frustration were burned away, tensions relieved, hurts assuaged, and new bonds forged. Hugh clenched his teeth as his crisis approached and prepared to pull from her body, but she wrapped her legs around him and drew him to a tighter embrace. "No," she gasped against his ear. "I want all of you! Now!"

Her words drove him to the final surge and he pressed his head against her throat, sobbing her name; as she rose against him, he felt that he was home after a long, stormy voyage. By the very act of completion within her body, she was saying that she was prepared to conceive another child—that she had come far enough along the road to want to bear one of his begetting.

In the aftermath, he continued to hold her close, reluctant to be parted, and pulled the coverlet over them both. In the dim light from the bed lamp, she reached up to stroke his face. "If a child comes of this," she whispered, "if we are so blessed, I want him or her to be born to a land at peace. Surely it will be over by then. Surely we can begin to think of living again."

Hugh ran his fingers through her hair. "The greatest impediment is gone, but my father and I have given our oath to Louis and we must move cautiously for the sake of all. A great deal rests upon what happens now."

"Upon my father, you mean?"

"Yes, upon your father. If any man can bring us through this, it is he."

She lifted her head to look at him. "Would you support him against Louis?"

"And be foresworn?" Hugh frowned. "We gave Louis our word of honour. Your father of all men will understand that. We need to know where we stand first, because otherwise how do we keep our balance?" He waited for her to bristle and say in high dudgeon that he should swear for her father immediately, but she remained quiet and thoughtful.

"So may I write to him?"

He hesitated. The fact that she was asking permission was a compromise on her part that melted him, but at the same time, he had caveats.

"You do not trust me." Some of the old anger bristled in her voice.

"It is not that," he said hastily, knowing he should not have paused because she was so swift on the uptake and hurts were still raw—on both sides. "I know you will do everything you can to mend the breaches. But our letters must be a joint effort."

She eyed him narrowly. "Of mutual trust?"

"Of blending," he said. "Like that blue belt we wove together, or the children we have made between us." He kissed her again to seal the words, and also for reassurance. A part of him was tense, waiting for her to remark that trust and blending were not the same things. He added, "There's always a place where the parts overlap and mingle, however different they are at the other edge."

She gave a reluctant laugh. "Oh indeed," she said. "Indeed, my husband." She licked her forefinger and thumb and leaned over him to pinch out the candle. The darkness enfolded them.

❖ ❖ ❖

The late February dusk was bitterly cold. Swathed in a fur-lined mantle, Mahelt stood beside Longespée and held her hands towards the recently kindled fire crackling in the hearth. It was just beginning to yield heat to the immediate area, but beyond the initial ring of cheer, the cold lingered. They had come to Thetford that afternoon and while the servants prepared the house, she had attended mass in the abbey and paid her respects at Ida's grave. She had given three cloaks in alms to the poor and three marks of silver in Ida's memory, and had laid a fresh wreath of evergreen upon the tomb.

Her father-in-law was in the church, giving Ida the time in death he had not afforded her while she was living, and saying his prayers while the candle burned down the wick. Perhaps he was reflecting on his own time too and the moment when he also would lie under stone in the priory church. The rest of the family had left him to his vigil and returned to the house. It had been shut up for months and was chill and musty, especially being close to the river, but at least this fire was burning well now and the bed linen Mahelt had brought with her from London was herb-scented and fresh. The prior had promised to send dishes from his kitchens, and while it would only be pottage and salt fish in this season, it would at least be hot. Hugh was outside talking to the grooms, Roger and Hugo with him. She could hear their voices piping in the yard as they played chase and the sound of their father's deeper tones in earnest conversation about the state of a horse with colic.

For the moment, in the long dark period of Lent, there was a truce while both sides recuperated and considered their stance and their options. Her father had been elected regent to reign on behalf of King John's nine-year-old son. He had offered amnesties and had reissued a more considered form of the great charter that had been negotiated and signed at Runnymede. Some barons had returned to the fold, but men were wary. Her father-in-law said that it was like being led into a chicken coop by a trail of crumbs and not knowing if a comfortable roost awaited—or the headsman's axe. That Mahelt's father was the one strewing the crumbs made little difference to his opinion. Hugh was reticent on the subject, only saying at the time the chicken analogy was mentioned that it was not a matter of being led into a coop, but of being clear-sighted and knowing who you were and where you stood. If you weren't on firm ground then how could you move forward? If you had given your oath to a man, then you could not renege on it, unless he reneged first, because that was your honour.

She turned to Longespée who, much like herself, had been staring into the flames in silence. "I am glad you came," she said. "For your mother's sake and for yours."

He gave her a twisted smile. "So am I, although I did not know how welcome I would be."

"Times have moved on," she said. "They have had to." She went to a baggage coffer standing in a corner, unfastened the ties, and brought out the small enamelled box that Ida had entrusted to her. "Your mother kept this close every day of her life," she said. "She wanted you to have it."

Gingerly, Longespée took the box, opened it, and looked down at the tiny shoes and the lock of hair.

"They are yours," she said. "They were all she had of you when she was forced to leave you behind. She grieved deeply over losing you and these were one of her greatest treasures."

Longespée gently closed the box. "Thank you." A muscle ticked beneath his cheekbone. "I shall treasure this too." He looked round as Hugh entered the room, his sons in tow, and tucked the box under his arm to shield it, his expression closing.

Hugh took in his half-brother's action while he sent the boys to wash their hands and faces. "She loved you," he said. "And so deeply that it was an unhealing wound—for everyone."

Longespée brought the box out again and looked down at it. "I am sorry I did not know her better." He rubbed his thumbs over the gilding.

"We all are—my father most of all. My mother had regrets throughout her life; my father's have begun since she died." He started towards the door. "I should go and fetch him."

"I shall come with you," Longespée said.

Hugh concealed his surprise. He and his half-brother might have a truce, but keeping each other's company was a different matter. Leaving the house, they walked the short distance to the priory, their way lit by a stable lad bearing a lantern. The river glittered like jet and the wind tossed through trees that were still stark but beginning to peep with bud.

Longespée cleared his throat. "I have been thinking long and hard."

"About what?" Hugh had an inkling what was coming because he too had been deeply pondering of late.

After a long pause Longespée said, "I have decided to go to the Marshal and tender my fealty to my brother's son, the rightful king of England."

"That will mean renouncing the oath you swore to Louis."

Longespée hesitated as they approached the abbey gate-house, then he put his head down and strode forwards into the precinct as if standing within hallowed grounds would give support to his next words. "I had to renounce John—because of what he did to Ela, and because I could not stand against Louis. I thought it would bring my brother to heel. It was never to overthrow the sovereign, and I shall not depose my own nephew in favour of a Frenchman. The young king's grandfather was my father."

"It has taken you a while to find your conscience," Hugh said curtly.

Longespée gave an uncomfortable roll of his shoulders. "I

couldn't let my brother behave as he was doing. Louis was the only alternative at the time, but now we have the Marshal and I trust him. I do not fear for England with him at the helm. Louis has called a truce and gone to France. Perhaps he won't return."

"That is wishful thinking. All he is doing is summoning more troops. He is not faithless like John."

Longespée jutted his jaw. "My mind is set. You may hate me for it; that is your entitlement. I would not have brother against brother; that is the last thing our mother would have wanted and we have been down that road too often to take it again."

"I do not hate you," Hugh said wearily. "But I do not have to like you or the choices you make. For our mother's sake and her memory, I am prepared to keep the peace."

They stopped as they reached the doors to the church. Hugh folded his hands around his belt and rested on one hip. "I gave my oath to Louis. So did my father; we are bound in honour to support him until he should dissolve that bond." He said nothing of Longespée's own honour. That was for his half-brother's conscience.

"I shall speak for you with the Marshal if you wish."

"We can speak for ourselves," Hugh snapped, and then heaved a sigh. "I am not ungrateful, but you take your path, and let me take mine. There will come a time when truces have to be negotiated and both sides will need good lawyers. What is fought for must be set down on parchment and in law, and that is as important as the fighting because it determines our future beyond the day."

Together they entered the church and walked in silence up the nave to the choir. Hugh's father had risen to his feet and was smoothing his hat under his hands. It was an old one, showing wear and the shine of grease, but the peacock feather in the band was new.

"This was her favourite," the earl said. "I wore it for her."

"She would have appreciated it," Hugh replied gently. After a respectful while he added, "Will you come to the house? There is food and warmth, and Longespée wants to talk to you."

His father inclined his head, but turned back to the tomb to lay his hat there beside Mahelt's fresh garland of evergreen. He crossed himself, bowed, and left the abbey bare-headed.

Forty-seven

*H*UGH WATCHED LOUIS PACE UP AND DOWN HIS CHAMBER in the Tower of London like a lean, enraged lion, his usually even nature deposed by a flush of angry frustration. Since Louis's return with reinforcements at the end of April, his cause had suffered a crippling defeat in battle at Lincoln in May. Then, a fortnight ago, fresh reinforcements sailing from France had been destroyed and scattered in a disastrous sea battle off the English coast at Sandwich. His English supporters were deserting him in droves to swear to the young king and his regent William Marshal. Louis had no option but to sue for peace.

Hugh was still at his side, because he had sworn Louis his allegiance and what did a man have if not his honour? Besides, his legal abilities, his knowledge of English law, and his kinship with William Marshal meant that he was in a position to negotiate the best for his family from the peace treaty. Hugh had fought at neither Lincoln nor Sandwich, but had spent his time in London as a core member of Louis's administration.

"Four days it has taken them to answer," Louis snarled, gesturing with contempt at the parchments on the trestle. "Four days! And now they want me to go before them dressed in my undergarments in token of my submission. I will undergo no such humiliation!" His eyes flashed. "I would rather fight to the death! You asked me to be your king because the one you had was unfit to be one, and now you subject me to this when I have tried to save you?"

Salomon de Basing, the mayor of London, rubbed worried hands. "Sire, the regent has brought up his troops to blockade us in. We must have peace. I fear for the city if we continue to refuse."

Louis curled his lip. "I will negotiate an honourable peace; I will not surrender, and I will not be shamed. The Marshal knows this."

"Perhaps if you were to wear a rich cloak over your garments," Hugh suggested. "Who then will know, other than those immediately around you? You will not be seen without your tunic by the greater public."

Louis cast him an irritated look. "I would know," he growled and paced the room again.

Hugh looked down at the parchments under his hands. Louis did not want to admit defeat—none of them did—but they had no choice. As the mayor said, London was under blockade and their situation could only deteriorate. But then again, his father-in-law could not afford to go for the throat because he had interests in France that he had to safeguard, and even a wounded dog could still bite viciously.

Louis returned to the table and picked up the demands again, scanning them with narrowed dark eyes. "Very well," he said. "If they agree to the cloak, I shall come and I shall yield." He lifted his gaze and fixed it on Hugh. "But if I pay this price, I expect something in return..."

❖❖❖

At the Marshal manor of Caversham, Mahelt embraced her father and was dismayed by how tired he looked, at the new lines on his face and the evident limp from an old battle wound,

489

but his smile was still there for her, and his embrace was like returning to a beloved place that was still home.

Her eyes filled and her father laughed at her foolishness. "We have weathered some storms, have we not?" he said. "No need for tears now."

"I'm not crying," she replied fiercely. "Or only with joy at seeing everyone. It has been too long."

She went on to embrace her mother, her sisters, her brothers. All were here save for Richard who was in Normandy. Will was in good spirits, although walking with a stick after having his toes trodden on and three of them broken by his destrier two days since. He hugged Mahelt and greeted her with a semblance of his old arrogant smile, although tempered by sadness and experience. Like Longespée, he had returned to the fold soon after his father had become regent, and in the months since then had gradually mended the rift with his parents. John's death had made such healing possible, and the atmosphere today was comfortable, even while the scars were still tender to the touch.

Her father tousled Roger's hair after the latter had flourished him a most proper bow. "Eight years old," he said, "and bidding fair to be a fine strong knight." He did the same to Hugo and eyed his toddling, fair-haired little granddaughter with gentle amusement. He embraced Hugh with the kiss of peace, which both were at pains to emphasise. All as one, the family entered the hall and sat down to dine and put on a show of unity to the world.

Nothing was said over the food where all was talk of social matters and family—of catching up the years and weaving them into the fabric of now like so many dropped threads, although Mahelt knew that words could never convey the same texture as the living experience, and so much had been lost.

At the end of the meal William and Hugh went off to ride the manor grounds while Will took Roger and Hugo outside for a lesson in swordplay with him and their other uncles. The women retired to Isabelle's well-appointed chamber on the floor above the hall. Gazing out of the chamber window, Mahelt watched her father and her husband set off side by side, her father riding on his favourite chestnut and Hugh on Hebon. Their horses matched strides in the golden September light, and a pair of her father's gazehounds trotted at their heels.

As usual, Roger's dinner had gone straight to his feet and he was running around the yard shouting and twirling, much to the amusement of his Marshal uncles.

Mahelt set her hand to her belly, and became aware of her mother's scrutiny on her, much as she was watching the men.

"I know that gesture," Isabelle said.

"It's only a thought at the moment," Mahelt replied. "Like this peace. It might come to naught, but I pray not."

"I pray not too," her mother said looking pensive, although she came to kiss Mahelt's cheek in pleasure at the news. "Your father needs a respite. I have considered tying him up some-times just to make him stop. He is past seventy years old and these burdens weigh on him."

Mahelt gave her mother an anxious look. "He is all right?"

"As far as I can tell." Isabelle gave an exasperated wave of her hand. "You know what he is like—refuses to yield an inch and pays no heed when I tell him to rest. Will takes what weight your father will allow him."

"I am glad that all is well between you."

Her mother's face clouded with memory for a moment; then she recovered herself and nodded. "It was a difficult time for all," she said, "and a terrible one, but we have weathered it. Your brother is home and, as you can see, he's even begun to smile again sometimes."

"Yes, I had noticed." Mahelt leaned her elbows on the ledge. Will had found himself a stool to sit on and was directing operations with his walking stick, as if it were a marshal's rod of office. Roger was taking on Walter, Gilbert, and Ancel all at once and she had to smile. A feeling of warmth swept over her. This was almost life as it had once been—and perhaps, God willing, a portent of things to come.

"How is your father by marriage?" her mother asked.

Mahelt screwed up her face and looked round. "His eyesight is failing badly and his knees give him constant pain. Hugh has taken over all the active business of the earldom." Her nose wrinkled further. "He still likes to have his say, even if it is only that the sauce on his meat is too rich and the bread not soft enough." She shrugged. "This conflict has taken much out of him—battered his pride—but it is my mother-in-law's death that has hit him the hardest, God rest her soul. He took her for granted and often thought her a nuisance, and now that it is too late he recognises her real value to him."

"I am sorry to hear that." Isabelle crossed herself. "Ida was a dear, sweet lady."

"I loved her," Mahelt said with simple conviction.

"And are you content with Hugh these days?"

Mahelt bit her lip at her mother's perception. "We have mended our differences—for now. I am learning how to rule the roost without seeming to—as you do with my father."

Her mother laughed ruefully. "Oh, I get my way some of the time, but I do not make the mistake of pushing at doors that will never unlock. You have to know when to seize the advantage and when to yield."

"My mother-in-law yielded every time, until she had no power of any kind left." Mahelt raised her chin. "I will not let that happen to me."

"As long as you know when to give a little too," Isabelle cautioned, sober now.

"That is what I am trying to do—but it isn't easy. I hope

Hugh and my father can bring about this agreement. Hugh says that diplomacy is every bit as difficult as battle, and he's right."

"Indeed he is," her mother said with an eloquent look. "On all counts."

Hugh and his father-in-law rode along a bridle path leading from the manor into the park. The sun was a golden benediction, illuminating the turning leaves and adding a touch of gentle warmth to the day. The horses paced eagerly, as glad to be out as their riders.

"So what does Louis say?" William asked after a while.

Hugh watched the dogs sniff and lope. "He says he will come to the Isle of Kingston and agree to the peace. He will wear his undertunic and braies as you desire, but only if he may cover them with his mantle and thus preserve his dignity."

His father-in-law grunted with amusement. "And he is a shy demoiselle," he said.

"Would you not do the same in his position?" Hugh asked and noted William's use of "demoiselle" to describe Louis. It meant not only a shy young girl, but was also a term for an untried young knight. That was far from the case, but he supposed that William's own long career gave him the right to use the word.

"I would do whatever I had to do, and if it involved exposing my underwear in public, then so be it." William gave him a shrewd glance, filled with the weight of experience. "I was an old man when they elected me to the regency and I have aged ten years since then. This conflict between English men, led by a French prince, should not be my life, but it is. I want peace so that I can settle husbands on my daughters and know the ones already married are in their homes and secure in their beds. I want to sit with my wife and enjoy the last rays of the evening sun."

"Amen to that." Hugh slapped Hebon's glossy neck. "We all aspire to such things."

They rode into a clearing and slackened the reins to let their mounts crop the grass. William said, "I have reissued the great charter that was the source of so much difficulty for both sides. To do that, I have had to be pragmatic and bring myself to new ways of thinking—accept different ideas. Sometimes a robe that no longer fits has to be cast off and a new one donned. Louis understands this too because he is a statesman as well as a soldier. We must make compromises without compromising our honour."

"As in wearing a cloak to cover the underwear?" Hugh said.

William's lips twitched. "Louis can have his cloak. I will see that there is no objection."

"Thank you, sire." Hebon tore at the grass and the bit chains jingled. Hugh watched a cloud of midges dance before his eyes, rising and falling. He cleared his throat.

"There is more, isn't there?" William said. "I know Louis."

Hugh sighed. "My lord says that if he is to return to France as soon as the treaty is agreed, he requires a payment of ten thousand marks in compensation for the damage he has suffered in England."

His father-in-law's eyes widened briefly before the usual neutral expression fell into place. "I see."

"You would be free of him for that sum. He promises to speak to his father about restoring Anjou, and will see to it himself once he becomes king."

"Louis is not a fool. I do not for one moment think he will honour such a vow. In his position, I wouldn't. It is the same as me saying I shall try to persuade the barons to allow him that money—it will never happen. Even if I agreed, I do not have those sorts of funds at my disposal. The country is nigh on bankrupt and you know it."

Hugh felt the heat of the sun on the back of his neck as he drew in the reins. Disputing with his father-in-law was not something he relished, but he knew he had to hold his ground. "Sire, you have the spoils of the sea battle at Sandwich—French spoils. I know how much was on those ships you took."

"Been adding it up, have you?" His father-in-law's tone was cooler now.

"It is part of my duty to my liege lord. Only a fool does not know what other men are worth."

"Or the price he is prepared to pay?"

Hugh inclined his head. "You have your lands in Normandy to consider and the goodwill of the French king is vital to your plans. No advantage will come of taking his son captive or digging in your heels."

William looked Hugh up and down. "You are your father's son," he said. "He has taught you well."

"I take that as a compliment, sire."

"As indeed you should. I have the greatest respect for your father and his abilities—not to mention his bloodstock." Having lightened the discussion by allusion to the horse he rode, he patted the chestnut's neck and added, "The Earl of Chester will never agree to such a thing."

"Not in a treaty, no, but in a private agreement...a pledge between men of honour."

William clicked his tongue to his mount and heeled him onwards. "So that is the golden border to this precious cloak of Louis's, and he would leave me perilously threadbare. Are there other demands I should know about hiding inside the lining too?"

"No, sire, only those I have mentioned. My lord is finished with England. All that keeps him here are his pride and the obligation of duty. If they can be satisfied, he will depart and we can all turn to the matter of rebuilding this land. As soon as I am absolved of my oath to Louis, I shall serve the young king—and the regent—to the best of my ability. This I swear on my oath."

"So the price of this peace is a cloak, ten thousand marks, and a charter of liberties to embrace both sides—and if it is not agreed, we move to a different game of chess."

"Yes, sire. One that nobody wins."

His father-in-law looked thoughtful. They rode in silence for a while amid the first light showers of autumn leaves from the ash trees. He halted the horse again as they curved round to the banks of the river. Looking downstream, Hugh could make out the earl's wharf and the barge drawn up there that would carry them down to London the next morning.

William watched the water for a while and sat very still, and Hugh sat with him, waiting, trying not to hold his breath, but staying within the calm of the moment. The sun cast gold coins on the water. Ten thousand twinkling spangles of light.

At length his father-in-law inhaled deeply. "I told you," he said, "I am an old man. I have outlived all of King Henry's children, some who were no more than babes when I was knighted, but I shall not survive their heirs. The work I have done is for you and for my children to continue. For my sons. For Mahelt and her sisters. For their children. Let the prince of France cover his nakedness with ten thousand marks, but, like his mantle, let it not be part of the written peace, because I fear that the Earl of Chester would not see it in the same way that I do."

"Sire." Hugh breathed out with relief.

The Marshal gave him a warm look that was almost father to son. "Hugh, take that daughter of mine and ride home to Framlingham. Go and build your life and raise my grandchildren in peace to be the best they can. That is an order, and one that I will not negotiate."

"Gladly, sire," Hugh said and felt as if all the coins in the water were brightening and glowing in his solar plexus. "More than gladly."

Forty-eight

*I*T WAS LATE BUT THE SKY STILL HELD A FLARE OF DUSKY turquoise to the west over Edmundsbury. Hugh and Mahelt stood on Framlingham's battlements and watched the stars together. Below the wall walk, in chamber, tower room, and bower, the castle occupants were finally settling down to sleep; save for the watchmen and the porter on the gate. Today they had celebrated Mahelt's churching, six weeks after giving birth to Ralph, their third son. He was dark-haired like her, but he was going to have Hugh's summer-blue eyes.

Her parents had come for the churching, as had several of her brothers and sisters. Hugh's siblings were all here too and the atmosphere was one of optimism. Even her father by marriage had taken an interest, holding his new grandson in his lap, saying that it would have been Ida's fondest wish to do this and, since she could not, he would do so in her memory.

Later, he and her father had held a long conversation concerning equine bloodstock. Both had gone down to the paddock to look at the mares and foals, her father limping from his old wound but still having to temper his pace to Earl Roger's slower gait and dimmer eyesight. Hearing the natural flow of their discussion, Mahelt had been pleased to see another fence mended and to hear talk not of war and policy, but of mutually satisfying everyday things.

Prince Louis had agreed the peace treaty at Kingston, his undergarments concealed by a rich mantle, and, the ceremony concluded, had sailed for France on the next tide, leaving those who had been under oath to him free to give their allegiance to the young king and his protector. Framlingham had been returned forthwith, and her father had immediately drafted Hugh into helping with the legal issues of government and matters concerned with finalising the peace.

She heaved a soft sigh that was part contentment and part letting go of the old and taking on the new.

"Profound thoughts?" Hugh asked and she felt rather than saw him smile, but could see in her mind's eye the way the laughter lines had deepened at the side of his eyes. He slipped his arm around her waist and tucked his thumb inside the belt she was wearing, the one they had part-woven together in blended tones of blue when their firstborn son was in swaddling. *Ne vus sanz mei, ne mei sanz vus.*

She answered his smile with the warmth of her voice, and leaned against him. "I was thinking that it is a beautiful evening and it is going to be a fine day tomorrow—and tomorrow after that. I shall take the best fleece from the sheep you gifted to me. I shall spin the wool, and dye it, and we'll weave another braid together, you at one end, me at the other, until we meet in the middle. And then we shall each have a belt, so that whatever happens, one will always be part of the other."

"That sounds like a fine notion to me," Hugh said, and by mutual agreement they descended the wall walk and strolled towards the narrow wedge of light spilling through the open hall door.

Author's Note

HIS IS THE PART WHERE I TAKE THE READERS BEHIND THE scenes and come clean on the historical background to the novel. If readers come across occasional anomalies between *To Defy a King* and earlier titles concerned with the Marshal family, I apologise. My research is ongoing and sometimes I come across material in the historical record of which I was unaware at an earlier time, but which I feel needs to be incorporated now. For example, towards the end of *The Scarlet Lion*, I have a scene where Mahelt is heavily pregnant in 1217, but I have since discovered that her third son was born the following year and *To Defy a King* reflects this. Again, when writing *The Scarlet Lion*, I was unaware of the siege of Framlingham, and this detail does add a new element to the history. I always strive for historical accuracy, but acknowledge that I am fallible, and that I am writing fiction, not a reference work. What I have tried to do is stay true to the characters and their life and times.

Mahelt Marshal does not have the fame or resonance in history that falls to her illustrious father the great William Marshal, but it has not made her any less fascinating to study. She is little mentioned in the narrative historical record. However, there are a few charters and documents that give pointers to her personality and her life—scattered bones that when collected together and assembled offer a glimpse of her character and illuminate the path even eight hundred years later.

She doesn't have a known birth date. In *The Greatest Knight* I've given a date of 1194, but I've revised this now and think she was most likely born some time in 1193. My excuse is that deeper research into previously peripheral characters brings new things to light that make for slight tweaks further down the line.

Mahelt was the third child and firstborn daughter of William Marshal and Isabelle de Clare. Their first two children were boys: William Junior and Richard. In charters and sources she is variously called Matilda, Maheut, and Mahelt, and I have chosen the latter, borrowing it from her father's biography, the *Histoire de Guillaume le Mareschal.* Following Mahelt's birth, two more brothers were born, Gilbert and Walter, and it wasn't until around 1200 that the next girl, Isabelle, came along. For seven years Mahelt was the only girl in her family and in that sense she had her father to herself and there seems to have been a special bond between them. The *Histoire* says of Mahelt that she had the gifts of "wisdom, generosity, beauty, nobility of heart, graciousness, and I can tell you in truth, all the good qualities which a noble lady should possess." These are stock phrases, formal and fairly common in such descriptions, and I take them with a pinch of salt. However, the *Histoire* also adds that "her worthy father...loved her dearly." This is interesting because following on from this remark, the other daughters and their qualities are mentioned, but there is no more of the "loved dearly" business. Mahelt is the only daughter who receives this accolade.

Of course even a doting father in the Middle Ages couldn't let such affection get in the way of politics and William approached Roger Bigod, Earl of Norfolk, and "asked him graciously, being the wise man he was, to arrange a handsome marriage between his own daughter and his son Hugh. The boy was worthy, mild-mannered, and noble-hearted and the young lady was a very young thing and both noble and beautiful. The marriage was a most suitable one and pleased both families involved." Roger Bigod was rich and powerful. His lands in East Anglia, where he dominated, were almost a kingdom in themselves, and he had sizeable estates in Yorkshire too. The family also had a royal kinship tie in that Ida, Countess of Norfolk, was the mother of William Longespée, Earl of Salisbury, King John's bastard half-brother. Longespée was also kin to the Marshal family through marriage, his wife Ela being William Marshal's cousin once removed.

When Hugh and Mahelt married in early 1207, Hugh would have been about twenty-four years old to Mahelt's approximately fourteen. The age difference, the arranged match, and the youth of the bride may seem shocking to a modern mindset, but to a medieval society this was business as usual. The age of consent was twelve for a girl and fourteen for a boy. It was judged that at this age, a person was capable of fulfilling a responsible adult role in society. Although girls were often married very young in aristocratic circles, consummation did not always automatically follow. There are written contracts in existence where families agreed on an age before which consummation was not to take place and I have mentioned such an agreement in *To Defy a King*. History tells us Mahelt Marshal and Hugh Bigod married early in 1207. Their first child was born some time before the end of 1209. The youngest Mahelt could possibly have been at the birth of their first son, Roger, was fourteen, and at the oldest she was seventeen. Her next child, Hugh (Hugo), was born three years later in 1212, and then there is another three-year gap to Isabelle in 1215 and Ralph in 1218. It's interesting to speculate that although contraceptive practices were banned by the Church, Hugh and

Mahelt may well have exercised them in one form or another.

The lines of the poem that feature in a few scenes are an excerpt from the *lais* of a female writer called Marie de France living and working in the twelfth century and come from the poem "Chevrefoil."

Mahelt's husband, Hugh, was given his first taste of government around the age of seventeen, when his father handed over to him ten knights' fees in Yorkshire for his own. By the time Hugh married at twenty-four, he was an accomplished landlord, soldier, and lawyer. He frequently accompanied his father on battle campaigns and in 1210 he deputised for him on the Irish campaign. Indeed, it seems likely that as Roger Bigod grew older, he delegated much of the active work of the earldom to Hugh. Both Roger and Hugh rebelled in the lead-up to the Magna Carta and it is likely that both of them had a hand in its drafting. Roger was an experienced lawyer and Hugh had followed in his footsteps. The reason for their rebellion is not known, but once they committed themselves to ousting John and accepting Louis of France, they remained staunch to that cause until Louis absolved them of their allegiance and returned to France. From that point onwards they remained in loyal service to the regent and the young king Henry III.

A thirteenth tax was indeed demanded in 1207 and was highly unpopular. People did scramble around trying to find hiding places for their goods and chattels—often in monasteries, which were searched. The constable of Richmond Castle really did have his keep taken away in punishment for trying to hide his possessions from the taxman! Churches and abbeys were routinely searched. Swineshead Abbey had its building fund confiscated because the seneschal of the Countess of Aumale had hidden his money there. During the interdict, when the clergy in effect went on strike on orders from Rome, King John ordered that their "wives" and children be arrested and sold back for ransom. Marriage amongst the clergy, once tolerated, had recently been banned and it was a cunning (if malicious) ploy on John's behalf to squeeze more money out of the Church.

Framlingham was besieged in March 1216 by King John and fell almost immediately, i.e., no resistance was put up. The defending constable William Lenveise surrendered to King John. From what can be gleaned, neither Earl Roger nor Hugh were present in the castle, but little Roger, Mahelt's son, was taken hostage and sent first to Norwich, then to Sandwich with Faulkes de Breauté. From there, he seems to have been kept in the household of William Longespée, Earl of Salisbury. There is no record of when he was returned to his family, but certainly he would have been home by the autumn of 1217 and probably before this.

No death date or burial site is recorded for Ida, Countess of Norfolk, although we know she predeceased her husband who died in 1221, because no arrangements were made for her during the settling of his estate. If I have misburied her bones at Thetford, then I apologise, but I think from my research that she would have been content to rest there with her husband.

William Longespée, Earl of Salisbury, did lead the English fleet to a great victory in the harbour at Damme, where he captured the French fleet, sacked the ships, and burned several to the water. He seems to have been an adventurous soul and to have lived his life writ large. His tomb can still be visited to this day in Salisbury Cathedral, and a very stylish gentleman he is too. At the disastrous battle of Bouvines, he was taken hostage and a prison tally from this time lists among the prisoners one Ralph Bigod, whom Longespée calls his brother. This list has been a vital piece of information in tracking down the link between Bigod and Salisbury. A letter still exists from Roger Bigod, Earl of Norfolk, to the justiciar Hubert de Burgh, asking for the return of the ten marks he owes him so he can put it towards paying Ralph's ransom.

King John's assault on Ela Longespée is mentioned in just one source: William of Armorica. Some historians discount it, saying that Longespée's likely reason for deserting John was that his small fortified palace at Salisbury could not have withstood a battering from the French. Personally, I think that it was a combination of the two—a moment when personal grudge and politics came together. John had a reputation for meddling with the wives and daughters of his barons; some of it unsubstantiated rumour and some of it hard fact. My own opinion is that John probably sexually harassed Ela, Longespée found out, the French invaded, and it was the last straw.

On a lighter note, I have to say Roland le Pettour really did exist. He held his lands in Langham, Norfolk, for the service of performing a "leap, a whistle and a fart each Christmastide before the King." The Latin amusingly describes the deed as *"unum saltum et siffletum et unum bumbulum."*

I have paused the novel at a time in Mahelt and Hugh's lives when they were looking forward to the future, having won through the crisis of King John's reign. However, there were further difficult times to come. Mahelt lost her beloved father in 1219, her mother in 1220, and Hugh's father died in 1221. Hugh himself died in 1225 at only forty-three years of age. It was sudden. One minute he was very much alive and attending a council at Westminster. A week later he was dead, leaving Mahelt a widow with four, possibly five children, the eldest of whom was an adolescent of sixteen years old. Mahelt moved swiftly, or those around her did, and within three months, she married William de Warenne, Earl of Surrey. He was the Bigods' neighbour with lands in Norfolk and Yorkshire and castles at Castle Acre and Conisburgh. He was considerably older than her—by my reckoning he was at least sixty years old.

Mahelt bore him a son and a daughter: John and Isabelle. I find it very interesting that in all of her charters from this time, she calls herself "Matildis la Bigot," never "Matildis de Warenne," or only as an afterthought. For example: a charter dated between 1241 and 1245, following the death of her second husband, has the salutation "...*ego Matildis Bigot comitissa Norf et Warenn.*" The "Warenn" is an official title like the "Norf." The "Bigot" is her personal name.

She did revert to her birth name again in 1246 when she was granted the Marshal's rod by King Henry III. All of her brothers and sisters were dead and thus the hereditary marshalship of England came into her hands. She became in her charters "*Matill Marescalla Angliae, comitissa Norfolciae et Warennae.*" I somehow sense a militant gleam in her eyes, and a taking-up of tradition that encompassed her ancestors, including her beloved father. She would be a Bigod, she would be a Marshal, but she would not be a de Warenne except in official capacity.

Mahelt Marshal was a strong woman who survived and learned wisdom through much adversity. I think she was greatly loved but not necessarily lucky in love. She died in 1248 and was buried at Tintern Abbey beside her mother, her bier carried by four of her sons.

Although the name of Marshal died out of the history books with the childless demise of William's five sons, Mahelt was a matriarch whose children went on to forge weighty links across the history of the thirteenth century and beyond. It is down Mahelt's line that the Stuart kings of Scotland claim part of their descent.

As in my other novels about the Marshal family, I have made use of the Akashic Records—a belief that the past is there in the ether to be witnessed by those who can access it. More details can be found about this strand of my research on my website. These records are responsible for, among many other things in the novel, the "over the wall" incident, the "return from Ireland bath" incident (Alison King who reads these records for me is still recovering from that one!), and the Ela and John "egg" incident.

I have also made extensive use of conventional research. For anyone wanting to read further on the period, I have enclosed a select bibliography. A full list of my reference works can be found at my website.

Select Bibliography

Atkin, Susan A. J., *The Bigod Family: An Investigation into Their Lands and Activities 1066–1306* (University of Reading, published on demand by the British Library Thesis Service).

Brown, Morag, *Framlingham Castle* (English Heritage, ISBN 1 85074 853 5).

Brown, R. Allen, *Castles, Conquests and Charters: Collected Papers* (Boydell, 1989, ISBN 085115 524 3).

Brown, R. Allen, "Framlingham Castle and Bigod 1154–1216" (*Proceedings of the Suffolk Institute of Archaeology*, XXV, 1951).

Carpenter, D. A., *The Minority of Henry III* (Methuen, 1990, ISBN 0 413 62360 2).

History of William Marshal, Vol. II, ed. by A. J. Holden with English translation by S. Gregory and historical notes by D. Crouch (Anglo-Norman Text Society Occasional Publications series 5, 2004, ISBN 0 9054745 7).

Holt, J. C., *The Northerners* (Clarendon Press at Oxford, 2002, ISBN 0 19 820309 8).

Karras, Ruth Mazo, *Sexuality in Medieval Europe: Doing unto Others* (Routledge, 2005, ISBN 0 415 28963 7).

King, Alison, Akashic Record Consultant.

Morris, Marc, *The Bigod Earls of Norfolk in the Thirteenth Century* (Boydell, 2005, ISBN 1843831643).

Norgate, Kate, *John Lackland* (Kessinger, 2007, ISBN 0548730954).

Painter, Sidney, *The Reign of King John* (The Johns Hopkins University Press, 1949).

Warren, W. L., *King John* (Eyre Methuen, 1978, ISBN 0 413 455203).

I welcome comments and I can be contacted through my website at www.elizabethchadwick.com or by email to elizabethchadwick@live.co.uk.

I post regular updates about my writing and historical research at my blog at http://livingthehistoryelizabethchadwick.blog-spot.com. You can also find me on Facebook and Twitter @ chadwickauthor and you are most welcome to join in!

For the King's Favor

FRAMLINGHAM CASTLE, SUFFOLK, OCTOBER 1173

OGER BIGOD WOKE AND SHOT UPRIGHT ON A GULP OF breath. His heart was slamming against his rib cage and, although the parted bed curtains showed him a chamber sun-splashed with morning light, his inner vision blazed with vivid images of men locked in combat. He could hear the iron whine of blade upon blade and the dull thud of a mace striking a shield. He could feel the bite of his sword entering flesh and see blood streaming in scarlet ribbons, glossy as silk.

"Ah God." Roger shuddered and bowed his head, his hair flopping over his brow in sweaty strands the colour of tide-washed sand. After a moment, he collected himself, threw off the bed coverings with his right hand, and went to the window. Clenching his bandaged left fist, he welcomed the stinging pain like a penitent finding comfort in the scourge. The wound was not deep enough to cause serious damage but he was going to have a permanent scar inscribed across the base of three fingers. The soldier who had given it to him was dead, but Roger took no pleasure in the knowledge. It had been kill or be killed. Too many of his own men had fallen yesterday. His father said he was useless, but it was a habitual opinion and Roger no longer felt its impact beyond a dull bruise. What did abrade him were the unnecessary deaths of good soldiers. The opposition had been too numerous and his resources insufficient to the task. He looked at his taut fist. There would be a lake of blood before his father's ambition was done.

To judge from the strength of the daylight he had missed mass. His stepmother would delight in berating him for his tardiness and then comment to his father that his heir wasn't fit to inherit a dung heap, let alone the Earldom of Norfolk when the time came. And then she would look pointedly at her own eldest son, the obnoxious Huon, as if he were the answer to everyone's prayers rather than the petulant adolescent brat he actually was.

Framlingham's bailey was packed with the tents and shelters of the mercenaries belonging to Robert Beaumont, Earl of Leicester—an ill-assorted rabble he had plucked from field and town, ditch, gutter, weaving shed, and dockside on his way from Flanders to England. Few of them were attending mass to judge by the numbers infesting the inner and outer wards. They were locusts, Roger thought with revulsion. By joining the rebellion against King Henry and giving lodging and support to the Earl of Leicester, his father had encouraged a plague to descend on them, in more ways than one. The plot was to overthrow the King and replace him with his eighteen-year-old son Henry—a vain boy who could be turned this way and that by men skilled in manipulation and the machinations of power. Roger's father had no love for the King, who had clamped down hard on his ambition to rule all of East Anglia. Henry had confiscated their castle at Walton and built a strong royal fortress at Orford to neutralise their grip on that part of the coastline. To add insult to injury, fines for the earlier insurgency had gone to assist the building of Orford.

Turning from the window, Roger sluiced his face one-handed in the ewer at the bedside. Since the tips of his fingers and his thumb were free on his bandaged side, he managed to dress himself without summoning a servant. From the moment he had been capable of tying his braies in small childhood, a fierce sense of self-reliance had driven him to perform all such tasks for himself.

On opening the coffer containing his cloaks, his eyes narrowed as he noticed immediately that his best one with the silver braid was missing. He could well guess where it was. While donning his everyday mantle of plain green twill, his gaze lit on the weapons chest standing against the wall. Last night his scabbarded sword had been propped against it, waiting to be checked and cleaned before storage, but now it was gone. Roger's annoyance turned to outright anger. His sword had been a gift from his Uncle Aubrey, Earl of Oxford, at the time of his knighting. This time the thieving little turd had gone too far.

With clamped jaw, Roger strode from the chamber and headed purposefully to the chapel adjoining the hall where mass had just finished and people were filing out to attend their duties. Roger concealed himself behind a pillar as his father walked past deep in conversation with Robert, Earl of Leicester. They were an incongruous pair, Leicester being tall and slender with a natural grace and good humour, and his father with a rolling pugilistic gait reminiscent of a sailor heading from ship to alehouse. His paunch strained the seams of his red tunic and his hair hung in oiled straggles, the colour of wet ashes.

Roger's stepmother Gundreda followed, walking with Petronilla, Countess of Leicester. The women nodded graciously to each other, smiling with their lips but not their eyes. There was little love lost between them, even if they were allies, for neither woman possessed the social skills upon which to build a friendship and Gundreda resented Petronilla's superior airs.

As they moved on, Roger's seeking gaze struck upon the flash of a lapis-blue garment and a twinkle of silver braid as his half-brother Huon swaggered out of the chapel, one narrow adolescent hand clasping the buckskin grip of a fine sword. A little behind him traipsed Huon's younger sibling Will, fulfilling his usual role of insipid shadow.

Roger reached, seized, and swung his half-brother around, slamming him against the pillar. "Have you nothing of your own that you must resort to thievery of everything that is mine?" he hissed. "Time and again I have told you to stay out of my coffers and leave my things alone." Taking a choke-hold on the youth's throat with his good hand, Roger used his other to unhitch the sword belt with a rapid jerk of latch and buckle.

Huon's down-smudged upper lip curled with contempt, although his eyes darted fearfully. Roger noted both emotions and increased the pressure. "I suppose you wanted to parade before my lord of Leicester and show off a sword you're too young to wear?"

"I wear it better than you!" the youth wheezed with bravado. "You're a spineless coward. Our father says so."

Roger released his grip, but only to hook his foot behind Huon's ankles and bring him down. Straddling him, he dragged the purloined cloak over his half-brother's head. "If there's a next time, you'll wear this on your bier," he panted, "and my sword will be through your heart!"

"Huon, where are y—" Having turned back to find her lagging son, Gundreda, Countess of Norfolk, stared at the scene with consternation and fury. "What do you think you're doing!" she shouted at Roger. "Get off him; leave him alone!" She forced Roger aside with a hard push.

Choking and retching, Huon clutched his throat. "He tried to kill me...and in God's own house...He did; Will saw it, didn't you?"

"Yes," Will croaked as if his own throat had been squeezed, and refused to look anyone in the eye.

"If I had intended to kill you, you would be dead now!" Roger snarled. He encompassed his stepmother and his half-brothers in a burning glare before flinging from the chapel, his cloak over his arm and his scabbarded sword clutched in his good fist. Her invective followed him but he ignored it for he had become inured to that particular bludgeon long ago.

Acknowledgments

$\mathscr{I}$ WOULD LIKE TO SAY A BIG THANK YOU TO THE PEOPLE WHO have helped behind the scenes while I have been writing *To Defy a King*. My husband Roger keeps the house ticking over around me while I disappear all day and sometimes most of the night to my study. My wonderful agent Carole Blake and the members of the Blake Friedmann Agency keep me in work and through their efforts my books are now available in eight different languages—a feat I would never have managed by myself! At my publishers, I would like to thank my editors Barbara Daniel, Joanne Dickinson, and Rebecca Saunders for their hands-on, but hands-off approach. They leave me to do it my way, but are there if I need help. I would also like to thank Richenda Todd for casting an eye over the finished manuscript and keeping me up to scratch where ages, dates, and names are concerned! Any remaining errors are purely mine!

My thanks go also to Alison King, my friend and fellow traveller, and I would like to apologise again profusely about Hugh's bath!

Online, I would like to thank the members of Historical Fiction Online and Penmanreview for book discussions and like-minded conversation.

Author Interview

You have been called "The best writer of medieval fiction currently around" by the Historical Novel Society. How and when did you first become interested in writing about the Middle Ages?

It's simple really. I had been telling myself stories since first memory, but I didn't write anything down until my teens when I fell madly in love with a tall, dark, handsome Frenchman in a children's historical TV programme called *Desert Crusader*. You can read the story of my love affair at my blog: http://livingthehistoryelizabethchadwick.blogspot .com/2008/04/tall-dark-and-handsome.html.

It was set in the twelfth-century Kingdom of Jerusalem and starred Thibaud, a knight in flowing white robes who galloped around the desert having adventures. Back then there were no DVDs or video recorders, so if I wanted more of this beautiful man, I had to imagine him. Filled with inspiration, I began writing a historical adventure romance novel and had an epiphany as I realised that I wanted to write historical fiction for a living. From that moment, my career path was set. Of course it was more easily said than done; it took me another fifteen years to achieve that goal—but I was determined. Since I wanted my stories to feel as real as possible, I embarked on a steep learning curve of detailed research. I think my teachers wished that I was as keen about my homework as I was about my external study! My first published novel, *The Wild Hunt*, won a Betty Trask award and is still in print. I say my first published novel—I have eight unpublished works in my drawer at home. I can say with a wry smile that it takes many years to become an overnight success.

You are renowned for being able to bring the past to life. Will you tell us a little bit about your research techniques?

I believe you need more than just reference works to write good historical fiction. In order to make the story leap off the page, the author has to bring the research into the world of 3D. I have a five-strand approach to my research and these five strands are woven together into a detailed and (I hope!) seamless braid.

1. Primary sources.
I read original charters, documents, and chronicles to gain a feel for the period.

2. Secondary sources.
I read numerous books on all sorts of subjects concerned with the period, generally from academic and university presses or specialist publications. I also use online study, but I am careful about the websites I use, as there is a lot of poor information out there as well as the useful material, especially on genealogy sites.

3. Location Research.

I visit locations mentioned in the novels where possible. So for example with *To Defy a King*, I travelled extensively in Norfolk, Yorkshire, the Welsh borders, South Wales, and Wiltshire. I didn't get to France this time around, but I have been there in previous years for research purposes. I like to get a feel for the places where my characters would have walked, even if the ground is sometimes very different now. I take numerous photographs and make detailed notes.

4. Reenactment.

This is part of the 3D element. I reenact with early medieval living history society Regia Anglorum. The society does its best to be authentic for the period and conducts living history experiments on a regular basis. I own numerous exact replica artefacts, courtesy of craftsmen who work for museums and the reenactment community. I know what it feels like to walk up and down castle stairs in flat shoes and a long dress. I have looked through the eye slits of a jousting helm. I have worn a mail shirt. I have used medieval cooking pots (better than stainless steel pans I can tell you!) and woven wool on a drop spindle. I can call upon the expertise of the members, many of whom are historians or archaeologists. There is nothing quite like experiencing it for yourself.

5. The Akashic Records.

This is a form of psychic research based on the belief that everything leaves its imprint in time and that if you have the ability, you can access this resource and look at the lives of the people who have gone before: their thoughts, their feelings and emotions; what they looked like and what they experienced. I don't have the ability, but I have a consultant who does, and I employ her skills. You can find more on this particular subject at my website under this heading. The result is a bit like conducting an in-depth interview with the historical person involved, or perhaps like seeing a documentary of their life in sensory detail. Visit www .elizabethchadwick.com/akashic_record.html.

What first drew you to writing about the Marshal and Bigod families?

You can't write about the Middle Ages and not come across the great William Marshal. He was one of the most powerful magnates in early thirteenth-century Europe, but he started his life as an ordinary household knight and worked his way up through the ranks with a combination of military prowess, charm, political astuteness, and good fortune. He was a jousting champion par excellence and in his later years became regent of England. We know about him because shortly after his death, his son commissioned someone to write an epic poem to celebrate his father's life. The *Histoire de Guillaume le Mareschal* is a very important document, because not only is it the first secular biography of an Englishman, but it gives a fabulous overview of the life and times of the thirteenth century. There are all sorts of need to know details such as what the aristocracy used for toilet paper, how much a soldier's horse cost, and the pleasure of drinking sparkling wine! Having decided to bring William into the limelight, I came across Roger Bigod whilst engaged in my research. Roger's career had many similarities to William's. They were both educated in the ways of power at the Angevin court and they both had to work their way up the ladder of royal favour. Where William's career was military, Roger's was judicial, but they were men who could do business together, and do it they did, when William married his eldest daughter Mahelt, to Roger's heir, Hugh. Unfortunately there is no epic poem about the Bigod family, but there were various theses, charters, and documents that came to my rescue and helped me piece together the story from their side of the fence. Again, it's one of power games and fighting to survive in a turbulent political climate.

Do you have a writing routine?

I work seven days a week and probably fifty-two weeks a year. The laptop always comes with me on holiday and I have been known to sneak away to the PC even on Christmas day! I am more of an owl than a lark. I am actually writing this interview well after midnight and will probably finish my working day about 1 a.m. I tend to answer emails in the morning and do routine work, and then gear up during the afternoon and evening to do the new writing. I write about 1,000 to 1,500 new words every day, except when I'm editing. I write about six drafts of the novel. Apart from the first draft, which is straight to PC screen, I like to edit the paper page, because I think it accesses a different part of the brain to screen editing and so adds in an extra layer. I also read the manuscript aloud to my long suffering husband (twice!) because the spoken word is different again and helps to pick up on things such as pace and repetition. I use music for inspiration, but I listen to it away from the PC. It would be too distracting to have it on in the background. But I do gain tremendous insight from listening to tracks whilst doing the washing up or preparing food. Each novel has a soundtrack that equates to the storyline. So, for example, the inspiration for the main love scene between Mahelt and Hugh in *To Defy a King* was Kiki Dee's "Amoreuse." The feelings of Mahelt's brother Will when being taken hostage and fighting against King John, were encapsulated by Bruce Springsteen's "Murder Incorporated." People are often surprised by this approach and seem to think I should listen to medieval music—which I do enjoy, but I also think that people's emotions don't change. Mind-sets might, but not the feelings, so I'm quite happy to use this century's music to bring people gone for eight hundred years back to life.

You are active on the Internet, on historical forums and networking sites such as Facebook and Twitter. How important do you think these are?

As an author I think they are very important for letting the readers know you are there and for being accessible, but at the same time, readers very quickly become irritated with authors who want to talk about themselves and nothing else. It's a little bit about giving something back, socialising and enjoying the interaction. I like meeting readers and talking to them, and not just about me. I'm a reader too, and I enjoy discussing novels with others, or indulging in historical chat. I see myself as an ordinary person who just happens to be a writer for a day job.

You have just said you like to discuss novels on forums, which begs the question, do you have any favourite authors?

I read voraciously across all genres. Historically speaking my favourite authors in no order are Sharon Kay Penman, Dorothy Dunnett, C. J. Sansom, Diana Gabaldon, and Lindsey Davis. I recently read *Wolf Hall* by Hilary Mantel and loved it. In other genres I am especially fond of Janet Evanovich's Stephanie Plum series. These are great to fit in between heavier reads to clear the air. I also enjoy the work of Katie Fforde and Jill Mansell, and I adore the earlier Terry Pratchett books, a particular favourite being *Witches Abroad*. Anyone who doesn't fall for the personality of Grebo is a lost cause!

Are you writing anything at the moment?

I am never *not* writing anything. If I stopped I'd have to do housework—perish the thought! I am currently at work on a novel about the Empress Matilda—no fixed title as yet. I feel that no one has ever got right up close to her to find out what she was really like. In the same novel I am also writing about Henry I's second queen, Adeliza, who has been very much ignored by history. I felt she really needed to be given a voice too. After that, who knows? Perhaps Eleanor of Aquitaine—again up close and personal. What did she *really* think and feel about various aspects of her life. If not Eleanor, whom I want to cover eventually whatever, then I have a couple of other projects up my sleeve that are very much in mind. Certainly I don't think I'll ever run out of material!

About the Author

*E*LIZABETH CHADWICK LIVES IN Nottingham with her husband and two sons. Much of her research is carried out as a member of Regia Anglorum, an early medieval reenactment society with the emphasis on accurately re-creating the past. She also tutors in the skill of writing historical and romantic fiction. Her first novel, *The Wild Hunt*, won a Betty Trask award. She was shortlisted for the Romantic Novelists' Award in

Charlie Hopkinson

1998 for *The Champion*, in 2001 for *Lords of the White Castle*, in 2002 for *The Winter Mantle*, and in 2003 for *The Falcons of Montabard*. Her sixteenth novel, *The Scarlet Lion*, was nominated by Richard Lee, the founder of the Historical Novel Society, as one of the top ten historical novels of the last decade.

For more details on Elizabeth Chadwick or her books, visit www.elizabethchadwick.com.

A Forgotten Hero
in a Time of Turmoil

The
Greatest
Knight

THE UNSUNG STORY OF THE
QUEEN'S CHAMPION

ELIZABETH
CHADWICK

"An author who makes
historical fiction come
gloriously alive."

—*Times of London*

❖ ❖ ❖

"Elizabeth Chadwick is
to medieval England what
Philippa Gregory is to the
Tudors and the Stuarts,
and Bernard Cornwell is
to the Dark Ages."

—*Books Monthly*, UK

A penniless young knight with few prospects, William Marshal blazes into history on the strength of his sword and the depth of his honor. Marshal's integrity sets him apart in the turbulent court of Henry II and Eleanor of Aquitaine, bringing fame and the promise of a wealthy heiress as well as enemies eager to plot his downfall. Elizabeth Chadwick has crafted a spellbinding tale about a forgotten hero, an ancestor of George Washington, an architect of the Magna Carta, and a legend of chivalry— the greatest knight of the Middle Ages.

978-1-4022-2518-5 • $14.99 U.S.